A TOKEN OF LOVE

ANN BOWYER

Published in 2013 by FeedARead.com Publishing – Arts Council funded

First Edition

A CIP catalogue record for this title is available from the British
Library.

http://www.annbowyer.com

Cover design and formatting: Richard Bowyer

Illustrations: Alice Bowyer

Dedication

To my family for their love and support

To all my writing friends for their unfailing encouragement

To the many Canadians who made this book possible

PROLOGUE

When Captain Palliser, on behalf of the British Government, explored the Canadian prairies in the 1800's, he realized the south-western corner of Manitoba and the south-eastern corner of Alberta as well as a large part of Saskatchewan were semi-arid and were the northern extension of the 'Great American Desert'. He cautioned this area was unsuitable for agricultural settlement, but his warnings were ignored by the Canadian government and the railway companies in their enthusiasm to settle the prairies.

This area now known as the Palliser Triangle is subject to periodic drought. At the beginning of the 20th century, new farming practices and new varieties of wheat were introduced and, even if rainfall was below average, a reasonable yield could be expected. However, if drought persisted into a second and even a third growing season, the consequences could be and, in the 1930's were, disastrous.

CHAPTER ONE

Canada 1932

Amy paused before stepping onto the sidewalk. It was empty – no one to pass the time of day or to enquire after the family. On the occasions when she was in town she wished for moments like this, when she could avoid saying how bad things really were, that the larder was bare or how impossible it was to satisfy the hunger of a grown man let alone three growing boys. But today was different. She wished gnarled old Billy was rocking in his chair, chewing on a piece of pemmican, making some wry joke. He, at least, would be a distraction and heaven alone knew she needed one. Today his chair was empty.

'Too darned hot,' he'd say.

She wiped her brow. Even the breeze was hotter than an oven, no wonder the place was deserted. It would be cooler in the General Store yet she hesitated, staring at the door, willing it to be locked, wishing with all her heart she didn't have to carry out her deed, wishing things had worked out differently. Her hand reached for the handle and her mind travelled down through the years to that first door – she had been young then …

* * *

Kent, England

February 1917

It was raining and the wind gusted through the nearby beech hedges, rattling the windows and rustling in the ivy. For the first time in her life she felt free from her mother's suffocating control. Holding onto her hat, she stared at the carved oak door and her gloved hand hovered over the ornate handle until, with a sharp intake of breath she found the courage to turn it. How times had changed. The country was at war and men were dying – thousands of them – and now her brother was here – in this improvised hospital. Oh, God, how she prayed he was all right.

Escorted along rows of beds, she averted her eyes but the images crept in – young men, faces contorted in agony – limbs bandaged, blood creeping through the stumpy ends where once a healthy leg or arm had been. The nurse stopped abruptly.

'This is your man, Miss Attwood. He's one of the lucky ones,' she said in an emotionless voice before bustling away.

It was a second before Amy realized she was alone with a patient shrouded in bandages, his eyes covered by thick gauze patches. She gulped. Was this really Freddie? It could be anyone. Out of the corner of her eye she could see a frenzy of activity – nurses scurrying between beds. She closed her ears to the cries of pain and held her breath in an effort to overcome the nausea caused by the stench. It felt like some terrible nightmare from which she would wake to the safety of her own bed.

Determined not to make a fool of herself, she tiptoed to the bedside.

'Freddie, it's me. Amy,' she whispered close to his face.

She could feel his breath, irregular and laboured. She looked for something familiar – his cheeks, his lips. It had to be Freddie. The nurse had said so. The bandages over his eyes were unexpected. Did they mean he was blind? He was a man of action and she couldn't bear to think of him being helpless. What would she do without him? He fought her battles, mediated between her and their mother. He was her hero.

She dragged a chair to the bedside and sat facing him.

'Oh, Freddie. Whatever have they done to you?'

'Why don't you hold his hand?'

She had thought she was alone but the words hadn't startled her; rather the words cosseted her in their warmth and there was a trace of an accent she couldn't identify. She half turned, wanting to see if his face was as attractive as his voice but stopped. Supposing he, like so many others, was hideously disfigured?

'Go on,' he encouraged. 'He'll know you're there then.'

She raised her hand, then put it down again.

'A man needs to know someone's here for him.'

She leant forward and placed her hand gently over Freddie's, looking for some movement of the fingers, some reaction. There was none.

'Lucky fellow, having a good looking girl like you to make a fuss of him.'

Holding her breath, she peeked over her shoulder. In one quick glance, she knew there were no horrific wounds – at least not to his face. Relief flooded through her and she stared at his bare feet before raising her eyes again. He was standing with the aid of crutches, one foot raised above the ground. Her gaze took in the bandaged leg, the stained night shirt and finally his lean face, shadowed with more than a day's growth of beard. Brown eyes stared at her and she felt heat flood to her cheeks. Had he been doing the same? Studying her? And did he find her as ... interesting?

'Sure it's a shock – seeing him like that.' He nodded in Freddie's direction. 'But he'll be right as rain once they get those bandages off.'

'He'll see?'

'Sure, he'll see. He'll be chasing you round the bedroom before you know it.'

She giggled and went hot with embarrassment. 'He's my brother ...'

'Oh – I thought ...' He broke off. 'He's been a bit incoherent. I thought you must be ...'

'Well, I'm not.' She didn't want to hear about her brother's ramblings. She glanced at Freddie, but there was no movement. 'Do you think they'll take the dressings off soon?'

'Possibly. Apart from the gas and the burns, I guess he got off lightly.'

Lightly? She fingered Freddie's bandages and wondered what a man had to endure to be considered badly wounded. Dead, maybe? Thank God, he was alive. 'Do you think he knows I'm here?'

'Maybe,' he said and began to hobble away.

'Were you – were you with him, when he got injured?' she called after him, anxious he shouldn't go.

'No.' His look told her he wanted to say more, but whatever it was, he changed his mind and limped away. Disappointed their conversation had ended, she turned her attention to Freddie.

* * *

When Amy visited the next day, the weather had improved and the sun sparkled in the leaded windows. She tried to work out which one was Freddie's, then admired the view across the formal gardens to the countryside beyond. It was such a pity the flower beds were neglected but so many of the men folk had gone to war. At home, their gardener had joined the local regiment and these days an elderly neighbour cut the grass and pruned the trees in the orchard.

The ward seemed lighter, airier. She walked along the rows, noting empty beds until she came to Freddie, who was propped up with several pillows. The voice, as she thought of him, was sitting on the end of the bed and, as if sensing her presence, turned and caught her staring at him.

'Hi. The patient's awake.'

'So I see,' she said, lowering her eyes and stepping past him to the head of the bed. Conscious of his proximity, she hardly trusted herself to speak and, oh heavens, she could feel herself blushing. She swallowed and tried to concentrate on her brother. 'Hello, Freddie. I came yesterday ... You were asleep.'

'Sis - sorry about the state I'm in,' Freddie rasped. 'George told ...'

She picked up Freddie's hand. 'Please don't apologize. I'm just so glad you're alive.'

'Wish I could get these damn things off ...' A bout of coughing interrupted him.

She replaced his hand on the bed. 'Soon maybe.' She had regained her composure. 'So you must be George?'

'And you, Amy.' He grinned as he got off the bed, muttering something about being caught by matron and held out his hand. His touch had the same alarming effect as his smile and she tried not to think about how he knew her name nor did she try to identify the accent which lay a slight emphasis on the 'A'.

'Do you know what happened to Freddie?' she asked as she removed her hand from his grasp.

George shook his head.

'And you?' She found herself asking in spite of her intention to keep the conversation strictly to her brother. Since leaving yesterday, he had been in her thoughts more than Freddie. 'What happened to you?'

He gestured to the rest of the ward. 'Same as everyone else, I guess.'

'I see some of your friends have gone home.'

'Home?' He snorted, then lowered his voice so Freddie couldn't hear. 'They're the ones who didn't make it ...'

'Oh. You mean ... they ... died?' She whispered, horrified. She assumed they had been lucky ... What must he think of her?

'And if you survive ...' He stopped mid-sentence. 'I'll be going back soon,' he said in a louder voice.

'Back?'

'To the front. Nice to be needed.'

She heard the irony in his voice and wanted to cry it was unfair. That he shouldn't go. That she didn't want him to go. How she hated this war. It had taken Freddie and Charles and now it was to take George.

They were silent.

George spoke first. 'Freddie'll be ok. At least, for a while. It'll take a bit to sort him out.'

Amy looked at her brother. 'What happened, Freddie?'

'Gas ...' he croaked.

She looked to George for an explanation, but he only nodded. Freddie's breath was coming in gasps and he lay exhausted against the pillows. She bent towards his ear.

'I'll come again later,' she whispered. 'I can see we're tiring you.' She picked up his hand and squeezed the exposed fingers tips. 'Get some rest. I'll come again soon.'

George grabbed his crutches and followed her. 'You live nearby?'

'No. Staying with friends.' She pulled on her gloves and wondered if George would be more informative than the nurse. 'My mother's unwell and couldn't manage the journey. Do you think we'll be able to take him home soon?'

'Maybe. Lucky fellow, having two ladies to dote on him.' He sounded envious.

'I expect your mother will be pleased to see you home.'

'I don't think so.'

His tone made her wonder about his background but his face didn't reveal what he was thinking.

'Don't you have any family?'

He hesitated. 'No.'

She raised her eyebrows at the tone of his voice. 'None at all?'

He didn't answer, but struggled to balance on his crutches and hold open the door.

'Tell me about the gas. I didn't know ...' She paused, allowing him time to follow her into the hallway but he remained in the doorway. 'Do you really think he'll be able to see again?'

'Sure. He's past the worst. They say if you survive a week, you'll live, but his lungs'll be shot.'

Amy frowned. 'How do you mean?'

'I'm no doctor.'

As if guns weren't enough, she thought and turned to go.

After lunch, when she returned, George was sitting on the landing, as though waiting to escort her. His smile took her breath away. Dressed in uniform, clean shaven, hair parted, moustache trimmed, he was the most eye-catching man she had ever seen. She stood motionless, watching him limp towards her.

'No crutches this afternoon?'

'Wanted to impress you.'

'You certainly have.' She drew in a deep breath. 'Let's go and see Freddie.'

Freddie was more settled, though she thought the iron bed and lumpy mattress far from comfortable and wished she could get him home.

As the days passed, she found she no longer dreaded her daily visit to the hospital. George was always there, exchanging jokes, discussing the progress of the war, cheering Freddie but mostly beguiling her with his broody dark looks.

A couple of days after the bandages were removed, Freddie announced some exciting news.

'They're letting me home,' he told Amy.

'That's wonderful. I must write and tell mother. Where's George? I know he'll be pleased.'

'He's gone.'

She stared at him in disbelief while visions of George lying in a muddy trench, his life ebbing away, flashed before her eyes.

'Gone? Not to ..?'

'The front? No. No. At least not immediately.' Coughing interrupted his words. 'He's gone to his battalion, that's all. Don't suppose it'll be long, poor sod.'

'What battalion, Freddie?'

'Winnipeg something or other.' He spluttered between coughs. 'Forget what he said. Funny names these Canadians have.'

Canadian. So that was the accent. His uniform was a little different, too. She had been too shy to ask but now she understood. Now it was too late. It was hard to cover her disappointment at not seeing him before he left, but any good-bye would have exposed her feelings and instinct told her he was not a man of whom her mother would approve. It was better this way – better he should go before she made a fool of herself. Mother had other plans for her future and she knew George would never be allowed to feature in them.

'He left this for you.' Freddie reached under his pillow.

Her hands trembled as she took the folded paper, holding it tightly, as though by doing so, she was holding George – protecting him – keeping him safe.

'Aren't you going to open it?'

'Oh – er – yes.'

The page had been torn from a small notebook. The slant of the handwriting was masculine with strong down strokes and there was an address. Her mind was racing ahead.

'What's he got to say for himself?'

She ran her eyes across the text and as she did, it was as though he was there speaking to her.

> **'Write to me. It'd be nice to get some letters – nice to know someone's thinking of me.'**

'He wants me to write.'

'Then you must. Every soldier deserves a letter from someone.'

Later, as she descended the stairs, she thought about the letter she would write. Of course, mother wouldn't like it but she would argue Freddie had said it was a soldier's right to have letters from home and he had no one else. Besides, wasn't he Freddie's friend?

> **'Dear George, I do hope this finds you well ...'**

No, that wouldn't do. She wanted something less formal but how did she begin a letter to a man she hardly knew?

'Amy!'

The sound of his voice burst into her reverie. He was at the bottom of the stairs, grinning up at her and she longed to run into his arms but a nurse appeared in the corridor and she suppressed the urge.

'I thought you'd gone,' she said when she stood beside him, still wondering what it would be like to be in his embrace.

'The Sergeant sent me for this.' He held up a folder. 'What luck. I thought I'd never see you again.'

A door opened and a soldier in uniform glared at them. She saw the stripes on his arm and was terrified George would be in trouble.

'You must go.'

They stood so close yet so far apart. He reached for her hand, his touch was electrifying. Dark eyes met hers.

'Good-bye, sweet Amy.'

She was consumed by a desire to draw him to her, to feel his arms around her, to feel his lips upon hers. She wanted to say so much but the moment was lost and he turned away.

'Wait.' She fumbled with the clasp of the gold locket which hung around her neck. 'Here, take this. It will keep you safe.' She wasn't sure it would, but it was important he had something to remember her by.

For a second, he held the locket, examining the exquisite floral pattern, taking in its unusual oval shape.

'I can't …'

'Please … I want you to have it. My picture's inside.' She could have added there was a space for his – that she wanted his to be there beside her own – that she thought she was in love with him. 'Take it,' she said instead.

'But ...'

'Go before you get into trouble.'

He closed his hand over the locket.

'I will treasure it – always.'

13

France

April 1917

*'The thought I might return alive to you keeps me
going. It's very noisy here, lots of activity, but at least
I'm away from the trenches. There's no privacy ...*

George leant against the wall and shifted into a more comfortable position, rearranging the paper on top of his Pay Book. It wasn't the most convenient writing place, but he had seized the opportunity. There might not be another.

There was so much he wanted to tell her. He stared down at the tiny picture in the locket. How beautiful she was – how much he was in love with her – how he dreamed of marrying her. She must like him or at least, be attracted to him. He pushed the locket into his jacket pocket and sighed. How futile it was. If he was lucky enough to survive, he wasn't stupid. He knew he would never be accepted by her family.

He began writing again.

'Has Freddie recovered? Write and tell me.'

Someone shouted. An officer was approaching and he hastily finished his letter.

'I think of you often. George.'

He hadn't said how often. She wouldn't understand.

It was Easter Sunday and, behind the lines, the French countryside was going to prayer. George listened to the church bells ringing and watched the troops marching to the front. Orders were crisply snapped and obeyed as they past local women, all dressed in black, their faces etched with fear. He knew what they were feeling. The apprehension was tangible. Even a large dog, which had been sniffing the air, loped off nervously.

Huge quantities of supplies and ammunition were being transported to the front and he, along with everyone else, knew there was to be an attack. The enemy knew. Of course, the bloody Boche knew, and would blast hell out of them the minute they stuck their heads over the top.

An enemy balloon floated into view. He heard shouts. A bi-plane dived steeply and machine guns rattled their deadly fire. Black smoke belched from the aircraft and its engine fell silent. He heard the explosion. Another life wasted. When would it all end?

The artillery pounded the enemy positions all day and, as dusk approached, orders came to move forward. He joined the line of soldiers into the long communication trenches, following his buddy, Alfie. Ankle-deep in mud, they made their way to the front, disturbing several rats along the way.

Alfie whistled through his teeth and George was grateful for the cheerful tune. Alfie could be relied upon to keep everyone's spirits up. They had met in Winnipeg and, when Alfie told him he was running away from home, they soon became the best of pals. He understood what it was like to run away. Since then, they had been everywhere together – starting with their medicals, their training in Canada, crossing the Atlantic, then more training in England before going to France. They seemed to do everything together – even managing to get injured at the same time, though Alfie's wounds were superficial and he was soon back at the front. He was the closest friend he'd ever had and he knew he could rely upon him.

There was a fine drizzle in the air. Once in position, there was little to do, but check their kit and wait. He noticed a few writing letters while others wrote in what he knew were forbidden diaries. Some prayed, some napped, but he couldn't bring himself to do any of these things. He had written his letter, he didn't keep a diary and he was so cold, he wouldn't be able to sleep even if he tried.

Alfie fumbled in his pocket for his watch, glanced at it and then produced a pack of cards.

'It'll kill a bit of time.' He began to deal. 'If anything happens, I want you to have my watch.' He patted his pocket. 'Keeps good time.'

'Nothing'll happen.'

They spoke in low voices.

'You never know. Sure cost a lot of money. I want it to go to a good home – not some bloody German ...'

'Shshsh. Nothing'll happen.'

The dark hours crept by, relieved only by the odd joke, a cigarette and a surprise delivery of chocolate bars and chewing gum. George bit into a Lowney's bar and, grateful for something normal, didn't stop to wonder how it had reached him. For a few seconds it reminded him of what he had left behind. He longed for the wide open space of the Prairies. What paradise – what peace. Even in winter, it was heaven compared to the mud and carnage of the trenches. He longed to stand up tall, the sun on his face, but instead, he squatted in a trench alongside the rats.

Now and then the monotony was relieved by a German star-shell, which shattered the twilight before falling to the ground and sizzling out. He saw his company commander check his watch and shivered. How much longer?

The drizzle became snow and then a blizzard.

There was a whispered order to fix bayonets.

'Good luck.' Alfie patted him on the shoulder.

'Yeah. We'll need it.' He said a silent prayer.

A great hush – thousands of men holding their breath.

One more minute ticked by, then a shot rang out. A second elapsed before the world around him exploded. The Battle for Vimy Ridge had begun.

* * *

May 1917

Buckinghamshire

' ... I fear for you all. Please write and tell me you are well. Amy'

16

She wanted to say so much more, how she longed to see him, how her heart ached but her mother always hovered in the room, making clucking noises of disapproval. Worse still, she had noticed the missing locket.

'It was a beautiful gift from your godmother. To carelessly lose it is beyond belief,' she scolded and Amy didn't like to admit what she'd done with it.

She put the pen down and looked out of the window. The spring bulbs were over, the last yellow heads surrendering to the warmth of the sun, but there was a haze of blue forget-me-nots and, beyond the garden, the apple trees in the orchard were in blossom. It was a day to be outside.

She could see Freddie sitting by the pond, engrossed in the newspaper. It was good he could read. There had been a nagging worry about his sight and, at first they protected him from the depressing news which always seemed to be the headlines, but it wasn't long before he thwarted any attempt to hide the newspaper. News of the battles continuing in France was reported daily, as was the number of casualties.

But the Canadians had been victorious – hadn't they? The papers had reported their victory at Vimy Ridge. So why hadn't she heard from George? It was she who couldn't bear to read the papers now. Damn the war. When would it be over?

She returned to her letter and read it through again, then folded it carefully and placed it in its envelope. There had been no word from George and, though shocking visions flashed through her mind, she couldn't believe he was dead.

The grandfather clock struck the hour. Midday. Lunch time and in the afternoon she was expected at "The Grange". Parcels for the front. Sewing for the poor. She was bored with it all. Work in the munitions factory would be more exciting. She wouldn't feel so isolated and she would be part of a team – doing something for the war effort. They needed nurses someone told her, but no matter how she pleaded, her mother still insisted she was too young.

Later, she set off carrying two parcels and a basket. Carbolic soap, chocolate and writing paper seemed most unexciting, but Freddie hadn't agreed when they discussed it earlier.

'Don't you believe it, sis. Soap's a luxury. There's enough rats to start a plague.'

She shuddered. Gas, rats, not to mention Germans...

She posted George's letter, then walked along the lane to "The Grange". Charles might be there. Gossip in the village said he was on leave from his regiment and she hadn't seen him for two whole years. Would war have changed him – like it had Freddie who jumped at sudden noises and couldn't tolerate complete silence? His mood would change in seconds – one minute he'd be fine and the next he was hostile and unreasonable.

She sighed for their lost childhood – years when her only worry was what to write in her English essay or how to explain the grass stain on her skirt. Peaceful, happy years and as normal as they could be for children growing up without a father. He had died when she was two and she envied Freddie's ability to remember him. But they were luckier than many children. Lady Margaret was a good friend and they had been fortunate to share Charles' governess. Her mother's greatest wish was for her to marry Charles.

Martha, the maid, opened the door and Charles, dressed in outdoor clothes, appeared from the parlour.

'Amy. How delightful.' In two large strides he towered over her, immediately taking the parcels, followed by the basket and placing them on the nearby table. Then he took hold of her hands and kissed her on the cheek.

'Nobody told me you were coming.' He studied her. 'My, how you've changed. Quite the young lady now.'

She saw the admiration in his eyes and didn't know how to reply. 'And you – ' She flustered. 'You're so much taller and thinner than I remember.' And handsome, but she hadn't the nerve to add that.

'The war. Makes one grow up very quickly.'

There was an awkward silence. 'It's wonderful to see you,' she said finally.

'I hear Freddie's home. Heard he was injured. Not too bad I hope?'

'He's much better, though his lungs will always be weak.'

'Gas?'

'I had no idea it could be so awful.'

A shadow passed across his face. He began to say something, then changed his mind and the smile returned. 'And Mrs Attwood? She's well?'

'Mother's very well and really pleased to have Freddie to fuss over.'

'Of course.' He changed the subject. 'I was going for a walk. Why don't you join me?'

'Amy has more important things to do.' Lady Margaret appeared in the hallway. 'We have lots of parcels to make up,' she said, emphasising the "we". 'Come along, Amy, dear. It won't do itself, you know.'

Charles frowned and she grinned. There was never any arguing with Lady Margaret, so she collected the parcels and the basket and followed her into the parlour. Through the window she glimpsed him heading towards the woods. It would have been so much more fun to be outside in the gentle May sunshine.

On the way home, she was surprised when Charles caught her up half way along the drive.

'Here, let me take that for you.' He took hold of her basket.

'Careful. There are eggs in there.' Food was precious and Cook had secretly given her four new laid eggs and two pork chops.

'Good ol' Cook. Doesn't change, does she? Still spoils you rotten. Remember chocolate cake? She always made chocolate cake if she knew you were coming.'

'Funny you should mention that. I was only thinking about it earlier. You know, the time when I hid in the schoolroom cupboard with an absolutely huge chunk of chocolate cake and got locked in by Smithie?'

He laughed. 'Yes and I still don't know how you managed to devour it so quickly, or how you kept a straight face when she let you out. You said were looking for a new reading book but, if she'd spotted it, there would have been real trouble. Smithie was a fearsome lady.'

'Oh, I didn't eat it.'

'You didn't?'

'Even I couldn't eat chocolate cake that quickly. No, I hid it in the cupboard and it was several days before I could retrieve it and by then it had gone mouldy. Most of the chocolate I see these days goes into food parcels.'

'You don't even have a little piece?'

'No, not the smallest. Your Mama is very strict.'

'I hope she doesn't work you too hard?'

Amy pushed a strand of hair out of her eyes and said nothing. Lady Margaret was a hard task-master, but how could she say so? Everybody was expected to do something.

'You mustn't let her, you know. I mean work you too hard.'

'She doesn't – couldn't.' Amy frowned. 'There's so much more I could do. If only mother would let me nurse –'

He grabbed her arm, bringing her to a stop. 'Quite right, too. I've seen some pretty awful sights ...'

'I'm much tougher than you think.'

His hold tightened and his face was grim. 'It's not for you.'

She glanced down at his hand, still gripping her arm above the elbow, then up at him. He let go and apologized.

'I did visit Freddie in hospital. I saw ...'

'You didn't see the half of it.' His eyes were troubled and the blue duller. 'It's slaughter. You saw the survivors – the few lucky ones who were nursed in England ...' His voice trailed off and she stared up at him, seeing for the first time, that he might bear no physical injury but mentally he was scarred. 'Please believe me, when I say it's no place for you. Freddie was very lucky. It's ... it's like lambs to the slaughter and there's no choice either. Go over or be shot for desertion.'

'Surely not?'

'I shouldn't have said that.' She heard his voice crack and he avoided her eyes. She watched him select a stone with his foot and kick it into the grass. When he looked up, he had regained control.

20

'I'm sorry, but it's the truth. I've seen strapping, big men reduced to jelly – babbling like new born babies. I've known men go mad after seeing their best mate's guts blown out … You've no idea, no idea at all.'

Alarmed at his outburst, she stared at him for several seconds before reaching up and touching his cheek. 'Poor Charles.' He held her hand to his face, then kissed the palm before letting it go.

As they continued walking in silence, Charles seemed distant. Was he there – reliving some dreadful battle? It was like Freddie all over again. She must choose her words with care.

'When it's over, I'm going into politics,' he announced without any preamble. 'I'm going to make damn sure nothing like it ever happens again.'

'Do you have to go back?'

She knew the answer by his expression.

'In a few days. I'm lucky. Most don't get home at all.'

They had reached the orchard and Amy opened the gate.

'Won't you come and see Freddie? And mother – she'd love to see you.' She sensed his hesitation. '

'No, I'd better not. Mama will be sending out a search party.'

He handed her the basket and reached to kiss her. Shocked, she turned her face away. He was a friend – a school friend. Her mother might wish for it to be more, but she longed for George …

'Charles, I, er – ' She saw his disappointed expression. As Freddie reminded her, every soldier needed to know someone was there for him. Before she could say anything more he had crossed the road.

'I'll call on Freddie tomorrow,' he said over his shoulder.

* * *

21

Belgium

November 1917

'... Received your letter today. It's wonderful to read about normal things. Nothing is normal here. Will it ever be? I can't tell you much, only that I am well ...'

Rain sheeted down. Men wallowed in the mud. Half of Passchendaele was flooded or so water logged, it was like a swamp.

George continued writing, wanting to explain his misery. How did he tell her about Alfie? He held the pen, but words wouldn't come and, even if they did, how would words be adequate? Alfie was dead. He repeated the words. They said everything, yet nothing.

They had fought together, endured the Flanders mud together – the cold, the drenching rain, the noise, the fear, the weariness. Together they had pushed the Germans back – gained the upper hand – thought they had made it. Sure, fire-fights had flared up throughout the day, but they had been away from most of them. They should have been safe. He dashed away tears. Alfie should have been safe, but, feet from him, Alfie had been in a sniper's sight. He hadn't realized, till Alfie's knees buckled under him and he fell forward, face down. Then he had seen the blood seeping out through his jacket. Frantically he had rolled him over, torn open his tunic, tried desperately to stem the flow. He had been helpless – helpless to stop Alfie's life ebbing away.

He began writing again, but this time he wrote of the vast horizons of the Canadian Prairie, his hopes of returning and how he'd rather endure the violence of a prairie thunderstorm any day. Word came they were moving forward and he pushed the crumpled, damp paper into his mud-stained pocket, hoping to finish it later and knowing his dreams of Amy were the reason he was determined to survive.

CHAPTER TWO

Buckinghamshire

April 1918

It was apple blossom time once more and Amy, on her way back from the village, hoped the early spring would signal the end of the war. Christmas had not been the usual happy festive event. Charles was in France and Freddie, against all their pleas, had returned at the end of November. Nothing had been heard from George since they parted over a year ago. He haunted her dreams but each morning when she woke she was no longer certain he returned her love. Had he found someone else or worse still, was he was dead?

The news of the war was grim and the few letters from Freddie caused great excitement but gave little clue as to what was really happening and she became more restless. George must be dead or surely he would have written? When she reached the orchard, the sparkle of the afternoon sun through the branches, dappled the mossy grass and she stood statue still, watching a rabbit graze in a sunny spot.

Soon there were several more rabbits. Enchanted by their antics, she became aware she was not alone – a solitary figure in khaki stood beside the gate.

'Charles?' At first she couldn't believe her eyes.

The startled rabbits darted for cover as she ran into his arms and he lifted her high, swinging her around in a circle. She could feel his heart beating and his blue eyes stared into hers.

'When did you get back?'

'Last night – late.' He embraced her and she allowed him to kiss her – a kiss that was not as earth shattering as she had believed it would be. She stared up at him.

'Thank God you're safe. It's wonderful to see you.' He looked so much older than his years, his face grey, the strain of war in his eyes. The thought he would have to go back seared through her. 'It isn't over, is it?'

He straightened his hat. 'No it isn't. It's awful – really awful. I only hope the Americans arrive soon.'

'The Americans? I thought …'

'We need more of them.' He stared up at the sky. 'I'm alive. Do you know that?' His laugh was on the verge of hysteria.

'No. No. You wouldn't know what I mean. How can you? You can't know how wonderful it is – to be here. To actually stand here – here in this orchard – in the peace of the countryside. Away from ….' His voice broke. 'Under an English heaven – you can't know what it means ...'

'Of course I do but please say you won't go away again.'

'I've got two days. I was in London, so they allowed me a pass. Tell me all the news. Mama tells me nothing and I couldn't find Cook. I saw Papa in London, but all he talks is politics or war and I'm sick of both. Tell me what you've been doing?'

Amy thought her life boring, but Charles was interested in it all – the monotony of mending and making do, the soup kitchen on Wednesdays, the gossip in the village, how there were now so few men, the women had to do so much more. The panic buying, food rationing – it all seemed to absorb him.

24

She insisted he came back to the house where Mrs Attwood got out the best china.

'We haven't heard from Freddie for weeks now,' Mrs Attwood said as she poured the tea.

'I always say, no news must be good news, Charles. Don't you think so?' Amy tried to hide the worry which she knew her mother shared.

He nodded. 'Of course. Freddie'll be fine. One day, he'll appear at the end of the garden, just –'

'Just like you.' She finished.

Mrs Attwood stirred her tea. 'I hope you're right.'

He stayed long enough to be polite. 'I'd better get home or Mama will be frantic – can't bear to let me out of her sight – bit suffocating, really.'

'I can quite understand how she feels. If Freddie was here I wouldn't let him out of my sight either. But it is so nice to see you Charles, and you will call again, won't you?'

Charles caught Amy's eyes, but he directed his words to Mrs Attwood. 'Tomorrow?'

Her mother beamed. 'We'd be pleased to see you.'

The door had barely closed behind him, when Mrs Attwood said in a loud whisper with a meaningful look on her face, 'He definitely has an eye for you.'

'Shshsh, mother.'

Amy was up early the following day. When she had looked out of the window at the clear blue sky, she knew it was going to be one of those incredibly warm spring days. She laid out a several outfits on the bed, holding each up and studying her reflection in the mirror. She still hadn't decided what to wear, when her mother called her.

'Amy, the post has arrived and thank, the Lord, there's a letter from Freddie.'

She didn't finish dressing but ran down the stairs. Maybe, just maybe there was a letter from George, too.

'Amy, for decency's sake, wrap that bathrobe round you,' Mrs Attwood said from the bottom of the stairs as she disappeared into the drawing room.

She tugged the garment about her and rushed after her mother.

'Freddie's written "2" on the front, so there must be another letter,' Mrs Attwood said, thumbing through the pile and reaching for her paper knife. 'It's the only one in this delivery so we will probably be reading his news in the wrong order.'

She watched with increasing impatience as her mother slit open the envelope. What did it matter what order they came in, it was from Freddie. If only there was one from George.

Her mother scanned the scrawling writing indifferent to her frustration.

'What does it say? Is he well?'

'Yes, yes. He's well … oh, and he's been awarded some medal.'

'Goodness. What did he do?'

'He doesn't say. It's very brief. Here, read it for yourself.'

The note was short but it was a something to tell them he was still alive, she thought, as she read the single page.

'Were there any other letters?'

'Yes, a couple.' She picked up the pile of envelopes and flicked through them. 'Nothing exciting. Bills mostly and this looks like a letter from my cousin.'

'Nothing for me?'

'No, dear.'

She watched her mother empty the contents of the other envelopes. Why was life so cruel? Every time the mail arrived her hopes rose, only to crash down again when there was nothing from George. Had he found someone else?

Later that morning, Charles and Lady Margaret arrived in a carriage drawn by two lively chestnut horses and he drove them all to a local beauty spot. While the ladies chose the right place for the picnic, he unloaded the hamper, which Amy looked at with a degree of guilt. She was certain it held more food than some of those who came to the soup kitchen would have in a week.

They spread the blanket out and the three ladies sat down but Charles strolled to the edge of the river and stood staring. She knew he was thinking about the war and longed to distract him.

'I fancy a stroll before lunch,' he said when he returned. 'Will you join me, Amy?' He offered her a helping hand. 'I'm sure, Mama, you have lots to chat about with Mrs Attwood.'

Lady Margaret didn't sound enthusiastic. 'Don't be too long, will you Charles? This is your last day.'

'You really have to go back tomorrow?' Amy asked as they followed the path alongside the river.

'It's such a lovely day, I don't really want to think about that.'

They walked in silence while Amy tried to find something else to talk about but everything was connected with the war.

'Do you …' he began before she could think of anything. 'Do you think I could take something of yours with me? A photograph perhaps?'

She thought about the locket she had given to George and had visions of him lying dead in a trench. She shivered.

'Do you have one?' Charles prompted.

'Er, no. I don't,' she lied. She didn't want to give Charles a copy of the picture in the locket. It didn't seem right.

'You must have one taken.'

'There's no time now.' She felt ashamed. She had heard how much photographs meant to the soldiers, especially those in the trenches. She wondered if her locket had helped George but it was so long since she had given it to him, it almost felt like a dream.

She glanced over her shoulder and knew the bend in the river meant they were out of her mother's sight. Charles caught her hand and turned her round to face him.

'A lock of hair would be almost as good as a photograph. What about that piece there?' He caught hold of a wisp which had escaped from her hair pins. 'Will you cut it for me?'

27

She giggled. He felt so close. She didn't want him to go away – didn't want to lose another friend.

'It's going to be hard going back, but it will be so much easier if I know you're waiting for me. You will wait for me, won't you, Amy?'

She looked away, unsure of what he meant. She didn't have time to expand on the thought before he captured her in his arms and kissed her, his tongue raking hers. She was consumed in a blaze of emotions and desires she didn't understand. His hand caressed her breast and excitement scorched through her.

'No, Charles. Not here. Not now.'

'I wanted to show you how much I want you – need you.'

She straightened her hat. 'You … you have, but …'

'You know I love you, don't you?'

'And I you ...' As she said the words, she felt a stab of guilt but for all she knew George was dead. He had no family – so there was nobody she could ask and she couldn't go on hoping for years. She was alive – they were alive. 'I think we'd better go back ...'

He let her go and they retraced their steps. Before they came into view, he stopped abruptly and when she turned to see why, he had taken off his signet ring.

'Here, I want you to wear this for me.'

She hesitated. 'On which finger?'

'On this one, silly.' He placed the ring on the third finger of her left hand. 'I want you to marry me. Will you?'

The ring was loose. 'Look it's too big. It'll slip off.'

'Oh.' He sounded disappointed, but then he spotted the silver chain she was wearing. 'Put it on that.' His finger caressed her neck.

She hesitated a second, then retrieved the cross and chain from beneath her bodice.

'Turn round. I'll undo it.'

Lifting her hair, he kissed her below the ear. She squirmed with pleasure and was disappointed when he stopped to undo the clasp on the chain before letting the ring fall, beside the cross, onto her chest. It

28

felt heavy with commitment and deceitfulness. Thousands had died and George was probably one of them, she told herself.

'Keep it safe 'til I return. When I get back, I must talk with your mother. Now we're secretly betrothed ...' He grinned. 'I shall think of where that ring is when I'm ...' His voice trailed away.

When they returned home, she made the excuse of fetching a book she had promised to lend him. Once in her room, she selected a small curl, snipped it carefully with the scissors kept on the dressing table and placed it inside a small prayer book.

'And don't tell me he isn't interested in you,' her mother said as they stood waving to Charles and Lady Margaret. 'His eyes hardly left you.'

She didn't answer until they were inside the house. 'He gave me his signet ring to look after until he returns.'

'So when do I expect him to call on me?'

'When he returns, he said he would. When he returns.'

* * *

Kent

April 1919

George shifted his weight. Would the train ever come? He looked along the platform. Soldiers – a continual stream of them – grey faces – haggard expressions. It was months since hostilities had ceased but only now were they going home. He thought about the word "home". Where was home? Canada? It had been three long years since he'd left. Should he go back? He'd lost so many friends – was there anything to go back for? It was a strange feeling – having no roots.

He could stay in England, but the idea didn't fill him with enthusiasm – in fact quite the opposite. It was always with a heavy heart that he thought of his family. How would his mother receive him after all this time? Eight years in which he had grown into his manhood. She probably thought he was dead. Would she recognize him? And what would his father say?

29

His mind travelled back through the years to his boyhood and the time he had run away to the docks. In his haste, he had forgotten his coat. The wind had whipped dust into the air and a fresh shower of golden leaves fell from the plane trees, which stood at regimented intervals along the street. He kicked aimlessly at the leaves which swirled at his feet and shivered again as the icy wind tugged at his shirt.

'A lazy wind,' he could hear his mother saying. 'Goes right through you.'

He took another swipe at the leaves and then traced his way along the cobbles. Instinct took him to the docks. Watching the big steamers arriving or unloading was always interesting. Often he played a game, trying to guess the cargo. If it was a boat from India it was easy – the aroma from the spices would hang in the air. Sometimes he would sit with Spike, one of the night watchmen and, if he was really lucky, Spike would share his sandwiches.

He glanced up at the sky – a violent mix of purple, pink and red. The moon was up already, not bothering to wait for the sun to disappear. The lamplighter was at work and the glow from the gas light threw his shadow lightly over the cobbles. It would be a high tide tonight. Spike had told him only yesterday it would soon be the Equinox

George touched his cheek with his forefinger and felt the bruise. His lip had swollen, too. He had only helped himself to a chunk of bread and hadn't Violet done the same? Yet he had been the one to receive the punishment. Under the table, his hands had curled into a fist in order to control the urge to retaliate. Then he fled from the house. It was so unfair. Even Ted avoided his father's wrath most of the time and he supposed Thomas would when he was older. Thomas had only arrived a few weeks ago, but already he'd taken over the household. Every time he as much as whimpered, he was picked up. Thomas's cries took precedence over everything. Let's face it, George, he told himself, they don't want you anymore.

'Oi! You boy.' George felt a hand grasp his shoulder. 'You're late. Come on. Get a move on.' The steely hand propelled him firmly him in the direction of the nearby gangplank. 'The cap'n wants to sail on tonight's tide and there's all them stores to stow.'

And so it was he found himself on a ship bound for Canada but, if he returned home, he wouldn't run away this time. He had seen the worst that could happen to a man.

Alfie.

He felt for the watch and immediately he was there with his best friend in his arms – the noise of the battle in his ears, the smell of death in his nostrils. If he went back, his father would have to accept him for what he was. What was he thinking? Was he really going back?

'Hey.' Someone pushed him on the shoulder. For a second he was back there at the dockside again. He turned, intending to say a few curt words, but the words died when he saw the man was a Captain and there was something familiar about him.

'Don't remember me, do you? I don't doubt you remember my sister.'

Amy? How could he forget? Each night, he went to sleep dreaming of her. Hadn't she been the reason he had survived?

'Freddie?'

He studied the Captain's face as they shook hands. He remembered the bandages and their removal. The voice was familiar.

'Still don't recognize me, do you?' Freddie shrugged. 'It must be at least a year since …'

'I – er – didn't expect to see you here. Thought you'd see the rest of the war out at home.'

'Couldn't bear to be out of the action. Fool that I was.'

'Where did you get to?'

'All over the place – then Italy. You?'

'Nowhere exciting. One trench is much like another.' George changed the subject. 'How's Amy? It's a while since I wrote.' Perhaps once he was settled in London, he could even call to see her on the pretence of visiting Freddie. He checked himself – Freddie was an officer. A friendly handshake didn't necessarily mean friendship.

'Why don't you come back with me? To Buckinghamshire – that is. Canada isn't just up the road is it? I'm sure Amy would be pleased to see you. I seem to remember you don't have any family. What d'you think?'

George didn't answer immediately. He was stunned by the invitation. He longed to see Amy, yet he hesitated. Would he be welcome? Freddie came from a very different background. Class didn't exist in Canada. In the Canadian army you earned promotion. Sometimes he doubted he had earned his own rank of Sergeant – it was more the result of so much slaughter – there really wasn't anybody else.

Freddie could see his uncertainty. 'If you've got other plans, I quite understand.'

'No. No. It'd be good.' He dismissed the consequences. This might be his only chance of seeing Amy. 'And it's real good of you to invite me, but what about your mother? Won't she mind?'

'Don't you worry. She'll be so pleased to see me I could bring the whole regiment to stay. Come along, there's a train due in ten minutes.'

George slept fitfully as the train took them into London and when he was awake, Freddie was not. He wanted to ask so many questions. He might have been resolute about facing his father, but the idea of seeing Amy again made him nervous. Would she have altered? The war had changed so much. Would she still have the gentle, soothing voice, the chestnut hair and amazing hazel brown eyes which seemed to see into his soul? The girl with an infectious giggle and a smile which lit up her face to reveal tiny dimples in her cheeks. From the moment he saw her, he knew she was the one for him. Never mind whether he would be welcome by her mother, the biggest question had to be, would she like him? Not like – that was the wrong word. It was obvious from her letters, she did. Why else did she write? But did she love him? Or more precisely, was she still unattached?

The connecting train took them to Amersham. From there they set off at a fair pace, hoping for a lift. They had walked a couple of miles in the fading light when a noisy vehicle bumped along the road behind them. The horn honked and they moved to the edge of the lane.

Freddie stared at the driver. 'Well, I'm jiggered. If it isn't Charles.' He dropped his bag, shouting and waving both arms in the air. 'We'll be all right for a lift.'

The car halted a few yards ahead and the driver peered out.

'Freddie Attwood.' Charles shook his head in disbelief. 'Where did you appear from? Did you write? Nobody's expecting you. Come on, get in. Amy'll be over the moon.'

'This is George. He's staying with us for a few days.'

George climbed into the rear seat. Freddie sat beside Charles.

'How long have you been back?' Freddie was anxious to know.

'Couple of months – they wanted me in London.' Charles put the car into gear and it jolted forward.

'I didn't know you could drive ...'

'Did a bit in France ... but I prefer driving this to the old crocks out there. She needs a bit of a spruce up after her war service – she was an ambulance, you know.'

'Ah, I wondered. I bet your father wasn't best pleased. He used to wrap it up in cotton wool.'

'That's the war for you. There've been a few changes while we've been away – this war's altered a lot of things. Even Mama is more down-to-earth these days.'

'Well, Charlie boy, I do rather envy you.' Freddie patted the leather seat. 'I didn't get the chance to drive anything with wheels. Did you, George?'

'Er, not really.' George had been listening to the conversation, feeling very much the outsider. As they trundled along the country lane, all he could think of was Amy and with the passing of every second, he felt more and more apprehensive.

When the car stopped, he stared at the house in despair. With imposing iron railings and huge chimneys, it was much larger than any house he had visited before. It was a far cry from the East End terraced house in which he had spent most of his childhood. He felt queasy. This was almost as terrifying as charging out of a trench.

'Come on, George.' Freddie was already out of the car and urging him to pass down their kit bags. He turned to Charles. 'Are you coming in?'

'I'd never be forgiven if I didn't.' Charles walked round the car to where Freddie was standing and said in a loud whisper. 'I didn't tell you the most exciting bit of news, did I? Amy and I are engaged.'

'Engaged? When did this happen?' Freddie held out his hand. 'Congratulations.' He shook Charles' hand vigorously and gave him a hug. 'You sly old thing. Amy didn't say a word, you know – not in any of her letters.'

'Oh, dear. I'll be in trouble. I expect she wanted to surprise you.'

'I always knew you two were meant for each other. Even as kids it was obvious.'

George stood still. What had he done, accepting Freddie's invitation? No wonder there had been no letters recently. What chance did he stand anyway? He hung back in the shadows, avoiding the shaft of light when the door opened. He was in two minds to slink away. Nobody would miss him and no doubt Freddie already regretted his impulsive invitation.

'Freddie. Freddie. How wonderful.' Amy wrapped her arms around her brother's neck and, as she did so, the light sparkled in the diamond ring on her finger. 'Why didn't you write?'

'No time, dear sister. It all happened rather quickly and I was on the train before I realized. Oh – and ...' He looked for George. 'I've brought you a visitor. George?' He squinted into the darkness. 'Come here, dear fellow.'

As if obeying an officer, George stepped forward.

Surprise registered on Amy's face.

'George?' She gaped at him and he stared back. Her beauty took his breath away and he had an overwhelming desire to lift her off her feet and run down the drive with her in his arms.

'How wonderful to see you,' she said recovering from the surprise of seeing him. 'Freddie, how did ..? This is truly amazing.' She beamed at him and for a moment he wondered if he was to receive the same enthusiastic greeting as Freddie. Then she held out her hand and the reality of his situation dawned. Her touch made his pulse race and when his eyes caught and held hers, the spark he had felt all that time ago in the hospital, surged through him. It was so powerful, he felt his knees buckle. It must be fatigue, he decided, as she removed her hand but her eyes lingered and he couldn't be sure whether she had felt it, too.

'Welcome to "Hazeldene".' She looked from him to Freddie and giggled. 'Fancy, my two missing heroes arriving together.'

'It sure is good of Freddie to invite me. I hope I'm not going to be too much trouble, 'specially to your mother.'

'Of course not. Any friend of Freddie's is welcome in this house. Do come in. You must both be very tired.'

CHAPTER THREE

Amy was still recovering from the shock at seeing George on their doorstep when she changed for dinner. The sensation of his hand in hers, the expression on his face told her he still loved her. Her emotions ranged from sheer joy at seeing him to the utter despair of losing him. She should have had faith – should have been stronger. Maybe he had written. Maybe his letters had gone astray. It wasn't impossible. Why, oh why, hadn't she waited?

'You're very quiet tonight, darling.' Charles put his hand over hers.

She cringed, wanting to remove her hand and avoiding his eyes.

'Am I? I suppose it's because it's nice to have you all in the house again – all safe at last.' She gabbled but Charles' attention was already on Freddie who was beginning to tell a joke.

'Is this in good taste?' Mrs Attwood interrupted.

Freddie laughed. 'Probably not, mother but it was the only way we could get through some horrific days.'

Amy glanced at George expecting him to be enjoying the joke, but his eyes were on her. Disconcerted she reached for a glass of water. Despite the flimsy blouse she had chosen to wear, she felt hot and was relieved when he made his excuses for an early night. When Freddie and Charles' conversation became boring, she decided she, too, would go to bed.

* * *

George had been glad to excuse himself as he found it hard to bear the way Charles looked at Amy. Otherwise, dinner had been pleasant enough, though he had been conscious of his position as an interloper and if he hadn't, he was certain Mrs Attwood would have reminded him. Freddie and Charles' conversation was light and entertaining and Amy, dressed in a pretty white lace blouse, was enchanting. In an unguarded moment, he found himself gazing at her and knew he had been foolish enough to allow Mrs Attwood to see. He was tired and as soon as he felt it wouldn't be rude to do so, he went to his room.

His bedroom was away from the rest of the family, not at the top of the house – Mrs Attwood had not insulted him by putting him in the servants' quarters, but nonetheless he felt a certain coolness towards him.

The bed was luxury after the years of soldiering – soft and inviting with crisp white linen. He hadn't got used to the quiet either and, even though he was exhausted, sleep didn't come easily. What a day. Even in his wildest dreams, he had never imagined at the end of it, he would be sleeping under the same roof as Amy.

She was everything he remembered and more – but she was unattainable. What a fool he'd been even daring to think she might be his. What hope was there for him? It would be better to make his excuses and leave. As he drifted into a restless sleep, he decided he would only stay the following day. Out of politeness, of course.

He woke with a start on several occasions wondering where he was and why there was no sound. At dawn he dressed and decided to go for a walk. He had never been to Buckinghamshire before. In fact he had probably seen more of France and Canada than of England, but the real reason for the walk was to see if some fresh air would clear his head. He was still a Canadian soldier and he had to decide whether to leave the army and stay in England.

The dream of courting Amy had sustained him through the dark days of the war, but the reality was so different. Should he stay in England – go home? Would he be welcome there? His mind was so occupied he failed to acknowledge the maid who unlocked the back door for him. He also failed to appreciate the gardens of which Amy had often written, but wandered aimlessly through the orchard and into the lane. He paused at end of the driveway to "The Grange" and wondered what lottery decided to which family you were born? Charles, it seemed, had everything.

It was over an hour before he returned and by then it was noticeably warmer. Unsure of the routine of the house and even more uncertain of what the day would bring, he was surprised to find Amy in the orchard. His heart did a somersault. Was she searching for him?

'Good morning.' He wanted to say so much more, but if he did, he would probably humiliate himself and embarrass her.

'Isn't it a gorgeous day?' Amy pointed at the sky. 'And so mild.'

George nodded.

'You were out early. I heard you go. Did you enjoy your walk?'

'Yeah, thanks,' he answered, wondering if she, too, had been unable to sleep.

'Did you go to the village?' she asked.

He didn't reply.

'When do you think you'll leave for Canada?'

'Haven't made up my mind. I might stay in England.'

'I thought ... You haven't any family here, so naturally I ...'

'I wasn't exactly truthful …'

'Oh?'

She caught his eye but he looked away. Didn't she know what she was doing to him? Her proximity was driving him crazy. He longed to kiss her, make love to her.

'No. I – er …' Words deserted him as he fought to hide his feelings.

'You have relatives here? Here in England?'

'In London.'

'London?'

He nodded and they continued along the path in silence. How did he explain his circumstances and was there any point in trying?

'Of course you must go and see them.'

'I don't think so.'

'No? You're not close?'

'It's not like that.'

'I see I'm prying. Sorry.'

'No, don't be.' Suddenly it was important she should know. It might be his only opportunity. 'I owe you an explanation.'

'No, you don't. It isn't any of my bus –'

'You see, I do have a father and a mother, but I haven't seen them in eight years.'

She stopped and stared up at him. For a second he allowed himself the luxury of gazing back. They were alone and the temptation to hold her in his arms was overwhelming. He bent forward, his lips drawn, as though magnetized, towards hers. He checked himself. He must never take advantage of her.

'Why haven't you seen them?' Her voice was low, sensitive. If he told her, she would understand.

He stepped back and it was a second before he replied. 'I ran away.'

'You ran away to ... to Canada? On your own? Whatever made you do that? '

He didn't answer.

'Have you brothers and sisters?'

'At the last count, two brothers and four sisters.' He laughed at her amazed expression.

'But ... You mean ... You mean you don't know?'

'I told you. I haven't been home for eight years.'

'You didn't write?'

'No.'

'But you must go and see them. I'll come with you if you like.'

He studied her face. He would like nothing better than to take her to meet his family. He would be so proud. Then he remembered Mrs Attwood's stern expression the previous evening.

'I sure don't think your mother would approve. After all, you are engaged.'

She looked down at the ground but not before he had seen the confusion in her face. He watched the colour rise to her cheeks. She

39

played with the ring on her finger as if trying to cover her embarrassing lapse of memory.

'No, of course, you're quite right. Come on.' She began to walk towards the house. 'It must be time for breakfast.'

Over breakfast the talk was of what young men returning from the war would do with themselves. Amy said Charles was thinking of going into politics. George said he hadn't any set plans and secretly thought Charles' sort could afford to go into politics, whereas he and thousands like him would have to find a job of some kind and, depressingly, he understood there were not too many of those. His instinct told him Mrs Attwood would not approve of his mother's politics or of some of her friends.

'I could go into the Indian Civil Service.' Freddie winked at Amy.

'Indeed, I hope not.' Mrs Attwood frowned. 'You've only just come home. How can you even think of going abroad? No, Freddie. It's time you settled down, like Amy. There's no shortage of suitable young ladies, you know.'

Freddie scowled. 'Mother, really. I want some fun. Don't you think we deserve it? I'm sure George feels the same, don't you, George?'

He opened his mouth, but Mrs Attwood cut across anything he might have said.

'Freddie, I am serious.'

'So am I.'

'Shall we go to the village this morning?' Amy interrupted. 'I've got some letters to post and I thought it would be nice for George to see the village. That is – if he'd like to.'

George placed his cup in its saucer and smiled. 'Sure, I'd like that. It'd be nice to see something of the area before I go home.'

'Home? I hope you're not planning to rush off just yet, old man,' Freddie said with his mouth full. 'We're going to have some fun.'

He looked at Mrs Attwood 'It really has been most kind of you to let me stay, but I think I should be getting back tomorrow.'

'Back? Back where?' Freddie raised his eyebrows.

'George has family in London,' Amy answered for him.

'Yeah and I'd kinda like to look them up before ...'

'Before you go back to Canada? Of course. I quite understand.' Freddie reached for some more tea. 'But you don't have to rush off just yet, do you? There's plenty of time.'

'Where in London do your family live?' Mrs Attwood asked.

He hesitated. 'East Ham ...'

Mrs Attwood's expression changed. 'Isn't that somewhere near the docks?'

He glanced at Freddie, who remained silent, but he could tell even Freddie knew East Ham was not Belgravia or Kensington.

Amy placed her napkin on the table and stood up. 'If you'll excuse me, I'm going to fetch my letters.'

* * *

When Amy came back downstairs she could hear her mother and brother in the dining room.

'I am not sure you should encourage him to stay longer. We're all to have dinner with Lady Margaret on Friday and – '

'For heaven's sake, mother. He's flesh and blood like you and me. He bleeds the same ...'

'Freddie. That is no way to talk.'

'You don't know the half of what we went through – all of us, mind. If you did, you'd welcome every soldier as a hero for that's what he damn well is and I'm sure Lady Margaret would agree.'

'Freddie, really. You know I don't like that sort of language.'

'Things have changed, mother, and you had better get used to it. Nothing will ever be the same and frankly, after what we've been through – all of us – I don't see why it should.'

'But he has no class ...'

Amy could no longer bear her mother's condescending tone and pushed open the door.

'Ah, Amy, dear. I have a letter, too.' Mrs Attwood glared at Freddie. 'I meant what I said. Tomorrow morning, he's to be gone.'

'But … he's my friend too.' She pleaded, knowing half of her didn't want him to stay – she was engaged now – it was too late – but her other half craved his love. 'You said you cared – at least that's what you said when you made me help Lady Margaret. You said they were all heroes.'

'Now the war's over, I want things back to normal.' Mrs Attwood swept out of the room, leaving Amy staring after her. How could she be so heartless?

'Don't worry,' Freddie said. 'I'll soon bring her round, but she's wrong if she thinks things will go back to the way they were. They won't. This war has changed everything.'

As the three of them set off on their walk, Amy chatted away, filling gaps in the conversation, desperate for the mood to be light-hearted and anxious George should not be made to feel inferior.

'What do you think you'll do – now you're home for good?' she asked Freddie. 'Seriously mind. I don't want to hear this silly talk about the Indian Civil Service.'

'Ha. Did you see how worried mother was?' Freddie laughed. 'Her face was a picture, wasn't it? I only said it because I knew she would take the bait, but actually I do have an idea. Quite a good idea, even if I say so myself. It'll need some capital, though. As I see it, motor cars are going to be the future and one day everyone will have one. They'll be plenty of work selling them and they'll all need repairs. I met a Major in France. Owned a bicycle shop. Streatham, I think. Said motor cars were the future and I think he's right. Wonder if he made it – last time I saw him he was in an ambulance.'

'Oh, I hope so,' Amy said. 'But motor cars? That sounds exciting.'

'If I'm successful I might open up a whole series of garages. You know, in several towns.'

'You'd need to have people working for you then, wouldn't you?'

'Of course. I could never do it all on my own.'

She turned to George. 'What about you?'

'Haven't decided yet.'

'You could work for Freddie.' She giggled. It would solve both of their problems. Freddie would have something respectable to do and George would have employment here. There was a dull ache of longing in the pit of her stomach. If only … She glanced up and was disturbed to find his eyes staring back at her. She felt exposed, as if he could see right inside her mind – her heart, even. She thought back to his arrival the previous evening – the surprise of seeing him, the blaze of desire which scorched through her, the self-control she somehow managed when even his handshake was thrilling. At dinner last night ... then in the garden ... she was certain he had almost kissed her. And she had wanted him to kiss her but, only now, did she grasp how much. The thought unnerved her.

In the afternoon Charles took them all for a ride in the car. Amy sat silently beside him, examining his profile out of the corner of her eye. How could she not be in love with such a handsome man? He offered her position, wealth – everything. George sat behind her and she was conscious of his every move. It was as though all her senses were tuned into him. It was too late, of course. Even if she wanted, she could never break her engagement. It was unthinkable. Her mother would never forgive her. She must put all thoughts of George out of her mind – it was dangerous to consider him as anything more than a friend of Freddie's.

'Good little nag, eh, Freddie?' Charles said over his shoulder, pointing out a particular horse which grazed in a field alongside the road.

'She is too. Will you ride her?' Freddie asked.

'Good Lord, no. The idea's to race her. Anyway, motor cars are more my style these days, aren't they, Amy, darling?' Charles patted her knee. 'I'm thinking of buying one myself soon. That is, as soon as I finish with the Regiment.'

'I'm planning to start up my own business.' Freddie leant forward to tell Charles about his idea and how he had seen the ideal premises in the village. 'Come to think of it, you'd make an excellent business partner. How about it?'

Their drive included a stop at a tea shop, where Charles plied them with cakes and sandwiches and as much tea as they could manage. He and Freddie were soon absorbed with motor cars and Amy became bored.

'Do you think you'll go back to Canada?' she asked George.

He leant forward and answered in a low voice. 'Tomorrow, if you'd come with me.'

She could feel his eyes on her. She daren't look up but reached for her cup and took a sip of tea. 'You shouldn't say such things.'

'Come with me,' he whispered.

'Shshsh.'

'You'd love it, you know. It's not like here – where it matters where you live and how you speak or who your father is.'

'Surely not.'

'Amy, you've led such a sheltered life. Haven't you noticed how your mother disapproves of me?'

'That's just her way,' she replied, but knew he was right – knew George would never be accepted.

'She sure is pleased it's Charles you're promised to and not me,' he said more loudly.

'Shshsh,' she mouthed again, glancing at Charles but he and Freddie were still debating the finer points of their planned venture.

'You know I'm right.' His voice was low again.

'Yes.' She fingered the spoon in her saucer. 'I know.'

'You don't love him, do you?'

The spoon clattered to the floor.

Charles looked in her direction before retrieving it and placing it back in her saucer.

'I think we'd better get back or I'll be in trouble with your mother, Amy, darling and it would never do to fall out with my future mother-in-law.'

For the rest of the day she avoided George and when, at dinner that evening, he announced he would be returning to London the following morning, Charles offered him a lift to the station.

'I'm joining Papa in London 'til Friday. There are a few affairs to be sorted and besides I want to organize the finance for Freddie and my new venture.'

Mrs Attwood's eyebrows shot up. 'What's this then, Freddie?'

'Don't get too excited, mother. It might not happen. Charles and I have a mutual interest in motor cars. They're going to be everywhere soon and we're thinking of starting a business together – selling and servicing them.'

Mrs Attwood frowned. 'Is this right, Charles?'

'Yes. I had a chat with Papa just before dinner and he's very enthusiastic about the whole idea.'

'That's all right then.' Mrs Attwood turned to Freddie. 'At least you'll be doing something useful with your time and not letting this new found freedom go to your head.'

As soon as dinner was over, George excused himself.

'George is going to look up his folks,' Freddie explained to Charles. 'He hasn't seen them for – what is it? Ten years?'

'Eight,' George corrected.

Amy could see her mother's disapproving expression.

'I'd like to be a fly on the wall when you explain where you've been and what you've been doing all this time,' Freddie said.

Charles patted George on the back. 'So would I. Half way round the world and back again – quite an adventure – even without the trenches. I don't blame you wanting an early night. Can you be ready for 6.30?'

'Sure thing.' He avoided Amy's eyes. 'Good night, ladies.'

When Amy retired for the night, she was astonished to find a note had been propped against her door. She sank onto the bed and examined the familiar handwriting. Oh, why did life have to be so cruel? In all that time, why hadn't he written – given her some hope he was still alive? She knew she should destroy the letter, but in an instant, she had ripped open the envelope. Inside was a note and her locket.

Darling Amy,

We both know how we feel. We only have to look at each other to know. I long to hold you in my arms and to love you. I know I have no right even to hope you might give up everything to be my wife, but wealth isn't everything.

In the circumstances, I think it only proper to return your locket. You'll find me at the above address.

I love you with all my heart.

Yours forever, George

She picked up the locket and, appalled at its battered state, struggled to open it. She stared at the picture inside. It was taken before she knew what heart ache was, she thought and snapped it shut. She re-read the letter. Did he really love her? And did she love him? Her mother would say she couldn't possibly love a man she hardly knew but George excited her in a way Charles never could. She had known Charles all her life. He was familiar. Was this the reason she didn't experience the flutter in her stomach, the ache in her heart which was present every time she looked at George? She wished for the hundredth time she hadn't given up on him – that she had trusted her instincts.

She looked at the address. East Ham. It might as well be the end of the universe. She read the letter several more times before placing it back in its envelope. Oh, God, what a mess.

CHAPTER FOUR

When Amy prepared for dinner at "The Grange", she spent much longer than usual in front of the mirror. All her waking hours had been tormented by her longing for George and he haunted her dreams but breaking her engagement was unthinkable. It would bring disgrace not only on herself, but on her family. She reminded herself that marriage to Charles would have its compensations – money and position. Now George had gone, she must forget him and try to be everything Charles desired. As she slipped into her favourite dark blue velvet dress, she told herself there was no other choice. This was her destiny. It was expected.

Although dinner was informal, her concentration wandered and George crept into her thoughts. She could write, but it would mean keeping it secret from her mother and she could never tell Charles. But it was one thing writing to George as a soldier at the front and quite another writing as an engaged woman in peace time. In any case, if she wrote, what would – could she say? Sorry but she was happily marrying a very rich man?

'Come along, my dear. The gentlemen wish to discuss politics,' Lady Margaret's voice broke into her thoughts and she horrified to see she was the last lady seated at the table.

Once in the drawing room, she stood at the window but the conversation bored her and her thoughts returned to George and whether he had been welcomed home. The evening dragged on and, tiring of the pretence at polite conversation, she asked Lady Margaret's permission to borrow a book from the library. As she crossed the hall, she could hear voices coming from the landing above.

'Come here, Martha, you little tease.'

She stood still. The voice belonged to Charles.

'Shshsh. Someone will hear.'

A loud giggle was followed by muffled laughter.

'Shshsh.'

'Leave your door unlocked tonight. I can't wait. I need you. Oh, you don't know how much I need you.'

She stumbled into the library, banging the door closed, not caring who heard. She shut her eyes, trying to obliterate the images which flashed through her mind. Her heart pounded. Charles and Martha? Martha – the housemaid? She sank to the floor. Thoughts crashed about in her head – the odd smile Martha sometimes had for Charles – his rakish wink back. Tears pricked her eyes, she gasped for breath, her anguish physical. Was it possible to die of a broken heart? Her body yearned for George, for the comfort of his arms, for him to take her away from this torment but she had thrown away her own chance of happiness ... Yes, admit it. She loved George and she had sent him away.

'Amy? Amy, are you in there?' Her mother's voice jolted her out of her misery.

How long had she been sitting there? Her watch told her it must have been almost an hour. She sprang to her feet, ran her hands through her hair and dabbed her eyes then snatched an open book from the table.

'Oh, there you are.' Her mother stood in the door way. 'It was most rude of you to shut yourself away in here.'

'Sorry, mother. I found a really interesting book.' She avoided her mother's eyes.

'Never mind that now. Hurry along. The gentlemen have joined us.'

Relieved her mother was more interested in returning to the others and hadn't noticed how upset she was, she smoothed her dress and took a moment to compose herself.

Charles was waiting at the entrance to the drawing room.

'Amy you look very pale.' He touched her arm and she jumped away as though stung. 'Are you feeling unwell?'

She shook her head, unable to speak. Maybe it was as well, for any words she might have uttered would have been words of accusation, revelation. She glanced at each of the male dinner guests. They would never believe her and, even if they did, they would only shrug. A gentleman was entitled to his dalliance ... wasn't he? Her

48

gaze finally rested on Charles and her hands itched to slap his face – to wipe away his concerned expression, so she balled them into fists and kept them at her sides.

The rest of the evening disappeared in a mist of automation. Later, when she undressed, her agony progressed into fury. She flung her dress into a corner and threw herself onto the bed, engulfed in tears of rage. She was trapped by the set of rules by which her class lived and how she despised them. Yet if she married Charles ... she would condemn them both to unhappiness. Even though she was young and inexperienced she had listened to adult conversation ... knew unhappy men spent more time at their club than they did with their wives ... knew of the adultery ... and now she knew she could never make Charles happy.

She slept fitfully, waking in the early hours to retrieve George's letter, falling asleep again with it held against her heart.

* * *

'Amy, you haven't been listening to a word I've been saying,' her mother complained over lunch the following day. 'Is there something wrong with your food? You've been playing with your fork for the last five minutes.'

'Sorry.' She smiled. 'Just dreaming.'

'Young love.' Mrs Attwood gave her a knowing look.

She was silent. It was important not to undermine the impression it was Charles she had been thinking of and it was equally important her mother should never guess what she was really thinking. Ever since she had got up that morning, a plan had been forming in her mind – a plan which would lead her to George. If he could run away to Canada, surely she could run away to London? It was, after all, only about twenty miles away. Very different to the thousands he had travelled. All she had to do was to find a way of getting to Amersham, from there it would be simple to get the train. She had the address. She would ask a policeman once she got to East Ham. But how did she get to Amersham? Walk? It would be a long walk, but if that was the only way, then that was what she would do.

'I'm going to visit my dressmaker tomorrow and I think you should come, too. It's about time we did something about your

49

trousseau. Lady Margaret said she would send the car down for us. It really is most kind of her, especially after your behaviour yesterday. Most kind of her.'

'Yes, mother.' She tried to inject enthusiasm into her voice, but failed. A visit to the dressmaker would fit in well with her plans, as the shop was on the edge of Amersham but it would be impossible to sneak away. Yet this might be her only chance. There had to be a way. She had to think of something.

'Lady Margaret and I were discussing the wedding last evening while you were so rudely absent. I don't know what got into you. Anyway, you and Charles must set a date. She thought June would be a good time.'

'Mmm.'

'She insists the reception should be at "The Grange". The gardens will be lovely then and the weather should be warm.'

'I'll have to discuss it with Charles.'

'Don't take too long. These things don't organize themselves in five minutes and June isn't that far away.'

By evening Amy had made up her mind. Somehow she would make the opportunity to get to London. Her mother sometimes spent a long time in the fitting room and usually she was left alone to read the magazines in the reception area. She would slip away. But how? And what would the consequences be if she was caught? She didn't dwell on that. She was not going to marry a man who was already unfaithful. She would marry the man she loved.

She removed her engagement ring before composing a letter to Charles. It wasn't easy and when she had finished, she placed the letter and the ring inside an envelope and sealed it. Then she wrote a note to her mother. She propped both letters against the mirror of her dressing table. Next she went to her wardrobe and swished the clothes along the rails before selecting a dark brown suit. It would be the right thing to wear to the dressmaker and it would be ideal for travel. A matching hat and a pair of toning shoes completed her outfit. She bundled a few items of underwear into her bag. That would have to do. A bigger bag would only draw attention.

In the event, it wouldn't have mattered how big the bag as she went to Amersham in Lady Margaret's chauffeur driven car alone. Her mother complained of a headache and stayed in bed but gave strict instructions on the dresses she was to select.

'Bring back samples so I can see them,' she instructed. 'Oh, and take that blue coat of mine. I want it altered to something more fashionable.'

The journey to the dress shop was so uneventful, she couldn't believe her luck.

'What time shall I collect you, Miss Attwood?' the chauffeur enquired as he opened the door for her.

'Oh, er ...' She had forgotten he would need to know what time to collect her. 'A couple of hours should be enough, thanks. No, wait. Maybe a bit longer. I have a couple of errands for mother,' she lied. 'Shall we say midday?'

As she closed the car door, she hoped he wouldn't notice her mother's coat still on the seat, then, waiting until the car had disappeared round a corner, began to walk to the station.

* * *

George paced up and down, stopping at the crossroads for the second time and staring along the street. He had played on these cobbles – run errands for his mother – but the last time ... the time he had gone to the docks and not returned. He never expected to see the place again. Hadn't he found a life for himself in Canada? So why go through this? Amy was spoken for – so why come back? Memories weighed heavily in his heart and his pulse hammered through his head. Did he really have the courage?

On the opposite corner was the shop. He remembered buying potatoes – it was always potatoes. Nothing had changed – the double doors opened straight onto the street. He screwed up his eyes trying to see if Mrs Wilson was still serving the customers, but he was too far away. He studied the houses. They didn't seem any different either but they were so much smaller than he remembered – all tightly packed together. And, with heavy clouds overhead, the street felt so grey.

He ambled back along the road until he stood opposite his house, except it no longer was. He tried to remember the layout, the bedrooms, the scullery and the living room but found he couldn't. It was very odd. He'd remembered his way here hadn't he? His eyes scanned the street. With little wind, the smoke from the chimneys rose straight up, black and sooty. The window ledges were covered in a layer of dust. He had forgotten about the soot and the grime.

Going home required guts. He stood and stared – he remembered the faded red curtains. He drew in a sharp breath as the door swung open and a young man stepped onto the street. It was Ted. There could be no mistake. It was like looking at himself in a mirror. He couldn't do it. It was a bad idea. He went to turn away, but Ted had seen him and was staring back.

'George?' He called as he crossed the street. He stood beside him and gazed at him with disbelief. 'Gaw blimey, it is.'

It was a second or two before either spoke.

'Well, I'm blowed. Where did you spring from?' Ted scratched his head and there was a moment's hesitation, before he took George's hand, shook it rigorously and gave him a hug. 'Where've you been all this time? Ma's going to be over the moon. Never been the same with you gone ...'

'Is ..?' George found he couldn't form the sentence, but knew he didn't have to spell it out. Ted would understand. He, too, had sometimes suffered their father's temper.

'The old man? Died a year back. Flu.' Ted's voice was flat and he eyed George's uniform. 'You saw action?'

'France.'

'They wouldn't 'ave me. Something to do with my ticker.'

George was concerned. 'Nothing wrong?'

'Not so as you'd notice, but they wouldn't 'ave me. I work at the docks – been there a couple of years. On my way there now, but I've got to see Ma's face when she sees you. Worth being late for. Must see 'er face. Gave you up for dead.' He gave George a nudge. 'Come on.'

Ted led the way back across the street.

'Where've you been all these years? Where did you get to?'

'Canada, then France.'

'Canada, you say?' Ted stopped and turned, then noticed the stripes. 'Blimey, a sergeant no less.'

George snorted. 'There wasn't anyone else.'

Ted ignored the remark and opened the front door. 'Ma's in the scullery.'

'Is she still into her politics?'

'Don't suppose you 'eard.' He lowered his voice. 'He – thingy – died, you know.'

George had forgotten about 'thingy'. It was the way they used to refer to Keir Hardy. Whenever he called they had to make themselves scarce. At the time George had never understood why and he was too young to even question it, but now he found himself wondering if there had been an attraction between Ma and Keir. He had heard it said he enjoyed the company of women.

'Can't say I knew. Sure would have remembered if I did.'

'Didn't want the war – neither did Ma, but his going ain't stopped her. Every night she's off out – some meeting or other. Says they'll be a Labour Government one day.'

'Do you think she's right?'

'Gawd knows? Don't suppose it'll make much difference to me. Come on, let's see what Ma makes of you.'

His mother's expression ranged from sheer amazement through to a broad smile. She stopped rolling out the pastry for the pie she was making, wiped her hands on her apron and stood facing him. But George had been wrong in thinking she wouldn't recognize him. He looked like Ted, and Ted, according to Ma, was the image of their father.

He thought about this for some time. No wonder he hadn't been popular with his step father and no wonder the old man had doted on Thomas. Thomas had been a baby when he left, but Thomas was his son, unlike him or Ted. They both reminded him of Ma's first and only husband. They had always known he was their step father, but were forbidden to speak of it. Now he was older, he understood what was meant when people spoke of the disgrace of living with another man.

What would Amy think? Or Mrs Attwood? What difference did it make anyway?

But what of Lizzy, Vi, Phee or May? His sisters had always been treated differently and he had never questioned why. He assumed girls didn't get it as hard as boys. He tried to remember. They were fair, unlike him and Ted. He had never thought about it before, just accepted it, but now, he comprehended, they were his half-sisters. And May? He remembered her arriving. Four sisters and two brothers. He stared at Ted, taking in the dark brown hair and the well-defined eyebrows. Ted must be his only true brother. Funny, he had never understood that before.

'What have you to say for yourself?' His mother's voice broke into his thoughts. He could see she was back in control – any trace of emotion, any hint of joy at the return of her first born, well and truly concealed. 'Where have you been all these years? You can't know the worry you caused. Had the whole neighbourhood searching, we did. Thought you'd drowned in the docks. You were always going there – couldn't keep you away.'

George raised his eyebrows. He wasn't going to apologize. 'Long time ago, Ma and I'm not a kid anymore.'

Looking up at him, she laughed. 'Yes, I can see. You've grown into a handsome fellow.' She patted him on the chest. 'You sound different, too. Come here, son.' She gave him a hug. It was the best he could hope for. His mother never believed in demonstrating her feelings.

'Pity Arthur isn't here to see you.' There was sadness in her voice. 'The flu – took it very bad.'

'Yes, Ted told me.'

'Let's sit down and you can tell me everything. Then we can decide where you're going to stay and what you're going to do with yourself.'

'I think I can decide what I want to do myself, thanks.'

'You're staying.'

It was a statement. Nothing changed. She was as indomitable as ever. Perhaps this was another reason why his step-father had taken it out on him – he never could suppress his mother.

Later, when they were all seated for their meal, he couldn't help comparing this dinner to the one with Amy. How different things had been with only Freddie, Charles, Mrs Attwood and Amy sitting together around the large highly polished table in Mrs Attwood's equally large dining room. Here, they had to eat with their elbows at their sides – not because it was polite to do so, but because there wasn't any room to do otherwise.

The cutlery was simpler too – a fork, knife and spoon – not the array which had adorned Mrs Attwood's table. He had been so careful to follow Amy or Freddie's example, wary Mrs Attwood would find fault in his table manners. Now he looked around as they chatted – Ma at one end of the table with Ted opposite, in his father's place. How weird it felt to be back. It was a different world to the one he had left behind in Canada and, after the years of soldiering, he didn't know if he fitted. Did he fit anywhere? Yesterday he had glimpsed yet another world, one which would never be open to him. Amy belonged there and his heart ached.

Ted, who had returned earlier with the explanation that he hadn't been selected to unload either of the ships which had docked, smiled as though he understood. He had offered George his place at the head of the table.

'You're the eldest. By right it's yours.'

He had declined. He felt the intruder. What right had he to usurp Ted's place? Ted had earned the privilege. He had taken the beatings, stayed with their mother.

He studied his brothers and sisters. First, there was Lizzy who had shown off her engagement ring, then Vi – appropriately named – as she shrunk back into her seat, allowing Lizzy all the limelight. Then came Phee or Phoebe, as she informed him she preferred to be called. She worked in a shop and travelled on the train and seemed to think she was better than the rest of them. She didn't clean like Vi or Lizzy.

Next came May – little May. He remembered her fondly as a pretty four year old, but now she was twelve and almost grown up and going through puberty by the look of her. He could see all the signs. She gave Ma a hard time.

Last there was Thomas. He could see the resemblance to his step father and he had Vi's eyes, but even at eight years old, he was willing to allow May to dominate him. Perhaps he would learn how to handle his bigger sisters. He hoped so, for he had rather taken to the lad.

Steak and kidney pie was his favourite and in spite of all the comparisons with dinner at Amy's house, he tucked into a large portion and came back for a second.

'If you're going to eat like this, George, you must see about a job,' his mother said, placing another helping of mash alongside the pie.

Of course, he'd pay his way.

Ted sensed his feelings. 'You planning to go back to Canada?'

'Might. Haven't made up my mind.'

'You'll do no such thing. You've just got back.' His mother spooned cabbage onto his plate. 'Besides, you belong here, with your family.'

He wasn't too sure where he belonged. Right now he wished he had somebody to confide in, a friend who would listen and sympathize, but, most of all, be on his side. He wasn't sure if Ted was that person. Alfie would have cheered him up – got him organized and probably, if Alfie had lived, he would be on his way back to Canada. But he was here – here with his family in a suffocating little house in a depressing, dreary London street. How could this compare with the quiet and solitude he had grown to love? He longed for the big blue skies and the dark black soil, the gold of a ripening crop – the silent white snow.

What was he to do? He had little money and, at that moment, no prospect of a job. Where was he to go? He had turned the problem over in his mind ever since leaving Buckinghamshire and still didn't know the answer. Amy. Would she reply to his letter? And if she did? What could he offer her? His home and family would embarrass her. He had been stupid writing the note and even more stupid for hoping she would give up Charles.

He slept on the sofa. It was a temporary arrangement until something more suitable could be arranged, as, by the time dinner was over and he had caught up with family news, it was late and nobody had the energy to move beds.

'We'll do it in the morning. Sleep well, son.'

56

The door closed and George settled under a blanket for the night. He rearranged the cushions a dozen times. His mind buzzed with information. Ma had suggested – no insisted – he stay in England and leave the Canadian Army. Hadn't she been surprised at that?

'To think you were in the trenches and I didn't know. I was the only one in the street with no one at the front.' He could hear her laugh. 'They all thought I was unpatriotic – you see I wasn't exactly in favour of the war.'

Lizzy whispered in his ear that Ma actively campaigned against it.

'And you were there all the time. And to suppose … Well, it's an ill wind … I don't believe you'd have come back if it wasn't for the war.'

She wanted him to get a job.

'You could try for something at the docks. Why don't you go along with Ted?'

Did he want to work in the docks? Was it really his type of work?

Then there was Lizzy's wedding. His mother wanted him to give her away but he wasn't sure. He had seen a look pass between Ted and Lizzy. It was obvious she wanted Ted to give her away.

He sighed. Lizzy's wedding was going to be the simplest thing to sort out compared to the rest of his problems. If only he had Charles' advantages. He wouldn't be worrying about a job or where he would sleep for the night.

By morning, he was going back to Canada. There was a chance his old employer, Aden Humphrey would need him. But he had let Aden down so would he want him? He had been relying on George to look after his farm and to look out for his wife, Edna, and the children while he was away fighting the war. Maybe he wouldn't be too impressed when he learnt that George had also volunteered for the army. But by the time George had left, boys were doing men's work – ploughing, harvesting, even manning the big threshing machines. All the same, if Edna hadn't insisted he take her into town and if he hadn't visited the General Store, he'd still be there. He wouldn't have gone to France and he wouldn't be here now wondering what to do. And he wouldn't have met Amy.

Women. It always came back to women. They didn't run parliament – didn't have a vote, yet they always got their way. Kitty was the reason he enlisted. He met her in the store. He remembered the conversation clearly.

'I like a man in uniform,' she'd said, fingering his coat. 'All your friends are in Europe, so when are you going?'

He was captivated by her big blue eyes and long lashes. How he wanted to impress her – to wipe the sneer off her face. Like a fool, he'd gone straight to the recruitment office and, like so many of his friends before him, he was soon in the trenches. Women. Hadn't they understood what they were sending their men to? Did they feel guilty now so many were dead?

Next day, at his mother's insistence, he went to the docks. It hadn't altered much in his absence – busier, perhaps, with more steamers. Cranes were unloading, men were carting, the place was heaving with activity. He recalled the fascination it held for him and his thoughts went to the day he had set sail for Canada. He never intended returning.

'Oi, not so fast.' A voice jerked him back to the present. A policeman grabbed a docker by his collar and subjected him to a thorough search.

In that second, he decided. It wasn't the life for him. He would go back to Canada. There was bound to be a shortage of farmhands – so many of the boys wouldn't have made it. He would tell them at supper – get it over with and then report back.

As he walked along the street, deep in thought, it noticed his mother was speaking to someone at the door.

'You can't possibly know my son,' he heard her say. 'He's been away for years ...'

The woman wore a dark brown hat with a large brim and a neat matching jacket. She was petite even though she wore strappy heeled shoes. Hardly the dress of a local girl. Surely, it couldn't be?

'Amy?' He ran along the road. 'Amy. What are you doing here?'

'George. Thank goodness.'

She was stunning – so fresh, her pretty face framed by the brim of the hat. He fought the desire to pull her into his arms.

'I thought I'd got the wrong address.' She gave him a thankful smile and looked back at his mother. 'There. You see, I do know him.'

He was speechless. Amy. His mind wouldn't focus and for some seconds he stood mesmerized, then remembered he had better introduce them.

'Well I never,' his mother said. 'You'd better come in.'

He showed Amy into the parlour, hastily gathering up his belongings from the sofa so she could sit down, then, not trusting himself to sit beside her, stood by the window.

His mother hovered in the doorway. 'Shall I make some tea?'

'That'd be nice, Ma. Thanks.'

'I thought of writing, but I had to come,' Amy said as soon as the door closed. 'I didn't know if a letter would get here in time.'

He searched for words to express how he felt, but found himself floundering. Amy here? In his mother's house? He looked, with chagrin, at the worn out rug in front of the fireplace and the chairs with their threadbare arms. He was ashamed that his army kit bag was still in the corner where he had slung it the previous evening. How shabby she must think him.

'I was terrified you'd leave for Canada before a letter reached you.'

He tried to concentrate on what she was saying but all he could think of was her engagement to Charles.

'Charles? What about Charles?'

Amy held up her left hand. 'I sent it back. You were right, he wasn't for me. It's over. He was … Oh, George, it was awful. He and Martha – they were … You know. Oh, it was awful.' She shuddered. 'Absolutely awful.'

He frowned. 'Charles – Martha?'

'They were ... You know –'

'But Martha? Who's she?'

'Lady Margaret's housemaid.'

'Oh.'

He thought he understood. He had seen the way Army officers behaved in French cafes. Usually, the men and the NCO's were not allowed to go to the same place as the officers, but he'd seen enough to know what went on. Once he even covered for one when he failed to make it back on time. Poor sod, he died the next day. How could he blame him for seeking comfort in the arms of a willing French girl? The truth was, he may well have done the same if the opportunity had come his way.

'What about your mother? Does she know you're here?'

Amy bit her lip.

'What? You mean … She doesn't?' He was alarmed. If he was ever to gain Mrs Attwood's approval he had better return Amy safely as soon as possible.

'I couldn't face telling her … I didn't know how to.'

'Does she know about you and Charles? That you've broken off the engagement?' He squatted beside her, gently shaking her arm.

'No. I mean yes.' Amy's big sorrowful eyes blinked back tears. 'I couldn't tell her so I wrote a letter.'

Women were amazing. How did they get themselves into such messes? It was as well they hadn't had to fight the bloody war.

'But you can't just run away.'

'You ran away.'

'That was different.'

'I can't see why?'

'It's obvious, isn't it? I'm a man and anyway I wasn't engaged.'

'What are you going to do?'

'You mean – what are you going to do?' He stood up and paced about the room deep in thought. What were they going to do? There was hardly enough space for him in this tiny house, so there was no prospect of Amy staying. It was an impossible situation and one of which Mrs Attwood would never approve. He wasn't sure his own mother would either, even though all those years ago, she had left her husband and gone to live with the man she loved. There was nothing else for it. He would have to take her home.

Amy was puzzled. 'No, George. I can't possibly ... Anyway, I thought – well, you said you loved me.'

He squatted again beside her. 'You know I do and I desperately want you to stay. Oh, Amy. I can hardly believe you're here.' He squeezed her hand and sought her eyes. 'Are you sure you know what you're doing? It isn't because Charles has hurt you? I couldn't bear it if you were using me to take your revenge.'

'How could you think such a thing? I love you. I wouldn't have made that dreadful journey if I didn't.' Suddenly she was anxious. 'You've changed your mind?'

'No. No. Never. But I have to be sure – sure you really love me and you know what you're doing. I can't offer you what Charles has. You know that, don't you?'

'You were the one who said wealth isn't all and you're right. I couldn't face it before ...'

'But, Amy, I can't offer you an easy life. Do you really understand what you're doing?'

'I don't care. I want to be with you. I know that now. I thought I could make Charles happy and I – er ... You see, it was what mother always wanted. She'll never forgive me, but I don't love Charles and we'd both be miserable.'

'You don't know how happy it makes me seeing you here, but we have to think carefully about what we're going to do.'

He went back to the window. The baker was delivering bread and the horse, hauling the cart, ambled along and stopped opposite. George made up his mind.

'You can't stay here, Amy. There's no room.'

'Where can I go?'

'Home.'

She shook her head. 'No. I'm not going. I can't. Don't make me, George. I simply can't.'

'Listen to me, Amy, darling. It won't be forever. I'm not doing this the coward's way. I want to marry you and so – I must ask your mother.'

61

'She'll never agree. You know she won't. You know what she's like. Please let me stay.'

'We'll talk her round – you'll see. I'm not running away a second time. We're going to do this properly.'

The door swung open and his mother stood holding a tray.

'What are you going to do properly?'

'Amy and I are getting married.'

CHAPTER FIVE

Mrs Mills drained her cup and placed it in its saucer. 'I think I should come with you. Returning this young lady will look so much better if I chaperone you. Besides, I might be able to add some weight to your argument. After all I do have first-hand experience of marrying for the wrong reasons.'

'Would you, Mrs Mills?' Amy said knowing how much easier it would be if they had the support of George's mother.

George raised his eyebrows as though gauging whether she really meant what she said. 'If you're sure, Ma. I mean, you're always so busy. Don't you have a meeting tomorrow?'

'Nothing that can't be re-arranged and, in any case, I'm never too busy to help my family.' She gathered the tea cups and lifted the tray. 'That's agreed then. We'll set off first thing tomorrow. Now I'd better go and see Mrs Wilson. See if she can let Amy use her spare room.'

'Do you think your mother really could persuade mine?' Amy asked as soon as the door had closed.

'Knowing my mother ... probably. But before we go back, I have to ask you a question.'

'Oh?'

He knelt on the floor in front of her and, with a serious expression on his face, took both his hands in his. 'Amy Attwood will you marry me?'

He was so solemn, she couldn't help giggling. 'Yes, you know I will. But you didn't have to kneel.'

'Got to do it properly,' he laughed and sat back beside her. 'Couldn't have you saying in years to come that I'd never actually proposed. There is one thing though …' his voice trailed off.

'What?'

'Stand up.' He yanked her to her feet. 'I want you to think about what you're doing,' he said in an earnest voice. 'I won't think any the less of you if you change your mind.'

'I wouldn't ever do that.'

'Nevertheless, I want you to have a good look at this room.'

She was puzzled. 'Why? What is there to see?'

He pointed to the hearth rug. 'Look at that for a start. Then there's the furniture. Not exactly stylish, is it?'

'Whatever are you talking about?'

'Turn round and look.'

She was baffled. 'What are you trying to tell me?'

'Everything is worn out – old.'

She stared at its shabbiness. It was old and, he was right, not very fashionable. But what difference did that make? She wasn't marrying the furniture.

'I want you to understand how different my family is to yours – how poor I am,' he continued. 'We don't have servants and there are no luxuries and, right now, I have no idea where we'll live. This is our best room and it's hardly as grand as your hall let alone your dining room. I want to be sure you understand what you're marrying into. Charles can offer you so much more …'

'I love you,' she said without hesitation. 'I don't care about anything else. We love each other, that's what matters.'

'We love each other now, but in five years, ten years when we have children and are struggling to make ends meet, when your hands are raw from housework, will you still love me then?'

Longing to be in his arms, she slipped her hand into his and squeezed it.

'I'll love you until I die and I don't care what I have to endure. I always will.'

'Enough to overcome all this?' He waved his arm in the air.

'How can you doubt me?'

'I need to be sure.' He put his arms around her and his kiss was passionate, leaving her floating in a heaven of fulfilled dreams.

'You've made me the happiest man in the world,' he said when they stopped to draw breath. 'As long as I have you, my darling, I have wealth.'

'We'll make it work, won't we?'

'Of course, we will,' he said and kissed her again.

* * *

They travelled to Buckinghamshire the following morning and it wasn't until Amy entered the house that the euphoria which had sustained her throughout the journey evaporated. She found her mother writing a letter in the morning room.

'Amy, thank goodness,' Mrs Attwood said, abandoning her task and crossing the room to hug her. 'You had me so worried. Where have you been? You've changed your mind?'

'No, mother. I haven't changed my mind. I've – '

'Who's this?' Mrs Attwood demanded, peering over Amy's shoulder.

Embarrassed at her mother's rudeness, she turned to introduce George's mother. There was an awkward pause and she looked from one to the other unsure what to say. It was Mrs Attwood who spoke first.

'It seems I have to thank you for bringing Amy back. It was most kind but we needn't detain you.'

She cringed at the coldness of her mother's words.

'George's mother arranged for me to sleep at their neighbour's house and it was really kind of her to – '

'I will deal with this now,' Mrs Attwood interrupted. 'As I just said, I am obliged to you for bringing Amy back but we wouldn't wish to delay you.'

'You're not in the least. Besides there are some other matters which need discussion,' Mrs Mills began.

'Ma, please,' George placed a restraining hand on his mother's arm. 'This is for me to deal with.' He turned to Mrs Attwood. 'I came to ask permission to marry your daughter.'

'Good heavens.' Mrs Attwood glared at him before returning to stand behind her desk. 'Is this some kind of joke?'

'No. It's a serious question to which I would like a serious answer.'

'Enough of this nonsense. Amy is already engaged to be married and, I would add, to a man of considerable wealth and position.' She turned to Amy. 'The letter you wrote to Charles is still sitting on your dressing table. He knows nothing of this stupid escapade.' She looked back at George. 'And so I'd be pleased if you would leave my house.'

'I'm sure your daughter's happiness is your greatest concern,' Mrs Mills said. 'For this reason, I want to tell you a little of my own experience.'

'Your experience?' Mrs Attwood glared at George's mother. 'I can't quite see what that has to do with Amy.'

'More than you might think. I know you have a very low opinion of my son, though I cannot think why. He has not acted or behaved in anything other than an exemplary manner which, I believe, is more than can be said of Amy's other proposed suitor.'

'How dare you?'

'There's something of which I think you should be aware,' Mrs Mills continued in a calm voice. 'Let me explain. My parents own quite a large estate in Oxfordshire and just like Amy, I was persuaded to marry a well-connected man – a man with wealth to match. I didn't love him. The marriage was a disaster. We separated. And then I found a man I loved – someone who also loved me. It hasn't been easy.'

'Good heavens. Do I take this to mean you are living with a man – out of wedlock?'

'You wouldn't wish that on Amy.'

'I wouldn't like to see her marry a bastard either.'

'Mother,' Amy gasped.

'I was married to George's father,' Mrs Mills said in a polite tone. 'I left my marriage with two children and George is one of them.'

'Amy, go to your room.'

'But mother, this is my future you're discussing.' She stood her ground. How dare her mother ban her as though she were a naughty school girl brought home by her teacher.

'I thought I could save you from lowering yourself to their level …' Mrs Attwood glared at Mrs Mills. 'You could do so much better for yourself … Think, Amy, if you married Charles you would have position and wealth.' Then she pointed at George. 'What has he to offer you? I'd hoped so much you'd come to your senses. I even made sure you didn't get … '

'Didn't get what, Mrs Attwood?' George was quick to ask.

Guilt flashed across her mother's face and Amy knew what the answer would be.

'What did you do with George's letters?' she demanded.

'I did what was best for you.'

'You knew how much those letters meant.' Her voice cracked. 'How could you let me go on thinking he was dead?'

'I – er – it was for all the right reasons.'

'Right reasons?' She screamed.

'Calm down. There's no need to shout at me.'

'Calm down?' How could she calm down when all she wanted to do was to shake her mother? All those months of longing, hoping, not knowing, the despair, the heartbreak. 'What did you do with them?'

Mrs Attwood sighed. 'I put them on the fire.'

'Burnt them? Burnt them? How could you?'

'Oh, Amy, my dearest, can't you see what you're doing?' She crossed the room and put her arm around her. 'Don't you realize I only want what's best for you.'

Disgusted, Amy twisted away. She had burnt her precious letters. How could she do such a callous thing? She had ached for George. If only her mother had known how much and to think that if Freddie hadn't spotted him on the platform she might never have found him again.

'I am going to marry George and there is nothing you can do to stop me.' She marched to the door where she stopped and turned. 'We love each other.'

* * *

Weeks later, as she lay listening to the steady breathing of Violet who shared the bed, she was still angry. How could she ever forgive her mother? The song of a blackbird filtered through her thoughts. She had never expected to hear the dawn chorus in London. Everything felt strange – weird, even. Nothing could have prepared her for a wedding day quite like this and it would be a relief when, as man and wife, she and George could escape the smothering attention of Mrs Mills who always made certain they were never alone. She suspected Lizzy had been pregnant when she married Albert and this was the reason for such restrictions. It was as though Mrs Mills was making doubly sure another baby was not conceived out of wedlock. True the organization of their wedding meant endless errands to run, but even George was beginning to lose his patience.

'She wasn't a suffragette for nothing,' he grumbled on one occasion. 'She has an answer to everything.'

She sat up in bed and hugged her knees, thinking about all the things which had happened in the last few weeks. Would she ever get used to her new mother-in-law? And what of George's siblings? Vi was all right – more than all right. She was her kind of person – the others were so noisy. Vi was to be her only bridesmaid. But the rest of George's family? Ted was thoughtful but she wasn't sure about Lizzy or Phoebe. Sometimes she thought they were laughing at her. But they had to get along, they were all going to be living in the same house. There would be no escaping to Mrs Wilson's when things got really unbearable.

She looked about the room. Hanging on the picture rail, shrouded in a sheet, was her wedding dress – or rather Lizzy's. She and Vi had spent hours sewing on the sequins Mrs Mills had cut from an old dress. The waist had been taken in, the skirt shortened and yesterday when she stood in front of the mirror she really felt like a bride.

She sat on the edge of the bed, yawned, then tiptoed across to the window to see what kind of day it was.

'You're up early.'

Vi's voice made her drop the curtain.

'Sorry, I didn't mean to disturb you.'

'I was half awake anyway.' She yawned and stretched. 'Today's your big day. Excited? Is that what woke you up?'

'I suppose … I'm a light sleeper. The birds outside – they woke me.'

'What sort of day is it?' Vi stretched and yawned.

'Dull. I think it's going to rain and I'd hoped so much the weather would improve.'

'Lizzy didn't get much sun either, did she?'

It was drizzling when Freddie arrived in his car to take her and Vi to the church and she was careful to lift her skirt to avoid the puddles which had already formed in the street. When she entered the church on Freddie's arm she could see George's family and friends but the sight of empty pews on the bride's side dismayed her and, for the first time doubts crowded in. She had never felt so alone.

She stood still while Vi arranged her dress.

'You look pale. You should have used some of that lipstick.'

Freddie squeezed the hand which, although she was unaware, was gripping his arm.

'Are you all right?'

She nodded.

She stared up the aisle at George's back but he might as well have been a million miles away and she in an alien land. She wanted to run out of the church into the rain and inhale great gulps of air but her legs wouldn't obey her. Her throat closed and she felt faint. This was all wrong. She couldn't go through with it. The organ struck up and she sensed all eyes on her. She felt the vibrations course through her body as the chords of the Wedding March began.

'This is it, sis,' Freddie whispered and patted her hand as though sensing her hesitation.

Then George looked over his shoulder. His smile was for her alone and her heart gave a familiar thud. Any qualms she might have harboured vanished. He was her whole world, her future.

* * *

The wedding party avoided the heavy downpour by dashing to a nearby pub to celebrate. Freddie, who was last and wettest, was soon telling everyone how he was responsible for George meeting Amy.

The chatter became louder and George, brushing a dust particle from his uniform, felt on the edge of things. Everyone was talking to someone. He took out his pocket watch and was disturbed to see Alfie's face staring back at him. Anger, followed by bitterness, swept through him, together with an overwhelming sense of loss. Alfie should have been here to be his best man and to witness him marrying Amy. The chatter in the bar became masked by the noise of battle and his mind lingered on the horrors of the trenches. He jumped at the sound of mortar fire and wrinkled his nostrils at the smell of gun smoke and then Lizzy's high pitched laughter pierced his thoughts. When he looked back at the watch Alfie's face had gone. Would the nightmare never fade?

It was nearly time to go. He shoved the watch into his pocket and looked across at Amy. She was so fragile, so dainty. Sometimes he thought if he held her tightly she would break. He sighed as he thought of the altered wedding dress. If only he was rich enough to buy her the dress she deserved, but she looked as beautiful as the bride in his dreams. She was chatting to Vi and he hoped they would become friends because he knew how alone Amy was and how much she had given up to marry him.

For a brief moment, he studied each of their guests until, at last, his eyes settled on Freddie. The only news Amy would receive of her family would be through him. He sipped his beer, cringing at the

70

memory of taking her back to "Hazeldene". He'd hated doing it, but he would not elope. He'd run away once – he would never do it again. It wasn't easy and he had been grateful for his mother's support. Amy was the most loving, compassionate girl he had ever met and at times he felt unworthy of her but it was true, Mrs Attwood had the right to demand to know what he could offer? And exactly what did he have to offer? Certainly not a title, certainly not position or money. All he had was his love.

'Drink up, son. Nearly time for you to leave.' Ma's voice interrupted his thoughts. He watched her drain her glass, noting the tell-tale pink in her cheeks and remembered the occasions in his childhood when his mother had drunk one glass too many. No doubt the wedding party would spend the rest of the day in the pub, but he and Amy had a train to catch.

'I guess you're right.' He finished his beer. 'Thanks, Ma, for everything and I mean everything.'

'That's what mothers do.'

She was never sentimental and he was surprised to see tears in her eyes.

'Two babies fledged and in two weeks.' She dabbed her eyes with a handkerchief.

'Hardly fledge. I did that a long time ago.' He laughed. 'Besides Lizzy's not too far away and you sure haven't got rid of me yet. But thanks anyway for making it possible. I guess I'd better tell Amy it's time to go.'

He tried to catch her eye. His wife. How his life had changed. In a matter of days, he had been discharged from the Army and, more importantly, landed himself a job. It was a menial job with the London Gas Light and Coke Company, but at least he could pay his way and support his wife and, although he might not be able to provide her with the things she had always taken for granted, he would love her like no other man. He vowed he would take good care of her. When at last Amy looked in his direction, he indicated it was time to go.

After Amy had changed into her going-away outfit, it was time to leave and everyone came to the station to see them off. They all spilled onto the platform and there was lots of kissing and hugging.

'Thanks for coming. I – we appreciate it.' Amy kissed Freddie.

'Keep in touch, sis and remember where I am if you need me.'

'I will and thanks.'

Freddie shook George's hand. 'I know I can trust you to look after my little sister.'

'Sure thing.'

He opened the carriage door and was delighted to see the compartment was empty.

'Come on, Amy.' He caught hold of her elbow and guided her into the train as Lizzy and Phoebe rained confetti over them.

'Oh, I nearly forgot. My bouquet.'

He lowered the window with the leather strap and Amy leant out. As she threw the posy, the guard blew his whistle and waved his flag. The train, with an almighty chuff and belching smoke, began to move. It was Vi who caught Amy's bouquet.

'I hope it brings her some luck,' Amy said, relaxing into the seat.

George placed their case in the netted overhead rack and sat beside her.

'I think I must be the luckiest girl alive.' Her fingers clasped the round, plain gold locket which hung around her neck. 'And I adore my wedding present.' She smiled, thinking how its shape and simplicity contrasted with the locket which had gone to The Front. 'We must find two photographs to go inside.'

George caught hold of her left hand and examined the gold wedding band. He wouldn't tell her he'd spent every last penny on it or, for that matter, the locket was second hand.

'In case you haven't noticed, we're alone at last.' He turned her hand over and planted a kiss in the palm before kissing her on the lips.

They spent three nights in a small hotel on the edge of Epping Forest, blissfully unaware of anything or anybody else. They walked and talked and made love and walked and talked some more. And then it was over and it was time to catch the train back to London and the reality of life.

When they arrived home, Amy wondered what was in the large pot simmering on the stove, but it smelt good and she was hungry. Dinner was in two sittings and together with Lizzy, Albert, Ted and Ma, they waited their turn.

'Let's have a drink, shall we?' Ma went to the sideboard for a bottle of sherry.

Lizzy passed the glasses around. Amy refused.

'Go on with you,' Ma said.

She looked at George, hoping he would rescue her, but he took the drink from Lizzy and placed it in her hands.

'Amy'll enjoy a taste. Let's keep the peace,' he said kissing her behind the ear.

'But, you know I hate the stuff,' she whispered. They were married now and he ought to understand how insignificant she felt amongst his loud and boisterous relatives.

'It'll do you good,' he said in a louder voice.

She frowned at him. He was supposed to be on her side.

'Right,' Ma held up her glass. 'A toast. To the newlyweds. She looked at Lizzy who held Albert's hand and then at George, who had his arm around Amy. 'I wish you all every happiness.'

There was a clinking of glasses and Amy looked at the dark liquid before taking the tiniest drop and finding it sweeter than expected. George and Lizzy, who were waiting on the others disappeared into the scullery, returning with bowls of steaming spotted dick pudding covered with custard. She watched him collect a stack of dirty plates and couldn't help compare this scene to the one at home where there was a maid to fetch and carry. Home? She chided herself. This was home now. At least for the time being – until they got a place of their own.

'When are you and George going to have a baby?' May bounced into George's empty seat, taking her by surprise.

'I – er – I don't know.' What could she say? They hadn't been married a week. In fact they hadn't even discussed the matter. She glanced down at May. She was so irritating – so forward – asking questions about the most intimate things – things she herself had only just begun to understand. She had found the whole business of making love a little shocking and George had told her on more than one occasion to relax. She knew so little about satisfying a man, but George kept telling her she was fine.

'Lizzy's showing already. What do you think it'll be?'

She glanced at her sister-in-law then smiled at May. 'We'll have to wait and see, won't we?'

'When you have a baby what would you like? A girl or a boy?'

'I think I'll be content with what I get.'

'Do you think you and George – '

'Second sitting,' Lizzy called.

Relieved to escape May's relentless questions, she found her place at the table.

'Back to work tomorrow, eh, George?' Ted pushed some vegetables onto his fork.

'What will you do tomorrow?' Lizzy looked in Amy's direction.

'It's washday.' Ma said before she had a chance to think of an answer. 'You can help me light the copper. There'll be plenty to do.'

She hadn't thought about this before, but what was she supposed to do while George was at work? Before she married, she wrote letters, read or played the piano and spent hours gardening. Here the garden was tiny and, anyway, she couldn't assume she could take it over. She itched to prune the bushes and the solitary rose could do with the dead heads removed. With only their room to tidy and clean, she would be expected to assist with the household chores. Her heart sank. She was bound to do everything badly.

George winked at her and his smile was reassuring.

'If you like,' Lizzy said, 'you can come and help choose some wool and patterns for the baby. Albert's mother is going to make the layette. She said she'd teach me how to knit and I thought I'd make a matinee jacket. Can you knit?'

74

She shook her head. 'But I can sew,' she said, wanting to show she could do something.

'But can you darn?' Ma said eyeing her.

She shook her head, afraid to admit she didn't even know what darning was.

'You'll soon learn.'

Her heart sank. The word "darn" didn't sound very exciting. She glanced around the table. Her in-laws were so different to anyone she had met in her entire life but, she assured herself, she and George would soon have their own home.

'What am I expected to do while you're at work?' she asked later when they were in their bedroom.

He helped undo the buttons on her blouse, his light kisses trailing down her neck. 'Whatever you feel happiest doing,' he said against her bosom. 'I want you to be happy.'

'I'm not sure about helping your mother. I'll be hopeless. I just know.'

'You'll be fine.' His lips found their way back to her neck. 'Anyway we'll get a place of our own soon.'

'Promise it'll be soon.'

'As soon as we've saved some money. Come to bed ...'

After George left for work the next morning, Amy sat writing a brief letter to Freddie, planning to post it when she went out with Lizzy. There was no morning room in which to sit and no newspaper to read. Everything had to be done within this one room. She looked around, comparing their tiny bedroom to the much larger one which had once been hers. She tried to console herself. Learning to be Mrs Mills would take time and there were bound to be things she missed. She loved George and that was all that mattered.

* * *

The excursion to choose knitting wool didn't take long and she was soon home. She didn't look for an excuse to linger. She still hadn't got used to the grime of the little streets and somehow Lizzy was not as much fun as Vi. Albert's mother was very nosey, asking all kinds of questions about her childhood and her answers, she suspected, would be passed on as gossip.

The remainder of the day was spent in the scullery, helping with the washing. She had no idea it could be such hard work and the dryness of her hands made her wonder how long it would be before hers looked as red and rough as Ma's.

In the afternoon Ma went to a meeting – something to do with the socialists, she'd said. Before she left, she demonstrated how to darn. Amy was left with a large pile of assorted mending, which she looked at with distaste. It wasn't as though any of it was George's. She selected a sock and held it up for inspection. It was hand-knitted and had stiffened with age. One of Thomas' she thought, noting there was already a darn in the toe. Now it had worn thin in the heel. She pushed the wooden mushroom inside the sock, found some suitable wool and struggled to thread the yarn through the eye of the needle.

She wished she had gone with Ma. Anything would have been better than darning socks. Ma had invited her along, but she had been brought up to believe politics was men's business. So she sat where the light was best and sewed countless buttons on shirts and blouses, darned at least six socks and was surprised at the satisfaction she felt at the growing pile of completed garments. She was finishing the hem on May's skirt when George returned.

'Do you think Ma will be pleased?'

'I'm sure she will.' He put his arms around her and kissed her. 'Come to bed. The house is empty. May's with her friends along the road. I saw her as I came home.'

'Thank goodness for that. She never stops asking questions, but where's Thomas?'

'Stop worrying. He's out somewhere. We have the place to ourselves.'

It was only as they relaxed after their lovemaking, she remembered Ma's instructions about dinner.

'She said to keep an eye on the range. The oven won't be hot enough and the pie will never be ready in time. My first day and dinner will be a disaster.'

76

'No, it won't. It'll be a little late, that's all. Come on, I'll give you a hand.' He jumped up and yanked her off the bed. 'Quick. Get dressed. I'll see to the stove.'

They heard the sound of the back door closing.

'Oh, no. It's too late.'

'Don't worry, I'll tell Ma, it's my fault.'

'But she'll know – they'll all know. Oh, how embarrassing.'

'Don't be so silly,' he chuckled. 'I sure bet she's done the same herself and more than once judging by the size of this family.'

'How can you say such a thing? Anyway, it's not the point.'

'All right. All right. I know what you mean, but I can't change things. We have to accept life isn't as private as we'd like.'

Several months went by and the only high spot in Amy's day was George's return in the evening. It seemed everything was shared with somebody.

'I wish we had more time to ourselves,' Amy said one evening as she closed their bedroom door.

'We'll have our own place soon, I promise.' George undid his shirt buttons. 'Just as soon as I've saved enough. We won't want to have children here.'

'At least we waited.'

He was puzzled.

'Until we were married – not like Lizzy.' She calculated Lizzy was at least three months pregnant at the time of her marriage.

'I take it from the tone of your voice you disapprove.'

'Our marriage wasn't arranged in a hurry because I was pregnant.' She slipped out of her blouse.

'Amy Mills you are beginning to sound like your mother.'

She finished getting ready for bed in silence. His words stung. Was it true? She knew her speech and her clothes were superior, but she had been so careful not to be arrogant. But there was still the time she had caught May mimicking her and once she was certain Lizzy and Phoebe were talking about her. As she opened the scullery door,

77

Lizzy stopped mid-sentence and looked uncomfortable. She was beginning to think she would never fit into George's family.

* * *

They had been married almost a year and Amy had begun to give up hope of moving into rooms of their own. Every time she enquired, George's answer was evasive.

'Soon, maybe,' he would say or 'I need to save more money.'

One morning, after he had left for work, she began to tidy their room but nausea threatened. She sat down to fold his pyjamas.

'Letter for you,' Ma said, standing in the doorway. 'Are you all right?'

'Yes, yes, thank you. I think it was the ham last night. Didn't agree with me.' She didn't add how fatty it was or how she disliked mushy peas. Or that, in her opinion, petite pois were so much more tasty.

Ma handed her the letter and turned to go downstairs.

She glanced at the writing and knew it was from Freddie. His letters were always interesting. He had started his garage business with money loaned from their mother and he had a new lady in his life. She sometimes wondered if the two were connected. She scanned the letter quickly, then re-read it. The news was so exciting, she felt she would burst if she didn't tell someone, but she was determined no one would know before George.

'Who was your letter from?' Ma asked later as they set off to the shops.

'Freddie.' She avoided Ma's prying eyes.

'Everything all right?'

'Yes, of course.'

As soon as George arrived home, she ushered him upstairs.

'Have you missed me that much …' He followed her into their bedroom.

'Shshsh.' She shut the door.

He reached for her, but she pushed him away. 'I've got a letter from Freddie and, you'll never guess ... there's a possibility of a job. Oh, I'm so excited.'

'And I thought it was me you wanted.'

'It's farming – like you used to do.'

George unbuttoned his work shirt, dropped it to the floor and sat on the bed to remove his shoes. 'What kind of job?'

She picked up the shirt and folded it neatly. 'It's on a farm near Freddie's garage. He said he's put in a word for you.'

'He has, has he?'

She ignored the tone of his voice and went to the dressing table to fetch the envelope. 'You'll be doing something you really like.'

She sat on the bed beside him. If only he would want the job as much as she did.

'Read it.' She pushed the letter into his hands. 'It sounds like the sort of thing you did in Canada. I know how much you miss Canada. It would be the next best thing and there's a cottage. Freddie says it goes with the job. A whole cottage to ourselves. Wouldn't it be wonderful?'

When he had read the letter, he looked up at her. 'Don't get too excited. I haven't got the job yet.'

'But you will. I know you will.'

'We don't know that. Anyway what about your mother? We'll only be along the road from her. Do you think it's wise?'

'What's wrong with that?'

'Nothing. Nothing. I thought you'd rather not – that it might be difficult for you – us. That's all.'

'Isn't here difficult enough? All on top of each other. Squashed in this little room. No privacy. May always being nosey. Don't you think it'd be nice to have a place of our own?' She slid her arms around his neck and kissed him. He must see it was their means of escaping this claustrophobic little room. 'Anyway, it isn't exactly next door. It's a few miles away and maybe, just maybe, if we were closer, mother might ... At least I could go and see her ...'

He grinned. 'All right, I give in. I know when I'm beaten and it seems a good offer on the face of it.'

He handed her the letter and Amy pushed it back into its envelope, but his voice told her there was a catch. 'You don't sound too enthusiastic.'

'I didn't say that ...'

'I thought you'd jump at the idea. The cottage ... It's so cramped here. It'd be worth it for a place of our own.'

He picked up his shoes and put them in the bottom of the wardrobe then slipped his feet into a pair of scruffy slippers. She watched, disappointed he didn't show more enthusiasm when all day, she had found it hard to hide her own excitement. She stared at the faded curtains and the equally faded bedspread and wondered how much longer they would have to live with this shabbiness.

'Shall we go over on Sunday?' he said in such a matter-of-fact way, it took a second for the words to sink in.

'You're not teasing me?'

'Would I do a thing like that?'

She flung herself into his arms and, even though the whole family was home, there was no protest when he took advantage of the situation.

CHAPTER SIX

The following Sunday, they caught an early train to Amersham.

'What do you think?' Freddie demanded to know as they inspected his new motor car.

'Very nice.' George ran his finger along the paintwork, admiring its sheen. 'Humber's supposed to be a good make.'

'It's the latest model.' Freddie opened the driver's door and George stuck his head inside.

'Never mind about silly motor cars, what about George's job?' Amy could no longer disguise her impatience.

'Amy's very excited,' George said, backing out of the car. 'I hope she won't be too disappointed if I don't get this job.'

'Don't worry,' Freddie said in a low voice. 'You'll get the job. Foregone conclusion. I've seen to that.' He turned to Amy. 'You look good, sis. Married life must be suiting you.'

'How can you be sure George will get the job?'

'Never doubt your big brother.' He waggled a finger at her. 'Sid Burton is the father of a very good friend of mine. He lost one of his best stockmen. I happened to be in the White Hart, when he was talking about it and he said if George was as good as I told him, the job was his.' He turned to George. 'What do you say, old man? Are you up for it?'

'Of course he is.' She grabbed George by the arm. 'You are aren't you? Oh, do come on. I can hardly wait.'

* * *

'I can't believe our luck,' Amy said later when they arrived at the cottage. It was one of three, all fronting a brick path, with tiny gardens and equally tiny windows. The interior was small and gloomy, but she could live with all its faults because it was theirs – all theirs.

'It'll need a good clean, but isn't it wonderful? I'll soon have it looking spick and span.'

Two weeks later, they left with two large boxes of assorted china, cooking pots and cutlery which they packed into Freddie's car. There was a bundle of sheets, two old blankets and a pair of faded red curtains, which Amy looked at with revulsion, until George reminded her of the state of their finances.

'And I thought you might need these,' Ma said, holding a broom and a mop, which George wedged into the car.

It was raining and she squeezed into the back while George sat at the front. She peered through the little oval window to wave farewell, grateful to be leaving dreary, wet London.

As soon as they arrived, she ran ahead, let herself in and stood quite still in the centre of the kitchen, taking in every detail. The big black range dominated the room and the stone floor was bare. It was as if she was in a dream. Would she wake up soon? She inspected the range, wondering how much food she would spoil, before she was able to cook George the special meals she planned.

The rain had eased by the time unloading was complete. Wet footmarks were everywhere, but to Amy it felt as if the sun was shining.

'I'll leave you two lovebirds to get settled in,' Freddie said, placing a box of groceries on the table. 'This should see you through a day or two.'

'Thanks. I hadn't ...' How could she forget something as basic as food? 'It's really sweet of you to do all this for me – us.' She tried to hide her incompetence and suddenly remembered the furniture upstairs. 'The bed – thanks for fixing that too.'

'The bed. An essential piece of equipment, I'd say.'

She giggled and, hot with embarrassment, delved into the box. 'Oh, some cheese.' She smiled her thanks. 'You must come for dinner as soon as we're settled.' Even as she uttered the words, she remembered the range. The thought she might not manage an edible meal for George let alone visitors, flashed into her head, but nothing could diminish her happiness. Privacy, at last.

'That'd be nice,' Freddie said. 'But I must go. Mother'll wonder where I've got to. Enid's parents are coming for dinner.'

'It's serious then?'

'Mother would like to think so.'

'But you? You're not so sure?'

'Early days yet.'

'You mustn't let her force you into a marriage. For goodness sake, Freddie, don't let her push you around.'

He looked uncomfortable.

'You've agreed to it already. That's it, isn't it?' Her mind raced on. Had he agreed to marry this Enid in return for that loan? She wouldn't put it past her mother.

'Enid's nice. You'll like her. I'll bring her over sometime.'

'Freddie, don't let mother bully you. She'd have had me marry Charles, no matter what. Just so I could be Lady Ashby.'

'Don't worry, sis, if I marry, it'll be because I want to.'

'Good, but make sure you marry for love.' It seemed strange telling Freddie what to do. It was usually the other way round. Her thoughts turned to the problem of their mother. Although she would never be able to forget she had burnt George's letters, she wanted to put the matter behind her. She was married and, in spite of all her faults, she missed her. 'Do you think mother might visit sometime?'

'Maybe.'

'She does know we're here? You did tell her?'

He nodded. 'Yesterday. She pretended not to be interested, but I know she was. Give her a bit of time. Now I must go or I'll be late. I'll call back later in the week and see how you're doing.'

'You could bring her with you ...' she suggested but before he could reply George appeared with the curtains over his arms.

'I think that's it. I didn't realize we had so much.'

Freddie went to the door. 'Cheers for now. I'll be over – Friday, probably.'

'Isn't this heaven?' Amy said as soon the door closed. She twirled around on the spot. 'Our own front door. Our own home.'

George enfolded her in his arms. 'Sweetheart, I have to see Mr Burton – see what's got to be done.'

'Now?'

'I need to know what's happening in the morning. Might have to do the milking. I sure wanna start right.'

She kissed him. 'Better go then. Sooner you go, the sooner you'll get back.'

'Wish me luck,' he said, leaving her standing in the middle of boxes and parcels.

She unpacked the groceries and discovered a loaf of bread, butter and a jar of pickle. Exactly what was needed to go with the cheese. Freddie was an angel.

Later, over supper they made plans for the garden.

'Vegetables, not flowers. That way we'll save money.'

'What no flowers? Not even roses? You know I loved my garden at "Hazeldene". I didn't understood how much until we were in London. We have to have some flowers, George. I insist.'

'Just for you, the rose on the back fence can stay.' He reached across and squeezed her arm. 'But we need as much ground as possible for vegetables. The more we grow, the better.'

'George.'

'Mmm.'

'There's something I have to tell you.'

'We haven't got any tea? Sure didn't expect none. Ma only has it because a friend of Vi's gets factory sweepings.'

'No, no. It isn't that. Anyway, I haven't lit the stove yet, so I can't boil the kettle.'

'It can wait until tomorrow. I've got to be up for milking and I'm tired. Aren't you?'

'Yes, but ...'

'We'd better make up the bed.'

'I've done that ...'

'You have? Good. I could fall into it right now.'

'George, there's something ... I think I'm pregnant.'

George placed his knife on the plate and gave her his full attention.

'Did I hear right?'

She nodded.

'Amy, that's unbelievable.' He smiled broadly. 'Son of a bitch, it sure as hell aint after what we've been up to. Oops, sorry about that ...'

She giggled. 'I do love you when you sound all Canadian.'

He reached for her hand, his face full of concern. 'How long? Are you feeling sick or something? You ate your dinner, didn't you?'

'Your face is a picture.' She leant across the table to kiss him. 'I'm fine. I felt a little sick the other morning but otherwise I would hardly know.'

'When? When's the baby due?'

'The end of January or may be into February.'

'Oh, Amy, I'm so excited. I can't wait to tell everyone about our son.'

'Son? It could be a daughter. Would you be disappointed if it was?'

He shook his head. 'As long as it's got all its fingers and toes. What do you want?'

'A boy. Definitely a boy.'

85

1923

George banged the door shut, shrugged off his coat and slung it on the nearest chair. He ignored the dirt on his boots and in two strides had slumped into the chair beside by the stove.

The room was gloomy. August, yet it felt like the middle of November. The rain had been ceaseless, penetrating every level of clothing, but he hadn't the energy to remove the rest of his garments and it was some minutes before he found the strength to remove his muddy boots. He sat gratefully warming his feet. Nausea gripped his stomach and it wasn't from the all-pervading tiredness. He struggled to focus his thoughts – to understand – to make sense of it all and failed.

The pot on the stove simmered gently. Amy always knew when a hot meal was required. The smell often made him lift the lid, but today he had no appetite. He rubbed his feet trying to get his circulation moving, then leant back, scratching his chin, rough with the day's growth of beard. His eyes roamed the room. This had been their home for three years. If they left here – where would they go? Back to London and Ma's?

His expression changed as he thought of Will and the joy their son had brought them. Then his eyes narrowed and he frowned. Amy would never tolerate going back and he couldn't imagine them all squashed in the little room they shared when they first married.

Canada? Whenever life seemed imponderable, his thoughts would veer off to impossible dreams. His mind went back to an evening spent with Army pals. There had been talk about land settlement – some government scheme. As a lad, Canada had been his opportunity of escape – but as a family man ... Anyway, Amy might not want to go. How could he blame her? It would mean leaving everything she loved and she had given up enough for him already. All the same, he wished he'd paid more attention to what had been said that evening. At the time, things weren't this bad and, besides, he was settled – they were settled, weren't they?

The queasiness returned. He had seen some dreadful things in his time, but today ... He swallowed. It was the hardest thing he'd ever done. Every single animal slaughtered ...

He closed his eyes and tried to erase the memory. He would have to tell Amy. He could hear her moving about upstairs. He would creep up later and look in on Will. Two years old. Where had the time gone?

And how did he explain this disaster? The farm had passed from father to son and Paul was a waster. It was common knowledge that he had run up huge debts and now Foot and Mouth. It might mean the end of his job, the house. The end of everything.

He tried to count his blessings. His employment had fed them and given Amy the home she wanted and what was more, he liked the work – enjoyed the contact with animals. There were no luxuries but Amy had adjusted to their new life and rarely complained.

He lifted his feet one at a time to feel the heat of the stove. He liked it here – would stay, if things remained the same.

But nothing is forever. He remembered how he'd often repeated those same words. Times when he'd been up to his ankles in mud in the trenches – when to step off the boards was to risk being drowned – when the war seemed never ending and when so many of his friends lost their lives. Nothing is forever. Those words kept him going. He'd promised Alfie if he survived he'd make the most of every opportunity and hadn't he done just that?

But even the good things don't last. Things were bad even before Foot and Mouth cast its ugly shadow over them.

All those beautiful beasts. His friends.

'Come along, Bessie. It's no good giving me the eye.' He would say to the big brown cow with the soft, gorgeous eyes.

He'd milk her cautiously. Most days she kicked out and if he wasn't careful, she'd kick over the pail.

When he'd finished with Bessie, there was Abigail and Gertrude. Then there was Maud, who only gave a good yield if you treated her right. He was the one who knew Gertrude behaved better if she was milked before Maud and Abigail liked him to whisper in her ear.

Now they were all gone – slaughtered. Such a waste. Such a damn, waste.

And he had led them … He had betrayed their trust. He swallowed and his heart felt heavy, his stomach sickened. He could see them lying in a pit – like his friends in the fields of Flanders. He kicked out at his boots, ignoring the lumps of mud which splattered on to the floor, then dashed away a tear.

'Life's so bloody unfair, Alfie.' He said out loud.

He heard Amy's footsteps on the stairs and managed to get a hold of himself, blowing his nose and wiping his eyes. He must tell her tonight.

'George. You gave me a fright.' She stood in the doorway with an armful of dirty washing. 'I didn't hear you come in. Why didn't you light the lamp?'

'Got a soaking. Thought I'd dry out.'

'Oh. Yes, hasn't it been an awful day. Not stopped at all, has it?'

George went to fetch the oil lamp and Amy dumped the washing on a chair and disappeared into the larder for potatoes to prepare for dinner.

'There's a horrid tummy bug going round. The girls next door have it quite badly,' she said, as she peeled potatoes. 'I thought Will had a temperature earlier, but when I put him to bed, he seemed all right. But you know what children are like – up one minute and down the next.'

She placed the pan on the stove. 'You're quiet. Is everything all right?'

'Been a hard day, that's all.' He was careful to keep his back to her as he placed the lamp on the table.

'I'd forgotten. Today ...' She hesitated. 'Did they?'

He concentrated on lighting the lamp. He couldn't bring himself to tell her. He needed time to compose himself. 'I'll go and tuck Will in,' he said and disappeared upstairs.

He entertained his son with a story and was pleased he had chosen one which was soothing and not just to Will. When he returned downstairs, Amy was piling vegetables onto the plates.

'Good, I'm glad you're here. Dinner's ready.'

He wasn't hungry, but sat at the table and pushed his food around the plate, while he tried to work out how to break the news.

'You didn't say ... Did they?'

He didn't, couldn't answer.

She looked at him with concern. 'I know it must have been a horrible thing to do, but wasn't it – necessary?'

He swallowed hard, trying to keep his emotions hidden. The word "necessary" grated. She'd never understand.

'There'll be new cows though, won't there? I mean, it won't stop them from having more will it? Just a bit of time to clean everything up, isn't that right?'

She made it sound so clinical, but they were his cows – each had their own personality and they were his friends. Nobody, but another herdsman, would understand how his heart ached.

She gave him a sympathetic smile, but he was unable to reply. Any words he formed dried to a lump in his throat. He got up from the table and put another log on the fire then went to the window, staring but not seeing, before closing the curtains.

Somehow he must explain a new herd wouldn't happen overnight. In fact, might not happen at all. And if he told her that Paul had gambled the farm away, she would soon guess Freddie was also gambling.

'What would you think of going to Canada?' The words slipped out and when he turned to face her, she was looking at him with astonishment. Fool, he cursed. If he was serious about taking them all to Canada, he should have made some enquiries, got the facts, so at least he knew what he was talking about.

'Are you serious?' She stared at him with raised eyebrows. 'What's brought this on? I thought it was all in the past. When we got married you said you wanted to stay in England. I thought we were settled. We are, aren't we, George? I mean settled?'

There was anxiety in her voice and he cursed himself for letting the words slip out. He should have taken more time, prepared the ground. No wonder she was alarmed. There had been no preamble, no hints. 'Yes. Yes, of course we are.'

'Then why this talk of Canada? When you took this job, you said you'd decided not to go back. That it was final. Have you changed your mind?'

'Take no notice. I don't know what made me mention it. After a day like today …' George shrugged and sat down again. 'Grass is greener sometimes, you know.'

'I know it's been a horrible day.' She placed her hand over his. 'But I've got something to tell you, which will make you feel much better.'

'Oh. What's that?'

'I think – well, no. I don't think. I know. I'm pregnant.'

'Really?' It was a second or two before the words sunk in and he tried to look pleased, but he had already been wondering how he was going to support the three of them. Now Amy was saying there would be a fourth.

'Mmm. Really.' She beamed at him.

'You're sure.'

'As sure as I can be.'

'That's wonderful.' He smiled at her. How could he say this was the last thing he needed right now? 'It's the best piece of news I've had in months. Oh, come here.'

They abandoned dinner and wrapped their arms around each other.

'I love you Mrs M.' He squeezed her close. 'How long have you known?'

'I've had my suspicions for some while, but I think I must be two months.'

'Why didn't you say before?'

'You seemed so preoccupied. Everything is all right?'

'Sure is, honey.' He tried to sound more positive than he felt. 'I guess it'll be another boy?'

'Of course. I told you, they'll all be.'

'And what if I'd like a little girl?'

'Bad luck.' She giggled.

'Little minx.' He tweaked the end of her nose and looked into her eyes. He loved her so much, how could he tell her tonight? It would spoil everything. Tomorrow. It could wait until tomorrow.

Days disappeared into weeks and then into months and, when the farm began the switch into pigs, George allowed himself to hope their luck had changed. But the horror of Foot and Mouth haunted his dreams much in the way the trenches still did and he felt unable to trust Paul, nor could he confide in Amy.

Early the following year, still unsure of his future at the farm, he enquired about emigrating under a government settlement scheme. There was no point in discussing this with Amy before he knew he was eligible. It would mean a tremendous upheaval and she would have to be totally committed or it wouldn't work. A farmer in Canada depended entirely on the support of his wife and family. It would mean giving up more than he had already asked and he wasn't sure if he could persuade her to leave her family forever. Family? What help and support were they? A brother-in-law who still played the field, even though his wife was pregnant and a mother-in-law who refused to accept him or acknowledge her grandson. What was there to stay for?

The day he was informed the farm was to be sold and his job threatened, the letter arrived. When he returned for lunch, Amy met him at the door.

'There's a letter for you. Looks very official. What can it be?' She handed it to him and went to finish laying out the cutlery on the table.

He studied the envelope, then tore it open.

'Dada. Dada,' Will clutched his knees. He lifted the boy, swinging him round in the air before placing him on his lap.

Amy hovered over them.

'Make us some tea, will you, sweetheart.'

He could see she was curious, but she went to the stove, picked up the steaming kettle and poured the water into the tea pot.

'What is it?' She asked as she placed a cup of tea in front of him. 'Mind Will doesn't knock it over.'

He was engrossed in his letter.

'What?' He looked up. 'Oh, yes. Thanks.'

91

'George?'

It was the news he was hoping for and it couldn't have been more timely. His mood lifted. Maybe Amy would be persuaded after all. He looked up.

'The letter? Who's it from?' she prompted.

'It seems there's good and bad news today, sweetheart.'

'Oh, do stop talking in riddles.'

He reached for his cup and took a sip of tea, deciding to tell her the bad news first. 'The farm's up for sale.'

'What?'

'Heard it officially this morning ... Sure is no hiding from this. We have to face facts and the truth is there's a good chance I'll lose my job and this house.'

She sat down. 'That's awful. Whatever shall we do?'

He didn't hurry to explain about the letter, knowing the problems at the farm would make the case for Canada. He wanted to make sure she understood their predicament.

'The new people – they must keep you on, surely? They must do – a good stockman like you.'

'Who knows what they'll decide.'

'I thought things were better now they'd switched to pigs. I don't understand. Why is the farm being sold now?'

George exhaled loudly and knew he would have to tell her the reality of the situation.

'The truth is, Paul Burton has been drinking and gambling his way through his father's money. He's borrowed against the farm and now the bank's going to foreclose. I'm surprised it hasn't happened before.'

'But that's dreadful.' She was studying his face and he knew he was in for a grilling.

'So this is what's been going on. I knew something was wrong – knew you weren't yourself.' She waggled a finger at him. 'Why ever didn't you tell me before? How could you carry on as normal and not give me a clue what was happening? What else have you been hiding?

Don't shut me out, George. We're in this together.' Her hand went to her tummy. 'All of us.'

'I didn't want to worry you.' He tried to sound as considerate as possible, hoping to smooth things over. 'Especially as we have this young man,' he added, ruffling Will's hair, 'and another due any day. What difference would knowing have made anyway? You'd have worried yourself silly. It's better you take care of yourself. No point in getting upset about things you can't change.'

'I am worried now.' Amy stirred her tea. A sudden thought struck her. 'But ... What about Freddie? He's very friendly with Paul Burton. I hope he isn't gambling.'

'I know he's your brother, but thankfully he's not our problem. We have enough troubles of our own.'

'But I can't help worrying.'

'Freddie might still be seeing that woman at the pub, but I don't think he's stupid enough to gamble his life's savings away.'

She sighed. 'I certainly hope not.'

'The garage is successful. He can probably afford it, unlike Paul.'

'But what are we going to do? Where will we go if ..?'

He couldn't help grinning.

'George, what are you up to?'

'How would you like your own place in Canada?'

Amy's eyes darted to the envelope on the table. 'The letter?'

'Ours for the taking.'

'What do you mean?'

'A homestead.'

'Homestead?'

'Farm. It's their way of saying a farm. It's official.' He handed her the letter. 'Read it. Sure is perfect timing.' He sipped his tea, his mind racing ahead. There would be cattle, horses, barns and acres and acres of wheat. Would she be as excited? 'We can go as soon as we've had medicals and interviews.' He wanted to jump for joy, but instead he bounced Will up and down on his knee and his words came fast and furious. He had to persuade Amy. It was a fantastic opportunity – their only hope. 'They're a formality, of course. The interviews, that is. It should all be straightforward. Of course I won't do anything, if you don't want me to, but it's the best chance we'll ever get.'

She scanned the letter, then read it again. 'It says Manitoba.'

'Sure. Remember I told you about Alexander? That's in Manitoba.'

'Is it really as cold as everyone says? Oh, George, I don't know what to say …'

'Think about it. Now I'd better eat something and get back.'

He watched her place a plate of food in front of him and knew she was not enthusiastic.

'Canada's a long way from home,' she said over lunch. 'What if I don't like it?'

'You'll love it.'

'How can you be so sure?'

'We'll have each other and the children.'

'But we won't be able to take a trip back here … It'll be ... forever.'

'True. We have to make Canada our home. What of it? It'd be different if our family was calling in every day.' He paused, wondering when she would give up on her stubborn mother, then decided to say what was in his mind anyway. 'The truth is, your mother doesn't exactly dote on her grandchild, does she?'

'Mother. I hadn't thought of her. What will she say? We'll have to tell her – give her the chance to make things up. I might never see her again. I'd rather go knowing we were, you know, at least talking to each other.'

'We're going then?'

She hesitated. 'I don't know … It's such a big decision and we've got to pass these medicals?'

'A formality. We're both fit, aren't we?'

'I need time … it's all right for you – you've been thinking about this for months – planning it behind my back.' She fetched a cloth and wiped Will's face.

'Don't say things like that. I didn't mean to go behind your back. There was no point in telling you until I knew for certain we could go. I wanted the facts and I only got those today. I don't think I could have told you sooner.'

'It still feels as if it's been done without me having a say.'

George slipped into his coat, wondering what more he could say to show her he hadn't meant to be devious.

'How soon will it all happen? The baby's due any day now …'

He finished doing up his buttons and turned to face her. 'I know, sweetheart and that's the reason I didn't want you worrying.' He sighed. 'It isn't going to happen tomorrow. These things take time. You know what it's like. There'll be all sorts of paperwork. I won't do another thing without your say so. Promise you'll think about it.'

She nodded and her face was serious.

'I've got to get back. We both have to want this or it won't work.' He squeezed her arm. 'Remember, I love you. We'll talk about it tonight.'

He gave her a peck on the cheek and patted Will's head. Then he was gone.

* * *

Amy carried the plates to the sink, then fetched the kettle, pouring the hot water into the sink to wash the dishes. She tried to think rationally. It was true the economic climate was harsh and jobs were difficult to find, but George was an excellent stockman and the country needed milk and meat.

Will brought his building bricks to where she stood and began to pile them one on the other.

'Don't build there, Will,' she scolded and dried her hands. She picked up the bricks which were scattered along the route between the sink and the table. 'Look it's better here.' She began to restack the

95

bricks. 'Mummy'll come and help when I've finished doing the dishes.'

Will screamed his annoyance, knocking the small tower to the floor. She ignored the tantrum and returned to her task.

Canada. The word was all pervading. Every thought, every action. If she said no, they were doomed and if she said yes ... Was George right? He was so sure and she'd never doubted him ever, so why now? She couldn't imagine life without him. She had to give him the benefit of any doubt. She had to.

She turned to clear the table, trod on a brick and yelping in pain, fell to the floor.

'Will,' she shouted. 'I told you not to play here. You silly child.'

He screamed and threw himself to the ground, arms and legs thrusting in all directions. She picked up a brick and tossed it to other side of the room. Damn, Canada. Damn the Burtons and damn being big and pregnant. The baby responded with a firm kick and she clasped her stomach. Dragging herself to her feet, she sat on the chair beside the stove waiting for Will to calm down, rubbing her ankle, thankful it was only bruised. The baby moved its position.

'It's all right,' she said to her unborn child. 'No one is going to hurt you.'

Her mind was still in turmoil when George returned at the end of the day.

He was the first to broach the subject over supper. 'Do we go?'

She dodged the question. 'It's such a big decision.' How could she make up her mind in an afternoon? She had so little information. George at least had the advantage of having seen the country. If it was just the two of them – but there was Will and the baby.

'Sweetheart, it's a huge decision. I know that. But I don't think there's much here for us.'

'They'll be no coming back, will there?'

'No. Not in the normal way of things. But why would we want to when we have our own place? We'd be working for ourselves. Think, honey, for ourselves. Any profit would be for us.'

96

His face shone with excitement. It was hard not to join in, but she wanted to be practical.

'What about the cold? And how do we get there?' The thought of travelling all that way terrified her. 'We'll have two children to consider, too, George and one will be a baby. What about them? Are there schools?'

He laughed. 'Sure, there's schools and people survive the winter. I don't deny it's cold, sometimes perishing cold, but we'd manage. Give it a chance, sweetheart. I know you'll love it and it's a fantastic place for children. Trust me.'

His eyes sparkled and her heart sank. She wanted to share his enthusiasm, but she needed to be sure it was right for her children – their children. It was the back of beyond and heaven alone knew what sort of school there would be. But if she refused to go, would he hold it against her for the rest of their lives?

'How do we get there? What do we take? What can we take?' Amy shook her head. 'It's too much to think about all at once.'

'We'll go by boat – from Liverpool, I think, or may be Southampton and then by railroad. The trains are real big out there.'

'You're beginning to sound all Canadian again.'

'I don't pretend it'll be easy,' he said and she knew he was trying to reassure her. 'I do know it'll be worth all the effort. We have to give it a chance. What else is there?'

She continued to eat in silence. His last remark reminded her again of their present predicament. His job was so much more – it was their home – their way of life. Maybe this was their lucky break. She turned the problem over in her mind while he chatted enthusiastically about the General Store where they would collect the mail, catch up with gossip and make all their purchases.

'All right, we'll go.' She stood up before she could change her mind and began to stack the dishes.

'You mean it?' He stared up at her and grabbed her arm. 'Are you sure – absolutely sure?'

She was far from sure, but she nodded.

97

'I don't want to start the paperwork if there's a chance you'll change your mind …'

'It's a big step, but … I don't see what alternative there is and if we don't, we'll always wonder, won't we?'

He stood up and put his arms around her. 'You won't regret it.'

'I'd better not.' She took comfort in the strength of his embrace.

'I want you to be happy, sweetheart.'

'I can't be if you're not. If going to Canada makes you happy, then we'll go to this Manitoba place.'

'I love you, Mrs Mills.' He kissed her.

'We will make a go of it, won't we?'

'Sure we will.'

The baby kicked and they both felt it. George placed his hand on her tummy.

'Seems like junior's in agreement.'

* * *

Amy's waters broke the following morning as she squatted to weed the garden. She wondered later, whether her fall the previous day had precipitated events, but, she hadn't mention it to George. Their next door neighbour went to fetch him, while his wife summoned the midwife. It all happened so quickly that, in spite of running all the way, George didn't get back to the house before the baby was born.

'Samuel's arrived,' Amy said as he entered the bedroom. 'I hope he takes the rest of his life more leisurely – he certainly didn't give me much warning.'

A look of relief flashed across George's face. 'Thank the Lord you're both all right.' He used his little finger to ease the shawl away so he could see the baby's face. 'He couldn't even wait for his father.'

She cuddled the baby close. 'He's a good weight even if he is a little earlier than expected.'

'A girl next time, eh?'

Soon the household revolved around baby feeding and nappy changing and, with a baby who cried incessantly, Amy became exhausted.

When the farm was sold later that month, George was fortunate enough to keep his job and in a matter of days a pedigree herd of cows arrived. On the evening of their arrival, Amy watched him place the envelope containing the paperwork for Canada on the top shelf of the dresser. He might not have completed his application, but the envelope was there, looking down at her. Reminding her. Secretly she hoped he would grow to love his job again and talk of emigration would be forgotten.

Sam was six months old, when one wet Monday, George arrived home half way through the morning. Amy was hanging washing to dry near the range and Will was playing at her feet.

'This is a nice surprise. Come to help with the household chores?' She chuckled at the thought of George bent over the wash tub but his face was serious.

'Is something wrong?'

He bit his lip. 'I've been given notice.'

She was stunned and watched in silence as he slumped into a chair.

'No? Surely, not?' she said in disbelief. Everything had been normal and George was good at his job, so what could possibly have happened? She knelt beside him, shaking his arm. 'Did I hear right? Have you really lost your job?'

He was silent.

'Why?'

'The place is going for building. Since Metro-land arrived on our doorstep the pressures for houses have only increased. Soon the whole place'll be covered in concrete.'

'But, I thought ...' She'd been about to say she'd thought things were going so well but the truth was her mind and her body had been absorbed in her children. Had she been blinkered? George was never one to unburden himself and now, when she thought back, conversations about work were all but non-existent. A bit like the war. A closed book and she had long since given up trying to prize open the

99

covers. She loved him so much. How had she missed seeing things were wrong?

'What are we going to do?'

CHAPTER SEVEN

Canada

April 1925

Amy squinted. In every direction, there was a vast empty whiteness creeping away into the horizon. Sometimes, as the railcar swayed and clattered along the lines, she spotted a house hidden amongst a small group of trees, as if sheltering from the icy wind. She imagined the family inside, the wife kneading bread, the children playing, all of them snug and warm. She stared, as the house disappeared into the distance, feeling a hollow in her stomach. It was as though she no longer belonged anywhere. Home might as well be on a different planet and, even if she could return, the thought of sea sickness still made her shudder. George said they'd been lucky – they had their own cabin.

'And another thing,' he said, trying to cheer her when all she wanted was to lie in a heap and die. 'Earlier migrants didn't get pillows and blankets or cutlery and china. They had to provide their own.'

'They probably weren't as sick as I feel right now.'

He wasn't sympathetic. 'You'll soon get your sea legs. Count your blessings. You're travelling in luxury compared to some.'

Maybe the 'Melita' was more comfortable, but they were third class and their accommodation was basic. Mealtimes punctuated the day and their only entertainment were books and card games or sometimes music played by one of their fellow passengers.

When she was able, they walked on deck.

'Sea. That's all there's ever to look at,' she complained one day.

'Huh. You might not be too pleased if there was a change of scenery. It would mean there was a storm or, worse still, an iceberg.'

She didn't need reminding of the Titanic.

Even when they docked at St John, it wasn't immediate freedom. They had to clear immigration – more queues and more stamps on more documents but, the uniformed immigration officer was kind, even teasing Will and at least they were spared quarantine.

As the train rocked, Sam lay asleep in her arms and she lifted him, trying to redistribute his weight. He stirred, but slept on.

George was right about there being no shortage of space in Canada. Even if she had only experienced it through a train window, so far everything she had seen was big. For a start, the train was huge and looked very strange with a series of big bars on the front. A cow-catcher, somebody explained, though it didn't exactly catch cows – just shoved any strays off the line. She felt insignificant, small and very ignorant. How would she ever learn to think of this wild country as home?

She closed her eyes. This was time to draw breath. There was little to do, apart from watch the scenery pass by and entertain the children. Their fellow passengers, all English, were also heading for unknown destinations but the air of excitement which had been present at the beginning of their journey, had long since disappeared.

Her mind went back to the day the Approval Certificate arrived. The document was headed the Department of Immigration and Colonization and, bearing the crest of the Dominion of Canada, looked very official. She'd never forget the elation in George's face when he opened the envelope.

'This is it, sweetheart.' He beamed at her.

She felt her heart drop into the pit of her stomach, but any doubts she might have had were soon brushed aside by George's enthusiasm. If only she felt the same.

He read the letter aloud. 'Enclosed please find Approval Certificate No 377, covering the acceptance of yourself and family under the Family Settlement Scheme.' He tugged her into his arms and whirled her round the room, while Will looked on in amazement. 'This is it, honey. This is it!'

She tried to appear as elated, but the very fact the certificate bore a number made her gloomy. Was that all they were? A number? For all the effort involved, the medicals, interviews, paperwork, it was demoralizing.

George filed the letter and certificate with their other papers. 'We'll need this when we get there, but the next thing is to book our passage.'

Finality struck home. She was leaving England and might never see Freddie or her mother ever again. But what choice had there been? Squeezing back into that tiny terraced house in London with George's family or a place of their own in Canada. If only her mother could have found it in her heart to offer them a home – it would have been temporary, of course. But she refused even to see her and George's mind was made up. It was his one opportunity and he was going to seize it. Decisions on what to take and how to pack, lists upon lists of things to do occupied her waking hours, whilst at night, she coped with a crying baby. The few items they could not part with were packed into a large trunk and then they were on their way to London, saying farewell to George's family before boarding the train to Southampton. The rapidity of their departure had been exhausting, the farewells tearful. Even Freddie had mopped his eyes.

Her reverie was broken by the sound of the whistle, a long, haunting, discordant note, so different from the trains back in England. The train slowed and eventually jolted to a halt, steam hissing from the engine.

George looked up from the book he was reading to Will and scratched at the ice which had formed on the inside of the window. He peered out, trying to establish where they were, but it was already dark.

'We'd know if it was Winnipeg,' he said and returned to the book.

They got underway again, sleeping fitfully, woken on one occasion by the train shunting and on another by officials who examined their tickets. When George looked out of the window the following morning he pointed to the huge rock outcrops and announced they had reached the Canadian Shield.

'When we reach the plains, we'll be almost there,' he said and began to tell Will about the herds of bison and tribes of Indians. 'The Indians used to hunt the bison, but not only for their meat,' he said with a knowledgeable look. 'They used the hide for clothing, dung for fuel and well, they didn't waste anything. They used it all. You'll see lots of Indians, Will.'

She listened in silence as he told them about the Sun Dance ceremony, not caring to admit, even to herself, how anxious she felt about seeing Indians. Would they really be friendly? George insisted they were, but it could only be fifty years since Chief Sitting Bull defeated Custer at Little Bighorn. The thought unnerved her. The Indians hadn't been friendly then, had they?

She looked down at Sam, who was curled against her and prayed they were doing the right thing.

'Not far now,' George said as though reading her thoughts and anxious to comfort her.

'It feels like it's been forever.'

'We'll find somewhere for you and the kids to have a wash. There'll be a hotel in Winnipeg. I can't wait. We'll get some good land. I feel it in my bones.'

She sighed. George was so sure of himself, so confident they were doing the right thing, while she – she was full of doubts. Would they have enough money? Where would the children go to school? What would they do if the trunk was damaged or worse, lost?

She glanced out of the window at the never-ending whiteness and was immediately downhearted. It was April and still there was snow. George had warned her the winters were long, but snow this late – is this what they had to look forward to? And the vastness. A rail journey in England would never take three whole days and yet still they were only half way across Canada. Would she ever get used to the size of the country? Already she had pangs for the hills of Buckinghamshire – even the dirty, cobbled streets of London had their attraction.

She was weary of entertaining the children for days and days. Weary of the train – its confinement, its sway on the tracks, even its mustiness, which lately had been overtaken by the smell of so many unwashed people. It would be pleasant to look out of a static window. What bliss to slide between crisp, clean linen, breath in the freshly laundered smell and fall asleep. She had lost count of the times George had told her how much better off they would be. He told her of the great boom before the war, when the price of wheat had peaked and tons had been exported. It would happen again. So why did she have these niggling doubts? Was it because they arrived in Canada on the 13th? She hadn't realized until she looked at the official stamp on their Immigration papers. It wasn't a Friday – she kept reminding herself.

'They said back in St John we might have to stay in Winnipeg for a day or so – just till they've sorted out the paperwork.' George interrupted her thoughts.

'Not more paperwork.'

'Be worth it all. You'll see.'

Winnipeg was not as unpleasant as she expected, nor did the dreaded paperwork amount to much. With their few belongings, they tumbled out of the train into a throng of mixed nationalities into a cold wind which cut through their clothing. She was fascinated by the differently clad passengers, men wearing high-shouldered suits, a Mounted Policeman, and a couple of cowboys in high-heeled boots and Stetson hats. Most were Europeans, some with families but some alone – many speaking a language she didn't understand.

An icy blast made her hoist up her collar and yank her hat down over her ears. She admired the shawl-like scarves adorning so many of the women and wished she had an extra layer but, grateful for her thick gloves, most of all she longed for warm feet.

Then she saw him – an Indian dressed in beaded leggings, a blanket and wearing moccasins. She couldn't help it – she stared at his jet black hair and large hooked nose. He appeared haughty and indifferent to everything around him. Nobody else took much notice, so perhaps George was right when he said they were harmless enough. Will was staring too and, aware of their bad manners, she caught his hand and distracted him by straightening his hat before he could say anything embarrassing or point rudely.

The stop in Winnipeg was brief. By the time she had washed the children and freshened up herself, George was back and in high spirits.

'We've got 200 acres.' His voice was jubilant. 'I can't believe we've been that lucky. I only expected a quarter section and what's more, there's a good house, sweetheart.'

Soon they were travelling again.

'Portage-la-Prairie is where the trappers used to cross the prairie from the lakes to the river. It's that narrow bit of land I showed you on the atlas at ...' He broke off and she knew he'd almost said "home". Maybe he felt a little homesick, too. The idea comforted her.

'All the rail lines go through Portage. Anyway that'll be our nearest town. Someone called John Stadnyk is meeting us.'

'Odd name. Is it foreign?'

He laughed. 'We're the foreigners, sweetheart.'

She smiled at her silly mistake. 'You know what I mean.'

'Maybe he changed his name. I remember a lot did. Or maybe his father did. Sounds kinda Russian. Lots of people are from the Ukraine. Anyway, he'll look after us – get us fixed up with supplies. I keep pinching myself. Two hundred acres. I'll be out ploughing by the end of the week.'

She glanced out of the window. Ploughing? That was ambitious with snow on the ground. She said nothing, but he must have seen her sceptical expression.

'You'll be surprised how quickly the snow disappears once the thaw comes. Before you know, it'll be very warm. First things first though. We'll need a wagon and team.'

'Team?'

'Team of horses. Then we'll have to see about getting some cattle and I'll need a plough and oh, a whole host of supplies. I hope this John Stadnyk knows the right people.' He held her hands. 'Aren't you excited?'

She nodded. Satisfied with her response he lifted Sam onto his lap. She looked away. She felt queasy with fear, not excitement.

After their arrival in Portage la Prairie, Amy stood on the main street, watching the progress of the horses and wagons. The melting snow meant there was mud everywhere and she was glad to be standing on the sidewalk. She was amazed by the number of cars and the width of the road – big enough to turn a wagon and team, George informed her. It was certainly the widest road she had ever seen.

Two ladies strolled by, both with the fashionable short hairstyle. Influenced by Vi, she'd had hers cut soon after the wedding. George disapproved, though she knew he had been careful not to say so. Most of the men were clean shaven and the shopkeepers wore waistcoats. George was right everyone did dress to go into town but it was very different to any city scene she could think of in England. There was only one stone building – everything else was wooden. Some buildings had false fronts, making them more prominent and there were no cobblestones. The sidewalk was wooden. Here, many miles from their farm, was the nearest place where they could shop for their needs.

They stayed with John Stadnyk's family for several days. At first George had refused the offer of accommodation, but was persuaded by John's wife, Ellie, who insisted Amy needed a rest and, after days of being in motion firstly on the ship, then on the train, she was grateful. Her whole body ached, her head buzzed and, when she looked in the mirror, her face looked grey. She thought lodging with another family would be as bad as living with George's mother, especially as John was a Pastor but right then she hadn't cared how moralistic or puritanical he was or how fusty Ellie might be. In fact it turned out to be the very best of solutions, for Ellie soon made her feel at home and even John was friendly. The house was big, perhaps not as large as "Hazeldene" but more than twice the size of the cottage they had left behind in England and all the rooms were comfortably furnished.

While George set about organizing supplies and equipment, Ellie showed her the finest stores, pointed out the best bargains and rescued her when she got into difficulty with the currency and even demonstrated how to use her stove and her sewing machine.

On one occasion when she was leaving the house with Ellie, she spotted an Indian squaw with braided hair and beaded costume, her baby on her back in what Ellie called a papoose.

107

'They're harmless enough.' Ellie tried to reassure her. 'You only get to see them when they come in from the reservation.'

Nevertheless she was wary whenever Indians were walking the sidewalks.

'It's such a shame you'll be so far from town,' Ellie said one afternoon when they were in the kitchen and Amy was helping to bake cookies. 'You sure are the nicest thing that's happened to me in a long time, but I figure we'll get to meet once in a while when you come in for supplies.'

'I'm so grateful to you. I really don't think I'd have coped without your help.' She was glad to have an opportunity to thank Ellie for making her feel less strange in a new country, but most of all she wanted to tell her how anxious she was, how she dreaded being alone and how George didn't understand. 'I know I shouldn't say this, but I wish I could stay here in town ....'

'You'll be fine.' Ellie tried to comfort her. 'Of course it'll take a bit of adjustment. Every prairie woman has gone through the same process, you know.' She gave her a cheerful smile. 'You'll be fine but make sure George brings you every time he comes into town.'

Though she'd like to feel confident, she wasn't but before she could say anything further, the conversation was halted by the shrill ring of the telephone. It was amazing how many households had telephones as well as electric power. Everyone was better off than George's family in the East End of London and even John did his rounds in a motor car. He had taken George out to their farm on their first day. But she still couldn't shake this feeling of disaster waiting to happen and neither could she forget they had arrived on the 13th. It's quite irrational, she told herself, when everyone is so optimistic and so prosperous.

Ellie and John's two sons were a little older than Will, but were soon friends. By the time it came for them to leave, Amy had learnt her way round town and Will had begun to speak with a similar accent to the local lads.

'I got lucky today,' George said on their last evening with the Stadnyks. 'There was a farm sale not too far from our place. I wouldn't have known, but Tom Sutherland told me.'

'Tom?'

He looked at her in surprise as though she had forgotten some vital piece of information, but she was certain the name had not been mentioned.

'I'm sure I must have told you. The Sutherlands will be our nearest neighbours. Anyway, I got a couple of cows and a plough – oh, and some harness. I sure am pleased with the plough. It hasn't seen much use by the look of it. Tom gave me a hand to get it all back. Decent of him, seeing as he didn't buy anything himself.'

She listened in silence as he ran through the items of furniture he had also acquired. She felt detached, as though it was happening to someone else. Later, as she climbed the stairs to bed, it was as though in a dream. Maybe she would wake in the morning to familiar things – English voices, horses hooves on cobbled streets.

By mid-morning the following day, the wagon was stacked high with their belongings and, together with a few last minute items of groceries, they were ready.

'Don't worry, you'll be fine,' Ellie embraced her.

'Thanks for everything,' she said, wishing there could be a telephone on which to chat to Ellie. There were sure to be a hundred things she wouldn't understand but she knew both telephones and electricity had yet to make an impact on rural life.

'Remember, there's lots of other woman like you. You won't be on your own.' Ellie said as if reading her thoughts. She turned to George. 'Next time you come to town, you must bring Amy and the boys. I know how isolated it can feel out there.'

He nodded. 'I guess it won't be long before we'll find something we need, but I figure Amy'll get used to managing without. We sure can't come visiting every day.'

The horses were keen, needing no encouragement and sloshed their way through the mud and puddles left by the melted snow. Blinking back tears, she allowed herself one last look back over her shoulder and waved to Ellie and John. She couldn't imagine why she felt so emotional, after all, she had only known them for a short time.

'When you're bigger, you'll be able to ride Buster,' George told Will. 'He's quite a steady old horse, aren't you boy?' The shire's ears bent back as though listening, then pricked forward so that it seemed to Amy, only she was apprehensive.

They crossed the bridge over the frozen river. Large craters were appearing as the ice melted in the heat of the day and they could hear it cracking. The air was fresh, the sun bright in the huge, clear blue sky and they felt its heat on their faces even though it was barely mid-morning. The track entered a wood which seemed to go on forever and in spite of her misgivings, she began to feel excited at the prospect of their house, but, when the horses halted her heart sank. In a country in which everything was huge, their house was so much smaller than she had hoped or dreamed of – hardly more than a hut in the middle of a forest with two windows and a door which opened straight onto the path. At the end of the path was the barn and a fenced paddock. George had warned the house wouldn't be as large as Ellie and John's but, he emphasized, it had a proper roof. They would be dry and warm. As she took in the peeling whitewashed wood and the shingle roof, she was not convinced. A former occupant had hung a horseshoe over a window and she hoped it was a sign of good luck.

'There's another room at the back,' George said, as if sensing her dismay. 'Don't worry, we'll all be comfortable. We're lucky – we've got a floor. Some houses round here only have dirt. Come on. Let's get sorted out.'

She gave him a disdainful look. He hadn't mentioned dirt floors before. She followed him inside, inspecting the living room with its table, chairs and stove, before wandering into the bedroom. Off the bedroom was a lean-to affair which George had alluded to as another room. She had seen these on the backs of many houses and thought they were the solution to an increase in family – some houses had several.

She dropped the bag she was carrying on the floor and looked about her. She sighed. It was no good feeling sorry for herself. They were here now and whether she liked it or not, she had to make the best of it. George would never agree to taking her back to town. But where to start? The place could do with a good sweep and it would be nice to get some curtains up at the windows. With beds and food to organize, she soon occupied Will with little errands but the noise of an engine caused them all to stop. George opened the door. A tall, sinewy man with a long nose and sharp eyes stood outside.

'Come in. Come in. Amy, this is Tom – Tom Sutherland. He's our nearest neighbour.'

'Nice to meet you.' She shook his large hand, feeling the rough calluses and wondered if George's hands would soon be like his.

'Sure is good to have people back on the old place. My wife sent this over.' He offered her a loaf wrapped in a cloth. 'Thought you might be glad of it. Janet'll be over tomorrow, but said to say if there's anything she can do, to let me know.'

'Thank you.' She smiled at him. 'It's very kind of her and I – we appreciate it. How lovely – it's still warm.'

'Just out of the oven. Janet would have come herself, but she couldn't leave the baking. Anyhow I see you folks are fine. George tells me he was farming out Alexander way before the war. Not like us. We came straight from the city – knew nothing about animals or crops or farm equipment or anything. Sure learnt the hard way and we were mighty pleased to find a neighbour or two to show us how.'

'We'll be grateful for any help you give us,' George said, glancing in her direction. 'And I know Amy'll be glad for some female company.'

'Sure. It gets lonely out here for our women folk.'

'Has this place been empty long?' She asked, unable to hide her curiosity about the previous residents. Had they gone back to where they'd come, much like she wanted to?

'Mmm. Let me think. Best part of two years now. Jack Donaldson's wife died and he gave up. Headed back east. Had family there.'

She wanted to know how his wife had died and whether they had children but, more importantly, with the house surrounded by trees, her fear of Indians had returned and she longed to ask whether there were any camped nearby. She glanced at George and knew he would be exasperated if she dared to ask. She folded the cloth and handed it back to Tom.

'Anyhow, I guess you've plenty to do.' He turned to go. 'Don't forget we're only up the track. Oh, I nearly forgot.' He stopped and faced them. 'Rumour has it there's a bear in the neighbourhood. Stan said he'd seen tracks up on the Indian trail near the river.'

'Oh, my goodness,' Amy gasped. Indians were one thing, but bears, that was something entirely different. A look from George stopped her from asking more.

'Didn't mean to alarm you. They aren't usually a problem.' Tom sounded reassuring but Amy's imagination was working overtime. George had never as much as hinted there might be dangerous wildlife.

'Just be on your guard, that's all.' Tom opened the door and George followed him out of the house. She could hear them discussing the possibility of ploughing.

'Even if the snow melts, the ground's way too hard,' she heard Tom say. 'Make sure you get your plough ready. S'long.'

When Amy slipped into bed that night, she nestled close to George, for in spite of the thick eiderdown and layers of blankets, she was cold. The doors were open so they could benefit from the warmth of the stove, but still the air felt very cool. The first night in their new home. She huddled still closer, wanting to feel his arms around her but, more than anything, wanting his reassurance. At first it had been Indians which jumped out of the shadows in her mind – now it was bears. But George was dismissive of her concerns and now he was sound asleep as though he hadn't a care in the world. His breathing was regular and untroubled, while she lay listening for any unusual noise which might warn of a bear. She tried to occupy her mind by thinking through the day's events, planning what she would write in her letter to Freddie and deciding the improvements she could make to the dilapidated shack which was their home.

George had bought a cow from Tom and tomorrow she was to learn to milk.

'When I get ploughing, I won't have the time,' he'd informed her.

She was not pleased. Milking was not on her list of jobs but then hadn't he said something about getting some chickens and pigs? Now, she was beginning to suspect, looking after these would also form part of her routine. She snuggled down under the bed clothes, closed her eyes and drifted into an exhausted sleep.

CHAPTER EIGHT

'Something's wrong with the water,' Amy said the moment George opened the door. 'I've just fetched some from the well and it's – it's disgusting. Here, taste it.' She held out a cup.

'I didn't like to tell you before – '

She saw his sheepish look. 'Tell me what?'

'It's a bit saline – that's all.'

'Saline?'

'Mmm.' He pursed his lips.

She looked at the cup and then back at him. The water had been fine yesterday. She frowned.

'Salt,' he said.

'I know what saline means. What I want to know is how did it get salty?'

'Happens sometimes, when a well's sunk – sometimes you can be unlucky.'

'You mean ... But, what are we going to do? We can't drink this – the children ...' Amy tipped the water back into the bucket. 'Anyway, it wasn't salty yesterday, so perhaps it's only this lot.'

George shook his head. 'Sorry, honey. It doesn't work like that. The well's salty. I confess I found out a couple of days ago and I ... To be honest, I didn't know how to tell you.'

She was puzzled. 'We haven't been drinking salty water, so ...'

'I boiled up some snow yesterday.'

She looked out of the window. 'But the snow's disappearing fast.' Yesterday she'd wished it gone, now, today, it seemed they needed it. 'What on earth will we do?'

'Make coffee.' George shrugged. 'Put up with it. There's not much we can do. We can't afford to sink another well and, anyway, I've got bigger problems to worry about. Ploughing has to take

113

priority. No crop – no money and with no money to see us through the winter, life would difficult.'

'But I can't give this to the children.' She stood with her hands on her hips. 'You'll have to take us back to town. There's no alternative. We can't manage without decent water.'

He shook his head. 'No way. We're here and we're staying.'

'But we – I can't ...' She was incredulous. He surely couldn't expect them to drink the stuff. 'We'll all be ill. For goodness sake, George.'

'No buts. That's the way it is. Besides it isn't that bad. It's only got a slight taste and we'll soon get used to it.'

She gave him a contemptuous look and went to organize the breakfast. She had woken chilled through and when she dressed, her clothes were like ice, the fire had gone out and Sam had begun to grizzle. It seemed he never stopped. Now George was telling her she had to put up with salty water. What else had he failed to tell her? She began to mentally list his failings. The length of the journey for a start and how small the house really was and then last night he'd told her she'd got to do the milking – it was to be her job. It was expected – he said – a normal part of a prairie wife's daily chores. Expected? Strange how he'd failed to mention it before. And it wasn't the only thing he had failed to mention. Bears ... every time she looked out of the window she stared into the shadows amongst the trees, certain one lurked out there.

As she stirred the porridge, she examined the cooker. George had also told her only yesterday that she would be expected to feed the thresher gang. A top rate spread, apparently, and comparisons were always made. There could be a dozen or more to feed. She hadn't thought much about it when he first mentioned it, but now she was using the stove, the magnitude of the task struck her. Yes, she had managed to tame the black monster which lived in their kitchen back in England, but any guests had been limited to Freddie and sometimes neighbours calling for the odd cup of tea. Now she was supposed to put on a banquet and all in the one room in which they lived. She banged the crockery and cutlery on the table. How were they to manage with salty water? She glared at George. When they were all sick he'd have to take them back into town.

114

'It's not all bad, honey,' he said, placing his hand on her shoulder. 'We'll manage. Besides, there's plenty of milk.'

She removed his hand and, ignoring the conversation he was having with Will, banged a bowl of porridge in front of him followed by a cup of coffee. Right then she hoped he'd choke on it but when she sipped her own, her mood lifted. It was passable. Just. And they probably would get used to it. Why did he always have to be right?

As she cut into Janet's loaf, she thought about the need for fresh water. The river wasn't far away ... She sighed. Another task – another burden. Pumping water from the well was arduous enough, but boiling snow or river water was not something she'd imagined doing when she had gone to sleep the previous night, nor was it something she would write home about. It felt like they had fallen at the first hurdle.

'I'm a bit concerned about the river,' George said as he ate his breakfast.

She spooned the last scrap from a bowl and held it out to Sam.

'Oh?'

'I thought I'd begin ploughing right where our land starts, but the river's up. It's thawing all right – the trouble is, it isn't fast enough.'

'What do you mean, not fast enough?'

'Upstream is thawing pretty fast and heading down at a heck of a rate, but the trouble is, the ice here is acting like a stopper.'

'Will it flood?'

He wiped his plate clean with a slice of bread. 'Already has. Hope it doesn't get worse. Tom warned me the soil could be difficult. Porridge was what he said and I think he's right. Up to my ankles, I was.'

'Surely, you don't have to start by the river ... I mean we've got so much land – can't you start somewhere else?'

'I'll have to but I hope the river doesn't rise too much or it'll hold things up. I got plenty of seed when I bought in the supplies. Tom said to use Marquis. Said it'd ripen sooner than other varieties. Seems the harvest gets going earlier with this new seed – sooner than it did when I was out here before. Have to be up early tomorrow – as soon as it's light. Last day of the holiday today, so make the most of it.'

She snorted. 'Holiday?' How could he describe this as a holiday when every task was more difficult than it might have been in England, not to mention all the extra ones she had now discovered were hers? She placed Sam on the floor and he crawled towards Will, who was playing at being a horse. Will heaved his brother in front of him, but Sam had either ideas and was quickly off on his knees.

'Hey, look at Sam,' George said and they watched Sam haul himself up, gripping the chair. Wobbling, he took a step, smiling up at them. Then he sat down with a thump, surprising himself. His face puckered into a cry and George picked him up.

'Never mind, Sam. It was a good try,' he said and still holding Sam, turned to the door. 'Come on, Amy, I think it's time you had a go at milking.'

'I'll do the dishes first.'

'No time like the present,' George said and set off to the barn.

Unenthusiastic though she was, she hurried out of the house after him, quickening her step in order to catch up, not wanting to be behind in case there was a bear lurking amongst the trees. George swung open the huge barn door and then fetched a three legged stool. He put his hand firmly on the cow's flank and pushed the animal over so that he could place the stool in position. He placed Sam in her arms and sat down on the stool. The cow bellowed and Amy stepped back not wanting to be anywhere near its hindquarters and was surprised when Will insisted on being right beside George while he demonstrated the technique. In no time at all, the pail had an inch of milk at the bottom.

'You're turn now,' he said and got up, taking Sam back into his arms.

She looked at the muddy floor with distaste and, holding her skirt up edged onto the stool, leaning forward yet reluctant to get too close to the side of the cow. Her hair tickled the animal's flank and its skin twitched. She reached for a teat which felt warm to her cold hands.

'She knows you're nervous.'

'Of course, I'm nervous. I've never been this close to a cow before.'

'Don't hang back. Put your head against her flank. That way, you'll feel if she's going to kick out … You'll soon get used to it. Easy goes or she'll never let it down. You have to sooth her. Say something nice.'

'Such as? It's blooming cold out here and hurry up?'

'Don't be silly. You know what I mean. Call her by her name and for goodness sake sound calm and she'll be fine.'

'Come on, Daisy, be good for Amy,' she said, hoping the nerves in her stomach were not reflected in her voice. The sooner this was done, the better, she thought, grabbing hold of a different teat. The cow, which had been munching feed, kicked out in alarm, tipping over the pail and the small amount of milk trickled onto the floor. She stood up, sending the stool crashing to the ground and the cow jumped in fright.

'You do it.' She burst into tears.

'Amy ... '

She turned, almost falling over Will and fled across the yard and into the house, banging the door behind her.

* * *

'No accounting for women, eh, son?' George sat Sam in the straw next to Will. 'Watch him for me, will you?' He placed the stool upright, sat down, whispered a few words to the cow and then began the whole procedure again.

When he brought the milk into the house, Amy was taking her temper out on some dough. He watched her punching it aggressively, turning it and repeating the performance and wondered whether she was pretending it was his head. He hadn't promised luxury, but so far he hadn't even provided some of the basics. No wonder she was angry.

'Where do you want this?' He indicated the bucket.

'What do I care?'

He lifted the pail onto the table.

'Not on the table. It's been in goodness knows what in that barn.'

He raised his eyebrows, wanting to tell her to make her mind up, but, instead, placed the bucket on the floor.

'And look at Sam. Did you have to sit him in all that mud?'

117

He considered saying something to make amends but decided it was safer to let her cool down. He shut the door gently behind him and headed back to the barn. Horses were safer – they didn't argue.

He checked the harness carefully and hitched up the plough, intending to work for an hour or so, before returning to the house. By then, it would be nearing lunch time and, in spite of his good breakfast, he knew he would be hungry. Besides, he didn't like being on bad terms with Amy and she might have calmed down by then. It was not like her to lose her temper.

He thought about their situation. Perhaps he should tell her how little money was left and remind her that the farm didn't come free. There was a mortgage to pay. It would take hours of toil before the ground would be ready for seeding and he wouldn't have time to milk or feed the chickens even, when they arrived. She must see he couldn't do it alone. He began to wonder whether she was suited to this life. Had he asked too much? He had never doubted their love, but for the first time he wondered whether she regretted not becoming Mrs Charles Ashby. Think how much more comfortable her life would be? The thought taunted him as he stood behind the plough and the horses took the strain.

They had left a comfortable house, friends and family and travelled half way across the world in pretty basic conditions. He glanced across the acres of land, patches of snow remaining only amongst the trees, wherever the sun had failed to penetrate. It wasn't a spectacular landscape and he missed the hills, but surely she would learn to love the prairie as much as he. It was the way of life he loved as much as the scenery and Amy had hardly experienced it. The house hadn't lived up to her expectations and, with the fire out, it hadn't been too warm when they woke. He hadn't given her comfort – he'd given her hardship. And she had left everything behind because he said they could make a go of it – because he'd raved about the great times. So certain was he they would be successful, he'd spoken at length about those, avoiding the downside. He had glossed over how hard this life was on women and now she was finding the reality a bit of a shock. Perhaps it wasn't surprising she was bad tempered.

He tried to think of what he could do to appease her, but his mind was soon occupied with the problems of frozen soil in one place and sludge in another. In very short order both he and the horses were up to their knees in mud. Tom was right. It was too early to plough and

118

his failed attempt had made a lot of extra work. For all his efforts, he had hardly ploughed a furrow and it took him the rest of the morning to extricate the horses and clean them up. Even the harness was muddy and he knew better than to skimp on cleaning. He couldn't afford for the horses to be rubbed raw because he'd neglected to remove all traces of mud.

Feeling dejected about his own disastrous efforts, he returned to the house, hoping Amy would be in a better mood. It was so frustrating to see the land emerge from the snow and be unable to get on it. He had 200 acres and the enormity of the undertaking was beginning to sink in. There was no question of failure – no option of returning to England.

'You're late,' Amy banged the saucepans together.

'Had a few problems.' He wasn't aware they'd agreed a time. Once the ploughing got underway, his lunch would have to be taken in the fields, but now was not the time to say so.

The meal commenced in silence.

'Hold your fork properly.' Amy took hold of Will's hand, removed and replaced the fork correctly.

'Don't take it out on the lad.'

She scowled at him. 'I wasn't. He has to learn some manners.'

He put his cutlery down. 'Look, I know things aren't easy, but I can only do my best. In time it'll get better, I know it will.'

She was silent and he began to eat again. Amy played with her food, eventually discarding her knife and fork.

'I want to go home.' She stood up. 'I wish we'd never come. You talked me into it. If I'd known it was going to be like this, I would never have agreed.'

He also stood up. Will looked from one parent to the other and Sam grizzled.

'I never told you it'd be easy. You knew it'd be hard, but you agreed. You agreed having our own place would be worth the hard work.'

'You didn't tell me there'd be snow in April and it would be so cold my clothes would be stiff with ice.'

119

'Sure the fire went out. That's no big deal.'

'No big deal? For goodness sake, George, if it's as cold as this now, what in heaven's name is it like in December or January?'

'Don't get so fired up about nothing.'

'Nothing? Is that what you call nothing – half freezing to death?'

'Don't exaggerate.'

'And what about all the other things you didn't tell me. You didn't tell me I'd have to milk the cows or that I'd have to cook for half the neighbourhood on this stupid, silly stove. You didn't tell me we'd have salty water and you certainly didn't say a word about there being Indians or for that matter, bears.' Tears welled up and she dashed at her eyes with her hand.

'Indians?' He said in surprise. 'Shucks, the few round here are never going to be a problem. And that bear, well now the thaw's here, my guess is, he'll head back to where he came from. Aw, come on, honey. Things'll get easier. You'll soon learn to milk. It isn't that difficult. We all have to start somewhere. I've had years of practice. Sure it's hard now and I know the water's a nuisance –'

'Don't patronize me, George.'

'What's that supposed to mean?'

'I'm not stupid. It won't get easier.'

'Of course it'll get easier. Summer'll be here soon, for a start. Oh, come here, honey.' He held out his arms.

'Don't you honey me.' She pushed by him. 'Don't touch me.' She banged the bedroom door behind her.

'Amy ...' He went to follow, but stopped when, with the change of temperature, he knew, Will had opened the front door. 'Will ..?'

Janet Sutherland stood on the doorstep, her face showing concern. Holding her hand was a fair boy about Will's age.

'We came to introduce ourselves to Amy and your boys, but I can see I've come at a bad time.'

He tried to cover his embarrassment – even if they hadn't been yelling at each other, the house didn't have thick walls. 'No. No, of course you haven't come at a bad time. Come on in, Janet. You'll have to excuse us. We were in the middle of – er – eating.'

Janet shook her head. 'I won't come in. I couldn't help hearing …'

He made a face, knowing no explanation was necessary.

'Maybe Will would like to come over for an hour or two. It'll give Amy a break. You could call later and collect him, or I could get Tom to bring him home.'

'That's real kind of you.'

'Oh, it's nothing. The least I can do. This life …' she indicated vaguely to the vastness of the prairie. 'Most men don't understand how isolated their women feel. That's the reason I called. It took me a long time to get used to things and I remember being glad of some female company. You get used to it, though. Give her time, George.'

Amy appeared from the bedroom shortly after the front door had closed and watched George clear the table.

'Fancy a cup of coffee?' he asked, hoping if he sounded cheerful, she would get over her bout of bad temper. 'The kettle's boiled.'

'Seems there's no privacy here either. It'll be all over the neighbourhood – that we fight and argue. Everyone will be laughing at us.'

'No they won't. Don't be so silly. Everybody has their bad moments. I know from what Tom told me, the Sutherlands haven't had an easy time, 'specially their first year.' He placed two cups of coffee on the table. 'Will's gone to play with Josh. We'll go and collect him later, then you'll see what nice people they are. Come here, you silly goose.' He opened his arms and she allowed herself to be hugged.

'I feel such a fool. What must she have thought?' she said to his chest.

He squeezed her tight. 'She thought you were going through the same problems as any other woman out here. Nothing's going to be easy, honey.' He looked down at her. 'I never ever said it would, but you know I can't do this on my own. We have to work together. Some chores I'm not so keen on either, but they have to be done and we have to help each other, not fight.'

121

He kissed her.

'Money's short, honey. We need this crop or … well, I don't like to think of the consequences. I need you to run things here while I'm out on the fields. When Will's bigger, he'll be able to help. All the children muck in.'

'I'm not much good am I?'

'Course you are.' He tweaked her nose. 'I wouldn't trade you for anything in the world. We'll have another go at milking tonight, eh? Friends?'

She nodded. 'Friends.'

It was another week before George was able to try ploughing again. By then Amy had become quite efficient at milking and was beginning to develop stronger hand muscles. He was pleased and relieved to read the letter she wrote to Vi, telling of her new skill as well as how Will loved to help with watering the animals. The letter she wrote to her mother, left out the description of milking and, instead, concentrated on their plans for the farm – new calves next spring and hogs and chickens soon. Maybe her mother might reply..?

* * *

On their first Sunday, George hitched the horses to the wagon and took them the mile or so to the schoolhouse where a church service was held every other week at three in the afternoon.

It was hot and, while they were awaiting the arrival of the preacher, Amy, holding Sam in her arms, stood beside Janet Sutherland in the shade of the only tree. Janet, she'd soon discovered when she had walked with George to collect Will on that first day, had an answer for everything. While George chatted with Tom, it wasn't long before she was spilling out all her fears and being reassured she was worrying needlessly.

'Bears sometimes wake up from their hibernation early and go looking for food but now the thaw is well underway the chances are it's gone back to its normal territory.'

'Where do they usually live?' She asked, hoping it was a million miles away.

'A good few hundred miles west, I think. It's only the second one I've heard of in all the years we've been here, so I don't think you should worry too much.'

When George went outside with Tom to inspect his bull, she took the opportunity to ask about Indians and though relieved that Janet was equally reassuring, Indians continued to skulk in the shadow of trees whenever she ventured across their lands and the sound of a snapping branch or the squawk of a surprised prairie chicken, had her scanning the scenery for signs of a bear.

Now Amy expressed her surprise at attending a church service in a school but Janet explained there were plans to build a church when funds permitted.

'The school's only ten years old,' Janet explained. 'But it isn't only the funds, you know, the men have to find time to build it, too. Oh, that's Josie Smith over there.' She gestured in the direction of the solitary motor car. 'She's the teacher here – boards with the McAllisters. The McAllisters were the first in the neighbourhood to get one of these new-fangled automobiles. Tom couldn't wait to get our Buick. Said he'd heard the McAllisters were thinking of buying a tractor. Whatever next?'

Amy was more interested in the schoolteacher, who was chatting to two young girls and a youth of about thirteen.

'She's very young,' she said, thinking this Miss Smith was not at all like Smithie who had taught her in what now seemed another life. Neither was Josie Smith a fuddy-duddy, but wore a pretty frilled white blouse and a hat with a narrow brim and, she noticed, she had an admirer or two.

'We're lucky to have her,' Janet replied. 'The school's getting bigger these days. Tom – he's a governor, you know – he said they've got fifteen pupils now.'

'Fifteen? And is it right, they're all in the same room?'

Janet nodded.

She studied the wooden building. It was very different to any in England. In her youth she hadn't gone to the local village school but there had been only the three of them, while here there were fifteen. Her Miss Smith had been strict and forbidding. Would this Miss Smith be as capable of keeping order? And how on earth did she manage to teach all the differing age groups? At that moment, the woman laughed and turned in Amy's direction, as though she sensed she was being scrutinized.

'I'll introduce you to her later. You'll be wanting Will along to school soon enough,' Janet said and then pointed out other new arrivals. 'There are the Chernitsky's. They come from Russia, you know. They say they're something to do with the Russian royal family – had to get out when there was all that trouble. I've been told he's got a metal plate in his head. He's odd enough, that's for sure.'

As Janet chatted on, naming each new arrival, she glanced across at George who, having tied up the horses, had sauntered off in the direction of the men. She caught the odd word – wheat and weather seemed to be the topics of the conversation. She looked for Will, but he had found Josh and was making friends with other children.

She was disappointed, when the preacher arrived, that it wasn't John Stadnyk, but linked arms with George and together with Will, they filed into the schoolroom, sitting or squeezing into the rows of desks. They were soon singing the opening hymn, accompanied on the piano by the schoolteacher.

Several times during the service, her attention wandered and during the sermon, she found herself staring at the back of Mr Chernitsky's head. There was no sign of anything metal. Disappointed, she looked at the others around her, trying to recall their names. Janet had reeled off so many. There was the Klassens also from Russia, the O'Neils from Ireland and the Jacksons and McAllisters who had come from Ontario and were, according to Janet, the two richest families in the district. Then there were the Jeffersons. Their house was the one with a dirt floor. Imagine – a dirt floor. It was hard enough keeping things clean with their wooden floor. Didn't Janet say that Marlene Jefferson had a grand piano? She couldn't imagine that standing on a dirt floor and what would all that dust do to its insides?

She examined her work worn hands and then glanced up at George, who smiled back and the sparkle in his eyes told her he was happy. Life might be strange and hard but, despite their worries, she knew he was content.

* * *

The days since the thaw began were very warm. George had forgotten how abruptly summer could begin in the prairies. Once the spring melt was underway, the temperatures rose and worryingly, so did the height of the river. But he had other troubles and didn't dwell too long on the possibility of bad flooding, concentrating instead on the acreage which had been cleared by the previous occupier and could be ploughed relatively easily.

At first Amy's anxiety about Indians and bears made her reluctant to go out alone or even to allow Will to play in the yard unsupervised but gradually her confidence increased and George persuaded her to bring lunch to wherever he was in the fields. They would picnic, while the horses rested and were fed. It was a sociable half hour with the children, but apart from this short break, he slogged on from first light to dusk every day, leaving Amy to cope alone. A milestone had been reached when ten acres had been ploughed and by working well into the dark, he also managed to harrow a couple of acres as well.

Early one Monday morning, as dawn was breaking, George was sorting the harness. The noise of several horses coming along the track heralded visitors.

'Thought we'd give you a hand,' Tom Sutherland said indicating his plough. 'Didn't see you yesterday at the service. The preacher – he missed you. Anyway, Stan and me – we got talking.'

'Yep,' Stan said. 'We guessed you could do with some help. So we brought our teams. Just tell us where you want to start.'

George couldn't hide his surprise. 'Really? What about your own places?'

'We're both well ahead now,' Stan said. 'We figured we could spare you a day or two. Tom saw you struggling a week or so back and guessed you were in a hurry to get on.'

George remembered with embarrassment how he'd freed the horses from the mud, but he hadn't noticed Tom go by. 'I should have taken more notice of what you said. The edge was fine, but the middle – well, the horses were knee-deep.'

Tom smiled. 'It isn't always easy to tell how bad it is.'

'It's real good of you to help like this, but can you really spare the time?'

Tom nodded. 'Sure can.'

'I don't know how to thank you.'

'Your turn'll come. All help each other out here. Case of having to.'

CHAPTER NINE

1925

August

The evenings were getting shorter and George sat at the table by the window recording their expenditure for the past week in his buff Land Settlement Board account book. Every cent had been accounted for and it was obvious more money was being spent than was expected to come in. He chewed the end of his pencil, flicking through the pages and thinking back over the months of work. The fine black soil had transformed into silvery green wheat, now so tall Will disappeared into it and Amy always worried he would get lost. He checked the crop every day, terrified some awful disease would occur before he could harvest the golden grain.

He turned to watch Amy darning his socks. Since their first argument, he couldn't grumble about her support though sometimes he had to remind her about little economies, like remembering to use the pig bucket for odd scraps of food and re-using the coffee grouts. On the plus side, there'd been butter making lessons from Janet Sutherland and now, with a couple of extra cows, surplus milk was converted into butter and traded at the General Store for other supplies. It eked out the money. A few chickens were running about the place and Will helped to collect the eggs. Soon they would be taking those into town, too.

She finished the sock she was working on and looked up.

'Your mother did me a good turn, teaching me to darn.' She grinned at him and picked up another sock. 'And I'm doing really well at knitting. Janet's been so patient. She helped me unpick that old jumper of mine. Look at all those skeins.' She indicated the pile of grey wool on a nearby chair. 'I'm going to make some scarves and mittens for the boys.'

Her words made him sad. He knew when they married he couldn't offer luxury, but it seemed it was only hard work and poverty he provided and now he was certain there was insufficient cash to last the summer, but with vegetables in the garden and chickens, eggs and milk, they wouldn't starve.

Tom Sutherland had loaned him his bull and he was thrilled all the cows were in calf and grateful the only payment was for Tom to have the pick of the female calves. He prayed, when they arrived, they wouldn't all be steers, but he also hoped they wouldn't need the attention of a vet – there was no spare cash for that.

'Shall I make some coffee?' Amy's voice cut across his thoughts.

'No – er - thanks.' He closed the account book. 'I think I'll go to bed.'

'How are we doing? Not too bad, I hope. We took a large batch of butter into town this week.'

'We're doing fine.' He didn't want to tell her how difficult things really were or that he'd rather starve than run up credit in the General Stores. No wonder he feared the worst every time dark clouds formed. A hail storm could demolish the crop in seconds and there had been no money for insurance.

Next year, he knew, there wouldn't be any help from Tom. In fact he must be prepared to return that favour sometime, so it was vital he got ahead with clearing more land of bush and scrub. Breaking virgin prairie was tough – very tough. Sometimes, when he looked over his shoulder, he would see the land lying over behind him like a strip of linoleum and if the plough hit the remains of a tree stump, yards of it unwound back into its original shape. Then there was no alternative but to go back and do it again.

He leant back in his chair and watched Amy patching a pair of Will's trousers and knew it would be a case of make do and mend for some time to come.

'Let's have an early night. I want to start on the hay tomorrow and I could do with your help.'

* * *

It was a bumper crop but the hay would have to feed the horses and cows through the long winter months. George mowed, raked it over and then during the next few days, they carted and stored it in the hay loft in the big barn. It was hard and exhausting work.

'It's too hot for this,' he yelled to Amy who was standing in the shade of a tree. She looked like he felt – exhausted and limp from the heat. 'We'll finish this bit and call it a day.'

The searing heat sent Amy into the house while he went to the barn. He knew that not many weeks ahead they could be plunged into icy weather and heavy snow, so, when he wasn't ploughing or hay making, he went logging. He began to saw up one of the recently felled trees but the saw was blunt.

'Damn,' he said in irritation. 'It's too bloody hot for anything.'

'I've brought you a jug of water.'

Amy stood in the doorway and he could see her frown of disapproval.

'You shouldn't creep up on me,' he grumbled knowing how she disapproved of bad language. He took the jug and tumbler she was holding. 'Thanks.'

He drained his glass in double quick time and was pouring another when a flash of lightning lit up the whole yard. The sky had been threatening all afternoon and now fork lightning stretched long terrifyingly, powerful fingers down to sizzle and scorch the earth, followed by a loud clap of thunder.

'The boys …' She turned and started towards the house.

'They'll be fine,' he yelled after her. 'But damn it, the hay won't,' he added as he dashed after her.

'I'm soaked,' Amy said, fetching a towel to dry her hair, while George, ignoring his damp clothes, slumped into a chair.

The wind and the rain battered the roof and lashed at the windows. Alternating between torrential downpours, lightning which lit up the whole room and thunder which deafened them, the storm lasted well into the night.

George gave up hope of completing outside chores and they went to bed earlier than usual and, in spite of the heat, Amy cuddled closer to him at every thunder crash. The house shook – the noise was deafening.

'Supposing we get a direct hit. We'll all be killed,' she said, clinging tighter. 'I'm glad the boys are asleep. This is far worse than back home.'

He hugged her. 'We'll be all right.' Then in the gloom, he spotted two little people in the doorway. 'Come on in, guys.'

All four crowded into one bed. The room became muggy and airless. He lay listening for the sound he dreaded most – the sound of hail hitting the roof, rattling the chimney or beating against the window. Sleep was slow to come even though they were all exhausted.

The air was fresher next morning and he rode bare backed on Buster to inspect the wheat.

'No damage. Some of the crops down, but I think it'll recover.' He said on his return. He slid down from the horse.

'That's a relief,' Amy said, following him, as he led the animal to the barn.

'I've seen hail leave a trail of devastation a mile wide. It can smash a crop to smithereens.'

'Why didn't you tell me?'

'No point in two of us worrying.'

* * *

They returned to their routine and Amy tended her vegetable garden or went berry picking with Janet. The variety of fruit amazed her and there were even wild strawberries. On one trail they came across Indians also intent on harvesting nature's bounty. Janet exchanged friendly gestures with them before they walked on to another area of wild bushes. Maybe she had been worrying over nothing, she told herself because Janet didn't seem at all concerned by their proximity. After each of these expeditions, she was even busier, bottling fruit and making jam.

'There's a letter for you,' George said, popping his head round the door on one very hot afternoon. 'Phew, it's like a sauna in here.'

She mopped her brow and scowled at him. He had escaped the grind and gone into town but, since the fruit she'd picked that morning was very ripe and in danger of going rotten, she was forced to stay behind. She would have given anything for the breeze sitting up on the cart behind the horses.

George placed the letter on the table, not waiting to know what it was all about. She glanced at the writing and knew why. It was from her brother. Wiping her hands on her apron, she slit open the envelope and sat down to read. Freddie wrote about the garage and the progress of his son Jonathan, but there was little mention of Enid and she wondered whether he was still seeing the woman at the pub. He went on to say how things were with her mother.

'How dare she?' she exploded aloud and threw the letter onto the table.

'She will never cope with a winter in Canada.'

The words blazed through her head. She'd show her. She'd show them all.

But it got her thinking and, later, she went to the cupboard in the bedroom and removed her best outfit. Once it had been the latest fashion and so smart, but it was years old now. She fingered the worn cuffs and knew it was looking shabby. She had given up everything for George and look where it had landed her. She looked at her hands. They were red and rough. She stood at the mirror examining her face. It was weathered and sunburnt. She went back to her wardrobe. It was non-existent when she could have been the best dressed woman in town. It would have been parties and balls and lots of new clothes – not this ceaseless make-do and mend and the never-ending grinding work. She sat on the bed, tears welling in her eyes. Maybe her mother was right.

'Mom, Mom,' Will burst into the room, clutching a small bunch of wild flowers. 'These are for you. Sam and me picked them.'

'Why, Will,' she gulped as she looked at the variety of pink, blue and yellow heads, wishing she had a book so she could identify them. 'How wonderful.' She hugged him tight fighting back more tears.

'Shall we put them in water?' she asked as she released him.

She dabbed her eyes. How could she doubt she belonged here? George was worth more than a million Charles and no amount of money, new clothes or grand titles could ever make her happier.

She picked up the vase from the window ledge intending to fill it with water but a shadow in the doorway made her look up. It was barely a second of eye contact but in that moment a scream had welled up from somewhere, followed by wave upon wave. The Indian scarpered, disappearing amongst the trees.

'Amy, what the hell …' George came running from the barn. He ran into the house, grasping her by the shoulders and shaking her. 'Shsh shshsh. Whatever's wrong?'

Amy stared at him in relief. It was several seconds before she could speak.

'There was an Indian, Daddy,' Will said from the bedroom doorway.

'There was, was there, son?'

'Sure was, Daddy. He went that way.' Will pointed to the woods.

He put his arm round Amy. 'Don't suppose he meant any harm.' He sat Amy in a chair. 'It sure is hot in here. Time for some refreshment, I think.'

As they sipped a glass of cold coffee, she was glad George hadn't made more of her foolish outburst. The truth was the Indian had spooked her.

'Sorry I was such an idiot …'

He squeezed her hand. 'Never mind that now. Just believe me when I say they're not a threat. Maybe curious – maybe some of them scrounge. But they're not dangerous. They need food and shelter, like the rest of us and, if it's hard for us, it's often harder for them.'

'I feel so – ' She wanted to say she felt scared and vulnerable, but Will's shout for help had them both scurrying to the door.

'Dad, Sam's on the barn roof.'

'What? How in the hell did he do that?'

They could see him, high above them on the slope of roof, sitting as though king of all he surveyed. He grinned down at them.

'He must have crawled out of those doors.' George pointed to the doors of the hay loft. 'I'll get the ladder but I sure don't know what we'll do it won't reach.'

Sam was soon rescued by George but the incident with the Indian had left an indelible mark in her imagination.

* * *

September

The fields ripened to gold and it felt like a huge landmark when George began the harvest. Amy spent back-breaking hours propping the sheaves in groups to await carting and threshing. At the end of the day, they fell into bed exhausted but triumphant.

George took them into town most weeks and they always called on Ellie. On one particular trip, George needed to call in on the harness dealer, which meant time spent with Ellie would be longer than usual. It was approaching the end of September and the two women sat enjoying homemade cookies and tea in the shade on the porch, while Will and Sam played with Ellie's two boys, Adam and Luke.

Amy sipped her tea and thought how wonderful it was to enjoy Ellie's company and wished for the hundredth time they lived nearer each other.

'I've got something I want to tell you.' Ellie placed her empty cup beside her chair. She seemed excited.

'Something nice I hope.'

She flapped her handkerchief about. 'These pesky flies.' She dabbed her forehead. 'It's so hot. I wish this weather would break.'

Amy was alarmed. 'We don't want any more storms. Not now. The threshers are due soon.'

'Don't look so worried. It's most unlikely to happen.' Ellie shifted herself to a more comfortable position in the chair. 'It's been so hot, I almost long for winter.'

'Not too soon. I'm not looking forward to it at all. Janet Sutherland said the snow used to creep in through the cracks in their first house. Imagine. She said she'd wake up in the morning and find tiny specks of snow in the creases of the pillow and she told me a friend of hers once found her hair frozen to the pillow.'

133

'Yes, I've heard those stories too, but they build the houses better these days. Anyway I kinda like winter, except when we get a white out, but even then you can be all sort of cosy indoors and I think I prefer it to the heat in my condition.'

'Your – your condition?'

Ellie laughed and nodded.

'You mean?' She had thought earlier that Ellie seemed a little plumper, but it had never occurred to her she might be pregnant.

Ellie smiled, her eyes sparkling.

'But that's wonderful. Congratulations.' Amy got up and gave her a kiss on the cheek. 'What lovely news. Is John as pleased as you?'

'John wants a daughter, but I told him he'll have to take what comes.'

She laughed. 'I'm so pleased for you both. When's it due?'

'March – towards the end.'

'But – ' She stopped. She had tried to put the matter out of her head, hoping it was a false alarm, but, with each passing day, she knew it wasn't. All the signs were there, only she chose to ignore them. Her heart sank. There was no escaping the fact she was pregnant and she was certain George would be horrified.

'But what?'

She could see Ellie frowning at her. She mustn't say any more. At least not before she had told George. 'Oh, nothing. Your news – it's wonderful. I'm really pleased for you. Do the boys know?'

She could feel Ellie's eyes boring into her.

'Don't tell me …' Ellie stared at her. 'You know what they say about a new house?'

She didn't answer but felt the colour rushing to her cheeks. She never was any good at concealing the truth.

'You're pregnant?'

Amy slowly nodded her head. 'I think I might be.'

'But that's wonderful. Just wait till I tell John. The two of us –'

'Don't tell him yet. Please. I only really just know myself. Felt a bit sickly a couple of mornings, but whatever you do, please don't tell John – at least not until I've had a chance to tell George. He hasn't a clue. You're the only one who knows and …' Now she had started to voice her thoughts, the words cascaded out. It was as though someone had freed out the stopper. 'The truth is, I don't really know how to tell him. He's got so many other problems and, though he doesn't tell me much, I'm not stupid. Oh, he tries to make out we're all right but I'm certain we're short of money. I'm so worried and I'm sure he is, because he's getting these dreadful dreams again. I thought they'd stopped but a couple of nights this week he's shouted out and woken us both up. He won't talk about it but I know it's the war.'

'Yes, I believe it left its scar on many a good man.'

'Whenever he's upset or worried, he gets these dreams but he refuses to talk about them. No matter what you say, Ellie, this couldn't come at a worse time.'

'I'm sure he'll be pleased, of course he will be.'

She was doubtful. 'We haven't got any baby things. We left them all in England.'

'You'll manage. It'll work out, you'll see. How many months are you?'

'I'm not sure.' Why hadn't she kept a better note? She had been in denial – something which was not going to be possible for much longer. 'A couple may be. I've lost track of the time.'

'Two months?' Ellie did a quick calculation. 'That means we'll be due about the same time. A girl for us both, do you think? What about you? Two boys each, it ought to be girls.'

Amy laughed. 'You can have a girl if you want, but I'll be content with another boy. Anyway I told George they'd all be boys.'

A noise from the side of the house made her uneasy. She looked over her shoulder and saw Luke and Will creeping towards them.

'Boo.' Luke jumped onto the decking. Will hung back.

Ellie wasn't amused. 'Luke – I said play nicely together and not on top us. Find the others and leave us in peace. Go on, off you go.'

Luke gave Ellie a stubborn look.

135

'Go on, the pair of you. Go find the others.'

They disappeared round the side of the house.

Amy was worried. 'I hope they didn't hear. Will repeats everything and I mean everything. Please, let's talk about something else. Remember not a word to John until I've told George.'

Ellie chatted on, excited at the prospect of their shared pregnancies, but Amy found it difficult to relax. She couldn't be sure Will hadn't heard.

'You must come and stay – at least two weeks before the baby's due. You can't possibly be out there on your own. I know John'll agree. I'll speak to him tonight.'

'No, Ellie, please. Please. Remember I haven't told George yet.'

'But you will – you must. Straight away.' Ellie smiled. 'He'll be delighted, I know he will. Promise me you'll tell him tonight.'

'I don't know how we'll manage. Oh, it's all such a worry.' How could she admit to Ellie she didn't want the child she was carrying, that, as the weeks past, she even hoped she'd miscarry? Ellie would be horrified. And how could she admit she hadn't told George because she hoped and prayed it wasn't true – that it was a bad dream. She changed the subject. 'Everything's a worry. This threshing business for instance. George says they'll be here sometime this week and I'm terrified I won't cook enough or it'll be so awful, we'll get the worst reputation. George says the gang always gives priority to the places where they know the food is good.'

'You're worrying over nothing. Why don't you ask Janet? I'm sure she'd help. She seems a good friend.'

She was appalled. 'I can't do that. George says the wives all treat it as some sort of competition.'

'I still think you're worrying about nothing. Cook what you're good at, only make a lot more. You must know how hungry George gets – the others won't be any different.'

When they said their good-byes, Ellie whispered the journey home would be a good opportunity to tell George her news.

She shook her head. 'I can't tell him in front of the children. It'll have to wait until we have a moment alone.'

Ellie raised her eyebrows. 'With the threshers coming, you might not get time alone. Tell him now before he finds out some other way.'

'What are you two whispering about?' George asked as he helped her up into the wagon.

'Nothing important.'

Ellie gave her a meaningful look and Amy knew her advice was sensible, but as the horses headed home, George was full of talk about the price of wheat and of the gossip in town. She hadn't the heart to dispel his cheerful mood but, as Ellie predicted, in the days ahead, she saw little of him.

The next morning saw her consulting her recipe books, inspecting the food store and touring the vegetable plot to see what would be ready before deciding what to cook. They killed four of their precious chickens and the day before the gang was due to arrive she baked so many pies and cookies, it was difficult to know where to store them.

It was almost eleven o'clock when George arrived back from Sutherland's farm where he had been helping the threshing gang. She was still baking.

'They're here,' he said shutting the door behind him.

She placed the latest pie on the table and closed the oven door. 'Thank heavens I'm nearly ready,' she said trying to sound upbeat but knowing she was dreading the whole thing. 'I thought I heard a whistle, but when I looked out I couldn't see anything. '

'They're up the track.'

'It's a pity they're so late. Will's desperate to see them.'

George smiled. 'There'll be time tomorrow. They came off Sutherland's and came down the track half a mile – best site we could find. Anyway, our crop's small so it didn't make sense to bring it all the way down here. Quite a business getting the outfit moved in the dark – had to go ahead with a lantern.'

'Do they expect anything to eat tonight?'

'No, Janet did us proud.' George patted his tummy and then noticed her frown. 'Don't look so worried. You'll be fine.'

She glanced at the spread of food on the table. 'I hope I've done enough.'

He inspected the huge quantity of cakes and pies, picked up a cookie and took a bite. 'Mmm. Tastes good. They won't go hungry with all this.'

'I hope not, but I'm worried about the space in here. We'll never fit everyone in. Do you think we could set up a table under the trees? It'd be cooler there. Janet said that's what other wives do. What do you think?'

'Yeah, yeah, later,' he said picking up his account book.

'George, we need to talk.'

'Can't it wait till tomorrow. I have some figures I want to sort out.'

At 5 am the next morning, before any alternative table could be organized, the gang squeezed into their living room. The large quantity of porridge she'd been stirring when they all appeared vanished in short order, as did the fried eggs and potatoes, which were topped off with freshly made bread and corn syrup. She cooked and served, cooked and served, all the time nausea creeping up on her. The heat and the flies were unbearable.

'Gee, this coffee's god damn awful,' one of the men said.

Another took a gulp and spat it out through the open door.

'What you done to the coffee, Mrs Mills?'

She felt the colour drain from her face. 'It's … it's the water …'

'Course, I remember now. Bad water here. We used to bring our own. We'll have to bring a barrel up from Sutherlands. Can you fix that, George?'

'Sure,' George said. 'Be here for lunch, boys.' He smiled around at them, glancing up at Amy, whose face was ghostly white. 'Are you okay, honey?' He whispered in her ear.

'It's stuffy in here. Need some air, that's all.' She bent over the stove, so he couldn't see the tears which threatened. The heat, the crush of bodies in their tiny living room, the flies, the nausea and now the coffee. How much more could she take?

He looked relieved. 'You've done well, sweetheart.' He patted her shoulder.

138

She gulped and turned to face him. 'The coffee. I feel so embarrassed.'

'Don't be. We'll get some water from the Sutherlands. I'll see to that. Just make sure you use it, especially for tea.'

After the men departed for the fields, she began the chore of clearing up and preparing the vegetables for lunch as well as the beef stew planned for the evening meal. The beef had been her one extravagance and had been purchased from the store when they were in town. Will, who earlier stood in awe of the threshing gang, was an enthusiastic helper, fetching and carrying dishes from the table and then vegetables from the storeroom, while Sam toddled after him. There was no time to stop and feel sorry for herself. Wearily she peeled potatoes and scrubbed carrots, all the time knowing she must tell George of her pregnancy. The faintness and nausea experienced that morning might not be possible to hide tomorrow. Maybe, when the harvest was safely completed, he would not be so worried about having an extra mouth to feed.

At mid-morning George arrived in the wagon with two barrels of water. He helped her set up a make-shift table in the shade of the trees as well as a bench made up with logs. She put out a bowl for hand washing and Will carried the soap and towels.

'George –'

'Can't stop now, honey.'

'But, George, I need to talk to you.'

'Later, later. We'll be back around twelve.' He leapt into the wagon, grabbed the reins and the horses set off at a fast trot, leaving a trail of dust and Amy staring after him. Would there ever be a right moment? When he was working on other homesteads and got home so late, he was asleep the moment his head hit the pillow and now the threshing gang was on their land, there was even less time to talk.

At lunch time, she was prepared for their arrival with a spread of food sufficient for an army and there were no complaints about the coffee.

In the middle of the afternoon, she and the children carried a bucket of tea and a large quantity of cookies out to the fields. The men driving the teams of horses which brought the crop in from the fields,

139

stopped only long enough to dip enamel cups in the bucket and gulp down their tea before they shook the reins and the horses set off again, the drivers shoving a supply of cookies into their pockets.

She let the boys watch a man stoke the steam engine.

'Stand well back,' she said, holding both their hands and eyeing all the moving parts. 'Those drive belts are dangerous.'

Tough, muscled, men forked sheaves with a regular rhythm onto the feeder, which carried the crop up into the big machine. Then, breathless with excitement and pride at the sight of their first harvest being thrashed, they went to inspect the grain as it came out of the shoot.

'Wow, when I grow up I want to be a steam engine driver,' Will said.

'It's smelly, hot and dusty work,' she told him, thinking her kitchen was sweltering enough but at least she didn't have to put up with the noise or the whiff of hot engine oil which right then made her feel nauseated.

When it was dark the gang appeared for their evening meal. There was little left of her beef stew and her blueberry pie was such a hit, several asked for third portions. Thank goodness she had made plenty.

'Mrs M,' George said as he slipped between the covers. 'You excelled yourself today.'

'There's something I want to tell you ....' She snuggled up to him. 'George?'

He was asleep, but she lay awake long into the night. It had been an exhilarating day and, yes, Mrs M, she told herself, you did excel. Not in a million years would any of her friends back in England have believed what she had achieved that day and, the thought gave her a deal of satisfaction but when she drifted off, her sleep was disturbed by dreams of hail storms, bad coffee and morning sickness.

At the end of the second day, the threshing gang had completed their task, but, with a broken belt on the separator, things had been held up and it was too late to move onto Jefferson's land, so Amy produced a second supper.

140

'They must be happy with the food, or they wouldn't have stopped,' George whispered. 'The only trouble is, they'll expect breakfast tomorrow.'

She had grown to hate cooking breakfast when the smell of food was so repulsive. It was as she placed the final plate of eggs and bacon in front of the man nearest the door that she was no longer able to hold back the nausea. She slipped out, hoping to be out of sight by the time she threw up. She reached the vegetable patch when the inevitable happened, but she had been followed by George, who had been followed by Will.

'Amy, are you sickening for something? Let me get you some water,' he said when he reached her. He put a comforting arm around her while she retched.

'Adam says his Mom does that every morning,' Will said in an important voice. 'His Mom's going to have a baby and he said my Mom was having one, too.'

'Will ...' She was sick again.

George looked at Will and then at Amy.

'Is that right?' He addressed her back.

She felt too wretched to answer.

He took hold of her shoulders, turning her to face him. 'Is it true?'

She avoided his eyes.

'Is it true?' He shook her gently.

Feeling weak at the knees, she nodded.

'Jesus ...'

She was feeling better now she had brought up the coffee she had drunk earlier and saw his look of astonishment.

'Why didn't you tell me before?' She could see the hurt in his eyes, then the anger. 'I hear it from my own son before you – before you bother telling me.'

'I ... how could I tell you? I tried.' She fought back the tears. How could she tell him she didn't want this child? 'You're never here but for the hours you sleep. There's never been a moment. Anyway I knew you wouldn't be pleased.'

141

'Pleased? Sure I'm pleased – pleased as hell. As if I haven't got enough worries,' he said in a loud voice.

She glanced towards the house, but the rest of the gang were still enjoying breakfast.

'We'll talk later.' He grabbed Will's hand. 'You can come with me and leave your mother to have a rest. You, young man, must learn not to repeat grown-up's conversations.'

'I didn't. It was Adam who said –'

'It doesn't matter who said what now.' Without another word, he walked Will back to the house.

She wandered around the edge of the vegetable patch to the log George had placed so she could rest in the shade. Now it was in full sun but she sat down, shoulders limp with fatigue, and stared around her. For once her eyes didn't see the growth of weeds or whether the carrots were doing well or even the dryness of the soil. Last night, she had been so triumphant but now she was full of remorse. She should have told him on the way home from Ellie's that day. All right it wasn't the perfect moment or private even. Will would have heard everything, but what difference would it have made? As if being pregnant wasn't difficult enough, now George was furious. Oh, why was life so unfair?

CHAPTER TEN

Mid-October

With the departure of the threshing gang, Amy's routine of chores resumed, while George continued to spend all daylight hours at neighbouring farms, only returning, exhausted, at night to fall into bed. She was weary of his lack of attention and the isolation until Janet called one afternoon.

'This will make up for all the hard work,' Janet said handing her an envelope. 'Tom says they should finish threshing today. I expect they'll be home early.'

'Oh. George didn't say.'

She looked at the envelope and wondered what else George didn't say. It was addressed to them both. Since he was hardly speaking to her, she had no idea of the progress of the thresher gangs and sometimes he even failed to inform her of his whereabouts.

'What is it?' The paper felt thick and expensive and the writing was precise.

'Open it and see.'

She reached for a knife to slit open the envelope. Inside was a card. She looked back at Janet. 'A ... a Halloween Party.'

'You sound as though you've never been to one. They sure are something else. Everyone will be there. They're simply the best.'

'How exciting. I can't wait to tell George.'

'You have to come. Everyone dresses for it.'

George came home for supper for the first time in weeks and unable to wait until he had finished eating, she retrieved the envelope. For a moment she allowed her fingers to enjoy the sensation of holding the luxurious white paper, while her mind raced on to the pleasures such an evening could bring. It was years since she had received an invitation like this and she knew it meant they were accepted as part of the community.

She propped the card against the salt pot on the table in front of him. 'It's from the McAllister's. Take a look.'

He shoved the last forkful of mashed potato into his mouth.

'It's an invitation. Our first party. Go on. Do read it.'

He picked up the card and examined it before placing it face down on the table. 'Expensive,' he said before mopping his plate with a slice of bread.

'Is that all you can say? Don't be such a kill joy. It's a party, a Halloween Party, and we've never been to a party together. Ever.'

He didn't reply.

'Do say we can go. Janet says everyone'll be there.' She gazed at him, not understanding why he wasn't excited but more than that why he couldn't forgive her. 'She told me the McAllister's have a big Halloween party every year. They used to have it in the schoolhouse but the roof was damaged in a storm a few years ago and since then it's been at the McAllisters. She says it's a lot warmer than at the schoolhouse.'

He grunted, picked up the invitation and replaced it against the salt pot.

'It's a beautiful house. Janet showed me when we went berry picking. It's huge – two floors and an attic too. I wouldn't have noticed the attic, but Janet pointed out these pretty little windows right at the top of the house. And there's a balcony at the front as well as a deck.' She sighed. 'They even have a rocking chair out on the porch. Oh, it must be wonderful to live in a house like that. And it has a furnace in the basement. Imagine the whole house nice and warm and Janet said there's hot water pumped to the kitchen. Hot water. Isn't that incredible? Wash day must be a dream.'

'Mmm.' George reached for another chunk of bread.

'And there are four bedrooms. If we had four bedrooms, there would be one each for the boys and another for a nursery. Wouldn't that be wonderful?'

'There's no reason why we shouldn't have a new house one day.'

'You're impossible, George Mills.' She shook her head and went to make coffee, but the invitation was uppermost in her mind. 'It'd still be nice to go. It looked a beautiful house. I'd love to see inside. Please, say we can go. The boys'll love it.'

He placed his knife and fork together. 'Of course, we'll go.'

'Oh, George.' She stopped what she was doing, wrapped her arms around his neck and kissed the top of his head. 'You are a tease. Why didn't you say so straight away?'

'That'd be too easy. Had to play you a long awhile.'

It was the first time she had kissed him in weeks and she knew how much she had missed him but she wasn't ready yet to forget the way he had ignored her. She went back to making the coffee.

'I can hardly wait – a whole evening out. It's so exciting and it'll be much more fun than gossiping after church.'

'You bet. Halloween in Canada sure is something else. We'll have a great time. There's always a feast – wouldn't miss it for the world, 'sides I want to talk to Sid McAllister about threshing.'

Amy poured the coffee. It was always farming. Why couldn't he think about her for a change? But it was the longest conversation they'd had in weeks.

'Threshing? Why?'

'Sid McAllister bought a tractor that's why. Used it for his harvest – didn't bother with the gang – did it himself or so Tom said. More profitable – saves the cost of the gang.'

'You're not thinking of buying a tractor?'

'Maybe.'

Amy was more interested in the party. For a moment she had a longing for England when a party meant going to the dressmaker, choosing the fabric and attending for fittings. She dismissed the thought. The lack of a new dress was not going to spoil the fun.

145

'I'll have to look at my clothes. I can't wear this old thing.' She indicated her blouse. 'Nothing fits these days.'

'I'll start hauling grain tomorrow and with the cash, we'll look at that sewing machine you've always wanted.'

He was keen to take his first consignment to the elevator at the nearby railway sidings. She'd seen these alongside the rail track right the way across Canada. They were visible for miles – tall, sentinel structures, punctuating the prairies – the place where the grain was graded and stored before its onward journey to the docks. Now it was time for their crop to be graded. It was a significant milestone.

'It's really going to happen at last?'

'Yep. It might be the smallest harvest for miles around here, but it's a beginning and more than I'd dared hoped.' He grinned at her. 'And when we go to town you must get a new dress.'

'A new dress and a sewing machine?' She couldn't believe her luck. She placed two cups of coffee on the table, thrilled at the prospect of a trip into town but even more excited by the prospect of a new outfit. 'When do you think we can go?'

'Soon, if the weather's good.'

'The weather?'

'Snow's due any time. Might not be able to get into town.'

'It won't be that bad, surely.' She sipped her coffee. 'I can't wait to have a sewing machine. I'll be able to make some things for the baby. Oh, all sorts of things ...'

'I haven't got a fortune to spend, but I sure can't have my wife looking dowdy, now can I? Especially when we go to the McAllister's and,' he smiled, 'especially now she's expecting my daughter.'

'It'll be a boy.' She was serious, anxious he shouldn't raise his hopes. 'I'm certain.' She felt her tummy and knew it would mean so much to him to have a daughter, but there was this absolute certainty – just like the times before and she had been right then, hadn't she?

'Third time lucky, they say.' He winked at her. 'And I've always wanted a little girl to spoil.'

'You've got me.'

He squeezed her hand. 'You know what I mean.'

'Three boys to work on the farm, that's what I think.'

'A girl to help with the chores. You'll need help with the cooking one day, you know. Threshing gang'll be here longer next time that's for sure. Next year there'll be a bigger crop and when I get a tractor an even bigger one.'

'You're set on getting a tractor?'

'The way I see it – it's the future. You see if I'm not right. Everyone'll have one. They don't get tired like horses and they don't need feeding all winter.'

'If you got a tractor to do the threshing, then they'll be no gang and I won't need a daughter to help me.'

He laughed.

'Anyway, aren't they expensive?'

'All women are expensive. I don't suppose a daughter'll be any different.'

'You know what I mean. Are tractors expensive?'

'Mmm, maybe.'

'How can we afford one, then?'

'May be I'll get us a loan.'

'Is that wise?'

'Half the farmers round here have loans – it's the way to expand, as I see it. There's no reason at all why our little farm shouldn't make us as rich as the McAllisters.'

'Really?'

'Maybe not as rich, but comfortable.'

'When we're as rich as the McAllister's we'll have money enough to hire some maids.' Amy laughed. 'I want better things for any daughter of mine.'

'So you think it might be a girl then?'

She shook her head. 'And when we're rich, there'll be money enough to have hired help with the ploughing, too. So it won't matter if it's a girl or a boy, will it?'

Relief flooded through her that at last they were talking again and it felt good. She had never known George to sulk before, but she had hurt him deeply and she hadn't known how to put things right. With the threshing over, George's mood lifted. And so did hers.

It wasn't only George who was so upbeat. When she was last in town, there had been a buzz in the air – a sense of achievement and satisfaction now the harvest was almost in. Everybody was relieved it had been accomplished before the onset of the winter snow and everybody told her the price for wheat wasn't too bad either. No wonder George was cheerful.

They were up early the day George began the task of hauling their grain to the elevator. He took Will along with him, sitting the lad on his knee and teaching him how to hold the reins. Every trip meant payment and with every extra dollar, Amy found he was even more amenable. Had things been that bad? He seemed happier at the prospect of another baby, but she hoped he wouldn't be too disappointed with a third son.

The weather became cooler and the nights had drawn in. The birds were migrating, flocks of geese streaking the sky as they headed south to warmer territory. The leaves turned various shades of crimson and yellow before falling to the ground and Amy rummaged through their clothes. Warmer things were needed but when she looked out the boys' woollies she was certain they'd shrunk.

She opened the door intending to call Will who was playing out in the yard. A strong farmyard smell filled the room and she wondered if the wind had turned.

'Will. Will, come here, please.'

'Is it important?' George's voice came from the back of the house.

'Yes,' she said walking to the corner of the house. 'I need him to … What is that awful whiff? Oh, my Lord.' She stared at them. Will was covered in mud.

'We're making us warm,' he said.

'What is going on?'

'Got to keep us cosy somehow.' George grinned at her and carried on layering cow dung onto the walls of the house. 'It's all good stuff. Makes good insulation. No point in wasting it.'

'It stinks to high heaven. I'll never sleep tonight with that smell inside the house as well as out.'

'It won't smell for long. First frost'll see to that.'

'But look at the state of Will. For goodness sake, George, he's covered in that muck. The child'll catch some unpronounceable disease.' She held up the jumper she was holding. 'I wanted him to try this on. Now he'll have to have a jolly good wash and look at all that extra washing.'

* * *

Winter arrived silently one night. The minute she awoke, Amy knew by the light in the room there was snow outside. She lay motionless and looked across at George, but he was asleep. He worked so hard, she thought, he deserved a lay-in. Most days he shovelled grain or felled trees. The wood pile outside the barn had grown into a mountain and there was another smaller stack nearer the house. The barn repairs were complete and everything was ready for the arrival of hogs next spring.

'What's in the bank has to last,' George often said. 'We can't afford to waste anything.' Then he reminded her, the chickens were unlikely to lay when it got really cold and the only vegetables available would be those in the store or what she had bottled. They would have to make things stretch as far as possible.

The room was icily cold. She snuggled closer under the covers. George grunted.

She yawned. 'I think there's snow outside.'

He turned onto his back, but his eyes were still shut so she reached across and rubbed the back of her hand across the stubble on his face.

'You have to wake up sometime.'

He rolled over.

149

'But it's much nicer here with you beside me.' He sat up, resting on his elbow, looking down at her. 'This is our time,' he said and kissed her.

They got up much later than usual that morning and Amy shivered as she dressed. She opened the curtains and looked out at the snow. There was a layer covering everything and on the inside, the window was thick with ice. Even the bucket of water, which she had left overnight by the fire had frozen. George went to feed the animals and do the milking, leaving her to attend to the fire, which was a tiny red glow in the ashes and needed urgent attention.

He was whistling when he returned with the milk.

'Not today,' he told Will, who had asked if he could go to see Josh. 'We're all going to town.' He banged his feet on the doormat. 'I want to visit the barbers and get myself smartened up for this Halloween party and I have to go to the bank.'

'And I want some candles for the pumpkins and we'll look in on Ellie.' Amy smiled at Will. 'You'll be able to play with Adam and Luke and, anyway, the snow will still be here tomorrow.'

'Sure, now it's here, it's likely set for the rest of winter.' George placed the bucket he was carrying on the floor and rubbed his hands together. 'We'll have to fix up the sleigh though. No wheels for a while, I'm afraid.'

George put some straw in the cart, covering it with a horse blanket. 'You'll be warmer there with the children, than up top with me,' he said and helped her to climb in.

The powdery snow had drifted in the wind and was heaped up around the farm buildings and the trees. It's a winter wonderland, Amy decided but, despite an additional blanket, which she had wrapped around the three of them, the wind cut through their clothing and gnawed at their faces. They pulled their hats down over their ears and wrapped their scarves over their noses. Only the muffled clops of the horse's hooves, the creak of the sleigh and the clink of the harness could be heard as they shushed along the track. Even the river had ceased to its noisy journey and, for now, seemed tamed.

'We'll be able to take a short cut soon,' George said over his shoulder. 'Once the ice is thick enough.'

150

After a while, he let go of the reins and pushed his hands in his pockets.

'My hands are freezing. The horses'll take us there. They don't need me to show them the way. They know if they go off the track, they'll sink up to their bellies in snow.'

A wagon approached and they recognized Tom Sutherland.

'You're hauling early,' George said after they had exchanged greetings.

'I want to get two trips in today before the weather sets in.'

'More snow, do you think?'

'Possibly before the day's out. Better make sure your wood pile's near your house. You'll need it.'

George laughed. 'Sure thing.'

'Have you heard the news?'

'What news?'

'You haven't heard? Seems Ellie Stadnyk was rushed to hospital.'

Amy felt herself go hot then cold with fear. 'Oh, no. Is the baby all right?'

Tom's eyebrows shot up. 'Didn't know she was ... Anyway, seems she was taken bad a day or so back. Heard it from Stan Jefferson when I was at the siding.'

They made the Stadnyk's house their first call. John opened the door. His expression was wretched and there were black circles beneath his eyes and several days' growth of beard on his chin. Amy thought he'd aged ten years since she last saw him.

'We came as soon as we heard,' she said, kissing him on the cheek. 'Ellie – is Ellie ..?'

George shook John's hand.

'Ellie's all right, but we've ...' He took a deep breath. 'She lost the baby.'

'Oh, John, I'm so sorry,' she said. 'Can I see her?'

151

'She's very down. Maybe you can cheer her up. She came home from hospital this morning. They said there was nothing else to be done.' Tears welled in his eyes. 'It's as though she didn't exist, but she did. I saw her. Perfectly formed – a little girl. They took her away.'

She hugged him. 'I am so sorry. Did Ellie ... Did she see?'

He swallowed and nodded. 'You go up. She may be asleep, but if she isn't, I know she'll be pleased to see you.'

She stood in the doorway, reluctant to enter, but, sensing someone was there, Ellie opened her eyes.

'Amy.' She began to sit up.

'Don't sit up. There's no need.'

'But I want to. I can't lay here forever feeling sorry for myself. I've got two boys to look after and John – he needs me.'

She crossed the room to give Ellie a big hug. 'Here, let me plump the pillows for you.'

Ellie leant forward and allowed her to adjust the pillows. 'Nobody thinks of the father, but John's hurting too,' she said as she settled back. 'I'm glad the boys don't really understand. John told them God decided she should be an angel instead.'

'I'm so sorry.' With tears threatening, she put her arms around Ellie again and held her close for a minute. 'Sorry isn't enough is it?' she said and, looking into Ellie's face, gently pushed a lock hair back from her forehead and away from her eyes. It felt dank and lifeless. 'But what else can I say?'

'We really wanted her, you know? We would have loved her.' A tear plopped onto the bedcover and she reached for a handkerchief to dab her eyes. 'John so wanted her. Why did God take her away? I wish I understood.'

Amy couldn't stop her own tears. She drew back. 'Sometimes – sometimes life is so unfair.'

They both wiped their eyes and she sat on the edge of the bed, holding Ellie's hand.

'It was our little girl.'

Amy looked away. 'Oh, I feel so guilty ...'

'Guilty? Why should you feel guilty?'

'Because ... I just do. I can't help it.'

She thought back to the time when she had first known she was pregnant – the time when she'd tried to think of a way to get rid of her baby – the time when George wouldn't speak of their child and she felt so miserable. She remembered trying to recall the conversation she'd once overheard between Lizzy and Phoebe. It had been about abortion. It had disgusted her at the time, but she knew she'd changed a lot since those innocent days when she hardly knew what it was to be married let alone pregnant. Yes, she should feel guilty. It was a terrible sin, but she had considered just that.

'I don't understand. Why do you feel guilty?'

She fingered the coverlet, not answering immediately. Ellie would never comprehend.

'I didn't ... You know how it was,' she began to explain. 'I couldn't even tell George properly could I?' She hung her head. 'I've never said this to anyone, but at first I didn't want my baby and ... You so wanted your little girl.'

Ellie nodded and dabbed her eyes again. 'John's little girl. John said she was too good for this earth. She's gone to heaven. Our little angel.' She blew her nose. 'But, Amy, you mustn't feel guilty. Whatever else you feel, please don't feel guilty.'

She didn't reply. She had voiced the feelings she had hidden deep down for so long and, although she had got used to the idea of another baby, looked forward to its arrival even, she still felt ashamed she could ever have thought otherwise. How awful was that? Not wanting her own baby.

Ellie tugged at her hand. 'Promise me something.'

She looked up and saw her serious expression.

'Promise me you'll pamper this baby. Spoil him whenever you think of me. Promise me. I want him to feel – well, ... special. Will you share him – even if it's only a little?'

'Of course, I will.'

'When he arrives, let me hold him – just a little. It'll ... maybe make my loss a little easier to bear.'

Amy swallowed hard and blinked back tears.

'Here feel.' She held Ellie's hand to her tummy and told herself she would love this child as no other. 'I promise he'll be the most wanted baby ever and you shall be his godmother.'

'And he'll be the most indulged godchild ever. There's something else. I've been laying here thinking and I … I want you to have all the baby clothes. They're over there.' She indicated the chest-of-drawers beneath the window.

'I can't do that. You'll need them for next time.'

Ellie shook her head. 'They said there won't be a next time.'

'Oh, no. That can't be right. Surely that can't be right? They could be wrong. Nobody can know for sure, can they?'

Ellie screwed up her a face. 'I think it's pretty certain I won't conceive again. Anyway I shan't need the baby things for a long time, so you must have them. Your baby needs them.' Ellie smiled at her. 'And, as his future godmother, I insist. I'll get John to pack them up right away – except the tiniest ones, of course.'

Amy looked puzzled.

'You are still coming here before the baby arrives? I meant it when I said you shouldn't stay all that way out of town. So many women don't make it in time. I've heard of women giving birth in complete stranger's houses. You don't want that. It'd be much better for you here. Come a week or two before he's due. You can bring the boys and, besides, it'll give me something to look forward to. I'll get John to have a word with George. He should be able to manage without you for a week or two. There can't be as much to do in winter – can there?'

* * *

A week later it was Halloween. The children were screeching with excitement and Amy, who had only manage to finish her new dress the previous day, was equally impatient for the day to pass. George was calm and practical and immediately after breakfast, placed two big stones on the stove.

154

'I'll wrap them in an old blanket and they'll keep your feet warm on the way.'

When they arrived at the McAllister's, several cars and wagons were there already. The porch was decorated with hollowed out, candlelit pumpkins and the house looked warm and inviting. Voices and loud laughter came from within and above it all, Amy could make out a fiddle playing a Scottish reel.

'Seems there's a few here already,' George said as he helped her down from the wagon. 'You go in the warm while I see to the horses.'

The boys soon disappeared for the bob-apple and other party games and she found herself alone, on the edge of things and feeling very much the newcomer. She noticed a noisy group of young men surrounding Josie Smith, the school teacher, who was dressed in an elegant deep maroon outfit which contrasted with her pure white skin. She immediately decided Josie was far too young and far too beautiful to be trusted to educate her Will. At that moment, Josie broke away from her conversation and crossed the room towards her. Every male in the room was watching and admiring, including George as he came through the door.

'I'm looking forward to Will coming to school in the spring,' she said as she passed by and, taking the arm of the nearest young man, went to join another group.

'Sure got an eye for that young lady,' George nodded in the direction of the young man.

'So has every other man in the room, including you, George.' Amy waggled her finger at him and took him by the arm. 'I think it's time you introduced me to Sid McAllister.'

The evening sped by far too quickly. It was a treat to be able to socialize and a delight to make new friends. She understood a little more about tractors after listening to George and Sid discuss their virtues, though the sums of money involved shocked her. It was academic anyway. They didn't have the cash. Besides didn't cars frequently get bogged down on the roads? What was there to say tractors wouldn't do the same?

She found Janet and was soon discussing the expensive and luxurious furnishings of their hosts' house, when some latecomers arrived.

'Look over there,' Janet said. 'It's the Jackson's. Didn't expect to see them here tonight.'

'Why? I thought the McAllisters and the Jacksons were as thick as thieves.'

'Not any more, they aren't. Didn't you hear? They haven't been talking since Sid bought that acreage from Mr Chernitsky. Put in a much higher offer right at the last minute. I heard there was a big row over it.'

'It looks as if they've made it up,' Amy said watching both Irene and Sid McAllister greeting their guests. 'They seem friendly enough.'

'Mmm. We'll see.'

'Why did the Chernitskys sell?'

'Needed the cash, I suppose. Mr Chernitsky hasn't been well and they had to call the doctor. Doctors cost money and Tom told me some of their crop failed. They got caught in that hail storm. Anyway, with a metal plate in his head, I wonder if he's quite all there. Claims he was a Russian Count if you please, but if that was the case, you'd think he'd have more money.'

The smell of warm honey and cinnamon wafted across the room.

'I think the food's ready and the cold's made me real hungry. Shall we go and see?' Janet led the way into the dining room.

George caught up with her and after they had eaten he whispered in her ear.

'Come and dance?' He placed his arm round her and guided her towards the front door.

'I wanted a few minutes alone with my wife, is that allowed?' He shut the door behind them. She could hear laughter and music coming from the nearby barn. Pumpkins lit the path. Overhead the moon shone down. It looked inviting, but he put his arms around her.

'I'm not much good at saying things, but … I know I've been rotten to you these past few weeks. Forgive me?'

'There's nothing to forgive. As you once said, we're in this together.'

'I suppose I did have something to do with it.' He grinned at her. 'I don't think you're quite clever enough to create a baby on your own.'

'George!'

'Ellie and John …' He became more serious. 'It got me thinking. We're lucky really, aren't we?'

She smiled up at him. 'I love you and yes, we're very lucky.'

He kissed her. 'Come on, it's cold out here. Let's go dance.'

Amy was sad when it all came to an end. Outside, the temperature had plummeted and she sat beside George on the way home and cuddled close for warmth. The night was still and above was a navy blue velvet sky glittering with stars. With the moon's light reflected in the snow, it hardly seemed dark. It was a wonderful, magical night.

CHAPTER ELEVEN

December

Winter isolated them in a white desert which glistened in the sunlight and was moulded and shaped by wind. The river had frozen and could be trusted to bear the weight of the wagon and team, enabling them to take a short cut to town, but the trips became less frequent and always waited until something vital was required. Icy stalactites hung from the roof of the barn and, most days the sky was without a hint of a cloud, the light so intense Amy had to squint or shield her eyes. Despite the incessant cold, it never made her feel miserable. It was so different to an English winter. She revelled in its novelty, entranced as the wind whipped the snow from the roof, sending it cascading to the ground, sparkling in the sunlight like a million diamonds. With the moisture frozen out, it blew about like fine sand. Jack rabbits, the size of dogs and bold enough to venture into the yard in search of food, intrigued her with their winter white coats, while the pretty Blue Jays fluttered between the trees and an enormous owl lurked behind the barn.

'I think it's going to be a hard winter,' George told her one day when he caught her scratching at the ice on the inside of the window. 'Tom reckons we're due one.'

'It's bad enough out there now.' She peered through the window. 'Surely it can't get worse?'

He shrugged. 'There's bound to be more snow. We can't expect to get through to spring without.'

'But there's already a foot. Surely not?'

'When it snows it's warmer.'

'But it'll soon mean we won't be able to go anywhere. I don't mind the sunny days. They're quite pleasant – if there's no wind, that is.'

'Wait until January.'

'You mean it really can get worse?'

'If we're unlucky it might. You might not like the snow, but it sure is better than when there's no cloud cover. After a week, it's tough. I remember one January. Someone said it was minus fifty five. Anyway, everything cracked with the cold – even the trees. They give up on the railroad then. Steel gets brittle at that temperature. Then there's frostbite. I've known men to lose their fingers or an ear even.'

As George predicted, more snow arrived and all trips were postponed. Getting to the Sunday service or up the track to visit Janet, Tom and Josh was too hazardous.

'I noticed when I was thumbing through our Eaton's catalogue, they stock decent underwear and I was wondering if there was some spare cash.' Amy said one evening as they enjoyed a game of cards together. 'Will's outgrown his vests and I need some new underwear. These pants are beginning to be uncomfortable.'

'Fifteen two, fifteen four and two for pairs.' He placed his cards down on the table and counted the remaining holes. 'I think that's it, Amy,' he said waving the winning peg at her. 'You should concentrate. You had a flush there.'

'How do you know?'

'Secret is to keep track of the cards not what's in Eaton's.'

'It's more interesting than your farming books and anyway, at least I can dream. There are even plans for houses, George.'

'Now don't go getting ideas. Underwear possibly. Maybe after Christmas.' He put the cards away. 'I think I'll turn in. Those coyotes kept me awake a lot last night. Wouldn't be surprised if they're sussing out our chickens. I wanna be bright enough to see them off.'

'The chickens'll be all right, won't they, George? I mean, it's not as though they're outside after dusk.'

159

'Coyotes are crafty.'

The last night or two, George, who normally slept so well, had been disturbed by the sounds of the pack. They sounded like wild dogs and she supposed that was what they really were. They were beginning to make her feel uneasy but, nonetheless, she didn't want him going out alone in the dark. There was the possibility of bears but she knew better than to say anything. George would do as only George would do. Her pleading would only increase his stubbornness so she was thankful when the coyotes didn't come calling for the next few nights.

She was busy making the Christmas pudding, when a blizzard closed in and, no matter how much ice she scratched off the window, nothing could be seen. The place was full of steam and when George opened the door to fetch wood, the wind banged the bedroom door shut and scattered the papers he had left on a shelf, leaving a sprinkling of snow on the floor. When he returned, he inspected the pile of logs already by the fire.

'That might last us today, but if this storm gets much worse, we won't want to bother fetching wood on the way back from the barn. I'll bring some more in now.'

By milking time, the wind was howling at the windows and rattling the chimney. They could hear it shrieking through the trees and she began to worry that even the house would be blown away.

'You're not going out again in this weather?' She said to George as she stirred the stew she was preparing for supper.

'No choice.' He slipped on an extra sweater and struggled into his coat.

'But how will you get to the barn? The snow must be over your boots. Please, don't go.'

He grunted and rummaged in the cupboard.

'What are you doing?'

'It's a white out – can't see a god damn thing.'

'George.' She frowned and looked at the boys, who were busy at the table. 'You know I don't like that sort of language especially in front of the children.'

'Don't be such a prude, honey and, sides, you won't stop them saying far worse once they get in that school room, that's for sure.'

'I sincerely hope not. We're not sending them to school to learn how to blaspheme. I hope Josie Smith is woman enough to keep those bigger boys in line, though I have my doubts. She's far too young to be a teacher. Why, she's hardly any older than some of the children she teaches. It would never surprise me if one of those youngsters made an improper approach.'

George stopped what he was doing and burst into laughter. 'Improper approach? Gee, honey, loosen up. You're not in England now. Anyway if there was the slightest chance of anything like that happening, which ever lad it was would get a damn good hiding.'

'If you speak like that here, what hope is there for Will?'

'He's growing up a Canadian and you'd better get used to it. He's already got the accent. Anyway, I've got more important things to worry about. I'm going to do the milking.' He held up a length of rope. 'I'll tie this to the door handle and play it out behind me. I should be able to follow it back to the house, when I've finished.'

He looped the rope around his waist. 'I've heard of men who never made it back from the barn on days like this. I'm not chancing it.'

She watched and knew nothing she could say would dissuade him.

'If I don't make it back, under no circumstances are you to come looking for me. I'll be in the barn. Don't leave the house. It's too dangerous. If you go outside, you won't see a thing and you'll end up lost and freezing to death. 'Sides your place is here. Stay with the boys.'

'Please don't go,' she pleaded. The thought of being alone in the storm alarmed her. 'Can't it wait until the morning?'

'Of course not. The animals come first. You should now that by now and anyway I remember you complaining how uncomfortable it was when you had too much milk. It's the same for Daisy.'

He tested the rope and, satisfied it was secure, opened the door. A blast of icy air struck him in the face, stinging his cheeks and making his eyes water. He struggled to close it. She ran to help and stood listening, but it was impossible to hear anything above the violence of the storm.

'Please, God, let him be safe,' she prayed out loud.

The wind had blown in more snow and she mopped up. The pot on the stove was bubbling so she returned to give it a stir. She had to keep busy. She corrected Will's writing, praised Sam's drawing, all the while listening to the moaning of the trees and the creaking of the house.

She stirred the stew once more and checked the pudding had sufficient water in the pot, then dabbed with a cloth at the condensation which had formed on top of the ice on the window, wondering if it would be possible to see the light of the lantern from the outside. Please God, let him get back safely. He said to stay in the house, but what would she do if she needed help? She paced up and down, every so often stopping to inspect the pudding and stir the stew, unaware she was doing either.

'Mom, when will Daddy be back?' Will looked up from his drawing.

'Soon,' she said trying to convey a confidence she didn't possess.

What if he didn't make it? What then? Whatever would she do – stuck here in the middle of the prairies, the nearest neighbour a mile down the track? She had never thought of the possibility of being here alone but then, George had never mentioned storms like this. Would she have agreed to come to Canada if she'd known? Probably not. She would tell him that when he came back, but … supposing the worst? What if he didn't come back and she was stuck here without him, what then? Work the farm alone? George was preparing Will for the time when he might have to take care of her and run the farm, but he was too young now. No, there was no way she could stay here – but how would she get to England? What money did they have? And, even if she found the money, there was the journey. However would she manage, with two small children and nearly six months pregnant, to travel halfway across the world to reach civilization and a questionable welcome from her mother? Return to London? It would be too awful to live with George's mother.

'Mom. What colour is a bear?'

She looked over Will's shoulder.

'I think it's meant to be a polar bear. They're white.' White like every other god damn thing. Stop it, she told herself. Just because George uses those words, there was no need for her to do so. Maybe bad language was something which evolved with the climate. Was that what happened? She so nearly let the words slip out and maybe if she had, she would have felt better.

Will inspected his crayons.

'White, Will, just white.'

'But I haven't got a white one.'

'Just colour everything else, then it'll look white.'

She stoked the fire and put on another log. George would need to warm up. The stew. She mustn't catch the bottom. She gave it another stir at the same time looking at her watch. A whole hour. He must have finished milking by now. Where was he? Had the rope become detached? Was he wandering around out there lost, blinded by the storm? Please God, she prayed again, let him come home safely.

It seemed forever before she heard him fumbling with the handle. She ran to the door and wrenched it open. The wind, the snow and George arrived together. They banged the door shut. He placed the milking pail on the floor, his face a greyish white.

'Not much – spilt some.' He inspected the contents. 'Quite a bit by the look of it. Wasn't too much to begin with anyway. Daisy didn't think much of my cold hands.'

He shivered, took off his gloves and rubbed his hands to get the feeling back. 'I don't think I've ever seen a blizzard as bad as this.' He removed his hat and began to tug off his boots.

She pushed the rug up against the door to stop the draught and tried to conceal her anxiety at the way the house groaned with every gust of wind. George was back, that was enough for now and she said a silent prayer of thanks.

The blizzard lasted for two days, piling snow against the door and windows, making it more difficult for George to reach the animals. On the third day it stopped snowing and, although the wind eased, it swirled the snow into the air and abandoned it in drifts several feet deep.

When George returned from milking, he didn't remove his coat. 'I'm going into town,' he announced. 'We need supplies.'

'Oh, good. Come on boys, we'd better eat breakfast right away,' Amy placed two steaming bowls of porridge on the table and tried to think of all the groceries she required. It would be wonderful to leave the house for a few hours.

George shook his head. 'Best I go alone. I think it'll be safer if you stay here with the boys.'

'But – '

'No buts.'

She ignored his words and employed another tactic. 'You can't go without something warm inside you. Eat some porridge. It won't take long. Then we'll all be ready.'

He grabbed a slice of bread from the table. 'I'm not stopping. I sure as hell don't like the look of the weather. I'll get something in town.'

She began to argue. It was so long since she'd been out in the fresh air and she wasn't going to miss the opportunity of seeing friends. 'I don't see why we all can't go. We've been stuck indoors for so long, it feels like a prison.'

'Yes, I know. I understand how you feel, but it's for the best. If I thought it was safe, I'd take you with me. You only have to look at the sky to know there's more snow on the way and the last thing I want is for you to be caught in a blizzard – especially now, in your condition.'

'But it needn't snow today.'

'It'll be here all right. Just poke your nose outside and look. There's another storm building. Believe me, Amy, I wouldn't go at all if I didn't think it was necessary. But I know how short we are on supplies and, if the weather really closes in, we could be cut off for weeks – till Christmas even.'

'Christmas? But surely –'

'No, Amy.' His face was determined. 'It's safer you stay. I've topped up the wood pile. Hopefully I'll be back in time for milking, but if you have to do it, make sure you use the rope.'

The milking? It was one thing doing it through the months of ploughing and harvesting, but now? Alone? The thought horrified her and she was stunned into silence. She watched him push his wallet into his pocket.

'I've already harnessed the horses. Give me your list. The sooner I go, the sooner I'll be back, but no matter how long it takes before I get back, you are not to come looking for me.'

It was useless to argue. She reached for the notebook she kept in the drawer of the table, tore out a page and handed it to him.

'I should be back to see to the animals.' He said, patting Will's head. 'You're to behave now, the two of you and look after your Mom.'

'Sure, Daddy.'

He kissed Amy. 'Don't look so worried. I'll be back before you know it.' He patted his pocket. 'I'll get everything on your list and may be some candy.'

'Oooh, yes, please, Dad.'

She tried to keep herself busy with household chores, tried to think of anything but the weather. There was plenty to do, but as she made beds and swept and tidied, attended to the fire and kneaded the bread, her mind was away with George.

The children played outside in the shelter of the yard for a while, but they were soon cold and back under her feet. They ate without George, but, she told herself, it was impossible for him to do the trip and be back for lunch. No, he would be back by mid-afternoon, hopefully before darkness fell. He would bring news from town, candy for the children and may be, as a treat, a newspaper for her. Best of all would be the mail – letters and Christmas cards from home. She looked forward to that. Tonight they would read them together.

Later she went outside to brush the snow from the windows and shovel snow away from the door. In the distance, there were deep black clouds lining up across the sky and the wind was beginning to get up. Weather, as George would say. In the summer they forewarned of a thunderstorm but now it would be snow. The clouds could be seen for miles across the flat landscape and they were heading their way.

She hoped George was well on the way home.

George was relieved when he finally left Mackenzie's store. The fuss over a parcel had delayed him and now he glanced up at the sky with alarm. The clouds were low and, by the look of them, heavy with snow and he knew it would be upon him long before he was home. Still thinking about the weather, he dumped the sack of flour and other supplies into the wagon and turned to go back for the rest of the groceries but a movement caught his eye. A black and white collie dog was nestled in the straw and looked nervously back at him as though expecting to be evicted from his warm bed.

'What are you doing here, boy? Wrong cart, that's for sure. Come on now. You must belong to someone.'

The dog resisted all attempts to coax him out so he returned to the store and shouted out 'Anyone missing a dog?'

There was no reply and Mackenzie shook his head. 'Sure aint anyone in the store.'

'There's a fair bit of weather on its way. I can't turn him out. Wouldn't be fair. I'll take him home. Can you put a note in your window, Mac?'

When he had finished loading, he set off at a fair pace. The horses were nervous and jumpy, as if they, too, knew a storm was heading their way. The full force hit them well before they reached the river and, having watched the clouds building with apprehension, he had already wrapped himself in the spare blanket he'd shoved in the wagon just before setting off. He made sure his hat and scarf were covering his face, leaving his eyes peering out into the whiteness. The temperature plummeted. The snow sliced horizontally into his eyes and the wind cut through him. He began to shiver. Everything about him was terrifyingly the same. Visibility was so poor, it wasn't long before he couldn't tell in which direction he was travelling. He could be upside down for all he knew. After a while, he began to feel he was going round in circles. His teeth chattered and his limbs were numb. He knew his life was in danger. There was only one thing left to do.

'It's over to you, boys,' he shouted above the wind. 'Take us home. Go on now. Take us back to Amy.' He released his grip on the reins, praying the horses would find their way and slid from his seat down into straw in the back of the cart. It was his only hope. The dog nuzzled him and they huddled together.

* * *

The bread was proved and baked, a pie was cooking in the oven and Amy was peeling potatoes. It grew darker. The children were squabbling. She was on edge and all her fears came rushing back. Supposing George didn't get home? Supposing he was lost? He had told her how men had gone missing and had never been found until the spring melt.

It began to snow. Just a dusting at first, drifting in the wind. Then the dust turned to flakes, scudding across the yard and hitting the window. Soon heavy flakes were piling against the glass. Still no sign of George. She became frantic.

'Mom, Mom, I can hear horses,' Will said.

She dropped a potato into the saucepan, wiped her hands on her apron and scratched at the window. She hoped Will was right, but she couldn't see a thing.

It was quite some time before George staggered into the house, carrying a large box of groceries.

Amy hugged him, feeling how cold he was and laughing with relief. 'Thank goodness you're here.'

'You never doubted me, did you?' He stood rubbing his hands. 'By golly, it's cold out there. My fingers are numb.'

'The kettle's hot. I'll make coffee. You need something to warm you.'

'Did you bring candy, Dad?' Will wanted to know.

'Sure did, but you'll have to wait till after supper.'

Amy inspected the contents of the box and held up the mail. 'Look how many letters we've got. You were ages in the barn. I began to wonder if it was really you we'd heard.'

'Had to see to the horses and I didn't fancy another trip outside tonight. 'Sides they deserved a treat.' He rubbed his hands. 'Without them I don't think I'd have made it back.'

167

'What do you mean?'

'They found the way home. Jesus, that storm is something else. At one point I didn't know if I was upside down even. Boy was I relieved to see our place.'

She wished he didn't use that word, but he was home and that was what mattered. 'You shouldn't have gone. You said it might be bad. We could have managed.'

'Maybe. But now we've got supplies to last us for weeks if need be. I gave the horses extra oats. Did the milking but there wasn't much. To be truthful I …' He lowered his voice and whispered in her ear. 'I gave it to a friend.'

'A friend?' She looked at George with suspicion. 'Why've you left him in the barn?'

He ignored her question and checked the wood box. 'I see you've topped it up.'

'And I cleared a path to the door too, but you wouldn't know.'

He laughed. 'Sure is a wicked night out there. I can't believe how lucky I am. If it wasn't for the horses …To be honest, I was lost and I damn well nearly froze. I don't know how they do it, but they found the river. I couldn't see a thing. Sure don't know where I'd have ended up without them.'

'Worse than last time?'

George nodded. 'Think so. There's already five foot of snow where its drifted. I was real glad to have a bit of company.'

'Thank goodness you got home safely. But why all the secrecy? Tell me, who's this friend?'

George put his fingers to his lips and, with a nod of his head, indicated the children, who were busy emptying packages from the grocery box and placing them on the table.

'Later,' he mouthed. 'We'll get no peace otherwise.'

When the children were asleep, they finished unpacking the groceries. There was candy for the Christmas stockings and letters and parcels from England. Amy looked at each of the envelopes, trying to identify the handwriting.

'Oh, wouldn't it be nice to have Christmas with the family?' A longing for England caught her unaware. 'Imagine if we were home in England, we could have invited everyone for dinner.' She sighed. 'It would be so lovely to have some company.'

George looked up from the newspaper. 'This is our home now,' he said and she knew he was determined not to allow her homesickness to ruin their Christmas. 'We've got our own place here and that's enough for me.'

She was silent. He was never homesick, or, if he was, he never let it show. After weeks shut up in their tiny house, she longed to be in a crowd – to enjoy conversations with family and friends. What she would give to visit Ellie or even Janet right now. She felt the baby move and thought how nice it would be to have some feminine conversation. Soon she would be with Ellie, she comforted herself. Hadn't George agreed she and the children should stay with Ellie at the end of January? She dismissed the thought she might not get there if the winter was really bad.

'Tell me about this friend,' she said, recalling their earlier conversation. 'I'm dying with curiosity. Don't tell me – you've found some wounded animal and taken pity on it. Was it caught in a trap?'

'No.' There was a wry smile on his lips. 'If you know me so well, you should know I'd put any animal caught in a trap out of its misery.'

'What then?'

'It took ages in Mackenzie's store. They couldn't find one of our parcels. Then I couldn't make up my mind what sort of candy the boys would like and while I was doing that John Stadnyk came in. Said Ellie was heaps better and looking forward to you and the boys going over. Tom Sutherland was in there too. Oh, and the McAllister boy. Just about everybody was in town collecting supplies. I guess they took advantage of the break in the weather. It was real busy.'

'Do get to the point.'

'I am. I am. All part of the story. Anyway when I got outside, he was there in the back of the wagon.'

'Who was?'

'This dog. A dog in the straw.'

'A dog?'

169

'Yep.'

'What sort of dog?'

'A collie, I think. The sort of farm dog most people round here have. I thought he must have made a mistake. Sure were enough wagons around. I went back into the store and yelled out to see if anyone was missing a dog.'

'And?'

'Got no answer. I hadn't the heart to turf him out, so I brought him home. Seemed friendly enough and he and I sort of kept each other warm in the back of the wagon. I guess I owe him.'

'He's in the barn?'

'Seemed best for tonight. Till we get to know him and if he's any good he'll be useful for rounding up the cattle. He'll have to earn his keep but for now, he's warm enough. We'll introduce him to the boys in the morning.'

'They'll love that. Will's always asking for a dog. But supposing he belongs to somebody?'

'Well, he can stay for now.'

'What do you think his name is?'

He shrugged. 'I called him Mac as I found him outside Mackenzie's store. Seems to answer to that, but I was offering some warm milk at the time.'

She smiled. 'Mac. Seems a nice enough name and if he's friendly, we'll keep him.'

CHAPTER TWELVE

The wind had deposited huge snow drifts against the house, making it impossible to tell where the roof began. When George battled his way out, he was stunned by the massive cliffs of snow. They were cut off. There was no doubt in his mind. It would take a colossal effort to clear a path. He felt vindicated in his decision to make the trip for supplies – it might be months before there was another opportunity to get into town.

He spent the day shovelling a narrow path to the barn. The wind blasted him with bullets of snow, gnawing at any exposed skin while his eyelashes felt as though they were freezing. He couldn't remember weather this bad before, but he didn't dare admit that to Amy. She was depressed enough already and he felt a wave of sympathy. She was pregnant, in a strange land and with precious little female company. No wonder she was so down but it would never do to let her know that sometimes things nagged at him or that he was also sick of the sight of snow and the battle to feed the animals.

In the barn, the dog wagged his tail and leapt about him, then shadowed him as he mucked out the horses and forked hay from the loft.

'Get out you silly dog,' he scolded when Mac tried to stick his head under the cow's teats and into the milk pail. He supposed the poor thing was starving, so took him back to the house.

'Can we keep him?' Will wanted to know.

'If no one claims him.' Amy searched the cupboard for an old bowl. She found some scraps of food, mixed it with a slice of bread and placed it on the floor. They watched him gulp it down.

At Will's insistence, Mac was allowed to warm himself by the fire. He stretched himself out on the rug, tolerating the lavish strokes the boys bestowed on him and even Amy was pleased to have his company whenever George struggled out to the barn. Mac's presence reassured her.

* * *

There was a break in the weather two days before Christmas and Amy was elated when George, who had managed to struggled up the track to see Tom, announced that, if they could get the sleigh out of the barn, it would be safe for them to attend the church service in the late afternoon of Christmas eve.

This might be the highlight of the entire festive season, Amy thought as she dressed the boys. It was a chance to get out and it might be their only opportunity to socialize.

'See the tree, Sam,' she said as she took in how well the schoolroom had been decorated. 'Oh, and look, there's a crib.' It was handmade and as she fingered the paper chains, was intrigued to discover they were made out of pages torn from old Eaton's catalogues.

After the service, they gossiped with friends. Mr Chernitsky's illness – serious, according to Janet – the Jefferson's new baby – born at the elevator apparently – the storm preventing them from getting to the hospital in town.

'And there was no woman to help. Imagine – only men. I suppose Stan should be experienced by now. He delivered his first, you know, in the back of their wagon.' Janet grinned. 'With their tribe, you'd think they'd know to set off to town earlier.'

Amy didn't find the thought of her baby arriving in the back of their wagon or in an elevator at all amusing. She felt the baby kick and was grateful they planned to be with Ellie in plenty of time. There would be no last minute dash if she could avoid it. But the knowledge the weather might deem otherwise, was always there.

Chatting with Janet, she kept her eye on George, who was asking everyone about missing a dog. Will trailed around behind him and with each negative answer, both their faces showed relief. She crossed her fingers. Will wasn't the only one who hoped Mac's owner wouldn't be found.

It was past ten o'clock when the boys hung up their stockings. Shrieks of excitement came from the bedroom.

172

'Father Christmas doesn't visit little boys who aren't asleep,' Amy said after she had scolded them for jumping all over their beds. 'If he finds you awake, he'll go away.'

As she shut their bedroom door, George put a finger to his lips, pointed to her coat and indicated they should go outside.

'We'll get the sleigh bells,' he whispered and quietly opened the door. 'That way they really will think Santa's on his way. That should make them behave.'

Giggling like naughty schoolchildren, they tiptoed to the barn. The night was very still and the stars so close Amy felt she could reach out to touch them. The bark of a coyote made her jump and one of the horses whinnied in recognition as they approached.

She waited in the doorway, while George found the bells. It was so different to any Christmas she could ever remember. There was no goose for dinner or fine table in Lord and Lady Ashby's dining room. Would mother be there and Freddie? Since she had disgraced them all, probably not, she decided. There had been no news of her mother and, though Freddie had scrawled a note, he hadn't said what he was doing. But in England, even if there was snow, it could never be like this magic, white wonderland. Still she couldn't suppress a longing for family, traditional festivities and friends.

'Got them,' George said, appearing from the darkness of the barn. 'Hey, Amy, look. Look up.'

He pointed to swirling, dancing lights – shades of turquoise, green and red – rising from the horizon and sweeping across the sky, spreading a translucent veil through which the stars still shone.

'My goodness. What's happening?'

'The Aurora Borealis – the Northern Lights.'

She stared. 'It's incredible. Like a magic curtain. Whatever causes it?'

'Something to do with the sun. It's beautiful, isn't it?'

He closed the barn door, put his arm around her and they stood spellbound, watching the lights dancing across the sky. 'A little compensation for living in such a cold wilderness.'

'Mmm.' She wondered if he knew she had been thinking of Christmas in England.

'The Indians believe it's the dead trying to make contact and if they whistle to the lights they'll conjure up the spirits.'

She shivered and he hugged and kissed her.

'You're cold. Here, we'd better get on with this before you freeze.'

He handed her the bells and was unable to suppress a smile as she pretended to be a reindeer, trotting along the path, bells held aloft. She stopped at the large heap of snow he had shovelled off the pathway earlier and turned, intending to make a return trip, then slid very inelegantly down into the snow.

He stopped laughing and rushed to her side. 'Amy, the baby. Are you all right?'

'Shshsh. They'll hear us,' she said but, with the memory of Sam's rapid arrival in her mind, her hand went to her tummy. She said a silent prayer. She wanted to get to Ellie's.

'Are you all right?'

She giggled and allowed him to help her to her feet. 'I think so. Just a bruised bottom by the feel of it.'

'Are you sure the baby's all right?' He still held her arm.

'Of course he's all right. Do stop fussing, I only sat down.' She brushed the snow off her coat. 'We've made so much noise, now the boys'll never go to sleep.'

'Hmm. After that exhibition, sure as hell there's not much chance of that.' He looked toward the house. 'I can't see them, but if they were looking, I bet they thought it was real funny seeing their mother cavort across the yard like a pregnant cow.'

'George!' She pretended to be angry, but they both burst out laughing.

'Can't see any faces at the windows,' she said. 'If they were watching, they must think they have the silliest of parents.'

Early next morning, after the boys had opened their parcels – wooden trains carved by George and matching hats, gloves and scarves, knitted by Amy – they exchanged gifts.

'Nothing very exciting, but it comes will all my love,' she said.

'Socks!' he shouted, feigning surprise. 'Exactly what I need and all the more special because you knitted them.' He kissed her.

'I didn't take lessons from Janet for nothing.'

'I can see and I'm impressed. Now your turn,' he said handing her a square parcel.

She carefully untied the string and removed the paper. Gone were the days when such things would have been discarded. She would save the string and paper for use another time.

'It's beautiful, George.' She fingered the picture frame. 'When did you find time?'

'Whenever I was working on the boys' trains, I'd do a bit. Sure had to hide it sharp, when you were about.'

She looked down at the picture of the four of them in England before they left for Canada. So much had happened since then.

* * *

The weather got colder in January – a whole week at fifty below freezing and, unable to do anything outside without fear of frostbite, everyone's tempers were frayed. The trees cracked, the odd branch snapping off, but the sheer beauty of it all took their breath away. It was a different kind of white out and one in which every twig was painted white with ice. With the arrival of leaden grey clouds, the temperature was more bearable but George was not so pleased.

'More snow,' he said watching it fall in heavy flakes. 'Spring'll be difficult. Sure to be floods.'

'Why? It'll melt and that'll be that.'

'Not here, honey. It'll lie around in big lakes on top of the soil – remember the soil will be well and truly frozen. It'll be weeks before it disappears and I won't be able to get seeding like I'd planned.' He

175

changed the subject. 'We must get you to Ellie's next week. Have you thought about what to take?'

They had to wait for a break in the weather before they could leave and, inexplicably, the temperature crept up to just below freezing. The air felt balmy, tempting them to think of spring.

'Don't let it fool you,' George said. 'We've still got March ahead and they say if it comes in like a lamb, then sure as hell it'll go out like a lion.'

He was fortunate enough to make his return journey before the temperature took a dive to below minus twenty that night. The house was quiet without Amy and the children but there was a pot of stew on the stove and Mac gave him a warm welcome, though the fire had long gone out. As he set about relighting it, he understood how lonely Amy must feel. No wonder she had pangs of homesickness. She was about to give birth and, even if he did make regular trips into town, it was most unlikely he'd be around when it happened. It was bad enough not being able to be with her when the baby was delivered, but he was miles away.

He warmed his hands and shut the damper a little, then sank into the chair, stretching out, warming first one foot then the other. Mac snuggled close.

The baby – if anything went wrong, what would he do? Right now, he'd abandon the farm to be by her side, but this was their home – their livelihood. There was no alternative. He couldn't leave the animals – the cows were in calf and needed to be kept an eye on, but supposing ... He stopped himself from thinking the unthinkable. She'd had two perfectly normal births, so why not a third? She was fit and healthy – had been all the way through, but supposing ... supposing it went wrong? That fall? A woman could die in childbirth. There, he had thought the worst possible thought. Now, it couldn't happen. Could it? And how did a man cope if the worst happened? How could he run the farm without her? And how could he bring up two boys and maybe a baby as well? Some would say, marry again and he knew of quite a few marriages which had been out of necessity. He couldn't imagine ever wanting another woman.

But there was another more alarming worry – something he had decided not to mention to Amy. When he had gone to harness the horses that morning, he had spotted fresh prints in the snow – large prints which told him there was a bear on the prowl and its tracks went right round their barn. He had checked the barn doors twice and was thankful he was up-to-date with maintenance. There were no weak spots a bear could make use of but a bear was a mighty animal and he prayed their stock would survive during his absence in town. And then, despite his hate of weapons, after he'd dropped Amy off at Ellie's, he had purchased a shot gun. It was hidden in the cupboard. The very thought of it being there disturbed him and, earlier, when he had held it up as though to take aim, the nightmare of the trenches had reignited.

He tried to shut his mind to such thoughts and concentrated on re-heating the stew. Perhaps while the family was with the Stadnyk's, he would put some whitewash on the walls and see to some of the draughts round the place, or even build that extra cupboard in the bedroom Amy was always on about. She'd be pleased with that.

And he had to make that big decision.

He had been turning the problem over in his mind ever since Halloween and his chat with Sid McAllister. Should he buy two more horses or should he get a loan and purchase a tractor? He had heard all the arguments but a loan was a big commitment and he had been brought up to save first and to owe nothing.

He took a sip of the stew. It was hot and tasted good. Whatever the decision, horses or tractors, there was much to keep him occupied.

* * *

Amy was enjoying the luxury of a town house.

'It's so lovely and warm here,' she said to Ellie after they had finished supper. The children were already in bed and John had excused himself on the pretence of preparing a sermon. She was grateful he had left them time for women's talk.

'I'm so pleased you're here and so are the boys,' Ellie said.

'Yes. Weren't they excited? I never thought they'd go to sleep. It was like Christmas all over again.'

Ellie laughed. 'I think they've quietened down at last.

'And you've no idea what a treat it is to have some female company. Oh, aren't I awful? I didn't mean to insult dear John and George has been so good these past weeks, especially now I'm so big. I can't help it but sometimes I long for someone else to talk to. Last summer he was out all day every day but if I was lucky there was Janet. Now he's under my feet nearly all the time. There's no happy medium and no escape. Sometimes it all gets too much and I feel like running away, and ...' Her voice trailed off.

Where would she run to anyway? Ellie might understand her longing to get out of the house, but if she confided everything – that she had seriously contemplated getting rid of the baby, that, if it hadn't meant admitting defeat, she'd have written to her mother begging for the fare home, she would be horrified. She was bound to tell John and he was bound to tell George. It was safer to say nothing.

'I haven't seen Janet in weeks,' she went on. 'It would be wonderful to see the end of the snow and know I could go and knock on her door.'

'Never mind, you're here now and it's really lovely to have you stay.' Ellie smiled. 'You'd better make the most of your time though. It'll go too quickly. How long do you have to go?'

'Three weeks, I think.' Amy shifted in her seat, trying to make herself comfortable. 'I don't remember being this big last time, but, even if I am huge, it will be bliss to be able to go to the shops.'

'Just because we've got sidewalks, doesn't mean it isn't icy. You must be careful not to slip and you've got to stay for at least two weeks after the baby's arrived. That is, if George doesn't mind.'

'No, I feel sure he won't mind. Oh, Ellie, I am so grateful to be here. I had this dreadful thought the snow would make it impossible to come.'

'I hope George doesn't mind looking after himself.'

'It'll make him appreciate me and anyway, I expect he'll enjoy a break from the boys – some peace and quiet. It can get a bit suffocating in the house with all of us together.' She sighed. 'It'd be wonderful to have more room and I mean a bigger house, not just another lean-to thing tacked on the back. Is it wrong to want a house like the McAllister's?'

178

'Patience, Amy. It'll come. George has ambition and determination. If you've got that and work hard, with just a bit of luck, things come good. People like the McAllister's weren't always so well off, you know.'

'With a bit of luck.' She sighed again. 'Maybe you're right. George is determined. He's already planning next year's crop. He said he's going to clear even more land once he's got the harrowing and seeding finished. He's even thinking about buying a tractor but I know that's expensive.'

'Now that's George's worry. Yours is to bring this baby safely into the world. I've prepared your room. There's the crib and all those little clothes …' Ellie's voice cracked. 'Sorry. It sometimes catches me.' She shook her head. 'Silly really. I should be over it by now.'

'Oh, Ellie. Me being here … It must be so hard for you.'

'Everyone says time will heal.' She gulped and blinked back tears. 'But it sure is hard.'

'Don't. Please don't torture yourself.'

She sniffed and searched for her handkerchief. 'Forgive me. I didn't mean for you ... I think I'm fine, then it up and hits me again. John won't talk about it and I need to. Sorry.'

'You've nothing to apologize for and if it helps, you must talk.'

She dabbed her eyes and Amy chatted on trying to cover the awkward moment.

'Anyway I'm so grateful to you for letting me stay. Did you hear about Marlene Jefferson? Janet told me they left it to the last minute, then the weather turned and the baby arrived at the elevator. It must have been awful. You can't imagine how thankful I am to be here and know I can get to the hospital in plenty of time. I don't know how we'll ever repay you.'

'Don't be silly.' Ellie had composed herself. She began to pile up the supper dishes. 'Have you thought about a name?'

'I like Robert, but George is convinced it will be a girl, so we thought maybe Laura.'

179

Ellie carried a pile of dishes through to the kitchen. 'They're both nice names,' she said over her shoulder, 'And you never know, you could still end up with a Laura.'

Amy picked up the cups and saucers and followed. 'No. I'm positive. Don't ask me how, but I just know. So it looks like it'll be Robert.'

'I sure hope George isn't too disappointed.' Ellie picked the kettle up and tipped the hot water into a bowl to wash the dishes. 'You know what men are like about daughters.'

'I should have thought three sons to help on the farm would be a bigger blessing. Anyway, perhaps it's as well it's going to be a boy. I think the prairies are very tough on girls.'

'You're right, it is and that's as may be, but let's think about tomorrow. Would you like to go to the store? Or – I know, we'll go out to tea. My treat. Some new tea rooms have opened. Real bone china, you know and gorgeous muffins and their cookies are to die for. Just about everybody goes there. John said he was working home in the afternoon, so we could leave the boys here.' Ellie's eyes sparkled. 'It'll do us good to get out without the children.'

Amy didn't have long to enjoy her stay in town for baby Robert made an unexpected entry into the world only a few days into March, catching everybody by surprise. Tom Sutherland was in town that morning and, Ellie, knowing he was bound to visit the store, sent Will and Luke with a message for George, but by then Amy was well into labour and had been taken to the hospital. It was late before he got the message – too late to set out and he didn't arrive until early the following morning. By then the baby was already several hours old.

'Handsome fellow,' George said, gazing into the cot. 'He's got more hair than I remember Will or Sam having.'

'You're not too disappointed, are you?

He kissed her. 'How could I be?' He smiled down at her, but she saw the disappointment in his eyes. 'As long as you're all right. That's what matters most. You. I need you, Amy.' He buried his face in her hair. 'I'm nothing without you,' he whispered.

They stayed locked together for some minutes before she stared up into his face. 'I love you, George Mills.'

'I am the luckiest guy on earth.' He kissed her again. 'If anything had happened to you, I'd never have forgiven myself ... You're the most important person in my world. Remember that.'

'You sentimental thing. I've no plans to go anywhere.' She squeezed his hand, knowing she wouldn't be running away from the white barrenness just yet. 'I don't know why you worried. I was fine and he was the easiest yet.' She smiled at him, anxious he should like his new son. 'Don't you think he's like Will?'

He leant over the cot to examine the new arrival. 'Mmm. Difficult to tell right now.' He grinned back at her. 'A real Canadian, eh?'

She nodded.

'One thing's for sure, when the boys get bigger, I won't have to hire so many hands.'

'Is that all you can think of?'

He laughed. 'I've got plans, honey, big plans. I'm hankering after more land. Would never be surprised if Chernitsky sells more of his. He's very poorly, you know and it would be ideal – we share boundaries.'

She remembered Ellie's words about George's determination. 'Do you really think they'll sell more of their land? Anyway, haven't you got enough to clear already? And, even if it does come on the market, it'll take more than a good harvest to afford it. Besides, didn't you say you wanted a tractor?'

'Possibly, but don't you worry your pretty little head about anything. It'll happen. It'll happen. All right Chernitsky's land might not be for us, but there'll be something else. You see if I'm not right.' He looked into the cot, smiling at the baby. 'Three sons is a fine thing for a man in the prairies.'

'I've done my bit then,' she joked, then became more serious. 'I'm sorry you didn't get your little girl.'

'I'm danged if I know how you knew. If you could tell me which of the cows was going to produce what, it'd make life a whole lot simpler.' He studied the baby's face. 'Well, Robert John Mills, you're going to be a farmer.'

Her stay in hospital was brief and she was soon back being spoilt by Ellie, who used any excuse to pick up the baby.

181

Amy was sorting washing. 'You'll make my life impossible if you pick him up every time he so much as squeaks.'

'He needed changing,' Ellie said, rocking the baby in her arms. 'Didn't you, my darling.'

'He won't get all this attention when he gets home.'

'No. That's why he should make the most of it now.'

'George said he was coming to collect me on Saturday next week – if the weather's right, of course.'

'But that's only just over a week away. Oh, Amy, I wanted you to stay for at least two weeks.'

'I feel bad enough staying this long.'

'Nonsense and you know it, but I suppose I can't blame George for wanting you home.' Ellie kissed the baby's head. 'In that case, you'd better not complain about me making a fuss of little Bobbie here. Next week he'll be gone.' She sighed. 'I have enjoyed having you all and it's been so nice to nurse a baby.'

For the journey home, George had filled the wagon box with extra straw and blankets and Amy made sure the baby was well clothed and wrapped in a shawl and several layers of blankets. She and the boys climbed into the back of the box and they left a tearful Ellie waving to them from the porch of the house.

It was very cold, the sky grey and the breeze carried with it a hint of a snow flurry. George was anxious to get home before another blizzard closed in. They passed the elevator at the siding, which was unusually quiet. There were only two wagons in sight, a sure sign, he told her, that hauling grain was not the thing to do on such a cold day.

As they approached home, he called over his shoulder to them.

'Look.' He pointed to the sky. 'That's what they call sun dogs.'

The sun was low, just above the horizon and around it was a sphere of light, the colours of a rainbow. It appeared as if there were three suns. Two jack rabbits in their winter white coats sprinted across the fields and a flock of snow birds swooped low.

'An auspicious welcome for our new son,' George said.

She shivered. It was an omen, she was sure, but she wasn't certain it was a good one.

CHAPTER THIRTEEN

1926

April

The mourners gathered at the school for the short service, filing in behind the coffin, the Minister leading the way.

> *'I am the resurrection and the life, saith the Lord: he that believeth in me, though he were dead, yet shall he live: and whosoever liveth and believeth in me shall never die.'*

Sometimes she doubted there was a God, Amy thought as she stood beside George. If there was, why did he make life so hard? She shifted her weight from one foot to the other, switching the baby into the other arm. He stirred slightly, his mouth curling at the corners. George always insisted he was smiling, but she knew better. It was wind. She could not remember an evening which had not been disturbed by his anguished cries – cries which went on well into the night – cries which twisted her stomach and nagged at her until her nerves were raw and she snapped at whoever or whatever was near. She rocked him remembering her promise to Ellie, wishing she could skip this stage of his childhood and that he was as big as the other two.

She glanced down at Will, who stood, motionless, very solemn and, priest like, his hands clasped together and wished they had sat further back – a place where he couldn't see the coffin. She had serious misgivings about bringing the children, suggesting she should stay at home with them, but George demanded they all went.

'It shows we care. We belong here now. Everyone will be there,' he insisted. 'Besides, it's a lesson in life.'

More like a lesson in death, she thought, but hadn't argued. George was a puzzle at times. He could be so loving, but sometimes he was hard on the children – especially when it came to life's most difficult lessons.

'They'll learn about life and death soon enough. Can't escape it, living on a farm.'

His tone shocked her, until she thought of the slaughter he had witnessed in Europe. It had deeply affected him, but no matter how she broached it, he would never speak of it. Lately, he might not wake up sweating to seek the comfort of her arms, but she always knew in the morning by the way he looked at his watch before placing it in his pocket, he had dreamt of Alfie. These days, she said nothing and, even though she felt shut out, she had long since accepted his inability to share this part of his life.

There was no war now, so why shouldn't their children be carefree? Why should they have to know about death at so young an age? Will was such a serious, conscientious boy and she was afraid the sombreness of the occasion would linger in his memory and give him nightmares. When they watched the horse-drawn hearse arrive, he had been so pale. He had his father's deep brown eyes and he was growing taller by the day.

'Mom, why do the horses have those blankets on?' he asked. 'Is it to keep them warm?'

She had suppressed a smile and whispered. 'They're special blankets called mourning drapes and they're black because we're honouring Mr Chernitsky.'

'Is he in the coffin?'

'Yes, love and we're here to say good-bye to him.'

The minister began to read a psalm.

185

'Lord, thou hast been our refuge …..'

She glanced down at Sam, who was leaning over the back of his chair. She could see Josh Sutherland grinning at whatever face Sam was making. She glanced up at George and was grateful he hadn't noticed.

She stared at the coffin and thought back to the first service she had attended in the school house – the time Janet had told her about Mr Chernitsky's metal plate and remembered staring at the back of his head. He seemed fit and healthy then. How could a man so energetic and full of life be there – there in the coffin?

They stood to sing the first hymn.

'Now thy earthly work is done:'

The tune was not familiar and she stumbled over the words, but even had she known them, her thoughts were elsewhere. She couldn't believe it was nearly a year since they had left England. It felt as though it was only yesterday. Her eyes travelled the room. Even from the backs of their heads, she could identify every person, knew all personally – knew of their problems, of their successes and their failures, their strengths and their weaknesses. Oh, how cruel the winter had been – it had snatched Ellie's baby – a child so wanted – and now it had taken Mr Chernitsky – a husband so needed.

She looked out of the window at the white wilderness which stretched to the horizon. The sky was leaden. Her heart sank at the thought that winter had not finished with them yet. She had had enough of the relentless cold. She yearned for spring flowers. Daffodils – glorious yellow heads bobbing in the gentle spring breeze. Bluebells – the bright blue haze amongst the vibrant green which was spring.

Out of the corner of her eye she could see George and knew he wouldn't have patience with these thoughts. He was a deep man – so deep – sometimes she wondered if she really knew him, let alone understood him. He didn't moan about anything but, instead, schemed. While he endlessly contemplated his next move, she had learnt to keep her thoughts to herself. He was, she thought, oblivious of her daily toil, the continual round of cooking, cleaning and washing – the boys squabbling and Bobbie's yelling. She lay in bed at night, too-tired for sleep and sometimes, during the day, she thought she would go mad and scream at them all. She even plotted her escape. George wouldn't miss her. He was too busy with his plans.

The hymn was over. They all sat down. Stan Jefferson was saying a few words. She listened to him explain how Mr Chernitsky had been injured as the family escaped from Russia and how he recovered in Germany. She strained her neck to make out Mrs Chernitsky, who sat at the front with her two girls, all dressed in black. Poor things. What were they to do, now they had been left alone? Since Mr Chernitsky's illness, she had lost count of the times George had been over to their homestead to chop firewood and to help with their animals. She had sent him with a saucepan of stew on more than one occasion and sometimes with a loaf of bread. He told her Mrs Chernitsky was planning to leave. It was a pity, he said, they weren't in a position to buy the land.

'How can you think of such a thing at a time like this?' she rebuked him.

'Someone'll buy it – sure as day follows night. The place has gone downhill since Chernitsky's been sick and Mrs Chernitsky's heart isn't in it. It'll go cheap and most likely the McAllister's or the Jackson's will get it. But why shouldn't it be us? Sure wish I had the money. You'll see – it won't be long before they'll be forced to sell up.'

'Where do you think they'll go? Russia?'

'Doubt it. I shouldn't think they'd welcome a Countess since they killed off the rest of their Royal family. No, they'll probably head east. I heard Mrs Chernitsky's sister lives in Toronto.'

Stan Jefferson finished what he was saying and she knew she had hardly heard a word. They stood to read the 23rd psalm. The baby stirred in her arms.

> **'The Lord is my shepherd: therefore can I lack nothing ....'**

Her thoughts drifted again. England. Her reminiscing had become a craving – a desire to pluck a pink rose and place it in a vase on her dressing table – a longing to walk down a leafy lane in the early morning dew or, as the sun set, smell the soft scent of honeysuckle as it drifted on the evening breeze. But things, according to Vi and

Freddie were not too wonderful in England either. Freddie wrote condemningly of the coal miners while Vi said there was talk of strikes and she was worried for Ted, who was heavily involved with the union movement. George had spluttered his amazement.

'Silly idiot. Isn't it bad enough having a mother involved in politics?'

Once the service was over, they filed out of the school room and, as they were not going back to the house, stopped to say a few words to Mrs Chernitsky.

'I'll be over tomorrow to fix that barn door,' George said.

'And you must come to tea,' Amy added.

They completed the journey home in silence, George's face was grim and he didn't allow the horses to dally. The day drifted by, but Mr Chernitsky's death had affected them both and neither was in the mood for conversation.

The next morning George returned from milking with a worried look on his face.

'Is there a problem?' she asked.

'I don't like the look of one of the heifers,' he said as he sprinkled a little sugar over his porridge. As soon as I've had this I'm going back.'

'What's wrong?'

He shook his head. 'Not sure. Just got a feeling. Flo wasn't interested in food at all this morning and that's not like her. Usually she's first in line.' He blew on a spoonful before putting it into his mouth. 'Might have to get the vet.'

'That bad? But that'll mean going into town.' She brightened at the thought of seeing Ellie.

'It'll also cost and might make the difference between getting more stock or even hogs.'

'Is a vet that expensive?'

'They don't come cheap.'

Immediately after breakfast, he returned to the barn. It was a gloomy day and tiny snow particles drifted in the air.

'Not more snow. Please not more snow,' she silently prayed as she watched him hurry down the path between the banks of snow.

He returned an hour later and by then snow was falling fast and there was a gale blowing.

'I need hot water,' he said, banging off his boots.

She knew by his face that things were bad. 'The kettle's hot.'

'Good, but we'll need more. Put a pan on.' He rummaged in the cupboard. 'A cup of coffee would be good.'

She placed a saucepan on the stove and made the coffee. 'Aren't you going for the vet?'

He shook his head. 'Isn't time – she's in labour. Anyway, I don't like the look of the weather. We're in the lap of the Gods now.'

'She'll be all right, won't she, George?'

He raised his eyebrows and gave her a gloomy look.

'The calf. Will it survive?'

Not answering, he gulped down his coffee while she tried to think of something cheerful to say. He went to the cupboard for the coil of rope and in doing so, knocked the rifle which he had hidden behind his old coat. It slid down from its perch and clattered at his feet.

'I thought you were against keeping firearms.' Amy said looking at the shot gun in alarm.

'Didn't like to tell you but I found bear prints round the barn. Thought it best to be prepared.'

'Oh, no. Not another bear.'

He placed it back in the cupboard. 'Never used the darn thing yet. Never want to. Insurance, that's what it is.' He picked up the rope. 'Wouldn't surprise me if it's a bear that's spooked the stock. Maybe caused this early arrival.'

The cow could be heard bellowing and she knew the agony it must be in. The noise tormented her while she tried to work out why George had kept the purchase of the shot gun to himself as well as how to keep the thing safely out of the hands of the children. The cupboard, she decided, needed a padlock.

She carried on with her chores, trying to keep things normal for the children. They couldn't afford to lose a cow or a calf. If there was a God, she hoped he would listen to her prayer.

'Mom, where's Dad?' Will asked when George didn't appear at dinner time.

'He's looking after one of the cows.'

'Isn't it very well? Is that why it's making all that noise?'

She nodded, hoping she wouldn't have to explain about it dying. George had been right when he'd said they would learn about life and death soon enough.

'Can I go see?'

'No, Will. Dad is best left on his own. We'll eat dinner, shall we?'

She hoped she would be able to tell Will and Sam about a new calf, but when George appeared half way through the afternoon she could tell by his face the news was bad.

'We lost the calf,' he said in reply to her unasked question.

Will stopped pushing his train and looked up.

'Did it die, Daddy?'

George nodded. 'Afraid it did, son.'

She poured water into a bowl so he could wash his hands. 'Couldn't you save it?'

'I think it was dead before it was born.'

She watched Will anxiously, but the boy seemed to accept his father's matter-of-fact explanation and resumed his game of trains with Sam. He picked up his engine and chuffed along the floor, mimicking the long discordant train whistle – a whistle which echoed across the prairies most days.

'Flo?' she asked.

'I think she'll live. We'll see tomorrow how she is.'

'Will she be able to have another calf?'

He was drying his hands. 'I might get the vet out. No point in keeping her if she can't.'

190

She put a plate of hot food on the table. She couldn't help feeling sorry for Flo.

He sat at the table and picked up the cutlery. 'Don't look at me like that. We're in this for a living. We can't carry passengers.'

'I know, I know. Just seems unfair. It's not Flo's fault, is it?'

He didn't answer but loaded his fork and shoved it into his mouth.

She stacked the saucepans in the sink all the while trying not to be sentimental. Sometimes life was harsh.

'The weather's turning milder,' he said when he had finished his meal. 'It's raining now. I might ride Buster into town tomorrow, though there's so much snow the next thing we'll know there'll be floods.'

'Floods?' It seemed there was always something to worry about. 'Are we safe here?'

'It'll have to rain a lot before it gets that bad. Most likely the roads'll be difficult. I seem to remember seeing a few cars up to their axles after a big dump of snow and, come to think of it, a fair number of lakes instead of fields.'

* * *

Amy felt let down when the following morning, having looked in at Flo, George once again insisted he went alone to town. She didn't bother to argue. What was the point, he always won and in any case, she didn't have the energy. But he surprised her with his quick return.

'Vet's up at Tom's,' he announced. 'I met him on the track and he's promised to look in. Saved me the trip.'

Later, after the vet had announced the prognosis was good, though not guaranteed and they had eaten supper that evening, it felt like a cloud had been lifted.

'I'm going to do a last check on Flo.' He said after the children had gone to bed. He pocketed some shot gun cartridges from a box now stored in the kitchen drawer then went to unhook his coat. 'Come with me,' he said, putting on his coat and picking up the shot gun.

191

Her apprehensive look was not lost on George but she grabbed her coat and then slipped her hand into his.

The night air was balmy after the bitter wind which, for weeks, had blown in from the Arctic but the rain had made little impact on the snow. She looked for grass or soil and was depressed when there was none. There was as much snow as ever and, in addition, there was a hazardous film of water on top. They had to tread with care and she was glad of George's steadying hand.

Flo was in one of the stables, away from the rest of the animals and bedded down with plenty of straw. She could see it was an effort to lift her head to acknowledge their presence.

'She looks so tired, poor thing,' Amy said.

'Wouldn't you be?'

'I suppose so, but I'm glad she made it. I dreaded telling Will we'd lost her – bad enough telling him about the calf.'

'He's gotta learn. 'Sides he seemed to accept it without any fuss.'

'Maybe,' she said, deciding Will took after his father in his reluctance to show emotion. 'He hides things, George. He broods over them. Just because he doesn't say much doesn't mean he doesn't feel it or that he isn't affected by it. He was really looking forward to the arrival of our first calf.'

'Didn't seem too bothered to me and in any case, there's no hiding the facts of life on a farm.'

'I suppose you're right,' she conceded. 'We all have to learn to accept life and death.'

'Of course I'm right. It's nature's way. It's likely as not the calf was unhealthy anyway. Nature doesn't do things for nothing, you know. Not like us humans. We kill each other for the most hideous reasons.'

They were silent and she knew he was thinking of the war. She studied his face noticing for the first time, the tiny lines about his eyes. He was thinner, too. This winter had taken its toll on them both and, though he would never admit it, losing a calf had been hard. She could tell by his gaunt expression. When would things start going right? Perhaps they were doomed to fail but it was more than she dared to suggest things might be easier back in England. In any case, she was

192

no longer sure they were. There was only one certainty – there was no money for the fare. They had to make it work, but as she looked at his tired expression, she knew he, too, was feeling the strain.

She turned her attention to Flo and sighed. It was then she felt his arm around her waist and he gave her a hug.

Within the circle of his arms, she turned to face him. 'Why don't you share your troubles with me?' She caressed his cheek. 'They're our troubles, you know, not just yours and, in any case, I thought we were here for each other.'

'I know, I know but I thought you understood – that I didn't have to spell things out.'

'I'm not a thought reader. Promise you'll share everything in the future.'

'Promise.'

He was a man of few words, but she was reassured and they stood for some minutes contemplating the scene, each with their own thoughts.

'Come on.' He broke the silence. 'There's nothing more we can do tonight. I think a glass of the brandy wouldn't go amiss. Even if we can't celebrate, I think I've earned it.'

She couldn't dispute he'd earned his tipple. The brandy bottle was almost empty and what did it matter there wouldn't be another? She waited while he closed the barn and slid the wooden bar into place.

In the stillness she could hear a rumbling sound. 'What's that noise?'

He turned to listen, shrugged and re-checked the door. They walked carefully along the track.

She stopped. 'Listen. A … a sort of banging.'

He tensed, standing motionless. 'That's it.'

'What do you mean?'

'The noise, silly. It's spring,' he said in a cheerful voice, the sad mood banished. 'It's the sound of spring.'

She gazed back, astonished when he grabbed her waist and swung her round, slipping and sliding on the watery ice.

'For goodness sake. Stop it.' She regained her balance.

'Come on.' He laughed and grabbed her hand. 'We're definitely having that drink. Spring's on its way and that sure is something to celebrate.'

'But, George ... Have you gone quite mad?'

'Of course not, honey. It's the river.'

'What is?'

'The noise. It's the ice cracking – that's what we can hear.' He laughed, his face lighting up in delight and looking years younger than only minutes earlier. 'There'll be no short cuts to town till next winter, but we'll be ploughing soon enough.'

After their little nightcap as they called it, they were soon asleep, Amy deeply but George dreamt of the trenches again. He woke with a start, certain the noise he'd heard wasn't part of his nightmare. He lay there, alert, listening. There it was again, muffled by the snow and he knew in an instant what it was. In giant strides was across the room and loading the shotgun.

Through the crack of the open door he could see the bear shuffling through the snow, pausing now and then to sniff the air.

The bang of the shotgun woke Amy.

'George. George?' Amy felt the empty space beside her. She knew instinctively what had happened and, grabbing her coat, ran to the door.

'George.' Relief surged through her when she heard him reply and seconds later he stood beside her. 'Thank God you're not hurt. What happened?'

'I scared him off – for now, anyway. Fired a warning shot and he scarpered soon enough. Let's hope he doesn't come back.'

CHAPTER FOURTEEN

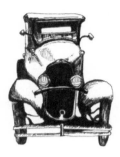

Overnight, winter gave way to spring, though it felt more like summer with soaring temperatures. Amy was both dismayed and disappointed at the sight of drab khaki brown grass. She stared at it in disbelief but George had seen it all before and was more concerned about the huge amount of water lying on the fields. Gradually it began to evaporate, the grass turned green, the sun shone and life took on a new and optimistic beat.

The Chernitsky farm sale was held exactly four weeks after the funeral. She thought it all too hasty, but he disagreed. The day after the funeral, George had called on Mrs Chernitsky and mended the barn door. She loaned him two horses and a sulky plough, which he was very pleased with. It had a seat and would save his aching legs, but he was disappointed and offended when she refused to sell them to him.

'I offered a fair price and you'd think she'd be pleased to take it, but I suppose she reckons Sid'll buy at the auction and she'll get a better price. I can't see him wanting horses though – not now he's interested in tractors. 'Sides what has Sid ever done for the Chernitskys? I've been over there day after day to feed her stock and I did a whole heap of repairs to their barn. That door was hanging off its hinges – had been for years, if you ask me, but there's gratitude for you.'

'Oh, well, we'll find out tomorrow and, in any case, if Sid's not interested in horses, then he probably won't want the plough either,' she said trying to humour him but a thought struck her. 'Didn't Sid buy some of their land? Maybe he's already struck a deal.'

He grunted.

'But don't you think the auctioneer would have advised her to wait?'

'More like he's after his cut,' he said from the bedroom. 'We'll find out soon enough.'

People from all over the district descended on the Chernitsky's homestead for the auction. Horses and wagons and a dozen cars were parked up on the trail and the dust they raised could be seen for miles. George scowled as more lined up behind them. Amy had seen that expression of hostility before and knew it didn't do to cross him. She hoped he wouldn't lose his temper when the selling failed to go his way.

'They can't all be bidding,' he grumbled as he helped her down from the cart. 'I bet they're just a bunch of nosey parkers.'

The word "vulture" popped into her mind but, with the sun on her back, she felt happier than in weeks. So what if it was a chance to pry, it was great to be out and about. He held her hand, complaining, as he went, that with this turnout, there wouldn't be many bargains.

The crowd was cheerful and nobody mentioned the recent dreadful weather even though there were still huge muddy puddles and they had to watch their step. Amy compared winter to being in labour or having toothache – it was long and painful, but once over, it was soon forgotten as everyone got on with life. Groups of women sheltered from the midday sun, caught up on gossip and laughed at each other's little jokes. Children played chase or hide and seek and men crowded together to exchange details on the progress of ploughing or what they hoped to buy. Everyone was speculating as to who might buy the farm. The grass was green again and the trees were sprouting leaves. The warmth of the sunshine had invigorated all living things into a burst of reproductive energy.

Later, when George inspected the cattle, Amy stood beside him contemplating the scene, suddenly grateful she was here and not in the little house in the East End of London. Vi's recent letter had told of unrest, revolution and a general strike. There had been no trains, factories had closed and only one or two newspapers had been

196

published. Hundreds of strikers had been arrested and Ted had been injured when a convoy of army lorries and armoured cars had arrived at the docks. Vi didn't go into graphic details but they were both relieved to read he had only been slightly hurt.

'Silly fool,' George had raged. 'He's lucky he's not in jail or worse, badly hurt.' He shook his head in disbelief. 'Why does he allow himself to get involved with such stupidity?' He tossed the letter onto the table. 'I'm glad we're out of it.'

She glanced about her. Standing here in the warm sun, it was hard to think of such goings on all that distance across the Atlantic ocean.

George caught her arm. 'You're miles away.'

'Mmm. I was thinking about home ...' She knew the moment she uttered the words, it was the wrong thing to say. He would never understand how much she missed some of life's little luxuries or how much, despite her faults, she missed her mother or the bustle of life in the East End or their tiny room even – when there was just the two of them.

'Here's home.' He squeezed her arm.

What could she say? She smiled at him and he winked back and in his look she saw her love radiated back at her. He was happy and that was what mattered most and the children were Canadian now – not English.

'Have you looked in the house to see if there's anything you need? I don't mind doing the bidding, but it's no good telling me later there was something you really wanted.'

'I did have a look,' she said, thinking how awful it was to have the whole world tramping through your house. She was embarrassed by the entire business and had made her assessment in record time, unlike some of the ladies who picked up every piece of china to examine the potter's mark and discussed the shape and size of the sofa. It was as though they were scavengers picking over a dead corpse. 'I don't think there's anything we need.'

'What about the butter churn?'

She shook her head. 'It's dented and not really any better than ours.'

'Right then. Let's find a good place to stand.'

The auctioneer, almost European with his gavel, clipboard and brown trilby hat, opened the sale. She thought the first lot looked like a heap of old iron but, amongst the following lots were pitch forks, rakes, wheelbarrows, carts and all manner of farm equipment. They waited patiently for the horses to come under the hammer and George was rewarded when his successful bid was no higher than the price he had already offered.

'That'll show her. It was a fair offer but now she'll have to pay the auctioneer's commission,' he whispered.

The sale continued and, although outbid on the cattle, George was ecstatic when he was successful with the plough. Amy lost interest and allowed her mind to wander as the auctioneer steadily made his way through the various lots, that was until the auctioneer turned to the farm itself.

'What am I bid?' There was a hush, all eyes on Sid McAllister. 'Shall we start at $2,000?'

Sid gave an almost imperceptible nod.

'Two thousand it is.'

'Three,' Alfred Jackson shouted.

'Three five,' Sid said and the tension mounted.

'Three five, I am bid.' The auctioneer looked at Alfred. 'Any advances.'

There was a pause. 'Four,' Alfred's jaw was set in determination. A murmur rippled through the onlookers and everyone held their breath, looking from one to the other. Would Sid dare to go higher?

'Four one,' Sid said with equal determination.

'Four one,' repeated the auctioneer, looking at Alfred.

Alfred lifted his hand. 'Four two.'

'That'll be it,' George whispered in her ear. 'And expensive at that.'

'Any advances on four thousand two hundred dollars?' The auctioneer held his gavel in the air and studied the faces around him.

'Going...'

'Four three,' Sid shouted.

Alfred Jackson opened his mouth but shook his head.

'Four three it is. Going ...'

The hammer fell and a buzz ran through the throng.

George guided her towards the horses. 'I wished I'd had a go at bidding for the land. It would've been good practice for when I've got the cash.'

'Next time, maybe,' she said, relieved he hadn't. In the frenzy of an auction it would be so easy to get carried away. 'Do you think the Jacksons will forgive the McAllisters for buying all of the Chernitsky land?' she wondered out loud.

He shrugged. 'Who knows? No point in not getting on with neighbours. You never know when you might need them.'

With the two extra horses hitched behind the wagon and the children reclaimed, they set off for home.

'We'll collect the plough tomorrow. It'll give us a chance to say our good-byes,' he said and began to whistle a cheerful tune.

'You sound happy. Isn't it strange how some sunshine seems to perk everyone up.'

He grinned. 'Yep, but that's not the only reason. This'll be a good year. You'll see. I feel it in my bones. This is just the start. Soon the McAllisters and the Jacsksons won't be the only wealthy people in the district.'

'What do you think Sid will do with the Chernitsky house? He won't want two.'

'Let it fall down, shouldn't wonder.'

She looked at him in amazement. 'Surely not?'

'If you had a house like his, would you exchange it for that?' He nodded vaguely in the direction of the Chernitsky house.

'Of course I wouldn't, but it's criminal to let it fall down.'

'Fire wood. That's about it. What else is he supposed to do with it?'

* * *

The day after the sale they called on Mrs Chernitsky to collect the plough and to wish her and the girls well in their new life in Toronto. They found her extremely agitated about the arrangements for their journey to Portage, where they were to catch a train east. They stood in the living room now bare of its furnishings, trunks and boxes stacked around the room. She told them, in her broken English, a family friend was to take them to town, but Tom Sutherland had called the previous evening with news her friend was sick.

She turned to George. 'You drive?' she asked in her deeply accented voice.

He was surprised at the question. 'Did a bit in the war, but that was a long time ago.'

'Goot. You drive.'

He was puzzled. He thought Tom would take them.

'Not fit.' She pointed to the trunks.

There was an awful lot considering how much had been sold at the auction and she was probably right, they and their luggage wouldn't all fit in Tom's Buick.

'Sure thing,' he said. 'I'll bring the wagon over in the morning.'

She shook her head. 'No, no. Drive car.'

He frowned. 'We don't have a car, Mrs Chernitsky.'

'Come. Come.' She grabbed hold of his arm and pulled him towards the door. Everyone followed.

She led them outside and round to the back of the house, where she removed the bar from the door of a dilapidated and long disused hog house. The door swung open. It took a second or two to adjust to the dark, but in the gloom they could see the outline of a car.

George stared at the black machine until he could make out the running boards, the spoked wheels and the canvas roof. He hadn't seen the car on his previous visits, but then there had been no reason to go into this disused hog house.

200

'This is … yours?' Why hadn't it featured in the auction? If Mrs Chernitsky couldn't drive, why would she keep it?

Will darted between them, running right round the car. 'Wow, Dad. Can I drive it?'

Amy laughed. 'Your feet would never reach the pedals. Anyway it isn't our car.'

'Why can't we have a car? Josh has.'

'No, he hasn't. May be Mr Sutherland has, but Josh doesn't drive it.'

Will wrinkled his nose which made Amy want to giggle. 'But he sits in the driver's seat.'

'That's as maybe.'

Mrs Chernitsky looked at George. 'You drive? Take to town?'

He examined the car. There were two large headlights and he could tell that under the dust, the paintwork was in good order. He opened the driver's door and peered inside. It smelt a little musty and he noticed a spider suspended on its thread from the roof. He stepped back to admire the vehicle. A Maxwell. He had seen the odd one in town, but now he was being given a chance to drive one.

'You drive?' Mrs Chernitsky repeated.

George's eyes were seeing more in the dull light. The tyres weren't flat and it certainly didn't look neglected. It was very strange. The car seemed to be in good order, but nobody had ever seen Mr Chernitsky out in it. Of that he was certain.

'I'm not sure …' It didn't seem manly to admit he'd only ever parked the odd car.

'You tek us, please?'

He didn't answer but looked at Amy, suddenly requiring her support and she tilted her head in agreement.

'Okay,' he agreed. 'I'll do it.'

Early next morning, he helped Tom pack the Buick, then together they put the last of the bags into the Maxwell, before Mrs Chernitsky and the girls squeezed into the little remaining space.

'I'll stay to make sure the engine starts,' Tom said, 'then I'll head off. I've got a list of things to do, so I'm not hanging around. See you in town.'

With Mrs Chernitsky leaning out of the car to watch him, he cranked the engine. Suddenly edgy, he half hoped it wouldn't start. He supposed he was being stupid, but his stomach was turning over, never mind the engine. Part of him was excited at the prospect of driving such a beautiful machine, the rest of him was extremely critical of allowing himself to be talked into doing it. It was years since he had sat behind the wheel and he was certain to make a fool of himself – crunch the gears or stall it, probably in town, when he'd feel an even bigger fool. Besides, the car was bursting at the seams. Despite Tom taking most of the trunks in his Buick, Mrs Chernitsky had an awful lot of luggage. It would never get underway with all the weight they had packed into it. Supposing they ran out of gas or worse still broke down. What on earth would he do?

The car burst into life without even the smallest cough. He wasn't sure if he was pleased but waved Tom off, praying for a safe and uneventful journey.

They bounced along the trail until they came to the road into town. It was worn into ridges by the wheels of wagons and where it wasn't bumpy and uneven there were deep puddles. He had visions of the car sinking to its axles in the mud and of missing the train. He was annoyed with himself when he crunched the gears, but amazingly within a mile, he began to gain confidence. He even started to enjoy the whole experience and was disappointed when they arrived. As they came to a halt, a mixture of pride and relief flooded through him. It was incredible how it had all come back – rather, the little knowledge he had. Having committed himself, he hadn't dared admit to Mrs Chernitsky or Amy, even, how limited his driving experience really was. This was his longest trip ever and considering all, he hadn't done a bad job.

'Where do you want me to take the car?' he asked as he deposited several bags beside the three large trunks Tom had already left on the platform. He assumed Mrs Chernitsky would expect him to take the car to her friend or at least the garage. He had arranged to get a lift back later with Tom and he planned to call in on John and Ellie.

The train was approaching and he offered the keys to Mrs Chernitsky.

'No, no. You keep.' She pushed the keys back into his hand.

Had she misunderstood? 'Shall I take it to the garage?'

She shook her head. 'No, no. You must 'ave. I vant … My thank you.'

He wasn't sure he'd heard her right, but the train hissed into the station in great clouds of steam, drowning any argument he might have made for not keeping the car.

'Mrs Chernitsky ...' he began to protest again, but she was already opening the door. He pocketed the keys and helped her onto the train. As he closed the door, he tried to say he ought to take it to the garage, but she was adamant. Seconds later, he was waving goodbye.

The train inched forward, belching huge clouds of smoke and steam as it got underway. He watched until it became a dot on the horizon, before returning to the car where he sat staring at the instruments quite stunned by the turn of events. Mrs Chernitsky wasn't so bad after all, but how was it he hadn't known about the car? Private people the Chernitskys. Didn't gossip. There were rumours, but nobody knew for sure whether the old man was a Count. Odd he had never seen the car before yesterday and nobody, he was certain, had ever seen them go to church in anything other than their wagon. Strange people. If he had a car – everyone would know. He'd be that proud, he would drive it at every opportunity. They would go to church and after, go for a jaunt, visit neighbours or go for a picnic. He laughed to himself. He had a car! Wouldn't Amy be surprised when he got home? He let his hands travel right round the steering wheel, patting the passenger seat with his hand.

'Yippee. Yep, you're all mine,' he said aloud before setting off for the store to leave a message for Tom.

It took some time to convince Amy of Mrs Chernitsky's generosity.

'Are you sure?' she asked over and over again, her face alight with excitement as she sat in the passenger seat. 'I can't believe it.'

He laughed – she laughed – they all laughed. He liked to hear her laugh. It was wonderful to give her such pleasure and he wished for the thousandth time, things would come right and he could give her all the things she deserved.

She got out of the car, shutting the door. 'I can't wait till we go to the service on Sunday. But I don't understand. Why didn't the Chernitsky's drive to church in this? Do you think he found it too difficult to manage? I mean driving isn't easy, is it, George? Oh, when can we go see Ellie?'

Will and Sam climbed in and out so many times, he began to get cross. Then they all nagged him to take them for a ride. He moved the car into the barn declaring he was too busy.

'But that's not fair, Dad,' Will said. 'You've been for a drive. We haven't been anywhere.'

'Don't be so mean,' Amy said with her hands on her hips. 'It's the best thing that's happened to us in ages. Do take us for a drive.'

He relented. 'Just up the track and back. That's all I've got time for. There's work to be done and we'd better get to it or there'll be no food on the table next winter.'

* * *

Now Will was at school, Amy, Sam and the baby went out to the fields to share George's lunch break. He spent long, tiring hours ploughing and seeding, returning deadbeat, his clothes dirty with soil and his face streaked where he had sweated in the sun. It was dark when he ate his supper and, then, too exhausted for anything else, he would leave Amy to clear away while he, aching and drained of energy, fell into bed. There had been no trip into town and, despite Amy's protests, they hadn't attended the church service.

'It's not fair. We have that beautiful car parked in the barn and we haven't yet been for a decent outing together,' she complained.

He gave her a guilty look. 'There's time enough.'

But all hopes of a trip into town were dashed when they were plunged back into winter with a massive deposit of snow and unpleasantly cold temperatures. Amy stared out of the window.

'I could cry,' she wailed in despair.

204

He remained cheerful. 'It won't last. It can't. You'll see. It's just a blip.' He hugged her. 'Next week, we'll be back to sunshine and summer.'

Three days of icy temperatures and snow followed by torrential rain – a twenty four hour storm, when going to the barn meant returning wet through. Water lay everywhere, rivulets appearing in the most unlikely places. The river burst its banks and flooded vast areas of prairie and Amy was horrified when George told her the seeds planted only the previous week had either been washed away or were covered in weeds from neighbouring fields.

'Stan's okay,' he sighed. 'His land is just that bit higher and his crop's already germinated.'

The safe arrival of five female calves compensated a little for the disaster of the floods and George allowed Will to help with the delivery of the last calf.

'He'll make a good stockman,' he told her later.

* * *

Finally the day Amy had been waiting for arrived. The first time they took the car to school for the church service. Amy beamed at everyone and detected a number of envious looks. Now, she thought they couldn't possibly be cast as the poorest family in the district.

'The Jefferson's certainly would never be able to afford a car,' she said as they drove home. 'They can't even afford a decent floor in their house.'

'We've only got a car because we've been very lucky,' he reminded her. 'And the same could be said for the floor in our house. If there hadn't been one, we'd have had to manage. I sure wouldn't have had time to cut timber for floorboards. Remember that.' He put the car into top gear and cast her a serious look. 'And there's no space out here for snobs either.'

She was silent. She hadn't meant to sound snobbish but sometimes her upbringing made her feel a misfit. Now, at last, in her heart she felt she was as good as the rest of them.

205

* * *

Bobbie was christened in July. Amy persuaded George to ask John if he would conduct the service and very early one Sunday morning, after George had finished the milking, they set off in the Maxwell. The christening was held in the church in town after the morning service, then they all went back to John and Ellie's for lunch.

'Here, let me hold my godson.' Ellie held out her arms.

'You look so much better than last time I was here,' Amy said.

'Yes. I think John and I have come to terms with things now.' She hugged Bobbie, who smiled up at her before blowing bubbles. 'Come on, little man. Blowing raspberries, that's no way to behave for your Auntie Ellie.'

Amy giggled. 'He hasn't learnt any manners yet.'

'You seem happier, too. Are things going better this year?'

'Not really. If I'm honest I'm beginning to think we'll never make a go of the place, but I know George'll never give up. Whatever sacrifice we have to make, he keeps on going but what else is there?' She didn't want to dwell on the awful spring and the poor crop. 'The car's the best thing that has ever happened to us and it's made such a difference to what we can do. I still can't get over Mrs Chernitsky's generosity.'

* * *

The summer was hot and arid with the risk of thunderstorms or worse a prairie fire and they were all edgy.

Amy planned to go berry picking with Janet. As she left, George was trying to mend some harness.

'Don't think we'll be that long,' she said. 'There's not much left to pick.'

George wiped his forehead and dumped the harness on his workbench.

'I'm going to town. That's beyond repair and I can't afford to be without a spare.'

'Can't it wait till we can all go?'

'Not really. The thresher gangs due tomorrow and I'll be expected to give a hand.' He saw her disappointment. 'Never mind. I'll collect the mail and buy a newspaper.'

* * *

With the repaired harness in one hand and a newspaper in the other, he was getting into the car when Tom came rushing along the sidewalk.

'Hey, George. Have you heard? The Municipality – they're doing some ditching and I heard on the grapevine, they're coming your way.'

'What? Really?' George was incredulous. 'Seriously? I didn't think anyone had any money.'

'Heard it from Sid and you know what he's like – nothing much he doesn't know.'

It would be their salvation. Better ditches would stop the flooding.

'That's the best news I've heard in years.'

CHAPTER FIFTEEN

1929

Spring

Amy didn't look up from her needlework when George shut the door with a bang.

'Damn the weather,' he cursed.

He didn't usually slam the door, but a gale was blowing and she could hear the wind and rain. It had been raining for days.

'God damn it, I've had enough of this confounded weather.'

She frowned at the sock she was darning and knew how he felt. The sock had been repaired several times and now she was mending the darn in the heel. She mentally damned the sock. She, too, was sick of the weather, but most of all she was sick of mending and making-do.

He struggled out of his wet clothing and hooked his coat on the back of the door. She could see a puddle forming. His actions reflected his mood. Though he said little, she knew he was depressed – had been for days. Now it was she who tried to be optimistic.

She went to the stove, where the kettle was steaming. 'Nothing a good cup of coffee won't fix.'

'Don't sound so godamn cheerful. No matter how much coffee I drink, it won't stop the rain or fix the river.' He tossed his boots into the corner. 'And I thought those new drains would solve the problem.'

She ignored the mud which splattered onto the floor. That was unimportant when they were facing a serious crisis. A late spring, combined with a slow moving weather system, had left them surrounded by water-logged fields.

'The river's still rising?'

'Yep. Seems every spring, it's the same.'

What could she say? If they lost most of the crop again it might not be a complete disaster, but it would be the end of any hopes of buying new clothes for the children. She couldn't help the pang of envy she felt every time she passed the Sutherland's or the Klassen's homesteads. Their harvests were always good. It didn't seem possible that, despite the extra drainage ditches, this could be happening again. All their plans ... No wonder George was angry. He had every right to be.

He sunk into a chair, a defeated expression on his face. Mac pushed a sympathetic wet nose against him and his hand reached out to pat the black head.

'Damn and blast the weather. What did I ever do to deserve this? Ma always said nothing in life is fair. Guess she's right – nothing is.'

She leant over the back of the chair, wrapped her arms around his neck and kissed his cheek. She longed to smooth away his troubles much as she did with the children but she felt so helpless.

'I can't believe this is happening again,' she said in a low voice.

'Neither can I.'

'You're right. It isn't fair. It simply isn't fair.'

'I don't reckon there's much hope of saving the crop.'

'No hope at all?'

'This is the worst it's ever been. You want to look outside. That big puddle on the way to the barn is almost a river. It's several feet wide and if it doesn't stop raining soon, it'll be in the godamn barn. It wouldn't be so bad, if we could re-seed, but it's never that simple. When the water goes, there'll be weeds washed down here from miles around.'

'This'll warm you.' Stirring the coffee, she placed it on the table, reaching for the cookie jar. They were his favourite – she had made them that afternoon.

'Thanks.' He took a bite, hardly noticing what he was eating.

She returned to her chair and inspected the pile of mending. There were two pairs of trousers as well as two more socks. It seemed she'd be mending forever. She picked up Sam's trousers and remembered Will wearing these very trousers on his first day at school.

'They held me down and pulled off my pants,' he had sobbed on his return in the afternoon. She still couldn't think of trousers as pants. 'And then,' he went on, 'they put them up the flag pole.'

She couldn't suppress a little smile. Poor Will. To him it had seemed like the end of the world but right now she understood. What were they to do? Sighing, she rummaged in her work basket for a suitable piece of material to form a patch. In the light of the oil lamp, it didn't look the right colour, but it was the best there was. When Sam finished with these, Bobbie would be wearing them and she would be patching them again.

* * *

George stared into the cup. It felt as if he was staring into an abyss. In the past, he'd always found a way, no matter how difficult, no matter the physical cost, but there was only so much a man could do and he alone could never defeat nature. In each of the previous years he had failed to make a single payment on the mortgage but on each occasion he had convinced himself the flood was a one off. Next year would be better. Now he was beginning to believe they were jinxed. He supposed he should have appreciated their vulnerability before. It was obvious the land was low lying and that, when the ice melted or if there were heavy rains or a late blizzard, the water would overflow onto their farm. He cursed himself for not realizing when he was first offered the place. Was that the reason they got 200 acres instead of the usual quarter section he'd expected? But forty extra acres could never compensate for the disaster a sudden thaw in spring could bring.

'There's no hope for us here, Amy.' He hadn't meant to voice his thoughts but he couldn't hide how bad things were any longer.

She looked up. 'Surely there must be something we can do? Next year will be better.'

'Hmm. Next year. We always say next year. How many years do we have to wait?'

He sipped his coffee and considered their plight. He felt certain they had been sold poor land and now he had been here long enough, he was equally sure he had paid an inflated price. Originally, he had been assured it was a grain farm and the asking price reflected this but it was obvious his land could never be that. Not when it flooded every year. It couldn't fairly be described as a stock farm either, not when the hay from water-logged fields gave cows belly ache and wasn't even safe to feed to the horses. Some weeks earlier, he had voiced his thoughts to the District Superintendent from Winnipeg. The Superintendent was there to keep an eye on all new settlers and had been sympathetic, even agreeing to mention their plight to his superiors. Nothing more had been heard.

He drained his cup and hoped the morning would bring better weather. 'Let's have an early night.'

The weather had improved the next day but, with the roads impassable, Will didn't go to school and breakfast was leisurely.

'I've got plenty of odd jobs to do, so I suppose there's no point in sitting around feeling sorry for myself. There's a pile of timber to split and the roof of the hog house is leaking. I might need a hand with that. You can help if you like, Will.'

'Sure thing, Dad.'

The boys disappeared into the other room and he went to the window, gazing out without really seeing. If he were to die, would the farm be worth anything? What sort of mess would he be leaving?

'I've been thinking. May be we should move ...'

Amy stopped what she was doing and stared at him in surprise. 'Move? Where did that come from?'

'I've been thinking about it for a while.'

'Are you serious? How can we move?' She wrung out the dish cloth and began to wipe the table. 'Where would we move to?'

'Another farm.'

'You're serious?'

'Of course, I'm serious.'

'But how can we do that? There's no money and anyway, you've – we've – put so much into this place. I know it isn't perfect, but you've done so much. The cattle and what about the hogs? You built the hog house yourself and look at all the repairs you've done to the barn and all that fencing ... You can't just abandon it all.'

211

'Don't you think I've thought about that?'

'But it's an awfully big step. Where on earth would we go? And, in any case, we haven't got the money.'

'I don't know any of the answers yet, but I'm working on it.' He sighed. 'All I want is the same chance as everyone else. That's all – the same chance as the rest of them. I don't know where we'll go or even if it's possible, but I do know we can't go on as we are.'

'Maybe this is just a bad year.'

'Another bad year? That's an understatement. It's real bad. Real bad. This time, we'll be lucky if there's anything for the threshing gang. Every year, it's the same. Spring melt followed by floods. We can't go on hoping ...'

'But our first year – I don't remember it being this bad.'

'May be, but surely you remember? The river still came up. I'm beginning to think our first year was a one off.'

'You mean ...'

'We were lucky. The good Lord, well, He thought He'd give us some encouragement.' He saw her frown. 'That's what happened, honey. Let them have it a bit easier to begin with. We got dealt a bum hand. This farm is doomed.'

She was silent.

'I've been thinking. If the people here won't do anything, maybe we can raise the matter with the government back in England.'

'In England? How do we do that? Surely it would be better to approach them here first.'

'I had a word with the guy from Winnipeg when he was here a month back. He made sympathetic noises. Said we're not the only ones. There's one or two others in the same boat and he did say he'd have a word with the authorities. But I – we can't wait forever. We can't afford to. 'Sides it was a British Government scheme which brought us out here and, as I see it, we're their responsibility. Ma'll know what to do. I'll write today. Might as well get it done, the weather the way it is.'

* * *

As soon as the roads were passable a journey into town to collect and post mail was possible but it was weeks before George received a reply. The day Ma's letter arrived, he left Amy outside chatting to friends, while he slipped inside the General Store. He even failed to acknowledge greetings from neighbours in his haste to rip open the envelope and scan the words.

'... suggest you write to our MP here in East Ham ...
you are still a British citizen ... they must do something.
Send your letter to me and I will see it gets there safely.'

After supper, he settled at the table, writing notes on scrap paper, firing questions at Amy, trying to get his thoughts into some sort of order and writing a draft. First he stated how the farm had been sold as a grain farm when in reality it was a stock farm and worth a quarter of the price. Then he wrote about the well which was saline and caused a general weakening of all the animals, costing more than double it should to keep and fatten stock for sale. He explained about the floods each spring and how things had not improved even though extra drainage ditches had been provided.

'I have put in four crops here and have never been able
to make my payments on this farm ...'

He put his pen down and paused for thought. The previous year had been so bad, he had even had to apply for credit in order to purchase seed and feed for the animals. The loan had been added to his mortgage and to make matters worse, the Land Settlement Branch had even taken control of the proceeds of the little crop they had, leaving them with a pittance. He had never dared to admit to Amy that the debt was increasing by the year. The injustice of it all infuriated him.

He picked up his pen again. This letter had to make a case – a good case for some form of compensation. He struggled with the rest of the letter before finishing with the hope the matter would be taken up with the Government and that he would hear something soon. He copied it in his best handwriting and they made the trip into town specially to post it.

Weeks, then months crept by and George began to think his letter had been ignored.

* * *

The reply came in an unexpected way. Nothing from London, but instead, a letter from the Land Settlement Board in Winnipeg and it offered another farm. George was ecstatic but Amy couldn't believe it and it made her wonder what had happened in London.

He was impatient to go to Winnipeg to sign the papers.

'Before they change their mind.'

She packed sandwiches and he loaded the car with eggs and butter for the store as he planned a brief stop in Portage before driving on to Winnipeg.

'Don't expect me back till late,' he said as he cranked the engine. It fired first time. 'Don't wait up for me,' he said as he kissed her. 'If I can't get back before dark, I'll stop over at Ellie and John's.'

'How long will it take to Winnipeg?'

He opened the driver's door. 'Haven't a clue, but if this baby behaves it sure as hell will be faster than with horses.'

'Wouldn't it be better to go by train?'

'No, no. It'd be much quicker and easier by road. No hanging around. Just drive straight there and back again. What could be simpler?'

'If you're sure.'

'Course I'm sure. 'Sides I never normally get the excuse to drive a long way. I'm looking forward to it.'

She watched the car disappear along the trail and wished she could have gone with him. Even if she hadn't any money to spend, she could look in the shops. She gave him a final wave and returned to the chores.

When Will returned from school, he helped with the milking and as dusk came, she knew George was unlikely to be back that night, but she didn't worry. Winnipeg was a fair distance. He'd probably stopped over at Ellie and John's.

It was late the following afternoon before she heard a car bouncing down the trail. Abandoning the butter churn, she ran to the door and was surprised to see it wasn't their car at all, but the Stadnyk's Ford. Mac barked and chased alongside, biting at the wheels and, as it came closer, she could also see George.

'It's lovely to see you, John, but why didn't you bring Ellie?' she said unable to suppress a yearning for female company.

'Ellie's at friends for tea. We weren't expecting George to call.'

She turned to George. 'But … where's our car?'

She saw a conspiratorial look pass between the two of them. 'Nothing to worry about.' He kissed her. 'Tell you later. Come on in, John. You must stop for supper. We've enough, haven't we Amy?'

'Of course we have.'

'No, no. I can't stop. I must get back before dark. Ellie doesn't know I'm here, but I wouldn't mind a cup of coffee.'

'We'll soon fix that.'

She picked up the kettle. It was already warm. 'Do tell me what you've done with the car? Did it break down or something?'

'Sort of.'

She disliked evasive answers and she could see his expression was sheepish.

'Whatever's happened? An accident? You didn't crash it, did you?'

'No, no, nothing like that but that doesn't matter now.' He grinned as he fished into his pocket and produced a folded document. 'Take a look at this,' he said, waving it in the air. 'This is our new farm.'

'Really? You're serious?' She could see by the excitement in his face he wasn't pretending. 'Is it near? Oh, let me see.' She cleared Sam's books off the table.

'Let's have coffee first. We must look after our guest,' he reminded her.

As she poured the coffee she fired questions at him. 'You haven't said where it is? Is there a decent house?'

'It's easier if I show you.' He opened the atlas and flicked to the right page. 'That's the border – that line there. This is too small a scale to see properly. Anyway we're not that far up from the States.'

'America?' She offered the cookie jar to John. 'I never thought we'd end up there. Well, near there.' She bent over the book. 'Show me exactly where.'

'I can't. It isn't marked. The farm's located south of Crystal City, but it isn't on this map.'

'Is there a school for the boys?'

'Sure, there's a school. The railroad goes there, so there'll be a Post Office and probably other stores.'

She looked up at his smiling face, but a sudden doubt crept in. 'Is there a river? There's no point in moving if there's any chance of flooding.'

'Need some water for the cattle, honey, but they did say in Winnipeg there was no chance of flooding down there. I made certain of that and they assured me there was no chance. None whatsoever.'

'If you're sure ...'

He laughed. 'It couldn't be better. Tomorrow. We start moving tomorrow.'

'Tomorrow?' She was horrified. 'I can't ... We can't move that quickly.'

'Don't worry, honey, it won't happen immediately. There's a whole host of things to arrange.'

John finished his cookie and drained his cup. 'I can see you've a lot to think about, so I guess I'd better head home. Ellie and I will miss you both, but when you're settled, we'll come for a visit. That is, if you invite us.'

'You bet,' George said.

'You'd better come or I shall want to know why,' Amy said. 'Oh, that reminds me. I sorted out Bobbie's outgrown clothes. Will you give them to Ellie for me? She'll know who can use them.'

'Sorting out already? Sounds like you're pretty organized.'

She felt awkward as she remembered how John had taken the loss of their child. 'We've so little space ...'

'You're right. Ellie will know what to do with them. Now I must get back.'

'Tell me, George,' she demanded the second John's car had left and they had waved good-bye. 'What have you done with our car?'

'Dried out a bit in the last couple of days.'

'Dried out? What are you talking about – dried out?'

'Look at all the dust.' He nodded in the direction of John's car.

'Oh, the trail.' She said with a note of irritation. She wasn't going to let him change the subject. 'You didn't answer my question. Tell me what happened. Where is the car?'

'Long story.'

'For goodness sake, do what you're always telling me. Start at the beginning.'

'The engine seized up.'

'How do you mean – seized up?'

'Ran out of oil.'

'How did it do that? Did you break something?'

He looked embarrassed but didn't answer.

'But it's all right isn't it? I mean you can fill it with oil again, can't you?'

'Wish it was that simple, honey. The fact is the god damn thing's seized up. It packed up right on the edge of Winnipeg and that's where I left it.'

'How do you mean – left it?'

'Some guy gave me a hitch to a garage, but they told me it needed a new engine and that cost bucks. There was no way we could afford it.' He shrugged and shook his head. 'I had to leave it there. Nothing else for it, I guess.'

It took a second or two before his words sunk in. 'You mean you're not going to get it back?' Her voice got louder. 'You've left it ... at ... at this garage?'

He bit his lip. 'We got a new farm. That's what matters, isn't it? We'll get another car as soon as we get on our feet. Things'll start to go good now, honey. I promise.'

'But that car was the best thing that ever happened to us.' How could he do this? The car meant freedom, a chance to visit friends and go on picnics – at least in the summer when the roads were passable. She tried to be logical. 'There must have been other garages – cheaper ones. Surely you looked?'

'I thought it was more important to do what I'd gone to Winnipeg for.' He pointed to the papers which were still spread out on the table. 'I thought that was more important. Anyway I only had enough money to get me back to Portage.'

'I can't believe it.' She banged the cups together and marched to the sink. Why did good news always come along with some bad?

'We'll get another. I promise.'

'Whatever shall we do next Sunday? And don't tell me we didn't always have a car.' She washed the cups and dumped them in the cupboard not caring whether they were clean or even if they chipped.

As they got ready for bed that night, he tried to reason with her.

'Honey, please,' he begged. 'I do know how much that car meant to you but – '

'You don't. You have no idea, none at all,' she yelled. She climbed into bed. 'It was my only pleasure – the only really good thing that ever happened in our entire married life and you just dumped it.'

'It isn't the only good thing and, anyway, I didn't just dump it. I didn't have a choice.' He climbed in beside her. 'It wasn't my fault the darn thing ran out of oil. I'm sorry, truly sorry and I don't like it when we fall out like this.'

'You should've thought about that before. You're selfish, George Mills, selfish. Haven't I always done my level best to do everything you've ever asked of me – everything? Sometimes it's not been just difficult but impossible but I've always tried. For you – always for you. What about me? How often do you think of what I want? That car

218

was my only pleasure. Oh, for two pins I'd go back to England. I might have an ogre of a mother but at least she cared about me.'

'How can you say that?'

'I should have married Charles. She was right and I've had enough. Do you hear me? Enough.' She turned her back on him, yanked the sheet up and fought back angry tears.

Things were no better the next day.

'I don't want to go,' she said over breakfast.

'Are we moving, Mom?' Will asked.

'I've – we've got friends here – Will's settled in school.'

'Are we moving, Dad?'

'Don't interrupt,' she snapped before turning back to George. 'It's miles and miles away from Ellie and it'd mean starting all over again.'

'No it wouldn't. For goodness sake, sweetheart, everything will come with us. We'll have a different house, that's all.'

'I've only just got curtains up at all the windows.'

'If I told you this is our only chance and we have to take it, would that make any difference?'

'You said that before.'

'It was different then.'

'Was it?'

'Yes and you know it. We didn't have a mortgage then. Now we have and I haven't made a single payment yet. The way things are, with floods every spring, I can't see how I ever will. They told me in Winnipeg this was a grain farm – they guaranteed that.'

They were silent for the rest of the meal.

'Will, go take Mac out. And Sam, you go, too,' he said when they had all finished eating. He waited until the door closed behind the children. 'Did you really mean it when you said you wished you'd married Charles Ashby?' he asked.

She began to clear away the dishes.

'Amy,' he held her arm. 'Please, we can't go on like this.'

'Watch me.'

Letting go, he sighed. 'I know I can never match Charles but I thought we loved each other – you ... Oh, what's the god damn use.' He strode across the room and banged the door behind him.

She washed the dishes, tears running down her cheeks. She did love him, damn it. But it hurt so much.

* * *

'I'll find that trunk we brought out from England,' George said over dinner. 'You'll need it for packing.'

Amy drew in a deep breath. She didn't want to move. That was the conclusion she had reached during the night. She had put so much into making this little house a home, she didn't want to leave it. While she tossed and turned, George, as usual, was soon in a deep sleep and she was left thinking through everything they had achieved over the years. She wasn't convinced the weather would always be bad. And then there was Ellie ... She didn't get to see her much now. If they moved all those miles away, would they ever meet again?

'I'm not packing anything. I'm staying here.'

'There isn't a choice.' George frowned at her. 'I showed you the paperwork. It's a done deal. This place is no longer ours.'

'Don't I get a say?'

'I had to sign there and then or risk losing the new place. It wasn't possible to consult you. You know the situation.'

'You didn't give me a chance to say what I thought before you went rushing off to Winnipeg. How was I to know you'd be offered a farm a million miles away?' She glared at him.

'It isn't a million miles away.'

'Might as well be.'

'All right. All right. I was wrong. We should all have gone to Winnipeg even though the animals couldn't be left overnight. It was a bad enough journey for me let alone bringing the children along, but, for all that, I can't change anything. This farm is not ours and we're moving to Crystal City, like it not.' Abandoning his coffee, George stood up and stomped out of the house.

The trunk appeared later that day. At first she ignored it but as they went to bed that night, she knew it was a battle lost. They were moving and that was that.

Within two weeks the entire farm, including all the animals and the contents of the house had been taken to the rail siding, where it was loaded onto a train for the journey south and when she closed the front door for the last time, she did so with sadness – something she had never expected to feel when they had first arrived. She had become attached to the tiny house in this flat and vast landscape. How or why, when it had meant so much hard work and so many sacrifices, she would never understand. She looked up at the horseshoe and thought about removing it. Then changed her mind. It hadn't brought them much luck.

An hour or so after they boarded the train, George went to check on the animals. The scenery began to change and she could see hills in the distance. Bobbie had fallen asleep and Will was reading. Only Sam was restless and difficult. He began to flick little balls of paper, made from an old Eaton's catalogue. One hit Amy on the arm and she gave him a long and meaningful look which he accepted as a warning. For a while he stopped till boredom set in again. Sam's latest and largest creation was aimed at Will, who was unaware and absorbed in his book. Sam had spent some time creating a heavier missile. He took aim, checked first, that Amy wasn't looking, then screwed up his eyes and aligned his fingers. It missed its target, hitting a man, who was walking through the carriage, squarely in the face.

'I am so terribly sorry,' she apologized as soon as she appreciated what had happened and tried to suppress a laugh. She glared at Sam. His antics would get them all into trouble. 'Stop that this minute.' She looked back at the man and was relieved he also found the incident amusing. 'I am so very sorry. I'll make sure he clears up the mess right away.'

'Kids – kinda boring a trip like this for them, ain't it?'

She nodded.

'Where you headed?'

'Crystal City.'

221

'Visiting relatives?'

'No, no. We're going to live there.'

'Farming? Them's yer animals back there?'

'That's right.'

'Out from England?'

'We've been here a few years now. We had a farm south of Portage.'

'And you're moving to Crystal City?'

'Yes. Where we were before ... it flooded in the spring, you see. Every year the Assiniboine washed our crops away.'

He shook his head and rubbed his hand over his moustache, a knowing look in his eyes. 'And you say you're headed for Crystal City?'

She nodded.

'Out of the frying pan.' He said in a tone which indicated he knew something she didn't.

'What do you mean – out of the frying pan?'

'Lady, you'll see when you get there,' he said over his shoulder as he continued walking down the car. 'But I wish you the best of luck.'

CHAPTER SIXTEEN

The sun's heat was ferocious and the wagon didn't offer any shade. They were squashed between items of furniture and large trunks, the children shrieking with excitement while George whistled a little tune. She felt weary and very grubby and she wasn't sure whether to be optimistic or pessimistic about their future, but the mood of the others was infectious and she began to sing songs and chant nursery rhymes with the children.

It had been a long, long day. The first sight of the farm was only possible as the wagon turned off the road onto a smaller track some miles from where they had left the train. The horses strained at the incline and she marvelled at the scenery. She was reminded they were not too far from the border, when a couple of cowboys, wearing chaps, stopped to enquire whether they had seen any stray cattle. The boys stared, Sam with his mouth open, while she eyed the holsters and the ornate handles of the pistols.

'No strays on the trail we've come on,' George assured them and she was relieved when they galloped away in a cloud of dirt.

'Wish I had a hat like that,' Will said in a wistful voice. 'And a neck tie.'

When, eventually the horses and wagon turned into the yard, she gasped in delight at the sight of the house. For the first time since George had returned with news of their move, she felt a surge of optimism.

'It's huge. You never hinted it would be this big.'

'You never asked.'

'I did but – '

'Amy, let it rest.'

She bit her lip. She might not have forgiven him but he was right, they couldn't go on like this but she wasn't yet ready to make peace.

'Well, anyway it's better than I thought,' she said in a half conciliatory tone.

'Didn't like to raise your hopes,' he replied in a gruff voice.

The children ran off to explore, Mac chasing after them, leaving her still staring in disbelief at the white-boarded house with its two storeys and veranda which ran along the front. It was almost as good as the McAllister's and she imagined sitting in a rocking chair, on a hot sunny day, in the shade of the porch. She wanted to pinch herself. Was this all a dream?

'It's amazing,' she murmured still not trusting her eyes. She gazed about her, turning slowly, taking in the detail – the dusty yard, the trees which gave shade as well as shelter and the tall barn, weathered silver-grey. Somebody had left a four pronged fork leaning against the door. Did they forget it or had they left in a hurry?

'This place is beautiful. I can't believe it – hills in the prairies. Little ones, I know, but they're there. I can't wait to write to Vi.' She looked back at the house and wondered why anyone would want to leave it. 'How many bedrooms are there? Oh, I do hope there's one for each of the children. I still can't believe it's ours. Wouldn't the McAllisters be impressed?'

George's eyes rolled skyward. 'Is that all you're worried about?'

'Of course not, but –'

'No time for buts. We'd better get that wagon unloaded. There's a lot to do before it gets dark.'

Amy sighed. After such a long journey, it was the last thing she felt like.

'Where are the boys?' She scanned the yard. There was a loud splash, followed by Mac's bark. 'The river. None of them can swim.'

George didn't answer, but was already running to the back of the house and she raced after him.

Sam and Will were stripped off and waist deep in water, splashing each other while Mac ran along the top of the steep bank, barking. Bobbie tottered around shrieking in delight, trying hard to remove his pants. Discarded clothing lay in the dirt.

'What the hell –' George caught Bobbie before he toppled into the water.

'It's lovely, Mom, Dad. So cool. You want to try it.'

'Will, Sam – What the hell do you think you're doing?' he yelled at them. 'Out this minute. There's work to do.'

'Owh.'

'Out.'

'Yes, Dad.'

'You didn't tell me the river was this close to the house.' She accused him.

'I might have done if you hadn't kept up this not speaking,' he yelled at her. 'And it's not a river. It's a god damn creek. Nothing more than a stream. It was on the papers. I showed you, remember?'

She drew in her breath. Cheek. He was the one who wasn't speaking and she hadn't set eyes on the papers since the day he returned from Winnipeg.

'There's no need to shout at me. I'm standing right beside you and what if the stupid creek floods …'

'It's tiny compared to the Assiniboine and look how deep the sides are. It's got a long way to go before it's a problem. It couldn't be better. We need water for the cattle.'

She hoped he was right and she envied the boys their dip. She longed for a wash, but there was work to be done. Lots of it. And, in spite of what George said, the creek was still going to be a problem. The boys would have to learn to swim and they would all have to keep an eye on Bobbie.

They returned to the front of the house and climbed the steps onto the porch. The children, half naked, raced ahead, running from room to room, their voices shrill and hollow, and their footsteps echoing.

She wrinkled her nose. 'Smells a bit musty.'

'Nothing a bit of fresh air won't fix.' He went to the window. The sill was grimy and there were three large dead black flies. Ignoring them, he lifted up the bottom sash.

She noticed a pile of dirt in a corner of the room.

'Look at that. I'll have to get sweeping tomorrow.'

'Been empty awhile.'

'I wonder when the last people moved out.' She returned to the hall and ambled into the kitchen. 'Good heavens. Come and look at this. I can't think why they left this behind. Do come and see,' she called to him. 'It has to be the largest stove I have ever seen.' She opened the different oven doors, rubbing dusty surfaces with her hands. It looked new and, wherever she removed the dust, the raised silvery decorations on the legs and doors gleamed brightly. 'It doesn't look as if it's ever been used.'

George stood in the doorway. 'I don't suppose a range like this is cheap.'

'Isn't it magnificent?' She had heard of several women who had transported their stoves hundreds of miles and it was by far the most impressive one she had ever seen. Even the McAllister's didn't compare. 'I wonder why they didn't take it with them. I know I would have.'

'A hot meal tonight, then?'

'You'll be lucky when there's so much else to do. But I still can't get over it. This amazing house and now this incredible stove.'

'Told you our luck would change.'

She allowed him to hug her. 'I can hear Will bossing the others about. We'd better go and see what they're up to.'

Upstairs were four bedrooms. The children had already selected rooms – or rather Will had decided and, before they reached the top of the stairs, they knew which was to be theirs.

'Mom and Dad will have the one at the front,' they heard him announce and when she peeped inside she was happy with his choice. The view from the window was across rolling countryside and the room was much larger than their previous bedroom, but it was its privacy which attracted her most. The boys would no longer need to go through their bedroom to get to theirs. In her mind, she began placing furniture – the bed against one wall, the chest of drawers under the window. There would be room for a chair. They didn't have much, but they would be comfortable and she would set to and make some new rugs for the bedside.

One afternoon, a couple of days after their arrival, Amy, dressed in her only good summer frock and straw hat, rounded up the boys and was about to leave the house, when cows came wandering up the track, shepherded by Mac. She watched as they were driven into the nearby field. George shut the gate.

'Where are you off to?'

'I thought it was time we enrolled the boys in school. I thought I'd be back by the time you got here. But since you're here, why don't you come?'

'Like this?' He indicated his grubby clothes.

'We could wait while you change.'

He shook his head. 'I'd like to. Next time, eh?'

Disappointed he could never spare the time and that they never had a moment together, she walked the children the mile to the junction where the tiny wooden school with its tin roof and sentry box lobby was located. They passed the flag pole, the union flag hanging limp, Amy pointing out the small bell house and reading the oval plaque above the door which said 'Melville School 1902'.

Through the open windows, they could hear the teacher's voice and then the door swung open and children of all ages spilled out. One or two of the older pupils hardly gave them a glance before heading for the nearby woodshed, where several brown ponies were tethered. Others shouted a cheerful 'Hi' before walking, mostly in ones or two's, along the trail. The bigger boys were dressed in faded indigo drills and one carried a large metal water container, which Amy knew would be brought to school the following morning, brim full of fresh water. Several of the girls had pigtails and one or two wore smocks.

Will watched enviously as the children mounted their ponies, two or sometimes three up.

They peered into the only room, where the school mistress, her back to them, was wiping the blackboard. On the table in the nearest corner was a globe and a small pile of readers. She spotted the illustration of "Mary, John and Peter" on the dog-eared cover and thought it could only be yesterday she was hearing Will read from one such book and now Sam was about to start school. Near the teacher's desk was a small and, she thought, remembering the chill of the church services at Will's last school, probably ineffective little stove. On the wall was a map of the world. The windows were along one wall and the sun streamed through, making the room uncomfortably hot. Several large flies crawled over the glass and more flew in circles overhead.

She hesitated, then clearing her throat, stepped into the schoolroom.

'If that's you Tommy Wilson ....' The voice was stern. The teacher turned to face them and they could see she was much older than Miss Smith. The light brown hair showed streaks of grey and was tied back and knotted into a severe bun at the base of her skull. Prim and proper was Amy's immediate reaction as she took in the plain white long-sleeved blouse – a garment which didn't have so much as a suggestion of a frill. There would no nonsense in this schoolroom.

'Oh, I'm sorry I thought – Well, it doesn't matter what I thought.' She smiled and Amy at once saw behind the stern façade. Blue eyes lit up and the forbidding expression disappeared in a warm smile, her face taking on a charm unnoticed before.

'New pupils I presume? But not this little one.' She wagged a finger at Bobbie. 'Not yet, anyway.'

Amy laughed as Bobbie hid behind her. 'I think he'd like to. He's not usually shy. This is Will and this is Sam.' She tugged Bobbie from behind her. 'And this is Bobbie.' He clung onto her skirt, while she explained they had moved into the area.

The teacher nodded. 'Ah, yes. They said there were new people on O'Brien's section. I'm Molly Everard.' She held out her hand and Amy shook it.

'I'm Amy Mills. Say hello to Miss Everard, boys.'

228

'Hello, Miss Everard,' Will said.

Bobbie hid his face in his mother's skirts. Sam said nothing, but stared straight ahead. She nudged him.

'Hello, Miss Everard.'

She suspected Sam was going to give the teacher a hard time but it was soon agreed the boys would start school the next day.

It was too hot to hurry, so they sauntered home, stopping under the occasional tree to benefit from its shade.

'Wish I had a pony,' Will said. 'I'd ride it to school like those other boys ...'

'You won't need a pony. It's no distance at all. They probably have much further to go than you.'

George was interested to hear about their visit to the school.

'Next year things might need to be different. Certainly in the summer,' he said, sitting at the table with the children who were waiting for their meal.

Amy appeared from the kitchen, a plate of food in each hand.

'Different. How?'

'Now I've had time to assess the place, it looks as if much of it's been ploughed at some time or other, so I mean to seed more acres than I've ever done before.'

She placed a dish of mashed potatoes and cold chicken in front of him. Even though the new stove motivated her to try all sorts of interesting recipes, she couldn't face the heat. 'That'll mean the thresher gang'll be here longer.'

'You don't get new cookers for nothing,' he said. 'And if the crop comes good I'll need some help. Will's getting mighty good with the horses. He could help with the hay. Might even try him on the mower.'

'Really, Dad?' Will's eyes lit up.

'Miss school? I don't think that's a good idea. How can you talk like that when they haven't even settled in yet? And in any case, they need an education,' she said and returned to the kitchen.

'Didn't do much for me.' George mumbled, helping himself to some pickle. He continued in a louder voice. ''Sides Will here's a big lad. He can handle a team very well.'

Will nodded. 'You bet.'

She reappeared, balancing three plates. 'We always agreed not before he was ten and then only if it was absolutely necessary.'

'Don't get all worked up. Will's a clever lad. Reckon there's daylight enough after school's out.'

'Do you think I could ride Buster to school, Dad?'

'Goodness gracious, no, Will.' She sat down. 'What did I say when we were coming home. You live too close to go to school on a pony.'

'And Buster's no pony.' George laughed. 'So you want a pony?'

Will nodded.

'Sure don't think we can justify keeping a pony, but I might run to a dog. What do you reckon?'

'Wow. A dog of my own? Do you really mean it, Dad? ' Will jumped up and down on his seat.

George explained that Jesse Carter, their nearest neighbour, had eight puppies looking for a home.

'While you were out, Jesse stopped by on his way to town. Said there was a bad plague of hoppers south of here.'

Will wasn't interested in grasshoppers. 'Gee, I can't wait. When can we go get a puppy?'

George rubbed his chin, feeling the day's growth. 'Well, let me see. I guess it depends. I reckon it depends on how you do at school.'

'If I do good, can I have one, Dad, please. Mom, please,' he pleaded.

'If you have one, he'll be your responsibility,' she said in a firm voice. It was all very well George giving the boys ideas, but she was not taking on any more chores. 'You feed him and clean him and train him. Understood?'

Will nodded.

'And he'll live in the barn. Now come on, eat your supper, boys.' She turned to George, ' What's this about grasshoppers? Are they a problem?'

'Could be. Let's hope they stay where they are.'

'What'll they do, Dad?' Will asked, shovelling into his mouth.

'Will, please. Smaller amounts on that fork.' She turned back to George. 'I suppose I know the answer. They'll eat the crop.'

George nodded. 'Guess so.'

'It seems there's always something. Now it's grasshoppers.'

'Jesse told me they can be bad. Eat everything. He said he'd seen a harness eaten clean off a horse.'

'Wow.'

She scowled at Will. 'It's probably an exaggeration.'

'Don't think it was. I've heard a few yarns like that over the years. 'Fraid it's a bit of a problem down here. Happens every so often.'

'Something else to worry about,' she said.

After they had eaten, George suggested they went for a walk.

'You haven't had time to have a good look round the place and even I haven't had time to inspect all the buildings. Let the boys clear up for a change. It's time they earned their keep.'

The heat was still in the sun but there was a slight breeze as they set out, following the creek as it wound its way through the pasture. George explained as they walked what he planned for each paddock and eventually they returned to the yard.

'The roof seems in good order,' he said when they stood inspecting the inside of the barn. 'That door up top could do with a new hinge.' He pointed to a door ten feet above their heads. 'Otherwise it seems fine. Impossible to tell if it leaks, though. That is, till it rains.'

'Everything's so wonderful here, I keep wanting to pinch myself and I still can't imagine why the last people left. You haven't heard anything, have you?'

'Jesse said Mrs O'Brien took sick. Don't know if there's anything more to it than that. Doctors are expensive. Remember the Chernitsky's?'

'Oh, well. What does it matter anyway? The most important thing is that we like it here.' She turned to go, but he moved to block her exit.

'Don't go. Not yet. We need to talk.'

'What's there to talk about?' She studied the floor not trusting herself to look at him.

'Sweetheart,' He sighed. 'You do know that all I want is to make you happy?' He said in a low voice. 'And I can't bear us being like this.' She could hear the pain in his voice. 'Amy, I love you.'

She looked up. His eyes were beseeching and she knew she couldn't hold out any longer and that if he touched her she would melt in his arms. He leant forward to caress her lips with his – like a butterfly – hovering – sensing. She didn't move but he didn't need encouragement and his arms slid around her, his tongue invaded her mouth, devouring her and she wanted him.

'God, Amy, I've missed you. Forgive me.'

* * *

In no time at all life fell into a routine. When Will was home from school, he spent his time playing with Spot, the new puppy. He fed and groomed him and taught him to sit and stay. Mostly Mac ignored the young incomer, except when his tail was nipped or if his quiet snooze was disturbed. Then he would slink off somewhere cool, usually under the porch. Some days Will spent hours trapping gophers.

'Vermin,' George said. 'The more you catch the better.'

Will would place his looped string around the gopher's hole and whistle. If he was quick enough, he might earn himself a cent. Spot and Sam sometimes tagged along, but he soon learnt that no gophers appeared when they were around so often went alone.

Most days Amy walked with Bobbie to wherever George was working to share lunch. It always seemed to be stiflingly hot and they

232

would sit in the shade of a tree. Often the wind blew up, raising dust into a spiral like a mini twister but the sun shone incessantly.

'We could do with some rain,' George said one evening. 'Do you know there hasn't been a single wet day since we came here? Seems there's no happy medium. Either we get too much or not enough.'

'There's the creek.'

'Even that's very low and pasture's getting short. If we don't get rain soon, I'll have to get Will to watch the cattle out on the road.'

'The road?'

'Grass is green all along the edge of the track. Precious little anywhere else.'

'Won't they wander off?'

'Where's to wander to? They'll be only too happy to stay where the grass is good.'

'Dad, Mom,' Will burst in on them. 'There's a big fire. Come and see.'

Alarmed, they followed him outside. On the horizon they could see a long line of flames which leapt higher with every gust of wind.

'I don't like the look of that and if the wind turns it could head this way and then we'd be in real trouble. I'm going to help,' George said and ran to the barn to get Buster.

Will followed. 'Can I come?'

'No, I want you to stay here. If the fire runs in this direction, your mother will need you.'

He was gone hours and when the sun set, Amy could still see a red glow in the distance but they were fortunate as the fire was extinguished a couple of miles away. Exhausted with the effort of carting water and blackened by the smoke, George returned with the news of a burnt out homestead.

'They lost everything – their crop as well as their house and we tried so hard to save that house. Ploughed a fire break and a dozen of us teamed up with buckets. Soaked the roof – used nearly every last drop of water. We tried everything, but the fire kept racing ahead of us and when we beat it out, it'd appear somewhere else and we'd start all over again. There was nothing we could do.'

* * *

The summer continued with months of intense heat and drying winds. When George inspected his crop, he began to be gloomy. After breakfast one morning, he walked out to one of the wheat fields and was horrified by the misshapen ears. The yield was going to be down. Why couldn't it rain for heaven's sake? It was just his luck. First too much, now too little. The previous year's wheat harvest was a bumper one – hadn't he read somewhere it was more than 500 million bushels? Everyone had had a goddamn good year. The Sutherlands, the Klassens, the McAllisters – hell, it seemed the whole world had had a good crop, except them. Amy had read Janet's letter to him. They had sent to Eatons for plans – they were building a new house.

He surveyed the whole crop. There was a strong wind blowing and he noticed that, along one fence line, soil had begun to pile up. Now that was a worry – the way the soil was blowing away. Rain would cure it. Surely the rain would come soon? Thank the Lord there were no signs of grasshoppers.

School finished as the threshing gang arrived in the district and everyone was kept busy with the harvest, but the heat which lasted through the night began to wear them down. Tempers frayed, children squabbled. Small dust storms often accompanied by thunder and lightning, blew dirt into the house and each morning Amy would sweep and dust, but the rain never came.

* * *

Early one afternoon at the end of October, George started hauling grain to the elevator. Their harvest was tiny and he had been watching the crop price for weeks. It wasn't good and he wanted to hold off selling, but they needed the money. He had been following Wall Street – prices were on the down. 'The economy's overheated,' someone said when they were talking about the greenback. Things, he suspected, were not going to get any easier. What did it matter anyway? He could no longer afford to delay.

234

As he got closer to the elevator, he slowed the horses. In the distance he could see the smoke of an approaching train. The mournful whistle echoed across the prairies. A crowd had gathered nearby. He thought it was odd they weren't queuing up to unload their grain, but he was in a hurry so didn't stop to enquire why they were standing about in the chilly wind. He drove the team straight up the ramp and into the shed, ignoring the odd shouted comment about the price. He knew it wouldn't be great – he'd already worked that out, but they needed the money. The move had cost them almost every cent.

Inside the elevator it was gloomy after the bright sunlight and it took several seconds for his eyes to adjust.

'Ninety cents a bushel. Still selling?' The operator said, making a note of the weight.

'No choice.' The price was dreadful – lower than he'd hoped. 'Things that bad?'

The man nodded. 'Reckon it'll get worse. Have you seen the Courier today?'

'Nope.' George shook his head.

'Sure don't make good reading. Several banks gone belly up.'

'What?'

The trap door in the back of the wagon opened and the golden grain flowed into the hopper beneath the driveway. The operator handed him a ticket which he shoved into his shirt pocket and, nodding his thanks, drove on out into the chill air. He wouldn't tell Amy how bad things were. She would only worry.

CHAPTER SEVENTEEN

Prairie School

'Sam forgot his lines today, Mom. Miss Everard wasn't very pleased,' Will said as he climbed into bed.

'Did not.' Sam stood in the bedroom doorway, half dressed, a defiant expression on his face.

'Yes, you did.'

'Never mind. As long as Sam knows his words in time for the concert and you will won't you, Sam?' Amy said thinking it was true that the middle child was always the difficult one. She spotted Sam's bare feet. How was it he never felt the cold?

'Wish I could have been Joseph, then I wouldn't have to be with Sam. He messes everything up.'

'The bigger boys are always Joseph.' She tucked Will's blankets in. 'You know that and anyway, you should help Sam. He's the smallest in the class.'

'But he's always in trouble …Miss Everard said – '

'That's enough now. I don't want to hear this tittle tattle and I'm sure Miss Everard is very capable of sorting things out.'

Will scowled at his brother who smirked back. Turning, she caught the look.

'Weren't you supposed to be clearing up your bedroom, young man? And if you've done that, why aren't you in bed?'

Sam recognized the tone of her voice and disappeared.

'Ruth Corbett forgot her lines, too, Mom. She's the other shepherd. Miss Everard said it should have been a boy. It'd be much better if it was a boy. It's not fair having a girl and Sam …''

She laughed. 'I expect Miss Everard ran out of boys.'

Will pouted. 'Well, anyway, Miss Everard told us all off, but I knew my words. It wasn't fair. She told us all off.'

She could think of a hundred ways in which things were unjust.

'Life's not always fair, Will. It's hard, I know, but that's the way it is. Anyway time for sleep, now.'

'Oh, Mom, Miss Everard said to ask you if we might borrow some sheets.'

'Sheets?'

'For the stage. She said we needed them for the stage.'

'But I haven't got any spare. I used the last one I had for your costumes.

He looked disappointed. 'I said you were bound to have some sheets.'

She shook her head. 'I haven't, sorry.' She smiled, trying to hide her despair at having to patch the patches on their sheets. 'Cheer up. Dad promised to find a tree for the schoolroom tomorrow. Miss Everard will like that.'

George took Will with him to cut wood and to select the Christmas tree. Amy watched them from the window as they set off on the horse-drawn sledge. While they were gone, Sam and Bobbie played upstairs and she got the sewing machine out, planning to finish the boy's Christmas concert outfits. She was pinning the last seam in Sam's costume, when Will burst into the house.

'Mom,' he panted. 'Mom, come quickly.'

'Whatever's the matter?'

'Dad. He's hurt.'

She dropped her work and stood up, pins sprinkling across the floor.

'Hurt? How?'

'He's cut himself with the axe. Please, come. Quickly, Mom. It's real bad. There's blood everywhere.'

She didn't bother with outdoor clothes or even with boots. Will held the door open. Halfway out, she stopped. 'No. No, Will. We'll need something to stop the bleeding – a towel. Anything.'

She returned to the sewing machine and grabbed the sheet she had been working on. It was the first thing she could think of and what did it matter about the costume? If George was bleeding they needed something clean. Together they ran from the house, following the trail made by the sledge right to the boundary where George sat, holding his leg. His fingers were red with blood which was oozing through his trousers. The sight of so much crimson on pure white snow was a shock.

'Oh, my God,' she said at the sight of the pools of blood. 'What have you done? Can you walk?' She looked at his white face. 'No, no. Don't even try. We have to stop the bleeding. Then we'll think of how we can get you in the warm.'

'It's not good.' He bit his lip. 'Can you get something round it – to hold it together?'

She looked away wanting to throw up. She swallowed hard. Remember the war? The hospital where they first met? Remember how desperate she was to nurse? There had been far worse sights then. She steadied her nerves before climbing onto the sledge beside him.

'We've got to raise your leg to stop the bleeding. Will, get something to rest Dad's leg on.'

Will ran over to the pile of logs which they had been about to load onto the sledge. George eased up his trouser leg. She took a deep breath, swallowed again, and then looked. It was deep – a long, gaping gash which exposed the bone. She tore the sheet into several wide strips and quickly wrapped one around his leg tying it as tight as she could.

'That's better. We'll soon have you indoors,' she said trying to be reassuring, while all the time terrified he would bleed to death.

The blood oozed through, so she applied a second and then a third layer. He was shivering and she wasn't sure if it was the cold or the shock. Probably both.

'We have to get you indoors, George.'

His face had turned grey.

Will returned with a log, but she abandoned the idea of raising the limb. He needed to be in the warm and by the look of things, it was urgent. She shivered. It was freezing and it had been stupid to come without a coat. She thought of sending Will back for one, then changed her mind.

'Can you lead Buster, Will?'

'Sure thing.'

'As close to the house as possible now and not too fast. Every jolt is going to be uncomfortable for Dad.'

Will took hold of the bridle.

'Steady,' he said as he urged the horse forward.

She sat on the sledge supporting George and held his hand. It was a rough ride and she could see him gritting his teeth at every bump. She said a mental prayer of thanks for Will's strength when, between them, they managed to drag him into the kitchen, laying him on the rug near the warmth of the stove. She grabbed a couple of gingham covered cushions and gently lifted his leg on top. He winced and she could see little beads of sweat on his forehead. Blood began to seep through the layers of linen so she found a towel and, ripping it in two, tied a strip around his leg.

He tried to inspect the size of the bandages. 'I'll never get my pants off.'

Will laughed.

'It's no laughing matter.' She knelt down and pushed a second towel under his leg, hoping it would protect the cushions. 'This is bad, George. You need to see a doctor.' She shivered. Now she was indoors, she knew how stupid she'd been. She wouldn't be surprised if she had frost bite in some of her toes and her fingers were painfully beginning to warm up. If they had taken much longer there might well have been two casualties but there wasn't time to worry about that. She looked up at Will. 'Do you think you could take me into town?'

'Sure, Mom.'

George closed his eyes. 'No, Amy. I'll be fine. Just fine.'

'You need to see a doctor. Will said he could manage the horses.'

'I'll be fine.' His teeth chattered. 'Just a bit cold. Get me a blanket.'

'But ...'

'Don't fuss, woman. I'll be warm in a minute and once the bleeding stops, I'll be fine. Might need to rest up a bit. I've seen enough bloody messes in my time to know. There weren't Doctors jumping out of the trenches when a man got half his head blown away. Just fix me some hot tea and put plenty of sugar in it. Two, no three spoonfuls. Have we got any brandy?'

'I still think you should see the Doctor. It's a bad gash – down to the bone.'

'Just get me some tea.'

She stood up. 'However did you do it?'

'Damn foolish thing to do. I only sharpened the axe yesterday.'

She sent Will for some blankets, put the kettle on the stove, then got out the cups and reached for the tea pot.

'Please let me get the doctor.'

'I don't need one.'

'George, it's bad.'

'Stop fussing. We can't afford a doctor.'

The tone of his voice made her stop what she was doing. She stared at him for several long seconds. 'Are things that bad?'

He didn't answer and she wanted to shake him – to make him understand she was part of this, too.

'Just how short of money are we?' She said in a moderated tone knowing he had hauled grain when everyone else had stopped. They couldn't afford to wait for a better price, he'd said. But it hadn't been that bad or had it?

'We didn't make much on the wheat.'

'You never said.' She saw his guilty look. 'How much did you get?'

'Not enough to see the doctor.'

'What do you mean?'

'It hardly covered the cost of threshing but if I'd waited for longer, we'd have got even less.'

'Less?'

'The price is still dropping.'

'But we'll be all right, won't we?'

He didn't reply.

She knelt beside him. 'Please, George, don't treat me like a child. Just tell me. How bad are things?'

He hesitated then the words spilled out. 'It's serious. The truth is I don't think we've enough money to see us through the winter and there's another problem. There isn't enough hay to feed the animals either.'

It was worse than she thought. 'Why didn't you tell me?'

'No point in worrying you. There's nothing you can do.'

'Oh, George,' she said holding his hand. 'We said we'd share all our troubles. Remember? When Flo lost her calf. We promised. We said we'd share all our worries – everything.'

'You were happy ... you love it here and it was Christmas. I didn't want you to worry.'

Will appeared with several blankets and she spread them over him, then went to pour a steaming cup of hot, sugary tea.

* * *

With George injured and unable to move about, Amy was grateful for Will's assistance at milking and feeding times. Terrified the wound would become infected, she still wanted to fetch the doctor, but he was adamant. He sent Will to fetch Jesse Carter and from then on Jesse called regularly. It was Jesse who delivered the tree to the school and Jesse who made sure there was enough firewood for her to keep the fire going. And it was Jesse who pitched the hay out of their loft for their animals.

As a school trustee, Jesse took his responsibilities very seriously, but then he was a solemn sort of fellow, Amy had thought, the first

241

time they met. He had sad eyes, which didn't often twinkle, a greying moustache and thin lips, which rarely smiled. Having lost his wife and only child in a fire some years back, he didn't have a lot to smile about. Most days he turned up in grubby blue work drills and a wide brimmed hat, which covered his receding hairline. He drank coffee with George, who would instruct him on what needed doing.

Amy fussed. How would they cope if George was crippled? If the leg became infected, who knows what might happen. She tried to put the thought out of her mind. Sam's shepherd costume still had to be made, so she found an old stripy towel which had been relegated to the dogs and washed it. It was a bit skimpy and thin, but when Miss Everard heard about the accident, she said she didn't mind, as long as he wore something.

On the evening of the school concert, Jesse appeared dressed in his smartest jacket under which he wore a matching waistcoat. He handed George a pair of crutches.

'You made these?' George said, admiring Jesse's handiwork. 'That's real kind of you.' He hauled himself up, pushing the crutches under his arms and with their aid, hobbled to the door.

'They're the right length. How did you manage that?'

'Lucky guess, eh?'

The schoolroom had been decorated and the tree stood in the corner, candles blazing, a golden star on top. A make-shift stage had been erected at the front and all the desks had been stacked out of the way at one end of the room. Everyone packed in, generating warmth not usually felt on a cold winter's day and when the concert began it never mattered who the current actors were, the applause was vigorous. Amy was relieved Sam remembered his few words.

Father Christmas arrived and excited children ran about while adults exchanged gossip, warming their hands around cups of coffee, made in an eight gallon cream can and kept hot on the stove.

'Mom, can you look after these?' Will shoved candy into her hand and ran off to his friends. As she placed them in her bag, she noticed Jesse chatting to Miss Everard who seemed to be taking in his every word. They looked like a couple, she thought and an amusing thought occurred to her. George had asked Jesse to join them for Christmas dinner and now she wondered what Miss Everard would be doing, but any hopes of match-making were abandoned when she overheard one mother telling another that Miss Everard was to join them for dinner.

Later, outside, horses were harnessed, sleigh bells rang in the still, crisp air and voices singing carols could be heard in the darkness as everyone departed for home.

On Christmas Eve, she and Will went with Jesse into town. As always, she was reminded of a grocery store in England, but it could just as easily have been a haberdashers, a shoe shop or even a milliners. The place was packed floor to ceiling with just about everything and smelt of kerosene, soap, spices, cheeses and dried fruit all mixed in with the strong aroma of roasting coffee. There were shelves of glass bottles, jars, tins and cartons and on the floor were cotton sacks of flour and potatoes and boxes of apples.

Jesse ambled off to chat to some friends who were drinking coffee, huddled round the stove at the far end of the store while Will gazed at the candy and she admired the selection of red, blue and green hand-knitted shawls on display. If only she had the money. She sighed. Things were bad but even before his accident, she'd had her suspicions. She might have been a silly young thing when they came out to Canada, but one fact she had long ago grasped was how everyone depended on the price of wheat. Even Bert Cooper who ran the store, would have been watching the price.

She turned her attention to the pile of books on the end of the oak counter – there to tempt someone like her. She opened 'The Great Gatsby' and began to read.

'Sure is a cold morning,' the storekeeper greeted her, looking smart in his brown suit and white shirt. At his neck was a matching brown tie.

Startled, she replaced the book on the counter.

'How's Mr Mills? How's the leg?'

'He's a bit better, thanks.'

'Give him my best wishes, won't you? Now what can I get you today?'

She produced her list. 'Some coffee, please, Bert, and I'd better take some sugar.'

'Suppose you heard young Ruth Corbett's got measles?' He looked in Will's direction as he placed the coffee on the counter.

'Oh, no. I suppose it'll be us next. Ruth was one of the shepherds with my boys at the concert.'

'There's been a bit of an epidemic so it sure won't be no surprise then, eh, Mrs Mills?'

'Let's hope we don't get it for Christmas.' She looked back at her list. 'Flour. I'd better take a bag.'

'Shall I take that?' He indicated her list. She nodded and watched him fetch a sack of flour then consult her list before gathering the other items – salt, baking powder, cod liver oil extract and 'Castle' Brand Superior Needles for the sewing machine. She had broken her last one stitching the towel for Sam's shepherd costume. She left Bert to it and sent Will to collect the mail, while she wandered around to see if there was anything she had overlooked.

The store became busy and she chatted to several neighbours while Jesse and Will loaded the supplies on the wagon.

'Now we've seen to the chores, what about you and me doing some man's work?' Jesse said to Will as they climbed in the wagon. 'Why don't we go and collect a tree for the house?'

It didn't quite make up for the lack of candy, she thought, but when they returned with a small spruce tree, it was fun decorating it.

On Christmas morning, Will appeared in their bedroom much later than expected. He complained of a headache and his face was very white. Amy reluctantly pushed a hand out from under the covers and felt his forehead. He had a temperature and while she slipped into her dressing gown, he slumped onto the floor at her feet.

'You've probably got the measles.' She helped him up and put her arm round him. 'Come on. Back to bed with you.'

'He must be sick,' George said, when there was no argument.

'Looks like I'll be doing the milking on my own today.'

'No you won't. I'll help. I'll use my crutches.'

For the first time for over a week, he hobbled across the yard, and sitting on the stool with his leg stretched out to one side, milked a couple of the cows. They returned to the house for breakfast to find that Sam and Bobbie had eaten all of the candy found in their Christmas stockings. Sam looked pale. She felt his hot head and knew he too was sickening for whatever bug it was. The candy did not stay in his stomach long and he, too, was soon tucked up in bed.

This is not how it's supposed to be, she thought as she prepared dinner. Now she hadn't one but three invalids to look after, but the more worrying thing was how George winced in pain whenever anything touched his leg. He wouldn't let her examine it, but she was almost certain it had become infected and when Jesse arrived, she asked his advice.

'Don't look good and it don't smell too good either,' he said inspecting the wound after George, with great protests, had allowed him to remove the bandages. It was a mass of dried blood and inflamed skin.

'I told him not to help with the milking, but he insisted. It really wasn't necessary and now see what's happened.'

'Doing the milking didn't make it septic,' George argued.

Jessie rubbed his large gnarled fingers along his jaw line. 'Without seeing a doc, it's hard to know what to do but you could try a bread poultice. Not sure if it'll work but that's what my mother swore by. Bread poultice. Reckoned it always worked.'

'Bread?' They both repeated.

'Yep. That's what she used.'

George looked doubtful.

'We have to try something,' Amy decided and went to the bread bin.

Under Jesse's instruction, she wrapped a chunk of bread in clean linen, placed it in a bowl and poured boiling water over it. Then, after squeezing out the cloth, she opened it out and placed it on George's leg.

His intake of breath was sharp. 'Shit. That's hot.'

Jesse was unsympathetic. 'Hotter the better.' He supervised as she replaced the bandages. 'Do the same tomorrow.'

Between running up to look in on Will and Sam, she worked in the kitchen, occasionally putting her head round the door of the sitting

245

room to join in the conversation. Bobbie played quietly with his lead soldiers and Mac and Spot were stretched out either side of the fire.

'Dreadful business – all those suicides,' Jesse said, referring to the Wall Street crash. 'Guess it could have been me. Thought about buying shares myself when I had a good crop in '28. Put it on deposit at the bank instead. Not so sure it was the right thing either with all these banks going out of business.'

'Some of these idiots borrowed money to buy shares. They were living in a fool's paradise and they got what they deserved. All too greedy. At least when the crash came, you didn't owe anything.'

Jesse nodded. 'Yeah, but I still aint too sure about these banks. My mattress might be a safer bet.'

George laughed. 'I wish it was my problem but at least we have a roof over our heads, unlike some of these youngsters. They've got nothing. I guess we ought to count our blessings. When I was in town last – before I put myself in dock – I counted at least six hoboes on the train headed west.'

'Riding the rods, yeah, for what good it does 'em,' Jesse said.

'Riding the rods?' She had caught the tail end of the conversation.

'Dinner smells good,' George said, catching a whiff of roast chicken.

'Sure does.' Jesse nodded.

'What do you mean riding the rods?'

'Hitching a free lift on the rail road. Hoboes - heading west, looking for work. No work round these parts.' Jesse shook his head. 'I heard things are getting pretty bad in Winnipeg and it aint no joke, this wheat price.'

George changed the subject. 'Tell me about the fair at Brandon.'

'Now that sure is a good show. I got a prize for my cattle once.' He beamed at them. 'Gee, you have to go. Next July. I'll take you.'

'It'd be something to look forward to,' she said.

The conversation continued over dinner but later, while she cleared away the dishes, both Jesse and George fell asleep. It had been the quietest Christmas ever, she thought when it was time for bed.

Each morning, Amy applied the bread poultice to George's leg but several days later, when she undid the bandage, it was still red and wild. She began to worry the infection was travelling up the leg.

'I don't like the look of this.' She pointed to the inflammation. 'Please let me get the doctor. He can take a look at the boys too.'

'Give it a bit more time.'

She was doubtful.

'Till the end of the week. Let's leave it to the end of the week.'

It was six days and six more bread poultices before there was any noticeable improvement to his leg and by then the boys were covered in spots and beginning to recover.

'I told you it'd get better, given time,' George said slipping his trouser leg over the smaller dressing Amy had applied.

'You'd better not put weight on it for a while yet. It still might open the wound.'

'I'll have to get on my feet sometime. We can't rely on Jesse to chop firewood and haul feed forever.'

The long winter months crept by and with very low temperatures and three hungry boys to feed, Amy began to worry about her store. The summer had been extremely hot and she had been too late with her planting to grow the variety and quantity of vegetables she relied on. The potato crop was very small and there had been a shortage of wild berries. At the end of November, George had killed a hog, butchered it then stored it in a big wooden box, which he had secured to the roof of the hog house where the meat froze but with the chickens no longer laying eggs and with the milk yield very low, they had made big inroads into their supplies. By mid-February, he was considering killing one of the cows in order to eke out the feed.

'There's very little pork left and there isn't too much in our store either,' Amy said when he discussed it with her.

'It might help then, if I kill one of the cows. The trouble is, they won't be that good for eating – no meat on them.'

'There's lots of goodness in oxtail soup. Better than starving.'

'Things aren't as bad as that.'

247

'Yet.'

He frowned. 'I've thought about asking Jesse if he's got any spare feed, but how do I pay him?'

She, too, had been thinking about their predicament and wanted to write home. Her mother had yet to reply to any of her letters, but the failure of the rains wasn't their fault and surely she wouldn't want them to go hungry? But there was no point in suggesting it. George would be never agree. If he couldn't feed his family, he would see it as his failure and he was so stubborn he would never ask for credit at the store either. Although she didn't approve of debt, she knew if the boys were starving, she'd swallow her pride.

Two weeks later, the day after Amy used the last potato, she shook out the flour sack and stared at the meagre amount in the mixing bowl. It would be a very scanty pie crust for dinner that day and tomorrow she knew there would only be soup. George would have to give her some of their few cents but how much food would that buy? They couldn't go on like this. Damn it, George, she would write home. She opened the kitchen drawer, found some notepaper and began to compose a letter to Freddie. He would understand. Maybe he could send her money without George knowing. Pen poised, the noise of banging furniture and screams from upstairs interrupted her thoughts and she abandoned the letter in order to act as referee.

George returned for lunch earlier than she expected and limped into the kitchen hauling a sack behind him.

'What have you got there?'

'Jesse sent these over. Said he meant to bring them at Christmas.'

'Potatoes. Oh, George, what a God send. However did he know?'

'Said he'd bring some hay over later. I guess when I got sick, he saw how little feed there was.'

She studied George's face. It had taken a lot for him to accept Jesse's help. 'He's a kind man.'

'He thinks a lot of you and the boys.'

CHAPTER EIGHTEEN

The Dirty Thirties

George stood beside Jesse's shiny new tractor. He had admired the paintwork and now he was inspecting the engine, trying not to show his envy and reminding himself a tractor would never make up for losing a wife and child.

'With all these banks going belly up, I didn't trust 'em with my money and when I lost Beauty, the team didn't seem the same,' Jesse explained, but he didn't need to justify the purchase. George could only imagine how thrilled he would be to put a tractor in his barn and then be able to forget about it till next spring. There would be no mucking out, no grooming and no tack to clean or repair. But more wonderful would be the lack of worry about feed.

'Holy cow – look at that!' Jesse pointed to a twisting funnel cloud, which was growing blacker and larger by the second. To the right were six smaller funnels snaking like elephants' trunks down to the ground.

He looked in the direction Jesse pointed. Tornadoes! All heading in their direction but one in particular, was terrifying. It was bigger and blacker and closer.

'Jesus! Quick. The basement. I'll get Amy.'

They ran towards the house.

George wrenched open the door to find Amy and Bobbie sitting at the kitchen table. She was admiring his drawing.

'Look Daddy.' He held the paper up.

'There's a twister and it's coming our way.'

Amy dropped the pencil she was holding. 'Oh, my God.'

'Where are Will and Sam?'

'Upstairs.'

'In the basement. Both of you. Now,' he yelled and turned to race up the stairs two at a time.

Will had been reluctant but George hurried him into the cellar.

'I wanted to watch,' he told Jesse.

'You don't go looking at twisters, son,' he said following them down the stairs into the basement. 'Best thing is to get out of their way – right out of their way.'

'It'll be all right, won't it? I mean the house ...' Amy looked at George but he didn't reply. He had seen tornadoes often enough, but this was the first time they were in its path. He remembered Ellie telling them about a cyclone hitting Portage in 1922. Freight cars were blown right off the rail track, houses destroyed, barns demolished. As he listened to the deep roar of the wind, his heart was heavy with fear. He could feel the walls shaking and, in the dim flicker of the candle, looked at Jesse to see if he had noticed, but Jesse was keeping Will occupied. He'd have made a good father.

'How fast does the wind go?' Will asked.

Jesse thought a moment. 'Now let me see. Faster 'n my tractor. Faster even than a galloping horse.' He shrugged. 'Who knows.'

'Gee. Really? Wish I could see it.'

'It aint safe, Will. Even when the twister's gone through, the storm can be pretty bad. Hail stones – sometimes as big as this.' Jesse held up his fist. 'Sure don't want to be out in that. Kill a man easy. I seen a herd a cattle knocked down dead by hail.'

Panic leapt into Will's face. 'Spot. Where's Spot? And Mac. I have to go get them.'

'No. No, Will. You stay here.' George barred the stairs. There was no way he was letting anyone risk their life for a dog.

'But Spot. He's out there.'

'He'll find somewhere to hide. Animals know what to do. He'll be fine.'

'Sure wish I left my cash in the bank.' Jesse grinned. 'It might have been safer after all. That wind could pick up a tractor, easy.'

'Your tractor'd better not demolish my house.' George wagged his finger at Jesse.

'How can you joke at a time like this,' Amy said.

George gave her a sympathetic look and put his hand on her shoulder. He'd experienced a twister once before, but she hadn't. 'Honey, there's not much else to do, is there?'

The children sat on a pile of empty flour sacks, but after half an hour, they were bored and he instigated a game of 'Eye Spy'. It entertained them, but it didn't take his mind off what was going on above. In the candle light they were beginning to run out of subjects when he decided to see if it was safe for them to come out of the basement.

'Stay here,' He said as he climbed the cellar steps. He opened the door a crack and listened to the roar of the wind. He could hear something banging outside. Was it the barn or was it the door to the house? He didn't remember shutting it and now he'd probably have to repair it but if that was all, he knew they would have got off lightly.

There was nothing out of place in the kitchen, so he pushed the door fully open and climbed the remaining two steps. He looked up and was relieved to see the ceiling. The thought registered that the house was still intact as, in the kitchen at least, the windows were unbroken. In fact everything was as they had left it. Through the window he could see a pail, rolling about in the wind and a scattered pile of wood, but the barn was still standing, though its door, as he suspected, was half off its hinges.

He exhaled slowly, hardly daring to believe their luck. He turned back to get the others, but Jesse was already at the top of the stairs and he, too, rushed to the window.

'Holy cow, it must have veered off in another direction. Gee a twister like that sure must have wrecked something. Better go check out your cattle.'

George opened the back door and they struggled against the gusting wind, banging the door shut behind them and crossing to the barn. The horses whinnied as they entered.

George went into the stalls, checking each horse for injuries.

'All right, Buster, old boy,' he said in a soothing voice. 'It's gone now and you're fine. Just fine.' He ran his hands down the horse's front legs and Buster snorted down his neck.

Outside, they spotted some minor roof damage. Next they walked down the track to check on the cattle.

'Holy smoke, look at that.' Jesse pointed to the line of cottonwood trees, which grew along the edge of the creak. Several of them had been snapped off feet from the ground, while two others had been uprooted. Beyond that, fences, wire and posts as far as they could see had been ripped up and rolled together by the force of the twister. Spooked and jittery cattle were wandering out onto the road.

'Where's that damn dog. He's never here when I need him,' George complained as he and Jesse ran about trying to herd the cattle into a paddock, where most of the fencing had survived.

'I guess he's hiding somewhere,' Jesse said. 'Can't say I blame him.'

The path of the tornado had been narrow but they had been spared severe damage. He hoped all their neighbours had been as lucky and returned for tools to repair some of the fences.

'Sure glad none of them is pregnant.' George hammered several nails to secure the barbed wire fence, which Jesse held in place. He stood up and examined his work. It wasn't perfect, but it would have to do until he could replace more of the posts. He studied the cattle. There were two calves. 'They don't seem too bad, considering. A month or so earlier and heaven knows what would have happened.'

Jesse nodded. 'Guess we was lucky the direction it took. I'll mosey on down to Corbett's' place. It headed their way.'

When George returned to the house, the children were making a big fuss of Spot and Mac.

'I found them, Dad,' Will said. 'In the barn, behind the wagon. They were real scared and Spot wouldn't come out for ages. Look, he's still shaking.'

'And look at my bread,' Amy said pointing to the small loaf which was cooling on a rack.

'We got off lightly,' George said. 'Very lightly. If all that's happened is a few head of cattle loose and a ruined loaf of bread, I'm not complaining.'

He slipped off his boots and sat in the nearest chair. He was weary and knew the following day he would have to patch-up fences and clear away storm debris not to mention any repairs the roof might need.

A week later, as he was coming out of the barn, he spotted a large cloud. He gazed at it, awestruck by its sheer size. It was taller than any mountain range and stretched in either direction as far as he could see, but it was more like a rolling cloud of smoke and was travelling at speed towards them. The sun became a reddish ball before disappearing and the sky became brown. It was only an hour since lunch, but it could have been twilight. Instinct took over and he ran into the house.

Amy was flicking through her collection of recipes, while the boys were playing at camps under the table.

'Quick all of you. Down in the cellar.'

'Not again.' She looked up from the recipe she was reading. 'Surely not again.'

'There's a storm headed our way. Don't mess around, it'll be here in seconds.' George picked Bobbie up and ushered them all into the basement.

It was some time later when they emerged.

'Just look at the mess,' Amy said staring about in horror and disbelief. She began to cough.

Dust hung thick in the air. It had crept in through windows and doors, settling on every surface and she held her handkerchief to her nose. The entire kitchen was covered in fine dirt – cups and saucers put out for coffee – the pile of neatly stacked ironing – even the dough, left to rise near the cooker.

'We can't eat this. Look at it,' she said, but knew she would have to scrape the surface.

A quantity of dirt had accumulated in one corner of the kitchen floor and they could feel the grit beneath their feet.

'Oh, George, this is too awful.' She was in the living room. 'How did it all get in here?'

'Through the cracks in the floorboards, I shouldn't wonder.' George peered over her shoulder. 'It's not as bad in here. You didn't have the windows open.'

'But it's a scorching hot day and it's unbearably stuffy. I have to have some windows open. You try baking in this heat. How often shall we have to put up with this?'

In the bedrooms, the floors, the window sills, books, shelves, toys – all were covered in a fine dust. They coughed and sneezed as they swept and dusted. She stripped the beds and washed the bedding but when she went outside to hang it to dry, the visibility was so poor she couldn't make out the barn. A thick fog hung over them. When she returned later to collect the washing, the sheets and pillowcases were a dirty grey. Tears crept into her eyes. They might be patched but she prided herself on white sheets.

For several more days the wind blew, a steady, hot wind and in spite of closed windows the dust penetrated everywhere. George spent one evening pushing old newspapers and rags into cracks in the floor boards and round the windows, sending Will and Sam to look for any he'd missed. It was three days before they could see more than a hundred feet from the house and over the next couple of months the wind blew almost ceaselessly, but they were grateful when the clouds of dust were only ever seen on the horizon.

* * *

That autumn was pleasantly warm and dry and there was a small harvest but George no longer felt excited in the way he had once. Instead he was depressed because there was no choice, he had to sell, whatever the price. They were desperate for the cash. He tried not to dwell too long on his worries and even though he didn't feel like celebrating, for Amy's sake, went along to the harvest dinner held in the Speer's barn.

'Reckon that soil came out of Saskatchewan,' Jesse said referring the dust storm. 'Archie over there says they want it back, but I heard it blew on all the way to Toronto.' He shook his head. 'Sure don't know what those city folks are going to do with it.'

He laughed though he didn't consider it a joke and changed the subject.

'I heard the Corbett family have given up. That storm – it could have been us.' Out of the corner of his eye, he could see Amy talking to Miss Everard and recalled how, after Jesse left on Christmas night, she had told him she thought they'd make a lovely couple. He hoped she wasn't trying her hand at match making.

'Yeah, I heard they went east. Got family in Toronto.' Jesse said with his mouth full. 'Bad do. Their house was a real mess after that twister went through. I heard they lost four cows.'

He wanted to ask whether there had been a farm sale, but what difference would it make? He didn't have any money. He glanced in Amy's direction and his stomach turned. She and Miss Everard were heading in their direction. He glanced back at Jesse and wondered if he knew what was about to hit him.

'Evening, Miss Everard.' He nodded politely. 'Have you come to tell me how bad my boys are doing?'

Miss Everard laughed. 'No and anyway, you know as well as I do, they're both bright boys.'

'Miss Everard – er – Molly, is joining us for dinner on Monday, George. Isn't that nice?' Amy's voice was smooth and she avoided his gaze. Inside he seethed. Jesse always came over on Mondays. He usually brought some of his potato wine and they put the world to

255

rights. Now he would have to watch what he said. The evening would be ruined. Women.

'I'm glad you're here, Miss Everard.' Jesse looked at George then at Amy, then back at the teacher. 'Do you mind if we excuse ourselves and talk school business for a minute?

'Sure, sure.' George immediately agreed. 'Amy and I have a few things to straighten out, too.' He grabbed her by the elbow and, guided her out of earshot, hissing in her ear. 'What do you mean by inviting Miss Everard. You know damn well Jesse always comes that evening.'

'That's the whole point, George. They'll never get together if somebody doesn't give them a push.'

'You shouldn't interfere.'

'I'm not. I'm merely er – facilitating is that the word? They'll never get together otherwise.'

'Facilitating? Facilitating?' His eyebrows shot up in amazement. Amy's choice of words was incredible. Was that what education did for you? Well, he was far more practical. 'For heaven's sake, Amy, what the hell are you going to feed them?'

'Oh, I'll think of something.' She was looking in Jesse and Miss Everard's direction and missed his worried expression. 'Look at them. Don't they make a handsome couple?'

He looked up at the rafters and shook his head. She was exasperating. Did she never listen to anything he said?

Despite his irritation with Amy, he had enjoyed the evening – one of the few chances there was to chat to neighbours. There were no sad faces. Everyone laughed and danced as though they hadn't a care in the world. He looked around at the smiling faces. Did they all have cash in the bank – cash acquired when the harvests were good? Was he really the only one with a shortfall?

The following Monday's dinner party was more successful than even he had dared hope and, rather grudgingly, he admitted to himself Amy was right. Jesse did have an eye for Miss Everard and, having watched them over dinner, he rather suspected she might also be attracted to Jesse. He wasn't too happy about entertaining the school mistress, though. He thought it might make difficulties for the boys, but Amy had made sure they were tucked up in bed well before their guests arrived. Later, when he went to fetch a book, he caught Sam at the bottom of the stairs, but that apart, the guests would not have known there were children in the house.

'What brought you to these parts, Molly?' Amy asked.

George looked up. He still found it difficult to call her Molly, but it hadn't taken Amy long to establish first name terms. He watched as she offered her freshly baked bread and wondered how she had come by the flour.

'My husband actually.'

'Oh. I – er, sorry I didn't know you were married.' She apologized.

He glanced at Jesse, whose eyes were down on his plate but he could tell by the way he was fingering the cutlery, he was listening.

'No, not many people do. You see, we got married hours before he caught a train to Winnipeg. He was a soldier and, like so many, he didn't make it back.' She held up her hand. 'And I don't wear his ring, so you weren't to know.'

'I'm sorry. I shouldn't have asked,' Amy said.

'Please don't concern yourself. It's all a long time ago now and I moved here because I was alone in the world and he had a sister and a mother. Mrs Holt died some years back and Susan and I – well, after that, we didn't get on too well. She sold up. I stayed. It was for the best.'

'So you became a teacher?' George said, wondering what was on the plate Amy put in front of him. He identified a couple of pieces of meat. It smelt rather good and, when he took a mouthful, tasted delicious. How had she managed to concoct such an appetizing meal out of the scraps he had seen earlier in the kitchen?

'I was teaching before I married, so it seemed sensible to go on with it, and, well, to be honest, that was the reason for keeping my maiden name.' Molly glanced in Jesse's direction and catching his eye, immediately looked away again. 'The school boards generally prefer unmarried ladies.'

'That's true,' Jesse nodded. 'Never could understand why.'

'George was in the Army, you know,' Amy said.

257

He felt their eyes on him.

'Everyone did their bit,' he said. Damn it. Why did she have to bring that up now? He didn't want to talk about the war. He felt for his watch and thought of Alfie. All the same, it would have been nice to ask what regiment Molly's husband had been in – whether he'd been at Passchendaele or Vimy, but the subject held too many horrible memories – memories he didn't want to think about. He was glad Jesse changed the subject, wanting to know what was being planned for the Christmas concert.

'Good gracious,' Molly exclaimed. 'I can't divulge such secrets. I would never be forgiven. The children put together much of that concert themselves, you know. I just choose the hymns and the readings.'

'But the songs? You must help with that, surely?' Jesse persisted.

'That's as maybe but it's still their choice.'

Amy turned to Jesse. 'What about telling us a bit more about yourself, Jesse. We've known you all this time, but you've never told us …' She broke off and glanced in George's direction and despite his warning look, ploughed on. 'That is you've never told me how you lost family. Why, I don't even know whether you had a son or a daughter.'

'Amy.' George frowned. Did she have no discretion?

To his relief, Jesse seemed very relaxed about being interrogated.

'Gee, I thought it was common knowledge. I forgot you folks are new here. Know you so well, thought you knew all there was to know about me.' Jesse paused then looked across at Molly before continuing. 'It was 1926. A fire – a prairie fire. I was told after, it was the biggest in years but I don't know exactly what happened. I'd been to Winnipeg to prove up my section and I remember I was feeling real pleased with myself ' cos I'd cleared enough land and had some real decent crops. I got the papers all signed and stamped and I thought I was set fair. I even made plans to buy another quarter section.' He drew a deep breath. 'Just goes to show. You never know what the good Lord has in line for you. I came back to find my neighbours charging about ploughing a fire break, fetching water from the creak and a team of 'em beating at the fire with anything they could get their hands on, but it was no good.' He shook his head. 'It was no good. I lost everything that day. My crop and both of them. Lizzy, my little girl and my wife.'

They were silent. It was Molly who spoke first.

'Jesse, that's terrible. It must have been awful for you.' She smiled at him and he smiled back.

George met Amy's eyes and could hear her saying I told you so.

'Yep. Gained a farm and lost a family all on one day. Spent the next couple of years re-building my house and learning how to be a bachelor again. The hand you get dealt, you can't change and 'sides, if you don't get a knock-back somewhere along, then you're damned lucky, that's what I say.'

'Seems we have a lot in common,' Molly said and the conversation passed onto lighter topics.

George noticed how Jesse laughed loudly at all of Molly's jokes and whenever Molly spoke, he could have sworn it was as though she was speaking specifically to Jesse.

'There, didn't I tell you it would be just fine,' Amy said as they stood on the doorstep and watched Jesse help Molly into his gig. 'I didn't know Jesse had such a fine carriage – ideal for the two of them.'

He grunted. He wasn't going to admit she was right. They waved as the horses set off.

'I bet we hear wedding bells soon.' She shut the door.

'I still think you should let nature takes its course.'

'Oh, don't be so stuffy. There's nothing like giving nature a helping hand occasionally. You've said so yourself and more than once.'

'I was talking farming. This is different.'

'I can't see any difference at all and besides it's time Jesse had a woman in his life. Didn't you notice how much he smiled tonight? I've never known him like it. Usually he's so dry and dull. It was nice to see him cheerful.'

* * *

Winter was approaching and, while he went about his preparations, George had a strange feeling it was going to be unpleasant. This foreboding was well founded when the winter snows failed to materialize. Temperatures were the warmest for years and he knew it was a bad sign. They relied on winter snows. He walked the fields, watching with increasing anxiety, the way the soil was caught up and whisked away. Dust devils. Tiny little tornadoes. Harmless – or were they? They could so easily become big dust clouds, lifting up his beautiful soil and taking it away. He bent down and scooped a handful, then held out his palm, watching the particles disappear on the wind.

They had been so happy when they arrived here. They both loved the house, the scenery, the creak, the hills, the town – everything. The boys were settled at the school. But without snow and its melt in the spring and with this persistent drying wind what chance was there of ever growing a decent crop? He looked down at his empty hand. The wind had taken everything.

CHAPTER NINETEEN

'I'm sick of washing up,' Amy said. 'Sick of it.'

Out of the window, she could see whirling dust – a black blizzard. It was as dark as night – yet another of the dust storms which had screeched into their area early in the New Year. It was too warm for snow and it felt as though the sun had taken a holiday. The high winds and darkness lasted for days and the dust was endless. Once she had caught Sam fingering an 'S' on the surface of his plate. Since then, washing up had become a ritual before as well as after dinner.

George was on his way to the barn, but stopped and put an arm round her shoulder and dropped a kiss on her cheek. 'I know it's hard, honey, but it sure can't go on much longer. Anyway – '

Whatever he had been going to say was taken away in a bout of coughing which racked his whole body and alarmed her by its force. When the coughing subsided, he suggested turning the plates upside down until she was ready to use them. 'That way only the bottoms get dusty.'

She considered this for a moment. 'Mmm. That's not a bad idea.'

He descended into another spell of coughing.

She grabbed a cup from the clean stack and filled it with water. 'All this dust. It's not doing you any good and it can't be healthy for the boys either.'

For weeks now, she had been concerned for his health. Freddie hadn't been the only one in the trenches to experience gas. George's lungs were weakened and at night his wheezy breathing kept her awake. She watched him take a sip of water before saying what they both knew had been in her mind for weeks.

'We can't go on like this ...' she began.

He lifted his coat off the hook behind the door. She could tell by the straightness of his back, he was resolute, but the lack of an answer irritated her. Could he not see this life was killing them all?

'I want to go home – back to England.'

'This is home.' He slipped into his coat and did the buttons up.

'You know what I mean.' She addressed his back. Why, after all this time, was he so stubborn? It was obvious, even to Will, things were verging on the impossible.

When he turned, his face was set with determination. 'We're not beaten yet.'

She wanted to shake him, but instead she exhaled a long breath. She must stay calm. She knew by experience, how losing her temper made him more determined and when they fell out, he slunk into himself and there were long silences between them. Now, more than ever, they needed to talk.

'Haven't we tried enough? Haven't we suffered enough,' she said in measured tones.

'I'm not giving up. This is our home.'

'But nobody would think any the worse of you – us. I'm so worried, George. Our stores are so low and the boys are always complaining they're hungry. I try to make things go as far as I can, but there's never enough to fill their stomachs.'

He avoided her eyes. 'Fares across the Atlantic don't come cheap. We haven't got the money.'

'Please let me write home,' she pleaded. 'Mother would send the fares, I'm sure she would.' His thunderous look made her change tack. 'Freddie, then. He's helped us in the past. Please – for the boys.' Her voice cracked and she fought back tears. 'I don't think I can take much more.'

'I forbid you to write. We don't need help. We're staying.'

He tied a scarf around his neck, lifted it up over his nose and, without another word, opened the door and went out.

'We're not just staying – we're starving,' she muttered and tears ran down her cheeks. 'Can't you see what you're doing to us all?' she sobbed as she returned to the dishes, not seeing if they were clean or dirty and no longer caring.

She wept again when she inspected the ironing. She held up a sheet and disgusted by its greyness, threw it back on the pile. If only they hadn't moved. It might not have been the most wonderful farm but at least they weren't starving. There had been nothing to spare, but they never went hungry. She thought of England and a pang of homesickness knifed through her, a terrible longing for the smell of damp mud and the lush grass of a Buckinghamshire field. If only it wasn't so far away.

What a mistake their move had been. They knew a thing or two in Winnipeg when they said there was no danger of flooding. And then there was that man on the train ... He had known, too, hadn't he? "Out of the frying pan?" They were well and truly in the fire now. No money, no food, no snow – only dust. Dust that got in food, up your nostrils, into your mouth, penetrated the inside of closets, and even got into bed with you. One morning when she sat up, the dust had rolled down the quilt like ripples across water. There was no escaping. She felt dirty – everything was dirty. Outside was worse. You were lucky if you could see a hundred feet. Where was the sun and the glorious blue sky, the vast whiteness, which she had once cursed, but for which now she longed?

* * *

Winter seemed interminable, but there was one bright spot when Jesse and Molly were married in early January.

'This has to beat household chores,' Amy said taking the glass George was offering.

'You were right. They are ideal for each other,' he conceded as he sat beside her in Jesse's living room along with the other guests who had been invited back after the ceremony.

'I do like it when I can say told you so,' she giggled but her eyes were on Molly, taking in the fashionable long waisted blue dress and T-bar shoes. A wedding should mean new clothes. Instead she felt scruffy in her threadbare brown suit which, she was annoyed to discover, had needed taking in. 'They're made for each other and I knew it the minute I saw them together.'

263

'I don't know how you do it. How could you tell?'

She laughed at his scepticism and touched her nose. 'Call it woman's intuition. And to think it might not have happened if I hadn't invited them over for dinner.'

'Huh. It would've happened eventually anyway.'

'I wouldn't describe Jesse as the fastest worker,' she whispered. 'If I hadn't given them a helping hand, who knows how long it would have taken.'

'Let's be upstanding for a toast to the bride and groom,' Bert Cooper's voice boomed out above the buzz of conversation.

They got to their feet.

'Molly and Jesse,' they all said in unison.

It was the highlight in an otherwise dull and dusty January. It meant another teacher had to be found for the school, but nobody seemed to mind. Amy felt vindicated and even George said he had never known Jesse so cheerful.

* * *

Somehow they survived winter with its appalling shortages.

'I reckon provided the rains come, there should be just about enough moisture in the soil for us to get a crop of some sort,' George said one May morning after he had inspected the ground.

She gave him a scornful look. Was he serious? She had had difficulty enough eking out the food this winter and if next was no better, she dreaded the consequences.

'Some sort of crop? Be realistic. The boys are growing. They need food. Good food and lots of it. If the rains don't come, we won't have vegetables to eat never mind anything else. Let me write home. I'm sure mother or Freddie would help. They're family and families help each other.'

'I said no and I meant it. The mortgage on this place is more than enough for one man. Apart from that, I've never borrowed a bean and I'm not starting now,' he said, his voice getting louder. 'And I'm not crawling to your brother or your mother or anyone.'

She pounded the rolling pin down onto the table, careless this was the very last pie she could make until they bought more flour. 'Damn your pride, George. Oh, why are you so obstinate?'

He banged his cup on the table, stood up and glared at her. 'You are not to write to your mother,' he yelled. 'Or Freddie, for that matter. I forbid it.'

She wanted to shout back at him, to rap him round the head with the rolling pin, throw the pie at him – anything. Why didn't he see what he was doing?

'You said you love me, so please let me write.' Careless of her floury hands, she put her arms around his neck. 'Please, George, if only for me.'

He reached up and caught her hands behind his neck. She held her breath. Had she won him round? Then with a sigh, he unwrapped himself from her embrace. 'I've got things to do.'

'Can't you see you're killing us? You'd rather see us all starve,' she yelled at the closed door.

* * *

The summer temperatures were high and the hot, drying wind blew unremittingly across the prairies. The soil, caught by Russian thistle, heaped up along fences until only the tops of the posts could be seen and by the end of June, although the crop had germinated, it was showing signs of severe stress. Any moisture had long since evaporated and the stalks were stunted. Things were bad, but George was still convinced rain would come. It only needed a thunderstorm and there was always a thunderstorm in summer wasn't there?

* * *

Amy was inspecting the shrivelled plants in the vegetable plot, while Bobbie poked about in the soil with a stick. Despite her watering, they were small. It grew dark and she looked up, dreading another dust storm, but the air was swarming – a cloud of grasshoppers so thick they blocked the sun. She stared for some seconds, stunned by the sight, astonished by the sound – millions and millions of whirring wings. She ran to the end of the row, lifted Bobbie into her arms and, as though her life depended upon it, ran to the house. By the time she reached the door, dozens were crawling in her hair. She stood Bobbie down and was horrified when she saw his hair, too, was alive with them.

'You look funny, Mom.'

'Yuk,' she said, standing on the doorstep and brushing them out of his hair, her hair and their clothes. It was hopeless. More arrived by the second. She opened the door and dragged him inside.

'Stay there, Bobbie. Stay there. I have to shut the windows.'

Ignoring the irritating pests which were crawling over her body and into her blouse, she rushed around the house, banging windows shut. Then she picked the insects out of Bobbie's hair, stamping on them as they fell to the floor. Next she stripped and shook out her own clothing. There were four dustpans full of dead bodies when she had finished clearing up and tears ran down her face. Bobbie stood watching and she turned her back to wipe her eyes.

'I can't take any more. Oh, George why are you so pig-headed? Why won't you let me write home?' she said aloud.

'Mom.' Bobbie tugged at her skirt. 'Mom, are the grasshoppers going to eat us?'

'No.' She turned and crouched down. 'No, of course not, poppet. We'll be just fine. You go and play, but you can't go out. Play upstairs. There's a good boy.'

What could she do to make George see reason? The rains were never coming. Didn't he know that? Just like the snows never came last winter and, now the grasshoppers were here, there would be nothing. They would all starve in this god-forsaken dust hole. Tears sprang into her eyes and she dabbed at them with her handkerchief. She would write home. She'd post the letter when she next went into town. George didn't always take her now Will was older. And if he wouldn't go back to England, she'd take the boys and go alone. She went to the drawer and found her pen and pad.

* * *

George had also seen the swarm of grasshoppers. He was walking along by the creek, Mac and Spot racing ahead. He planned to inspect

266

a field up towards Jesse's place and thought he would call in and scrounge a cup of coffee – see if married life was still suiting him. The sight of the muddy channel alarmed him. The cattle needed water. He changed direction and headed towards a slough which was usually full of water in the spring. If need be, he could bring the cattle up there to water them.

The cloud passed high over his head, temporarily blotting out the sun and then on down towards the house. He stopped and watched it disappear and instinctively knew it had settled on the wheat – his wheat. Tears of frustration crept into his eyes. Damn it. The sun had already shrivelled the crop. Now there were grasshoppers. How much must a man take? He looked up to the heavens. God, why have you forsaken me? Have I sinned that badly? First you send floods and now you send drought and grasshoppers. What have I done? What are you trying to tell me? Go back to England? He kicked at the earth and watched the dust disappear on the wind. No, he would not give in. Never. Never.

He rubbed his eyes with the back of his hand. He had come through a war – nothing could be worse than that. He owed it to Alfie and all the others he'd fought alongside. This was his country, his land and he would never give it up. He whistled the dogs and walked on to the slough, determination in every stride. There would be water there.

* * *

'Hi,' he called when he returned to the house. He tried to inject some cheer into his voice, though he didn't feel any. He had found very little water at the slough. 'Did you see that swarm of grasshoppers go over?'

Amy closed the writing pad and pushed it out of sight into the drawer of the table. 'Swarm. Oh, yes. Grasshoppers. They swarmed all right. All over me and dozens got into the house. As if I don't have enough to do. I swept up four dustpans full of them.'

'Did you kill them?'

'Of course I did. Ugh.'

'They're eating our crop,' he said, but didn't add there would be nothing left when they were gone and there was nothing he could do about it. He wondered if the pad she had pushed into the drawer was a shopping list or whether, despite all he had said, she was writing home. He didn't ask – he couldn't face another argument.

'And they've eaten my vegetables. I know what this means, George. I wasn't born yesterday. I know only too well what it means.'

'It might not be that bad, honey.' He tried to make light of it.

'Not that bad?'

He saw her withering look and knew there was no way he could conceal the truth.

'For heaven's sake, George, for once, face facts. It's a total disaster and you're deluded if you can't see it.' She opened a cupboard and grabbed some plates which she placed face down on the table. 'I have to get tea. The boys'll be home from school soon.'

He knew he had to say something – do something, but what? 'Honey, I want to talk to you.'

'I can write home?'

'No. Not that.'

'There's nothing to discuss then, is there?'

'I thought I'd …' He reached in his pocket and felt the smooth metal of his watch. Alfi would understand. 'I know we're short of cash, so I'm going to take this into town.' He held out the watch. 'It must be worth something.'

'Alfie's watch? You can't sell that.'

George sighed. 'I don't know what else to do.'

For a fleeting second there was compassion in her eyes as she put her arms around him and they stood for some minutes locked together in silence. Then he looked down at her and kissed her.

'I'll sell Alfie's watch and we'll get through this, you'll see.'

* * *

Next morning they went into town. Amy couldn't bear to listen to Bert and George bargaining, so she took Bobbie's hand and went to collect the mail.

'I hear you got grasshoppers,' Bert was saying when she re-joined them at the counter. She could tell by George's face, the deal had been struck. 'Sure been a bad season. Everyone's the same. Heard they stopped the railroad. Made a real slimy mess. Train slithered to a halt. Couldn't grip the rails. They'll eat anything. Shouldn't be surprised if we get no crop at all this year.'

'No need to be so cheerful, Bert,' George said and picked up the sack of flour.

Amy shuddered at the thought of thousands of grasshoppers – munching their way right across Canada. She picked up the remaining packages and hurried to the door. She didn't want to discuss grasshoppers or the drought or the lack of money with Bert or anyone else for that matter. They had sold Alfie's watch and that had been hard enough.

'Is this all we got?' She stared in disbelief at the few items they had between them. She had given George a much longer list.

'Bert said it wasn't worth much. I gave him the list and he picked the items he reckoned we'd need most.'

'Oh.' She scowled at him. Bert had offered them a loan. She had overheard that much of the conversation.

'I won't accept credit,' George said as though reading her thoughts.

They loaded the wagon and sat Bobbie in the back with the supplies. Amy climbed up beside George. She tipped the brim of her hat to shield her eyes and mopped her brow with her handkerchief, then glanced over her shoulder at their meagre purchases.

'Those won't last long. I already make pies with more air than anything else. What do I do when I've used up that measly bag of flour?'

George didn't answer but picked up the reins. The wagon moved off and the journey was completed in silence.

* * *

The grasshoppers left the way they had come – in a huge cloud which obliterated the sun and when George walked the fields, there

269

was nothing left – everything devoured by an army of chomping insects. He stood with his back to the house and stared at the empty field. What should have been a golden carpet of wheat was brown and threadbare. His beautiful crop – gone. Bending down, he ran his hand over the stubs and wept.

When he stood up moments later, he was resolute. There had to be a way. The early pioneers had survived. He would. Men had left their farms at times like these and found work in towns. But what work was there? None. He thought of the hoboes – all in search of work. In the last year things had got pretty bad and there had been crowds of them, jumping into the rear car as the train clattered slowly along and slinking away when there was any sign of a ticket collector. So what chance did he have of finding work when so many others were already looking? May be if he went back to Portage he could join a threshing gang. There had been rain there – north of them. There might be a crop to thresh. It might be worth a try.

* * *

When Amy inspected her vegetable plot, she was overwhelmed by the devastation. The dog had followed and nuzzled her hand, as though in sympathy.

'All that hard work, Mac and for nothing.'

For several days her mind had been preoccupied with what they could sell. She was cross she hadn't thought of it before. If Bert had taken George's watch, then he would surely take her jewellery. Indoors, she went up to their bedroom and found her jewel box, tipping its contents onto the bed, turning the few items over to inspect them. The necklace Freddie gave her one Christmas, the little silver cross which was a Christening present, the battered locket which had gone to the Western Front. Then she picked up the gold locket. She studied the two pictures inside. George had been so handsome then and now he was thin and his hair was greying. She stared at her own picture. She had been young and beautiful. She stood at the dressing table and studied her reflection. A gaunt face stared back. She put the locket to her lips, then gently closed it and placed it back in the box. She had made a decision.

After the children had gone to bed, they sat on the porch together enjoying the cooler twilight air. It was still – the sky purple and red – a rare perfect evening. As the sun disappeared over the horizon, they sat in the stillness, taking in the beauty.

'I've been thinking ...' she broke the silence.

'Please don't start, Amy.' His eyes were closed. 'I'm too tired to argue and you know I don't want you writing any begging letter –'

'Oh, listen, will you. Today I had an idea. Why don't we sell my locket? It must be worth at least as much as Alfie's watch – probably more.'

George yawned and stretched his weary limbs, giving her a weak smile, then slowly shook his head. 'No, I don't think that's a good idea.'

'But we need the money.'

'I said no.' He closed his eyes again. 'Let's leave it, shall we?'

She stared at him in the dimming light and knew it was futile to argue. Their purchases might keep them going another week or so and, if she was really very careful, possibly a month. But what then? She remembered the partly written letter and resolved to finish it. She might have promised to love and obey, but surely in these circumstances, God would forgive her?

'Jesse said he and Molly were going into town tomorrow. Now we don't have any chickens, I need some eggs. I can't do much without them. Do you mind if I go?' He didn't reply and when she looked, he was asleep.

The next morning, as soon as the boys had left for school, Jesse's wagon arrived in the yard and, since George had declined to accompany her, she went alone with him and Molly.

'We won't be long,' Molly said as they got down from the wagon. She was holding a large round tin in her hands. 'Just wanted to drop some cookies into May. She's not been too well and I said I'd try and visit ages ago. We'll meet you in the store in about twenty minutes.'

Amy crossed the road. It was hot and it wasn't even midday. It was also very quiet. Even Billy's chair was empty. In her bag was her locket. She hesitated at the door, but the moment had come to seek out Bert Cooper. She wished so very much it wasn't necessary, but her locket must be worth something ...

271

* * *

Late the following afternoon, when George returned to the house for tea, Amy was refereeing an argument between the boys.

'Will, you're sitting there, and Sam there. I'll have no more arguments. Now go and wash your hands, all of you. Will, help Bobbie.'

George stood staring out of the window.

'What's wrong now?'

Her voice startled him. 'There's a storm brewing.'

'I thought it felt close, but that's what we need isn't it? I know we haven't got a crop, but at least the pasture will be better for the cattle and in any case, didn't you say water was beginning to be a problem?'

He turned to face her. He had been watching the clouds build for the last half hour.

'I think we'd be better off in the cellar. I saw several twisters on the horizon earlier and I've got this feeling.' How did you explain instinct? Maybe a man's was different to a woman's. Amy's seemed to be tuned to people, but his was a kind of animal instinct – a gut awareness deep inside that something terrible was going to happen. 'I think there's a good chance there's more on the way. I don't want to chance them heading our way.'

She went to the window and looked at the eerie light. The sky was heavy and soil was being whipped up on the wind. 'It seems fairly normal to me.'

'Just the same, I think we should take our supper and eat it in the cellar.'

'Do we have to? It makes so much work. We've seen twisters before. It doesn't mean they'll come in our direction.'

'I'd rather not risk it.' He opened the door to the cellar. 'I'll light the candles and put some sacks out for the boys to sit on. I'll take a couple of chairs down if you want and we'll have supper down there. The boys will think it a fine adventure and I sure as hell would feel a lot safer.'

The children were eating their food when the storm hit. There was an incredible rumble. He felt the vibration through the floor but sat helpless knowing with certainty that the twister was ripping through the house. Sam stood up in terror, his plate falling to the floor.

Bobbie ran into Amy's arms. 'Mom, Mom ...'

She stared at George, mouth open, an expression of horror on her face. The noise was deafening – as if a train roared through. The candles flickered and it was airless. He put his arms round her and felt her sobbing.

It was a long time before he felt it was safe to emerge from the basement and by then, the candles had burnt low and the heat was intolerable. Pushing the door open, he knew by the feel of the breeze on his face, that his worst fears had been realized.

'Is it bad?' Amy called.

He didn't – couldn't answer. He just stared. The table had been lifted and thrown against the wall, disintegrating into so much firewood. Papers and china were strewn about. He crunched his way to the window. The glass was missing, sucked clean out and the curtains, blowing in the wind were in tatters – shredded beyond repair. Beyond he could see only sand. Everywhere he looked was sand. He was stunned.

'George? George?'

He went back to the cellar door.

'You'd better come up.'

'It's all right isn't it?' She climbed to the top of the stairs. 'Oh, my Lord.' She held her face in horror. 'This is terrible. The windows ... my curtains.' She looked down at her feet and picked up a broken teapot. The lid was complete. 'Oh, George. This was part of a wedding present from your mother.'

Will, Sam and Bobbie were at the top of the steps.

'Can we come out now?'

'No,' she told them. 'It's safer there.' She looked at George, who stood with his back to her staring out of the window. She made her way round an upturned chair and put her arms about his waist.

'Let's go home, George. Let's go back to England.'

273

CHAPTER TWENTY

'I'm not going,' Will stamped his foot. 'I'm not. I'm not. And I'm not leaving Spot. He's mine. You gave him to me.' He raced out of the kitchen. Through the open door Amy watched the dog bound towards him, tail wagging as together they ran up the track.

She stood looking after him. What could she say? How did you comfort an eleven year old? How could she expect him to understand why they couldn't take a dog to England? Why they had to go at all? He loved the farm – adored the horses, was so good with the cattle. Canada was the only home he'd really known. Her heart ached. Why was life so cruel?

It had never occurred to her before what effect returning to Europe might have on the boys. Will would have to leave all his friends – everything he knew and cared about, including Spot and they were inseparable. When the creak had water, they swam together. Then there was the time Spot found a skunk. Oh, what a whiff. How they laughed and laughed as the dog ran for miles trying to escape the awful smell. So many happy memories.

But he wasn't the only one making sacrifices. George. Her heart went out to him and there was still the dreaded sale. It loomed over them, coloured every aspect of their life, every decision they made.

'What good is it trying to sell anything?' he said almost every day. 'Nobody's sold any grain. Nobody's got any money and even if they had, what use is stock to them? What are they going to feed them on? We'll end up giving it all away.'

She remembered the Chernitsky's auction and the way people trampled over the house. She glanced at their makeshift table with its drab cloth and blinked back tears of despair. Nothing was white any more. The house was a wreck and so was she. But, no matter what the future held, it was not here. She would never forget the moment when they had climbed over furniture and staggered, shell shocked through the frame where the door once hung, to see what other damage the storm had wrought.

'Christ almighty ...' George said as he scrambled over an upturned feed trough which was wedged across the door. He helped her over the obstacle and they gazed in silence at the piles of sand heaped in all corners of the yard.

'The roof ...' she could see it was badly damaged and the house had an obvious lean.

He didn't stop to see what other destruction the storm had inflicted on the house, but ran out onto the trail.

'Where the blazes did this lot come from? Amy,' he called to her. 'Look. It's – it's everywhere.'

She came to stand beside him and in whichever direction she looked all she could see was sand.

'Jesse told me once of a special place,' he said in a low voice. 'An Indian burial spot where there was quicksand and spruce and not much else.' It was a second or two before he went on. 'Acres and acres of sand, he said. The Indians said it was sacred. I reckon that's what we've got here. Sacred sand.'

She had never seen a man weep before, but when she had got into bed that dreadful night and had cuddled up to George, she felt his body shake and knew he was crying and then she had cried too. Silently, in each other's arms, they cried. It would take years before their land would grow anything again.

* * *

The expected letter arrived from England several weeks later. Jesse had dropped by and brought the post with him. She glanced at the envelope George handed her, identified the familiar stamp with the King's head and she knew why he hadn't stopped for coffee. She eyed the Buckinghamshire postmark, and studied the writing she'd identified in an instant, putting off the moment when they knew their fate. Don't open it – let's stay, her heart cried out. She looked up at George but he had turned away, his shoulders stooped like an old man. He closed the door behind him and she knew in that instant he was a broken man.

Her hands trembled as she looked at the single sheet of paper. The note was brief. They were all to come home. "*All*" had been underlined twice. It was as though her mother had been here privy to their conversations, as though she had heard George argue over and over that he should stay. That he would find work with the threshing gangs up at Portage and send for them when things got better. She looked inside the envelope at the tickets.

* * *

It was some time before she realized Will was missing. He had come home from school, but she hadn't seen him since. He hadn't said he was going anywhere, yet when she looked out in the yard, there was only Sam and Bobbie.

'Have either of you seen Will?' she asked before crossing to the barn, where she stood in the doorway, staring into the shadows. It was very quiet. George must be out somewhere and surely Will would be with him? They had become closer lately. So much so, she often felt excluded. It was as if they blamed her for everything.

She was about to leave when a startled chicken squawked its way out into the sunlight. Then she heard George's voice. He was talking in quiet tones to Buster. In the gloom she could make out his arm round the shire's neck. She stood for a second and listened.

'This is it, old boy. You and I are destined to tread different furrows from now on. You've pulled your last plough – at least for me. My days are over.' The horse nuzzled him.

She turned and ran out into the yard. That horse had trodden every step with George, seen him home through the blizzards and, of all the horses, was the most loved. She stifled a sob. What had she done? She had broken their hearts. Would they ever forgive her? She dashed away the tears and gulped large mouthfuls of air. No, she was the sensible one. She was the practical one. Now it was up to her to find the strength to see it through. It would never do for all of them to dream of how things might be.

But where was Will? She looked in the empty hog house, which tilted precariously since the storm, calling for him as she went. No sign. She returned to the house and found Sam and Bobbie sitting on the steps.

'Are you sure you don't know where Will is? He must have said something.'

They shook their heads.

'Sam, did he say anything to you on the way back from school? Did he say he was going to catch gophers or something like that?'

'No, Mom.'

* * *

At tea time, Will was still missing.

'What's happened to that boy? What does he think he's playing at,' George raged.

'Don't get cross with him. He's upset over being parted from Spot. I expect they'll be back soon.'

'Upset? Upset?' George drew in a deep breath. He wanted to say how miserable he felt, but what was the point? When the farm sale was over that would be it. His life's work gone. What future was there for him in England? He glanced at Amy – didn't she understand jobs weren't any easier to come by there? She was so sure Freddie would help them – give him a job in his garage. But supposing he didn't? Or supposing he did and they didn't get on? He'd agreed to go back, but were things really going to be any better? How was he going to pay his way? The thought he might be in debt to Amy's mother for years infuriated him. He cut through his slice of bread and stabbed at the jam. He wasn't hungry. He threw his knife on the table and stomped out of the house.

* * *

Will was still missing when she sent the others to bed, but she didn't clear the table as George had not returned either. When it started to get dark she became anxious. Where were they? She went to the barn. The horses whinnied as she checked in each stall. She even poked around in the little hay there was in the loft.

She called their names. No answer. When she returned to the house, the light was fading and she lit the oil lamp and picked up the letter from her mother. She studied the tickets and still holding them, slumped into a chair, tears trickling down her cheeks, slowly at first, then in floods. She wept for what had happened to them, for George

277

who had sacrificed everything and Will who would lose his dog and a way of life, then she wept for herself.

How long she had been sitting there, she didn't know, but the sound of a horse and wagon approaching brought her to her senses and made her hurry to the door.

It was Jesse's wagon and in fading light, she could see Will. Beside him was Spot.

'Reckoned you might be missing this fellow.' Jesse tilted his head in Will's direction.

'Will.' Relief flooded through her. She ran down the steps. 'Thank goodness. Where have you been?'

'Found him down at the railroad.' Jesse dropped the reins and jumped from the wagon. 'Lucky I was passing. Reckon he planned on a trip to Winnipeg. Sure is no place for a lad.'

'Oh, Jesse, thank you. Thank you for bringing him back. Will, whatever were you thinking of?'

Will stood beside Jesse and gave her a defiant look.

'I'm not going to England. You can't make me. I'm not going.'

'None of us want to go, Will. None of us. It's just something we have to do.'

'No it isn't. Dad wants to stay. I know he does. I could stay, too.'

'That's enough, Will.'

He looked up at Jesse. 'Couldn't I stay with you and Miss Everard?'

'Will, I said that is enough and in any case, it's Mrs Carter now.'

Jesse looked at her over Will's head as though trying to gauge how he should answer. She shook her head.

''Fraid not, son. Your place is with your Mom and your Dad. Things ain't that bad. I reckon when you get back to England, you'll soon forget about old Jesse.'

Will ran into the house.

'Things not easy?'

'No, Jesse, things are awful. Will's taking this very badly. I can't blame him really. We have to find a home for Spot and he's, well ... You know he's very attached to that dog. And George ...' Her voice cracked and she blinked back tears. 'He didn't stay to eat his tea and I don't where he is. Oh, Jesse, what did we ever do to deserve this?'

'There now, don't you worry, he'll be back.' He put his arm round her. 'Sure don't understand the good Lord sometimes. I guess there's a reason, but I can't figure it out. Why one house is blown apart and another left standing.' Jesse shook his head and rubbed the stubble on his chin. 'And this sand is something else ... I guess it'll be years before any of us grow a crop. You might not be the only ones leaving.'

'I wish we didn't have to... That there was some other way ...'

'You've had more 'an your share of bad luck, I'd say.'

'Yes,' she sighed. 'I think you're right.' Then she tried to sound more cheerful. 'What about some coffee? At least, we've still got some of that and George might be back by the time it's ready. You'll stay?'

'No, no. Thanks all the same. I gotta head home. I said I'd be back in daylight. Don't you go worrying about George. He can handle himself. A man needs space, you know. Get his thoughts together.'

'Are you coming to the sale?'

Jesse shook his head. 'Nope. I reckon George and I can reach a deal on anything I want.'

'Oh? Have you agreed on something then?'

'Sure, but I'll let him tell you.'

She was rummaging around in the closet when George returned. Earlier in the day she had found the trunk and had partially filled it with some of their belongings. She went downstairs intending to make fresh coffee for him, but he had already put the kettle on the stove.

'Where did you get to, George?'

'Is Will back?'

'Yes, yes. Ages ago. Jesse found him at the station, but where've you been?'

'At the station?'

'I think he was running away.'

'Running away? God dammit, Amy, how much more must a man take?'

She put her arms around him. 'Shshsh. Shshsh. Don't go on so. Jesse brought him back. He wouldn't have got far, you know that. Anyway, he's back safe and sound and that's all that matters.' She hugged him tight. 'Where did you get to?'

'Took Mac and went for a walk. Thought I might find Will. Is he all right?'

She sat down. 'Not really.' She blinked tears back. 'It's all my fault.' She put her head in her hands.

'No, it isn't.' George patted her shoulder. 'It's not your fault the rains didn't come and it's not your fault a tornado ripped our house apart and dumped the best part of a desert on us.'

She looked up at him. 'But it's my fault we're giving up and going home.'

'No.' He shook his head. 'I'd have come to my senses eventually.' He pulled out a chair and, ignoring its rickety legs, sat facing her. 'Even if I'd gone up to Portage and been lucky enough to find work, it'd be years before I'd saved enough for you and the boys to join me. I don't want that – miss my boys growing up and I couldn't live without you. You see, while I was walking, I got to thinking and I kinda turned things over in my mind – came to a conclusion.'

'Oh?'

'Yep.' He took a deep breath. 'I guess it's hard for me say this – to admit even, but it's true. We're finished here.. They never should have ploughed this place up. Never should have taken all the grasses out. Guess that's what held the soil down. Now it's all blown away and all we got is sand. It'll be years before they get it right – before there's any hope of growing anything.' He looked into her eyes and she could see he was not only sad, but exhausted. 'Too late for us ... '

'You really think so?'

'May be, just may be if we'd had a bit of money behind us, we could have ridden this out, but we haven't. Fact is, there's nothing left – nothing at all and with no money we'd pretty soon have no food. In fact, I sometimes wonder how you manage to make things go so far but you always were a good little housewife.'

He didn't notice the guilt she felt certain was written all over her face. How could she admit that they would have run out of food over a week ago if she hadn't gone into town with Jesse and taken the opportunity to see Bert about her locket. Better that he shouldn't know.

'I only did what I had to.'

'Maybe, but I'm grateful.' He picked up her hands and squeezed them. 'I guess I got lucky when I didn't take a loan for a tractor. What good's a tractor now?'

The kettle was steaming and she added the water to the remains of the day's brew. She had to eke out the supply even though it tasted like dishwater.

'Anyway, Will will be pleased when I tell him Jesse's going to have Spot.'

'He said you and he and agreed something.'

'Spot was one of his pups.'

'At least he'll have a good home, but what about all the other animals? It doesn't make that any easier, does it?'

'Come on, cheer up. You should be pleased. You got your way. We're going back.'

'Got my way? How can you say such a thing? How can I be pleased?' She stopped stirring the coffee and glared at him. 'Going back to my mother's is not clever for any of us but what choice do we have? I wanted our life here to be a success just as much as you and I worked as hard. All right, I know I was grumpy about things when we first came to Canada and yes, you're right, I was a snob. It was all so strange, but … I got used to it. And I … I know you won't believe me when I say I do like it here. This dust … it won't last forever. Don't you think I wish we could stay? Stay for the day the rains come.' She sighed and began to stir the coffee again. 'We've made some wonderful friends and it breaks my heart to see Will hurting. I don't want to go but we'll starve if we stay and when we get home … There's bound to be a big inquiry. My mother didn't send those tickets without a price tag. Oh, yes you can be certain there'll be demands and conditions I'll have to fulfil and she's bound to rub in the fact she never ever agreed to us marrying. Oh, yes. I'm pleased all right.'

'Honey, I'm sorry. I didn't mean it to sound quite like that. I know I've been an idiot and an obstinate one at that and I can't blame you for being angry with me but I am trying to be reasonable now. Come here, you silly goose.' He stood up and held open his arms and she allowed herself to be comforted.

* * *

On the day of the sale, George had arranged for Jesse to collect Amy, Sam and Bobbie and take them to his place. Together with the two dogs and Buster hitched to the back of the wagon, they left. He and Will watched as they drove away.

'Come on, son,' he nudged Will. 'We're in this together, aren't we? Man to man?'

'Sure, Dad. Man to man.'

Side by side they watched each animal, each implement and each item as it went under the hammer but when the horses were sold, Will ran off and George watched him go. He, too, wanted to cry but it he had to see this through. The sale slowly progressed, but it was as he expected. Nobody wanted to buy cattle. Nobody had money to spend. The herd was virtually given away, along with all the farm implements and other household equipment they were not taking with them.

'Not much left after you settled with the auctioneer,' Jesse said when George held out the few dollars the auction had raised.

'Sure isn't much for a life's work.' George pocketed the money and they went to join the others for tea.

'You're not going back there tonight,' Molly said, handing George a cup of tea. 'I've made up beds. It's all agreed. You're staying here.'

'But, Molly –'

'I insist.'

At seven o'clock a car entered the yard, followed by several carts and carriages. Amy looked out of the window.

'Are you expecting company?'

'No,' Molly said. 'But you are.'

The room was soon crowded with friends who had come to say farewell and wish them good luck and though it was a sad occasion, they laughed and shared experiences and memories with them all.

When it was time to go, Bert Cooper sidled over to George and pressed an envelope in his hand.

'My watch?'

'It's of more value to you than it is to me.'

He held the packet out to Bert. 'I can't take this. We owe you.'

Bert pushed his hand away. 'So does half the neighbourhood and most of them will never be able to pay.' He shrugged. 'What's the difference?'

'But ...'

'I want you to have it. It means more to you than it ever could to anyone else and 'sides there's no way I could find anyone to buy it.'

He grinned. 'I guess you're right. Who would buy a watch when they need food in their bellies?' He placed the envelope in his pocket. 'Thanks, Bert, but you must let me pay you. I've got some cash from the auction.'

'Wouldn't hear of it. Look on it as a gift.' He put his hand on George's arm, preventing him from removing his wallet. 'I mean it. It's the least I can do and I sure hope things work out for you. You take care of that Missus and those boys of yours.'

* * *

Early next morning the click of the bedroom door closing woke Amy. She felt for George but the bed was empty and she guessed he had gone to see Buster.

On her way to the kitchen, she looked in on the boys. It had been a late night and they were still asleep. Jesse was brewing coffee. He handed her a cup.

'George's seeing to Buster.'

'Yes, I thought he would be. When we get to England, there won't be another horse. He'll miss him.'

'England. That reminds me.' He picked up the paperweight on top of the nearby bureau and retrieved an envelope. 'In all that kerfuffle yesterday, I forgot. When I collected the mail yesterday, I got yours.'

She stared at Freddie's handwriting before ripping it open and scanning his words.

'Not bad news?'

She looked up. 'No, not for once but I must tell George ...'

She found him leaning over the gate post. He heard her approach, turned and smiled at her.

'I'm glad we're alone. I've got something for you.'

She was puzzled. 'Really?' She thought she'd accounted for all her belongings and she couldn't imagine what else he might have. 'Did I leave something behind?'

'I suppose you could say that but it wouldn't be true. Actually Bert gave it to me.' He held out his hand. In it was her locket.

'Oh.'

'Is that all you can say?'

'It was the only way ...'

With his other hand, he fished out his watch. 'He gave me this back, too.'

'Alfie's watch.'

'When he was leaving last night, he gave me an envelope – said I was to think of it as a gift.'

'He's a kind man. I don't think he'd see anyone starve.'

'Why didn't you tell me?'

She didn't answer.

'It wasn't only me who kept secrets then? But what I don't understand is, why? I don't mean why you went behind my back. That's obvious but why didn't you sell your other locket? I know you still have it. This was my present to you on our wedding day … a token of my love.'

'I didn't want to do it, George, but there was no food – nothing. It was the only way. I know you're upset because I chose that.' She pointed to the locket he was still holding and knew he was hurt. 'I couldn't part with the other one. Truly, I couldn't. Remember when I gave it to you – all those years ago. I remember … wanting you.'

His eyes softened. 'And I you.'

'If only that Sergeant …'

'Or that nurse.'

'I gave it to you because it was the only way a little bit of me could be with you. I know it sounds silly, but I thought it would keep you safe.' She smiled at him. 'And it did. If you like, it was a token of my love. I could never part with it. It's part of you – and me. All those dents … they mean something.'

'I see,' he said, considering her words. 'Turn round and let me put this back where it belongs.'

He undid the clasp and she stood still while he fixed the locket around her neck, then he turned her to face him.

'There, back where it belongs. I suppose we'd better get back. Jesse'll be wondering what's happened to us and the boys will be causing havoc.'

'Wait,' she said remembering the letter and pushing it into his hand. 'You must read this. It's from Freddie and for once, it's good news and I mean good news.'

He looked doubtful but began to read.

'You enjoy driving, don't you? A chauffeur's job would be better than no job at all and there's a house, George. It would be a start and if you didn't like it, you could always look for something else.'

He looked up at her and, as though unconvinced, re-read the letter.

'It says chauffeur handyman,' she said, slipping her arm through his. 'And I think you're the best handyman in the world. Look at all the things you've had to fix.'

'Huh, a case of having to.' He scanned the letter again. 'I can't quite believe this. It's a bit of déjà vu.'

She laughed. 'We'll be all right, George. You'll see. We'll have a house of our own and you'll have a job. I knew Freddie would help us somehow. He might have his faults, but he's always been good to us.'

'Yes, I guess you're right.'

'You know I am.'

He put his arms around her and held her close. 'And we still have each other,' he whispered against her hair. 'I will always love you, no matter what the future holds. You'll always remember that, won't you, Amy?'

Through mists of tears she nodded. 'I love you, George Mills, always have and always will.'

EPILOGUE

Conditions in the Palliser triangle were extremely bad for the best part of ten years, with 1936 having the hottest summer temperatures ever recorded, while the winters were cold in the extreme. Drought, plagues of grasshoppers and crop diseases such as rust, made conditions difficult while high winds blew away the topsoil sometimes hundreds of miles out into the Atlantic ocean.

The drought of the 1930's was preceded by the Wall Street crash of 1929 and millions of workers in Canadian towns and cities found themselves out of work and on relief. During this period farming families in their millions left the dustbowl. How many is uncertain as no records were kept. For those who remained, their cattle starved and their crops failed and relief was slow in reaching them. In the words of James Gray, who wrote The Winter Years,

> *'... people all across the West discovered there was no essential relationship between income and enjoyment of life.'*

Somehow they survived and finally, with the outbreak of war in 1939, the depression came to an end. Better farming techniques were introduced and millions of acres of land in Saskatchewan and Alberta were taken out of cultivation and restored to grass.

Lightning Source UK Ltd.
Milton Keynes UK
UKOW05f2100201013

219393UK00001B/14/P

9 781782 997542